GUACAMOLE DIP

GUACAMOLE DIP

From Baja... tales of love, faith—and magic

DANIEL REVELES

SUNBELT PUBLICATIONS
San Diego, California

Guacamole Dip
Sunbelt Publications, Inc
Copyright © 2008 by the author
All rights reserved. First edition 2008

Cover and book design by Laurel Miller
Project management by Jennifer Redmond
Printed in the United States of America by United Graphics, Inc.

No part of this book may be reproduced in any form without permission from the publisher. Please direct comments and inquiries to:

Sunbelt Publications, Inc.
P.O. Box 191126
San Diego, CA 92159-1126
(619) 258-4911, fax: (619) 258-4916
www.sunbeltbooks.com

11 10 09 08 07   5 4 3 2 1

LIBRARY OF CONGRESS CATALOGING-IN-PUBLICATION DATA

Reveles, Daniel.
Guacamole dip : from Baja—tales of love, faith, and magic / Daniel Reveles. — 1st ed.
    p. cm.
ISBN-13: 978-0-932653-83-3
ISBN-10: 0-932653-83-9
1. Tecate (Mexico) — Fiction. 2. Baja California (Mexico : Peninsula) — Fiction.
    3. Mexico, North — Social life and customs — Fiction
I. Title.

PS3568.E785G83 2008
  813'.54—dc22
                          2007031048

Cover Painting "Plaza de Tecate" by Russel Redmond

For Valerie

Tu y yo.
Juntos lo hicimos,
juntos lo haremos,
juntos siempre.

Tu y yo.

A Note from the Author

*I*f it wasn't for a few special people you would not be holding this book open on your lap and I would be in therapy on the Oracle's couch in Delphi. This is the fourth book of tales from Tecate I have offered my readers. I have run up a huge debt with Valerie Ross, previewer and most assiduous critic since the very first enchilada was served up in 1994. I will never stop thanking Michael Ross who once again made the long drive to Mexico to retrieve the guacamole from somewhere in the viscera of a dysfunctional computer. Sitting in the car for two hours waiting to cross the border had to be a lot more fun than a day at the beach. I owe you. Thank you, Michelle "Eagle Eyes" Ross. My thanks to Gabriela Schneider and Hernan Franco Martin for making the CECUTEC library available to me. Sonia, my trusted housekeeper of many years, and endowed with unexplained powers, succeeded where I failed to produce a floppy disk by means of undisguised sorcery. *Gracias.* How can I ever repay Tracy and Dean who abandoned their margaritas at the Diana and rushed to the rancho to perform what was to me high tech *brujeria*. And then, there's Jennifer Redmond, editor and in-house Titania at Sunbelt who can make anything happen with a wave of her magic wand. I have never seen Jennifer without that special smile. OXO. Señorita X, *adios y que te vaya bien.*

— *D.R.*
Tecate, B.C., Mexico

Contents

Aperitivo

*T*I'm so glad you could make it down to Tecate today. Let's take a shady bench here in the plaza and watch a live show as good as any musical you'll see on Broadway. Our plaza is the stage where the everyday drama of life in Tecate unfolds. Mariachis, wandering musicians, singing pushcart vendors, and the steam whistle at the brewery provide the music. Costume and choreography are pure improvisation. I have a lot of new people I want you to meet and I'll tell you their stories—stories of love, and faith, and witchcraft. You'll laugh, you'll cry, you'll make new friends, but, fair warning, you might leave behind a piece of your heart. Of course, some of your old friends are back. Look! There's Peter Lorre. Well, okay, it's really Trinidad Contreras, our Peter Lorre look-alike. Treenie is a certified state-licensed matchmaker. In adherence to Truth, I should add that Treenie is a certified state-licensed anything you need him to be for a fee. That frightful little gnome walking toward the kiosk is La Cucha. It's said that she lives under the bridge near the Padre Kino School and snatches away little children. I hope it's a joke. La Cucha is Tecate's news satellite. She sees everything, hears everything, assumes everything, then disseminates it all over town. If she comes by our bench we'll be on the evening edition. There's the Sno-Cone man. The whole town knows his deep dark secret. But nobody's telling! Glance over at the man with a guitar in his lap getting his shoes shined. That's Antonio, Tecate's favorite balladeer. I'll make sure he sings a couple of songs for you while you're here. The dark man buffing his shoes is Cepillos.

Now, Cepillos is not your ordinary shoeshine man because nothing in Tecate is ordinary—he's a forensic scientist. In Tecate what you see is not necessarily what you see.

Pay no attention to that huge cloud of black smoke. It's not a terrorist. That's Father Ruben's pickup pulling into the church parking lot. The Padre is always running a little late. You'll meet him later and you'll like him immediately. That pretty girl in the backless turquoise dress? That's Señorita X. No, she's not a story, but you'll meet her later. Of course, we'll stop in for coffee with Los Cafeteros, Tecate's Chamber of Deputies that convenes every morning at La Fonda over a pot of coffee and drafts legislation for Vicente Fox, and El Boosh. By their second pot they turn profound and deal with heavy questions like, can we love too much?

I've often been accused by critics of being the natural enemy of truth. But the charge is an injustice. Tecate lives in its own reality. Those of you who have read my previous chronicles of Tecate are not likely to arch an eyebrow in an expression of disbelief when El Shorty comes riding into town on a big black and white Holstein cow that backfires. I can solemnly swear on my margarita that I write only what I see and what I hear.

The people you're about to meet on the following pages are not digitally enhanced characters invented just to make them entertaining. Their reality may not be your reality, but they're all real Mexicanos, people I see and talk to every day, people you would meet yourself if you took a shady bench in the plaza, sipped a margarita at the Diana, or strolled into the marketplace and ordered a love potion or boy-repellent from the *curandera* or sought the services of one of our local witches, purveyors of spells and curses. That's Tecate. As to witches, when I first arrived in Tecate I questioned everything. Twenty-five years later I still question everything but I doubt nothing. There must be a reason why the *botanicas* always sell out of *ojo de venado*, a powerful amulet that immunizes against *brujeria*. Do I have one? Yes! Do I wear it around my neck? No. It hangs on the computer!

Like any responsible author, I believe in full disclosure. The author is not responsible for convulsions of laughter, pernicious yawning or soggy handkerchiefs. If you suffer from nervousness, dyspepsia or hives, consult your medical professional before you continue reading. If you are pregnant or presently nursing, limit your dosage to one story in a twenty-four-hour period.

Let me begin with "Rain," the novela of seventeen-year-old Consuelo and thirty-nine-year-old Doña Socorro brought together by Fate, disguised as circumstance and coincidence. All Tecate is still talking about Consuelo and Doña Socorro. It's a story that proves what the ancients left written on papyrus over a thousand years ago: Love is without limits, the full power of Love has never been measured. And it's a good thing for us they did it on papyrus. If the wise men of the ancient world had saved their knowledge in the C-drive the whole file on Love would be lost to us today. Come, finish your mango Popsicle, and join me at my corner table at La Fonda for a margarita, mariachis, and a little bit of magic.

—*Your Servidor.*
Tecate, B.C., Mexico

Rain

Metaphorically speaking, the story of Consuelo and Doña Socorro puts me in mind of two letters, both pleading for rescue, sealed in two different bottles, put adrift in two separate oceans, and eventually washing up on the same shore. The slightest change in tide or current would have altered the course of events and I wouldn't have a story.

It is safe to say that everyone has experienced the passion of fear at some point in their lives, for the few seconds it takes to answer the ring of a phone, to several hours while we wait for the doctor to come out of surgery and tell us what we fear to hear. When the fear has passed, it leaves us drained of mind and body. Fear is a form of death. Consuelo Hernandez lived in a permanent state of fear; fear of hunger, fear for her mother, fear of the man who lived with them, fear of being beaten, fear of being violated. It was more than any seventeen-year-old girl in full bloom of her youth could be expected to cope with. I always felt Fate had dealt unfairly with Consuelo. Even her name was an irony: Consuelo, *comfort*. It seemed to me she was the one in need of comforting.

My story begins in Ciudad Obregon in the state of Sonora. Consuelo sat in the gloomy kitchen of the shack she called home eating a cold tortilla. A 40-watt bulb under a dirty white plastic shade filled with dead moths shed a sullen light over the room. Her mother had come in earlier, around seven o'clock, reeking of beer. She brought a plastic container of meat, potatoes, and some rice which Consuelo had a strong conviction her mother had stolen from the cafeteria at the bus terminal where she worked.

"Here's dinner," she said. She smelled like a brewery. "Don't save anything. Emilio eats before he gets home. I'm going straight to bed. My kidneys are bothering me tonight." It was never the alcohol in her body. It was her kidneys. This was not an unusual occurrence.

There was no means of heating the food for lack of butane in the cylinder and the three hundred pesos to buy a refill. Consuelo served her three step-siblings the lukewarm food straight from the container and ate what they didn't, which wasn't very much. At eight o'clock she had them all in bed. By half past ten she was making every effort to keep herself awake. Consuelo chewed her stiff tortilla and listened to the night noises coming from the other room. The other room was neither bedroom nor living room but an unfinished room with a cold concrete floor that served as both. At one end was a television set, two rusted chrome dinette chairs, and an old sofa covered in cracked green vinyl—her bed. The rest of the room was paved with mattresses for the three little ones, Paulo, three, Clara six, and Julia, seven. The only bed was for her mother and whoever she chose to share it with. These days it was Emilio, father of three-year-old Paulo. The two girls were the work of a bricklayer and a farm hand respectively. The men never stayed long after the arrival of their by-product.

Consuelo couldn't remember anything about her real father. Her mother told her he ran off shortly after she was born then drank himself to death one sip at a time. She was left with a mother determined to do the same thing. It shamed Consuelo that she could only feel disgust, yet if someone were to ask her if she loved her mother, she would say she did, just as all beings love the woman who gave them life whether that love is deserved or not. But deep in her heart, Consuelo knew she couldn't respect her, and this brought her a pang of guilt for she knew also she didn't adore her.

Her two older brothers were luckier. They escaped long ago. She wouldn't recognize them now if they walked in the room. But where could a girl go? And how far could she get? She never had more than a few coins in her pocket. She was trapped. An after-school job was out of the question. Her mother needed her home to look after her trophies left by various "husbands." She had girlfriends her own age that had a comfortable home with the stability of a mother and a father who looked after them, to see they were properly fed and clothed. They had a father who came home from work sober, eager to play with them. On weekends their *real* father and mother took them to play in the park or to the local *cine* for a matinee. Her friends didn't wear second hand clothes. They didn't sleep on a mattress on the floor or on a broken sofa. They had their very own beds with fresh-smelling white sheets and warm blankets—and a real bathroom! Her friends were all happy at home. And safe. Consuelo had no acquaintance with happiness and she never felt safe.

She should have been a beautiful girl. All the essential elements were there. She was like a flowering tree in winter, dormant, all twigs and branches, no full round blossoms to give her shape and form, no graceful foliage. Her pretty face was tawny, the color of comb honey, smooth as varnished pinewood, but painfully thin and gaunt. The lights were out in two round dark eyes that should have sparkled with the joy of youth, a smile would have made the pale mouth sensuous. Her hair was the purest black and should have shimmered when struck by the rays of the sun, but it was dull and lifeless, and drooped to her shoulders with something of a sigh.

Gentle sounds of breathing came to her from the next room. The three little ones wheezed softly at different intervals. They sounded like toy whistles playing in three-part harmony. It was almost funny. Her mother snored frankly in a deep alcoholic fog. The clock on the wall said eleven-thirty. She wanted to be in bed on her sofa before Emilio walked in a few minutes past midnight. Not asleep, but wide awake and fully clothed. Prepared.

Consuelo fought back sleep for another quarter hour listening to the raindrops plunking on the roof. It wasn't a heavy rain—not yet—but a round wet spot was already spreading like dark syrup on the plywood ceiling. She was glad she didn't have to use the bathroom. You had to go outside to get to it. A parade of roaches now marched along the baseboard but she made no attempt to squash them with her shoe. It was time to close up for the night. The back door was already locked with a bent nail but that didn't matter anyway. Emilio would come in through the front door with his own key, drunk, horny, and mean. She removed the meat knife from the drawer, turned out the light, and groped her way back into the other room.

Still fully clothed she got under the covers on the sofa, arms bent at the elbows tight against her body, the meat knife clutched in her hand. It wasn't long before she heard the tinkle of keys in the lock. Emilio was home.

She felt cool wet air on her face as Emilio stumbled in. The astringent smell of tequila and greasy food filled the room. Emilio drove a night taxi. All the *taxistas* met at Tacos La Chinita for calf-head tacos after their shifts then moved next door to El Acapulco to play pool and get drunk. She did not need the benefit of sight to know his every move in the dark room. She heard the thud of his leather satchel containing the day's cash receipts as it landed on top of the television. Emilio was only two steps from her bed. He didn't move. He just stood there breathing. What was he doing? Why wasn't he going to his bed? Then she heard him step closer. A large hand was now rubbing her back. Her fingers clasped the meat knife.

"Are you awake, little one?" he whispered.

Consuelo held her breath and feigned sleep. She was hoping he would move away as he usually did when she didn't respond. It didn't work. His hand moved lower, fondling her *nalgas*, squeezing and cupping first one side then the other.

"Are you asleep, Consuelito?"

"Stop making so much noise, *viejo*, come to bed. It's late." Her mother's voice was the answer to a prayer.

The hand on her bottom moved away quickly and he clomped his way toward her mother's bed. Consuelo listened. One at a time his shoes hit the floor. The jingle of a belt buckle and the whir of a zipper told her he was taking off his pants. She heard him shrug out of the rest of his clothes and the soft shush as they hit the floor. She wouldn't feel safe until she heard the squeal of the bedsprings when he fell into bed. No sound came. All quiet. Too quiet. Then she heard the soft padding of naked feet walking across the concrete floor.

He was coming back!

Consuelo froze where she lay. He was standing right next to her now. She heard a movement and perceived he was kneeling on the floor beside her. He belched and the smell of tequila and undigested food attacked her nostrils. She was sure she would vomit right into her pillow. She felt him gather up her hair and gently pull it away. His rough lips were kissing her neck and nuzzling her ear. The hand was back squeezing and massaging her bottom again. Cold fear paralyzed her. She couldn't move, couldn't scream. She felt a painful twinge in her bladder and she knew in another second she would be wetting the bed.

"Hey, *viejo*, where are you? Come to bed now, I have it all warmed up for you."

The kisses and nibbles ceased. The thick hand stopped playing with her bottom. "Shut up, *vieja*, I'm coming right now. I'm coming to beat some sense into you and teach you a little respect."

Bare feet now could be heard retreating toward her mother's bed. Consuelo tightened her grip on the knife. She heard the twang of the springs as he fell in like a sack of potatoes. Consuelo was ready to make her move. No sound came for long agonizing minutes. Then she heard her mother moaning softly. Emilio was grunting and straining. He sounded like he was lifting weights. Suddenly he let out a hoarse scream then all was quiet until he began to snore like a chainsaw cutting oak. Emilio was under the anesthetic. Nothing would wake him now until noon.

Consuelo felt her body relax. She dared to resume breathing. But she just couldn't take anymore. Life was becoming unbearable. It was time to make a decision. And to Consuelo it was now a critical decision of life or death. Now was the moment! Now or never! Could she do it? She *had* to do it. God would forgive her.

What would happen to her if they caught her? Consuelo wasn't sufficiently coherent to answer her own questions.

Silent as a wraith she slipped out of bed exactly as she had slipped in, fully clothed, the meat knife tight in her right hand.

II

Socorro Castellano was rummaging through the attic of her mind, an occupation she always undertook on rainy days without really understanding why she did it. This is where she stored all her yesterdays. And here they all were, carefully wrapped in sadness cloth just as she'd left them eighteen years ago. She undid the frayed ribbon and that rainy afternoon at Leopoldo's country estate in Cuernavaca came back.

"*Socorro, mi amor, I love you so much. I don't ever want to stop kissing you.*"

"*I love you too, mi amor.*"

"*God, you're beautiful all over! I can't stop looking at you. I could stay like this forever.*"

"*Ay, corazón, you have me on fire. Maybe we'd better slow down.*"

"*Can you feel that? Is it nice?*"

"*Sí, I can feel it.*"

"*And that?*"

"*Yes! It's too nice—I think we'd better stop.*"

"*Stop! But I love you. Don't you love me?*"

"*If I didn't love you we wouldn't be doing what we're doing. Now, come on, let's get dressed before the others come looking for us.*"

"*I can't stop now, I'm too far gone—oh! oh!—*mi amor*—I love you! I love you! I love you!*"

The wrappings fell away from another yesterday. It looked the same now as it did that painful Saturday morning with her parents at home in Mexico City.

"*How could you be so stupid! So indecent!*"

"*Mamá, I know I was stupid, now I need your help.*"

"*Help! You're a little late for that!*"

"*Please, Papá. Beat me if you want, but just listen to me!*"

"*What's to listen to? I have two sons and two daughters and you are the first one to bring disgrace to this family!*"

"*Socorro, you know your father has to work closely with the most important people in the capital. His reputation means everything. It's a matter of pride—family pride. What could you have been thinking?*"

"*Where can I hide? How can I face the new delegates, the mayor, the governor? They'll laugh me out of the city. And my adversaries! You've given my opponents all the filthy dirty scandal they need to ruin me.*"

"*Who's the father? Leopoldo, I suppose.*"

"*Sí, Leopoldo.*"

"*Have you told him?*"

"*Sí, Mamá, he knows.*"

"*I'll call that fathead this very minute! I'll see to it that—*"

"*The family left for Europe two weeks ago, Papá, they'll be away for six months.*"

"*Whatever are we to do? We can't take her to Dr. Avila. Everyone will know.*"

"*I'm sending her to my sister in Guadalajara immediately. I'll deposit sufficient funds in your bank account to see you through. Your aunt will find you competent medical care.*"

"*Papá, you're treating me worse than you would treat a servant! I've seen you show more compassion for one of the maids that gets pregnant.*"

"*The lower class needs our compassion because they are the victims of poverty and ignorance. You're not!*"

"*What I did was wrong, yes, but I'm your own daughter!*"

"*And that makes it worse! Have you no pride? I'm putting you on the morning flight. You can have your bastard child over there!*"

And there, under another pile of old yesterdays, Socorro found that awful day in Guadalajara and opened it.

"*When will they bring my baby in to me?*"

"*There now, you just get some rest,*"

"*But I want my baby!*"

"*Doctór will be along soon. Just relax, oh, here's doctór now.*"

"When am I going to see my baby?"
"Your baby died a few minutes after birth. A little girl. I'm so sorry, señora, we did everything we could but we couldn't bring her back to life. I'm so sorry."
"I named her Laura...."

Socorro opened her eyes. The bedroom was pitch dark, she couldn't even make out the furniture. She listened to the rain thrumming on the roof tiles. It sounded like thunder. A warm rain ran down her face.

"Buenos dias, Doña Socorro, *Como amaneció?"*

She must have gone back to sleep! A soft gray light came in through the windows and there stood Navidad next to her bed with a steaming cup of hot chocolate. Navidad was her loyal housekeeper, a tiny native of Oaxaca. Her skin was copper plated, her hair covered her back like a black shawl held in place with a turquoise comb. She was dressed in the clothes typical of Oaxaca she made herself, a white blouse with white embroidery, the long skirt, three shades of lavender. She jingled with rings and bracelets and the dangly silver earrings grazed her shoulders. Navidad stood no taller than the doorknob.

Sleepy-eyed, Doña Socorro sat up. The little gold medallion with the baby's name she wore around her neck was still pressed tightly in her hand. *"Buenos dias,* Navidad, *gracias.* It's been raining hard all night." She released the medallion and took the cup with both hands.

"These March rains usually come over the Rumorosa in the afternoon. They don't last long when they come in the morning. You watch, by noon the sky will be blue and innocent, the sun will melt our bones. Morning rains are like a spoiled child's temper tantrum, sobbing and fussing for a couple of hours, then docile as a newborn kitten." Navidad was more than a competent housekeeper, she was Doña Socorro's weather channel.

Navidad watched her lady sip the chocolate gratefully. "Your breakfast will be ready when you come down."

Doña Socorro finished her chocolate, bathed, dressed, and went down to the large hacienda-type kitchen. Navidad knew just what she liked, fresh mango, *pan dulce,* and good strong coffee she brewed with a stick of cinnamon. As was her custom, Navidad had disappeared. Doña Socorro planned her day. She would run errands and get them all out of the way for the week; the bank first, the power company to pay the light bill, the telephone company, and if she had time, a walk through the *fruteria* for fresh fruit.

It was warm and drippy when she left the house at nine and headed for El Emporio, Tecate's biggest ready-to-wear store which she had opened on her arrival eighteen years ago. Of course, she started with the proverbial hole in the wall, but she carried what people wanted and was good with customers. In a few years she was able to open the big store two blocks from the plaza and buy the big colonial house with huge living rooms on the ground floor and five bedrooms upstairs. It was a lot of square meters for one person, but she felt comfortable and secure.

No one would describe Doña Socorro as gregarious. Courteous, yes, but she had a tendency to keep people at a distance, exchanging a reserved but cordial *buenos dias* with her neighbors and a wave to those at a distance as she walked the three blocks to her shop. She'd never been in her neighbor's houses. They'd never been to hers. No one knew Doña Socorro any better today than they did when she arrived in Tecate.

She'd only walked about a block when she suddenly stopped and looked down at her feet. She was still in her bedroom slippers! She started back. "I'd leave the house without *calzones* if I didn't have them on!" she scolded herself. She returned home, slipped into shoes, and saw that she had also left the money for the cash register on top of her bureau.

There was little to do in the store this morning. She only had two customers who knew exactly what they wanted, found it, and paid. Chatting with each one took longer than the transaction. That was one of the many things that amazed Doña Socorro about Tecate. No one was ever too busy to stop and exchange pleasantries. The people here were warm and gentle. They would rather miss their bus or sit in traffic through another red light than fail to exchange greetings with someone they knew even if they had said the same things only yesterday. In Mexico City you'd get lynched.

Doña Socorro put a sign in the door that said "Back at 2PM." It was a lie, of course, but in Tecate time on a clock was optional. She stepped into the street. The steam whistle at the brewery ripped the warm air. The pious strains of Ave Maria blared from every radio in Tecate, drifting from the hills of Cuchuma, to the river, across the plaza, and slipping over the barbed wire fence into the United States without a green card. The sounds of noon in Tecate. The sidewalks were dry, the sky was a flawless blue tile. The sun burned her shoulders and she was glad she carried her parasol. Navidad always got it right. If she told her there would be a blizzard in July she would dress for it without question. She headed in the direction of Banco de Londres.

Everyone in Tecate would agree that Doña Socorro was a beautiful woman. She was. But the assessment was an over simplification. At the precarious age of thirty-nine her skin was flawless, not a crease, not a line anywhere, smooth as a Dresden figurine, her face a classic cloisonné. Every facial feature was in harmony. She had a high forehead, gorgeous eyes, and a full voluptuous mouth. Her shoulder-length russet hair was thick and luxurious. But that was about as far as the description could go for no one in Tecate knew anything more of her beyond what they could see. But on the inside there existed a perennial sadness. The dark eyes appeared to be guarding a secret. Her mouth, though pleasant to the eye, would curve with the promise of a smile, but the smile never matured. No one in Tecate ever heard her laugh. Doña Socorro made no attempt to bribe nature with cosmetics. Her clothes, while they were of obvious quality, were lusterless, mostly grays, browns, dark blues, and sometimes black. Even her voice was gray. Everyone in Tecate knew Doña Socorro for there are no strangers in Tecate and she'd been there since she was twenty-three. But no one could tell you her civil status; was she married, divorced, single, widowed? Did she have children in some other town? For lack of evidence no one addressed her as señorita which would imply a single status and therefore assumed virginity. And they couldn't very well make the assumption that she was married or had been married, and call her señora. But with respect for her maturity it seemed correct to everyone to rely on Doña, a venerable honorific. Doña Socorro was on good terms with everyone, but with an austerity and aloofness that discouraged friendship. It was only natural that men should approach her in the early days of her arrival. Doña Socorro was not hungry for attention. She sent them off with a bad case of frostbite.

The bank was a madhouse when Doña Socorro walked in. It looked like an airport during a blizzard when all the flights have been canceled or delayed. Long lines at all the counters reached to the door. Crowds gathered around every customer service desk. There was hardly a place to stand. Some people leaned against the walls and waited.

"Doña Socorro! *Buenas tardes!*" The effusive salutation came from Señor Jimenez, the portly manager of Banco de Londres with a perennial smile. "Come in, come in, the coffee is fresh!"

"Sr. Jimenez, you are *muy amable. Gracias.*" Socorro followed her host to an inner office. He held a chair for her. While Doña Socorro put down her briefcase and got comfortable Sr. Jimenez made a trip to the credenza and back with a cup of fresh coffee, one sugar, no cream. Sr. Jimenez knew his customers. She had been a major account for many years.

He pushed a small plate of *empanadas* toward her. "I can win the struggle against mortal sin, but I have no will of my own when it comes to these *empanadas* the sisters bake at the convent. You can't leave without trying one of these. Apricot!"

"*Gracias,*" she declined. Doña Socorro was here to conduct business.

It might have been a scene in someone's living room. The bedlam on the other side of the door was forgotten. Consistent with Mexican custom it would have been crude to come immediately to the point. They talked about last night's rain, the heat wave, and other harmless gossip. It wasn't until Sr. Jimenez offered his guest a second cup of coffee that he discreetly pressed a buzzer and a pretty young secretary stood at his side. Doña

Socorro opened her briefcase and handed her a bundle of cash, all organized and held with rubber bands, and a deposit slip. By the time the second cup of coffee was finished Doña Socorro's transaction was done. The secretary was back with a receipt for sixty thousand pesos. Doña Socorro would never be expected to stand in line. Sr. Jimenez walked her to the door like a favored guest where they exchanged courtesies and Doña Socorro was on her way to her next errand.

III

When Consuelo got off the smelly Tres Estrellas bus in Tecate the only thing she had was a splitting headache and a painful memory. Were they looking for her? What would they do to her if they found her? The night she ran away was as vivid in her mind now as it was three days ago; the old lecher snoring, the canvas bag sitting on the television. It was too dark to see what she took. She just grabbed a bunch of paper money. That was the last time she would have to defend herself in bed. She put the meat knife back in the drawer and ran for the bus terminal. After buying her ticket to Tecate she was left with twelve hundred pesos. It would have to do for food and a place to stay until she found a job. She had no luggage. There was nothing to pack. Her total possessions were what she had on; a pair of frayed blue jeans held up with a pink belt, a yellow blouse, a green cardigan and her underwear. A strand of red yarn held her hair.

She came ready to go to work. It wouldn't take long to find something—anything. Consuelo was the kind of girl that wouldn't turn anything down. The price of rooms was exorbitant. She had to search the *colonias* on the outskirts of town to find an affordable room. Consuelo was on intimate terms with poverty but she was unprepared for El Rincon, the corner forgotten by God. She went up one street and down another until she found something affordable. It was nothing more than a small storeroom in the back of Tapiceria Lopez, an upholstery shop run by an old man and his obese wife.

"I can let you have it for six hundred pesos a month." Six hundred! thought Consuelo, that's half of what I have. "There's no place to cook. You'll have to eat out. But there's a toilet and a laundry tub out back."

After a long day of hunting Consuelo knew it was the cheapest thing she would find. "I'll take it, señora."

"I need the first month in advance."

Consuelo knew that was coming from her experiences earlier in the day. There was a second hand store in the neighborhood where she bought a metal cot, a thin mattress with a dark stain in the shape of South America, and a blanket.

After five days Consuelo was sick with despair. She was down to three hundred pesos. That would have to do for food and bus fare. And if she didn't have six hundred by the end of the month she'd be out on the street. She was determined to find work today—anything. Her clothes were clean. She'd just laundered everything yesterday. Her underwear was a little damp but that didn't matter. It would dry as she walked the streets. The day was hot.

By the time she reached the plaza she was tired, thirsty and hungry. She called on eight stores—she counted them—no work. Nothing. She wanted to cry. She dared to buy herself an ear of corn and a lemonade. There were still two blocks on the other side of the plaza that she hadn't called on. The corn filled the empty place in her stomach, the lemonade brought relief to her parched throat, and somewhat restored her spirits. Her search continued on the next block. There was a pharmacy, a stationers, a florist and—and a sign in the window!

SE SOLICITA EMPLEADA

Consuelo had to read it twice to believe it. The name on the front of the building read El Emporio. Clothing was displayed in the large window, menswear, ladies apparel and accessories, children's clothing and baby clothes. Consuelo's heart leaped. Quickly she checked her appearance in the reflection in the window, tucked her blouse, ran her fingers through a fugitive strand of hair, and pushed through the door.

The store was larger than she had imagined, the aisles wide and deep. It had the pleasant smell of new clothing. The only inhabitant was a severe-looking woman in dark gray pants and a matching jacket over a black blouse. The woman didn't smile. Consuelo was immediately intimidated. She wanted to run but she managed to produce a pleasant smile. The woman wasn't old but it would be safe to address her as señora.

"*Buenas tardes,* señora. I came to see about the job."

Doña Socorro allowed her to approach. She looked at the scruffy little sparrow in frayed blue jeans with a pink belt, wrinkled blouse, and atrocious green cardigan with a missing button. She had a hard time keeping employees. Doña Socorro was a demanding employer and expected the same enthusiasm for work as she demanded of herself. They didn't last long. This one was poorly dressed but at least her hair wasn't purple and she didn't have a ring in her nose.

"Have you any experience in retail clothing?" she asked in a cold voice.

"No, señora."

Her voice turned to ice. "This is a clothing store."

"The sign didn't say. It just says help wanted."

"I should think it would have been obvious," she snipped. Doña Socorro knew herself better than most people who think they know the inner self. She recognized what in her mind were her two greatest faults. Her absent-mindedness was a major annoyance and she was prone to give voice in advance of thought. She had to admit the sign in the window was vague. "How old are you?" She spoke to her in the familiar second person. After all, the girl was only a scruffy child.

Consuelo took an instant dislike to the woman. She was ready to turn around and walk out. But she didn't dare. She needed the job desperately, and besides, she had no experience in sticking up for herself. "Seventeen, señora."

A runaway maybe? "Where do you live?" It was more demand than question.

"El Rincon."

Doña Socorro shuddered involuntarily. A runaway without a doubt but she didn't ask any more questions. She didn't want to know. "What can you do?"

"I can do anything you ask of me, señora."

Doña Socorro was not impressed. Her tone was tart. "I can use someone to come in every day and clean."

"I could do a very good job of that."

"I pay three hundred pesos a week and I expect you to be punctual." It was a gruff take-it-or-leave-it voice. She did not expect the girl to last more than the first week.

Consuelo was afraid her heart would leap out of her mouth. "I can start today if you like."

"What's your name?"

"Consuelo Hernandez, *servidora*."

"Be here tomorrow morning at nine ready to go to work," she ordered sharply and turned away.

"*Si*, señora, *gracias*." Consuelo fled before she would burst into tears. Three hundred a week! That's twelve hundred a month. My rent is six hundred. I'll have money for food, a few clothes, and money left over! *Gracias a Dios*!

Consuelo was already waiting at the front door when Doña Socorro appeared in a black suit to open the store at ten minutes to nine the following morning. She didn't like the woman any better today than she did yesterday but her life depended on this job. She managed a smile. "*Buenos dias*, señora," she said pleasantly.

"*Buenos dias*." It was more of a grumble than a greeting. Consuelo felt her answer was nothing more than minimum duty to common manners. She didn't even return her smile.

Doña Socorro was quick to notice the girl was in the same clothes she had on yesterday but they were clean. It must be all she owns, she thought. She must have washed everything yesterday then stood around naked until they dried. Doña Socorro got right down to business. "The first thing you will do every morning is to sweep the sidewalk in front of the store then sweep the gutter. Everything goes in that big barrel marked AYUNTAMIENTO XV. Tecate does not provide street cleaners. Each merchant is responsible to keep his portion of the street clean. They assess a fine if the inspector comes by and sees it hasn't been done."

"I understand, señora."

"Follow me."

Socorro led her the length of the store talking as she went. "The floors must be cleaned every day. Do not get the floors wet. Work with a mop that is barely damp enough to gather dust."

"*Sí*, señora."

"Use a soft cloth to dust the sides and tops of the counters, being careful that you don't raise even more dust."

"*Sí*, señora."

They passed a U-shaped counter where the cash register was located and a small table with a coffee pot. "When you clean here you have to be careful not to move my notebooks." They walked on. "This is the storeroom where I open shipments that come in almost every day. You'll mop the floor, and dust the shelves. The empty cartons need to be flattened to fit in the trash barrel out front." Socorro led the way a little farther. "Through that door is a utility room. It has a bathroom, mops, brooms—everything you need to do your job."

"*Sí*, señora. I might as well get started." Consuelo entered the utility room, found what she needed and went to clean the front of the store.

Scrubbing and cleaning and washing was something Consuelo had been doing since she was six. By noon she had the store spotless. She was getting hungry. Breakfast had been a piece of *pan dulce*, a banana, and a cup of coffee at seven-thirty. It was a long ride from El Rincon. It required two buses. She'd leave for work at five in the morning if necessary but she was not going to be late. That frosty woman would probably beat her. Her stomach was complaining but she was too timid and too embarrassed to ask permission to go down to the plaza and get a taco. By two o' clock Consuelo was lightheaded. She was going to have to ask that woman with an ice cube for a heart permission to go out.

Doña Socorro came up at that moment with her key in her hands. "I usually close from two to three. Do anything you like but be back here promptly at three. I don't want to wait for you."

"*Sí*, señora." Consuelo ran out of the store and across the plaza where she devoured two meat tacos, an ear of yellow corn, a cup of ice cream, and a tall orangeade.

In the weeks that followed the two women grew accustomed to one another's demeanor like a dog and a cat that have called an uneasy truce, but they didn't know each other any more than they did the first day they met. Their only exchange of conversation was limited to instructions and "*sí*, señora." Consuelo no longer gave her the benefit of the doubt. She was simply a cold, bitter woman by nature with no feelings for anything or anyone. Doña Socorro was pleasant enough to her customers but she never smiled, never laughed. The woman was a rock.

Doña Socorro was surprised to see her employee waiting for her at the front door a few minutes before nine every morning. They exchanged the statutory *buenos dias*, but neither meant it. Having a cleaning girl that showed up was one less thing for her to worry about. She wouldn't last, of course, they never did, but at least this one was always on time and kept the place immaculate. But once Consuelo learned her routine Doña Socorro had nothing further to say to her save a few necessary words related to the store. They didn't even talk about the weather.

One morning after about a month on the job Consuelo went directly to the utility room as usual and came out with her brooms and dustpan when Doña Socorro rushed in. "What are you doing?" she demanded.

"I was just going to clean out front."

"Leave that for now. I need you for something else."

"I can have it done in a few minutes, señora."

"I said leave it!"

Consuelo jumped at the woman's tone of voice. She put everything back and waited for instructions.

"Two large unexpected shipments came in. I need your help to unpack and arrange the merchandise before a third shipment arrives later this morning. Follow me." Consuelo followed. "I'll open the cartons, and call out each item. You will check against the bill of lading then take the merchandise out front and arrange it on the proper counters."

"*Sí*, señora."

And so they began. "Twelve pairs white athletic socks."

"Twelve pairs white athletic socks. Check."

"One dozen T-shirts with fiesta print."

"One dozen T-shirts with fiesta print. Check."

And so it went until everything was checked in, counted. and arranged. Without another word Doña Socorro walked into the store. A man with a clipboard was standing at the door.

"*Buenos dias*, Doña Socorro."

Doña Socorro bristled. She knew who he was and why he was there. "*Buenos dias*, Jorge."

"I'm sorry to do this, Doña Socorro but it's past ten and the street in front of your place hasn't been done."

"No need to apologize, Jorge. It's your job. You are paid to see that city regulations are complied with."

"I could go do another street. You could have it done by the time I got back. Save yourself two hundred pesos."

"That won't be necessary," she snapped. "I'll go this afternoon to *tesoreria* and pay the fine."

"Oh, there's no hurry, Doña Socorro. They give you fifteen days."

"I'll be there this afternoon!"

Jorge handed her the citation, gave her an embarrassed smile, and left just as Consuelo came in from the utility room with broom and dustpan.

"It's a bit late for that now."

"Too late?"

"The city inspector has come and gone." She held up the citation. "This is a two hundred peso fine. I thought I made it clear to you when you came to work here that the front of the store was your first duty. "

"But señora—"

"It's useless to explain, Consuelo, now see if you can manage to get the rest of the merchandise put away. I'm on my way to pay the two hundred peso fine. Two hundred pesos! I might as well have thrown them out on the street. Or given them to the beggar on the corner who could at least buy groceries for his family."

The rest of the day was dismal. Neither spoke. I hate her! Consuelo fumed. I absolutely hate her! Doña Socorro attended her customers and stayed at the cash register making entries into her ledgers. Consuelo kept busy and stayed out of Doña Socorro's vicinity. There was plenty to do. She flattened all the cartons and stacked them into neat bundles preparatory to tomorrow's trash pickup. She swept up the lint and plastic peanuts spilled during the unpacking then mopped the floor and dusted the storage shelves. This done, she cleaned the sidewalk and the gutter out front and scrubbed the utility room. For whatever reason Doña Socorro did not close at two for lunch. She kept herself busy with her ledgers and attended whatever customers came in. She didn't tell Consuelo to go get something to eat and she was too timid to ask. By five in the afternoon her head was throbbing, she was over hungry and exhausted. How inconsiderate, how vindictive! I hate her! Consuelo repeated to herself. She waited until there were no customers and approached Doña Socorro at the cash register.

"It's five o'clock señora, will there be anything else before I go?"

"No. Be on time tomorrow, do your job properly. I ask nothing more."

The injustice of the severe reprimand for something that was not her fault brought Consuelo tears of anger and frustration. She controlled her voice. "I found this. You must have left it on the windowsill of the utility room." She handed her a heavy envelope.

No answer. Doña Socorro did not acknowledge the courtesy. She took the envelope without comment as Consuelo went out the door. She realized instantly what she had done. It contained two thousand pesos in cash she'd intended to put in the cash register but with the unpacking and the checking and the stacking it had completely gone from her mind. Again! It might have gone out with the trash and she'd never have known it.

The next morning there was no sign of Consuelo. The street in front of the store was littered with candy wrappers, paper cups, empty cigarette packages, and a child's shoe. The gutter was worse. Doña Socorro was livid. She would have to speak to the irresponsible girl about the importance of punctuality. Well, it's no surprise, she complained to no one, I didn't really expect her to last as long as she did. The lower class is all the same, ignorant and hopeless! I'll have to dismiss her today. She got busy with other things, and as was her wont, totally lost track of the time. There were a couple of early customers, a few cartons of new merchandise to open. She used this time productively, honing the angry words she would throw at the little tramp when she came in, then tell her she was no longer needed.

By ten-thirty Doña Socorro realized Consuelo wasn't late for work. She wouldn't be in at all. What can you expect of these people?

"*Buenos dias*, Doña Socorro."

She looked up to see Jorge with his clipboard. She was incensed. "*Buenos dias*, Jorge," she answered without meaning it. "I know why you're here. Give me the citation. I'll go in and pay it this afternoon."

"But Doña, I can always come back later and—"

"I said leave it with me, Jorge!" Her voice sharp enough to cut a brick. "It's my responsibility."

Refusing to look at the litter, Doña Socorro took a few minutes to go to city hall, pay her fine, and return to her store. It turned out to be a busy day. When the last customer finally walked out at eight o'clock she closed up and started for home. She made use of the short walk to nourish her anger. God, the lower class is *imposible*! If only they weren't necessary. I have a thing or two to tell that stupid girl in the morning. By the time Doña Socorro got home she was seething with fury.

Navidad greeted her at the door with her beauteous Indian smile, the lights of Oaxaca flickering in her black eyes. "You worked late, Doña. You look tired. I have your favorite dinner all ready for you. *Calabazas* in salsa and chicken in *mole*."

Doña Socorro declined dinner. "I'm too tired to eat, Navidad, I'm going straight to bed."

She was still angry and she wanted to *stay* angry.

Navidad made no answer and returned to the kitchen. She was worried about her señora.

She'd seen her solemn and serious before, that was Señora's nature, even vexed. But never like this. Señora had a scorpion in her stomach.

Up in her bedroom Doña Socorro threw off her clothes and yanked on a cotton nightgown she didn't particularly like. By the time she was between the sheets Navidad came in soundless but for the tinkle of her bracelets and the rich smell of cinnamon flowed into the room.

"You must put something in your stomach, Doña, something sweet to drive away the scorpion." She handed her a plate of golden banana slices sautéed in butter and sprinkled with cinnamon and sugar. They looked like big gold coins.

"*Gracias.*" It was impossible to frown at Navidad but she couldn't even summon a smile. She took the plate from her and inhaled the delicious aroma.

"It looks like we'll have some rain tonight but tomorrow the sun will smile on us and a new life begins. Sleep well, Doña." Navidad quietly jingled away.

If Doña Socorro possessed any passion at all, it was for bananas sautéed in butter sprinkled with cinnamon and sugar. She brought the plate up to her nose. The spicy fragrance nearly coaxed the sulky mouth into a smile. It would have required no effort to wolf down everything on the plate and two more just like it. One bite, she knew, would make her feel better and all the bitterness would disappear. But Doña Socorro wanted to savor every drop of the nectar of her fury. She threw the plate on the nightstand, turned out the light, and lay in the darkness staring up at the ceiling with clenched teeth in the perverse comfort of her anger. Sleep came in the company of a soft rain.

The ring of the phone at half past three in the morning startled her out of sedation. She groped for the instrument and answered with a groggy *bueno*?

"Socorro! Did I wake you?"

"Mamá, mamá! Is it really you?

"*Sí, mi amor,* of course, it's me."

"Oh mamá, mamá, you've made me so happy!"

"Your father and I are flying out tomorrow."

"Oh mamá, it's been so long. I can hardly wait till morning!"

"Papá has his own plane, you know."

"An airplane!"

"Yes, *mi amor*, an airplane. He takes it to the office every morning then flies home and puts it in the garage. We'll bring bananas and—"

Bananas! "*Bueno*? Mamá, mamá, are you there? *Bueno, bueno!*"

Doña Socorro bolted up in bed. The room was cold and her nightgown was soaking wet. The nail polish smell of bananas was overpowering in the pitch black bedroom. Rain against the windowpane sounded like someone was throwing gravel at her window. She tried to pull the clammy nightgown over her head but she was clutching the little gold medallion in her sweaty hand. "Dear God, will the dreams ever go away?" she asked the darkness. It's been eighteen years. Eighteen years! Lost to pride, the most destructive of all human traits. How many sons and daughters, brothers and sisters, are pulled apart by pride? Her heart couldn't hold any more. Doña Socorro began to cry.

Navidad had it right. The next morning the sun smiled on Tecate, the air smelled freshly laundered. When Doña Socorro came around the corner she saw the trash scattered on the sidewalk in front of El Emporio. She ignored the litter, jabbed her key into the lock, and stopped. Memory, her unwanted companion, was back. *Crazy dreams, airplanes, bananas!* A voice from the past...*victims of poverty and ignorance...a matter of pride*. She retrieved her key.

On the corner of the main plaza Doña Socorro saw "la burra," the local yellow bus gasping for life with its doors open, and boarded. She knew why she was on the bus, she knew where she was going, but she wasn't prepared for what lay ahead. It took half an hour to the end of town where she was told to transfer to the blue and white TRANSPORTES SUB URBANOS. Here she endured an hour in a broken seat jouncing and lurching over dirt roads strewn with potholes the size of craters. This was one of the rare times Socorro regretted not owning a car. It was not that she couldn't afford one, she could easily afford to buy any car she wanted. It was that she simply wasn't fascinated by motorcars like most people in Tecate. She bought a Honda Accord soon after her arrival in Tecate and paid someone to give her lessons. Her first lesson consisted of a simple turn around the block. This was going to be easier than she thought until a hay truck suddenly backed out of a driveway. There was a horrendous explosion and she sat in a blizzard of hay and dirt. Sixty bales of high quality alfalfa were now scattered on both sides of the street. A number of ducks and chickens, understandably excited from their close call with death, fluttered in all directions. She walked home and never got behind the wheel again.

When the blue and white bus slammed to a stop and the doors hissed open, Doña Socorro knew she would never walk again. "El Rincon," the driver called out. "El Rincon *de los damnificados!*" and she limped out. Her whole body ached and she knew her spinal column was irreparably dislocated. She stood on a corner assessing a wooden shack with a Coca-Cola sign that gave it the appearance of a grocery store. A black poster with yellow lettering on the door read, WE VOTED PRD. Cautiously she stepped inside. It was dark and for a moment she thought she had just walked into someone's living room by mistake. Little children in someone else's clothing played on the bare concrete floor. A baby, innocent of its legacy, slept soundly in a cardboard carton. There were no aisles or counters. It was one small room with a long table where some sorry looking grocery items were put out. The place reeked of rotting vegetables and kerosene. When her eyes accustomed to the dark a figure came into focus. A tired-looking woman about her own age sat in a chair watching the children. Socorro made inquiry. The woman did not recognize the name Consuelo Hernandez but the description matched the young girl who came in and bought a banana almost every day.

"The girl lives at the Tapiceria Lopez. It's on the next street. Just walk to the corner and turn left." The woman began to struggle out of her chair. "Come, I'll show you."

Doña Socorro looked at the swollen ankles. "Oh no, you mustn't bother. I can find it."

"No bother, señora. I'll just take you as far as the corner. I have trouble with my legs. It's the diabetes, you know."

The woman's obvious sacrifice to do a total stranger a good turn brought Doña Socorro a twinge in the vicinity of her heart and a flush of embarrassment. They reached the corner. "Just follow this road all the way to the end, about two long blocks, and you'll see it. Tapiceria Lopez."

"*Gracias, muchas gracias! Muy amable!*" Doña Socorro gushed sincerely. She felt she wanted to do something for the poor thing, but what? The woman was poor but not without dignity. Any type of remuneration would have been a slap in the face. She repaid in kind. "*Gracias*, may God visit you and reward you for your kindness." She started down the dirt road.

Both sides of the street were banked with a high berm of dirt left by a road grader last winter. That left only the middle of the street for cars, pedestrians, and dogs. She had to be careful not to turn an ankle in a pothole or stumble on the concealed outcroppings of rock that poked out of the ground like icebergs. Every time a car rumbled past she was left choking in a tidal wave of yellow dust. The street was lined on both sides with pathetic little hovels, some of brick, some of scrap lumber with a blue plastic tarp for a roof. Crazy zigzags and meaningless scribbles taking the form of letters in black and red and purple were sprayed on every wall. Used clothing hung on fences with a "for sale" sign. Ugly cats sulked under the shade of dead cars rusting in front of nearly every shack. Street dogs, victims of nature's practical joke, looked as though they were on their way to a masquerade party. The wiry tail of a terrier waved to her from the hind end of a boxer. A cocker spaniel wearing the pointed face of a Pomeranian followed her for a few steps then went off to sniff at a silky collie wearing the face of a Doberman. She had to step around a huge rat still twitching from a head wound. Everyone on the street must have been cooking. The smell of hot lard and fried beans hung in the dusty air. I'm walking through the natural habitat of the destitute, Doña Socorro thought, a dynasty of poverty, hunger, and dirt. Crime must breed here like mosquitoes in stagnant water.

What misery, she thought. Doña Socorro could accept poverty. She'd never experienced it, but it was something she could at least understand. Hunger also. But filth, never! She thought of Consuelo. She's poor. She may not get enough to eat, but she's clean! Doña Socorro saw the upholstery shop up ahead, a plywood shack that wouldn't be there tomorrow if the wind picked up. She shuddered. Thank God I'll never have to do this again. A voice spoke to her. *Consuelo does this every day.* It had never entered her mind. Consuelo did this every day, twice a day. And she was never late. She must start out at five in the morning!

Either there was no door on Tapiceria Lopez or it was open, Socorro couldn't be sure. She walked in. The strong smell of new fabric was pleasant. A man the color of varnished maple was busy guiding a piece of fabric under the stitching needle of an ancient Singer. *Clickety-clickety-klunk. Clickety-clickety-klunk.* An enormous woman in flowered smock and pants sat cutting a pattern with a pair of shears. She looked up from her work.

"*Buenas tardes,*" Socorro's voice was tentative.

"*Buenas tardes,*" the pair answered.

"I'm looking for Consuelo Hernandez."

"Through there," the woman answered and tossed her head in the direction of an open door at the back of the shop. "Just knock on the back door."

Doña Socorro thanked her, passed though the doorway, and stepped into a small yard littered with car seats stripped naked to the springs. There, on the side of the shack was a wooden door. Closed. Her authoritative knock rattled the sagging door like an earthquake. No answer. She rehearsed her speech. She had something to say to this girl and she was ready for her. Maybe the girl didn't hear. She'd try another series of knocks, louder this time. The door opened and Consuelo stood in front of her wearing only jeans and a towel draped around her neck. Doña Socorro noticed the bra would never survive another washing. Consuelo's hair was wet, black, shiny. She smelled of flowery soap and shampoo.

Their eyes met, cold and silent. Doña Socorro thought she was ready for the confrontation. She wasn't. Neither spoke. She looks like a child, Doña Socorro thought. She *is* a child. Seventeen. My Laura would be seventeen now. Her hand came up to her breast involuntarily to caress the gold medallion. Seventeen years, she sighed in silence, seventeen years and the pain of the past still festers in my heart.

Doña Socorro looked into the youthful face in front of her, the large eyes timid as a fawn. She gathered herself up and squared her shoulders. She didn't mumble, didn't look down at the ground. She spoke in a firm, resolute voice. "I have done you a terrible injustice, Consuelo, I came to beg your forgiveness. I don't deserve it but I hope you'll come back to me." Suddenly Doña Socorro was overcome with emotion. She didn't wait to hear the answer. Fighting for self control, she turned and walked back the way she came, through the street with no hope, watering the dirt road with her tears.

When Doña Socorro returned to El Emporio late in the afternoon she was emotionally drained. I'm delirious, she thought when, for no reason she could credit, she was replaying a scene in a high school class of twenty-five years ago where they were required to read La Iliada de Homero. No wonder! I feel like Hector must have felt when he was dragged behind a chariot. She thought of that big comfortable house waiting for her. What I need now is an hour in a deep hot bath with scented oils. She put her key in the lock and turned. The idea took form in her mind in the same instance as the click of the lock. Would it work? Why not? Yes! The hot tub could wait. She summoned Navidad.

The next morning Doña Socorro opened the store earlier than usual. She wanted to be there before Consuelo arrived. Her mind was crowded but right now there were other things to do. She put cash in the cash register, arranged some baby clothes that had come in yesterday. It was nearly ten when Doña Socorro looked at her watch and realized Consuelo wasn't there. The girl was never late. A half hour later she had to accept it. Consuelo wasn't late. She wasn't coming.

Doña Socorro stepped out front and assessed the overnight accumulation of litter: papers, Styrofoam cups, candy wrappers, an aluminum beer can, a red plastic sandal, and several large dark coils left behind by homeless dogs. Anyone, a passing boy, the beggar on the corner, would have performed the unpleasant task for a few coins. Without so much as a flinch she went to the utility room, returned with broom and dustpan, and got to work. She gathered all the litter from the gutter and deposited everything in the municipal trash barrel on the corner.

We get what we deserve, an inner voice said.

Wednesday morning the scene of the previous day was repeated. The collection of overnight litter was the same as yesterday with the exception of the red plastic sandal and one less extrusion. One of the dogs must have changed his route. Doña Socorro set to work and listened to her thoughts. *She's won't be in today either.* Doña Socorro had to admit the painful truth. *She's never never coming back, I stepped over the line. I can't believe how much damage we do to others when we've been hurt. Why do we do it?*

Before she left the house Thursday morning Doña Socorro checked to make sure she had shoes on her feet, the cash envelope in her bag, and headed for the store. She waved a listless *buenos dias* to her neighbors along her route. It was time to face reality, she told herself. Consuelo would never be back. I'll put the sign in the window first thing this morning. She turned the corner, waved to the news vendor and suddenly her vision went blurry.

Consuelo!

There she was in her rumpled jeans with the pink belt and that faded yellow blouse. She held a broom in one hand, a dustpan in the other. "I borrowed these from the flower shop next door."

Doña Socorro thought her heart would burst fighting back the joy in her heart that threatened to spill into her eyes. She wanted to throw her arms around the child and say *you're back, you're back! I thought I lost you!* She did neither. Don't get all misty-eyed, she told herself. This doesn't mean she's forgiven your inexcusable behavior. It simply means she needs the money.

"We'll open late today," Doña Socorro said in a colorless voice. "I didn't have time for breakfast this morning. Let's get a coffee and pastry in the plaza."

They walked the two blocks without words. Both had something to say but neither knew how to begin so they just walked along pretending the recent incident never happened. They crossed the plaza, entered the Panaderia del Parque, and found a table for two near the window.

"*Buenos dias*, Doña Socorro, coffee for two?"

"Yes, and a pastry. What do you like, Consuelo?" She saw the girl hesitate. "I myself prefer the palm leaves. No one makes them better than Juanita." Consuelo nodded in agreement and Juanita smiled her appreciation.

They sat facing each other with nothing to say until they were served. Doña Socorro was now ready to begin her presentation. Consuelo lost no time in biting into her palm leaf dusted with sugar which immediately shattered.

"They're crumbly but they sure are good," Doña Socorro said, and now her lap was full of crumbs too. "I've decided that I need a full-time assistant more than I need a cleaning girl. There is so much to do and I just can't do it all. It means more responsibility but it also means a bigger salary. What do you say to that?"

Consuelo turned shy. "Yes, señora, I think I would like that but am I really the right person for the job? I have no experience, remember." She hesitated. "I don't want to disappoint you, señora." Consuelo didn't say, *I haven't gotten over what happened,* but she didn't have to. It was apparent.

Doña Socorro marched right on. "Of course, it will take some time to learn all the details of the store, but you're a quick learner. I think you would do a great job." She waited for Juanita to bring refills. "But I think it would be best if you lived closer. It's an arduous trip now, it'll be even worse come winter."

A gloomy shadow appeared on Consuelo's youthful face. She dropped her eyes and stared down into her cup. "It's all I can afford, señora," she answered in an embarrassed whisper.

Doña Socorro felt like biting her tongue. Her voice turned soft, warm. *"Ay, mi amor!"* The endearment escaped and her hands were holding Consuelo's before she knew she'd done it. Consuelo couldn't remember anyone ever calling her "my darling." Two warm hands gently enfolding her own brought Consuelo a flood of silent tears. Never in her life had anyone—no, not even her mother—laid a loving hand on her. She'd never felt a reassuring touch, a tender kiss, no one ever put their arms around her. She wanted to wipe away the tears from her face but she didn't want to lose the feel of Doña Socorro's warm hands gently caressing her own.

"That's not a problem. There's a spare room at the house. It's yours if you want it." She handed Consuelo her napkin and watched her dry her face to give her time to answer. Consuelo remained silent. Doña Socorro pressed on. "No one's using it. Why waste it? You might as well enjoy the convenience of walking to work."

Consuelo crumpled the soggy napkin in her hand and managed a timid little smile.

"Gracias, señora."

"Good, that's settled—and stop calling me señora. My name is Socorro. And I prefer to be spoken to in the second person. I hate the sound of *usted."*

"Socorro," Consuelo whispered. *Succor.* It made sense.

Doña Socorro, too, saw the irony. The girl in front of her was named *comfort.* "And you were baptized Consuelo. I never thought about it before." She took a final sip of coffee and returned the cup to the table. "Come, let's get the store open and get to work!"

And at that moment the cold, austere Doña Socorro became Socorro. She took Consuelo's arm, put it through hers, and they crossed the plaza in gentle silence.

Together they organized the stock and put out fresh merchandise. Occasionally, Socorro left her alone while she waited on customers. Consuelo studied the front window. It looked the same now as it did when she came to work five weeks ago.

"Would you mind if I did something with this window?"

"Mind? By all means do what you want! I never get around to it."

"There's a little wicker basket in the back. I thought we could put a baby doll in it and surround it with all the baby things."

"*Magnífico!*" Socorro actually clapped her hands. "Go down to the toy store and pick out what you want." She handed her a two hundred peso note. "And anything else you need."

Consuelo was only gone a few minutes. In less than an hour she had the big window dressed. A sweet baby in pink lay sleeping in the basket surrounded with pink booties, gowns, and one-piece flannel trundle outfits. She dressed two boy mannequins in shorts and tank tops and placed a soccer ball at their feet. The shapely girl mannequin got a black T-shirt and pair of rather tight pink jeans. Consuelo arranged her so that her smooth *nalgas* faced the street.

"Come outside a minute, Socorro, and see if it's okay." It was the first time she'd called her by her first name and addressed her as *tu* and not *usted*. It felt strange but she liked the sound of it.

"This is wonderful!" Socorro exclaimed when they stood out on the sidewalk. "You know, when I first came to Tecate I noticed that no one bothered to arrange displays. They still don't. They just pile stuff in the window. And I'm just as bad. From now on you're in charge of windows!"

Two older women stopped to look in the window. "*Ay, comadre* isn't that adorable!" They walked inside.

"I can't leave the store alone, Consuelo, but this would be a good time for you to go to the house and see if your room is adequate." Socorro followed the *comadres* into the store.

Consuelo suddenly became timid again. "Oh, Socorro. Are you sure it's all right? I don't want to impose on you in any—"

"Stop!" Socorro was laughing while she said it. "I don't want to hear such nonsense. The room is sitting vacant. Go see if it's all right, we can go for your things later." Both women knew there were no "things" to bring back later. "Go to the corner of Nayarit and walk three blocks. It's No. 26. Navidad will show it to you."

Consuelo walked the two long blocks with a light heart and a skip in her step. No one had ever been kind to her before. No one. Like a stray dog, Consuelo accepted each day as it came and took whatever scrap was offered. It was probably no more than a cot in a storeroom, but she would be living five minutes from work. She could meet people and make friends. And she liked Socorro. Even alone it embarrassed her when she remembered accusing her of having an ice cube for a heart. A black wrought iron gate with No. 26 came into view. She let herself into a small garden and rang the bell on the old door of heavy oak.

"*Buenas tardes.*" Consuelo, who was not tall, had to look down at the diminutive figure that opened the door. That's as far as she got.

"Señorita Consuelo, *pase usted a su casa.*"

Consuelo stood stunned for a moment. No one had ever called her señorita before and certainly never spoke to her as *usted*. But her moment of wonder didn't last. Navidad swung the door open wide. The warm Indian smile and the sparklers in the deep black eyes left Consuelo no doubt that she was really in "her house."

"*Gracias.*"

"*Pase, pase!*"

Consuelo followed Navidad through a long *estancia* with a view of a garden where a small fountain babbled like a happy child. They ascended a long staircase paved with rose-colored mosaic then down a dim hall. Navidad pushed open another oak door and with the same language of the eyes native to Oaxaca, ushered her in.

"*Lo que se le ofresca,* Señorita Consuelo. *Para servirle.*" And with that Navidad disappeared. "Whatever you need, Señorita Consuelo, I am here to serve you." A standard Mexican recitation, but from Navidad, came across to Consuelo as genuine and sincere.

Consuelo walked the rest of the way into the room feeling she was wide awake in a dream. She didn't know where to look first. The huge bed, white, with blue, red, and yellow hummingbirds flying across the headboard dominated the room. It was covered with a green and yellow flowered comforter and matching pillows. A bed! *I've never slept in a bed!* She threw herself onto it at once. I'm never getting up, she laughed to herself. But she did, and discovered a matching dresser with the same little colored hummingbirds on the drawer-fronts and a big mirror. A tall carved armoire stood in the far corner. On one wall was a yellow brick fireplace with a raised hearth. She swept the whole room with her eyes again and discovered another door. A bathroom! A real bathroom, with a massive tub of green porcelain with matching basin, and a real toilet. She used it immediately. No cockroaches crawling near her feet. No big, black, hairy spiders. What luxury! When she went to wash her hands she discovered a bowl filled with rose-shaped soaps. She felt like a princess.

Still in a dream state Consuelo returned to the bedroom. She admired the dresser. *I'll never have anything to put in here.* She slid open the top drawer. Somebody must have left their things in it. There was a neat row of panties in pretty colors—and matching bras. The next drawer down held T-shirts, some awfully cute blouses and a sweater. Was she in the wrong room? Then it all clicked. *No one left these things here. They've never been worn—they're intended for me!* She ran to the armoire and threw open the doors. Pants, skirts, dresses, a coat!

Consuelo began to cry.

A customer was just leaving when Consuelo entered. She spotted Socorro still at the cash register and flew the entire length of the store to throw her arms around her. She had so many things to say to her at once that she couldn't say anything at all. The two women, both with wet faces, held each other tight in a fierce embrace.

Socorro yielded to a joy she hadn't felt in eighteen years. "Let me look at you," she sniffled.

Consuelo held out her arms and made a graceful turn. She was in a pair of baby blue jeans with a pink daisy embroidered on each back pocket. The navy blue jersey gave Consuelo new feminine lines that weren't there before. She made an effort to blubber her thanks but the words wouldn't clear the thickening in her throat.

Socorro was pleased with her choice. "We'll have to do something about shoes."

And so it was that the seeds of friendship found fertile soil in the hearts of a seventeen-year-old-girl and thirty-nine-year-old women. For Consuelo El Emporio was more than just a job. For the first time in her young life Consuelo felt safe. She had a real home, a trusted friend, pretty clothes, and money in her purse. In her favor was the resiliency of the young. Day by day, her old fears began to fade and in time the scars in her soul began to heal.

A slow but inexorable change began to take form in Socorro. Consuelo was more than an employee to her. For the first time in eighteen years she had someone to think about besides herself. The child was sensitive and vulnerable. Consuelo needed someone to look after her and she fulfilled Socorro's need to feel useful. Socorro learned to smile, to laugh again, to rekindle friendships. Gradually her new sense of self-fulfillment began to leach away the past and she came into the store one morning in a gaily flowered silk dress!

Together they ran the store like two partners and they never failed to have a good time doing it. When they closed up and went home Navidad would fix them dinner. They would take their coffee into the living room and talk away the evening like two girlfriends. Socorro remembered, Consuelo learned. When Consuelo was running a low grade fever Socorro would put her to bed. She did not leave her to the servant like her parents did to her, but looked after her herself before she left in the morning, again at noon, and sat at her bedside in the evening. If Consuelo had cramps Socorro would assert her authority and send her home early then bring her *pasiflora* tea to soothe the distress of the first day of her *regla*. On weekends they would take a taxi to Rancho Tecate Country Club for a lavish dinner or walk to La Fonda and listen to the mariachis.

Over time the girl and the woman grew together. They knew what the other was thinking and even knew what they were going to say before they said it. So it wasn't unusual when one Friday Consuelo perceived that Socorro seemed nervous and more absent minded than usual. Something was obviously troubling her mind. As soon as she had the merchandise organized she would go over to her and see what had her so antsy. But she didn't have the opportunity. Socorro came to her.

"Consuelo, *mi amor*, would you mind running some errands for me this afternoon? I've got too many things on my mind."

"So I've noticed! Whatever it is, put it in my hands and out of your mind."

"You're wonderful! Right after lunch I want to you to make the bank deposit. Then go to Rosita's shop and see if the ceramic plate I ordered has come in yet."

"That's all? I can do that in a flash and come back and help you here."

"Oh!" It was more of a gasp than an interjection. "I almost forgot. Take the phone bill to the Telnor office and check the amount against the charges. I think they made a mistake."

"I may be a couple of hours but I'll take care of everything. You just calm down and relax, okay?"

"*Eres un amor!*"

Banco de Londres was Consuelo's first stop. It was one of her favorite errands. She thoroughly enjoyed Sr. Jimenez's extravagant reception into the inner office. The bowing and the "*Buenas tardes*, señorita, *sí*, señorita, coffee, pastry? You simply must, señorita." It was as much flirtation as it was courtesy. The trip to Rosita's was something of a wild goose chase but she finally concluded that the ceramic plate had not arrived. Her visit to the telephone company office was tedious. No one at Telnor offered you coffee and pastry. She stood in a long line that never seemed to get shorter. It took half an hour just to get to the girl at the counter and then she was referred to someone else. It took nearly an hour to come to the conclusion that there was no error in the billing.

Consuelo was gone two hours. Two hours! She was ready to drop into a chair. It was after three when she walked into the store and she headed straight for the coffee pot. *Dios mio!* The place was full of customers.

"There she is!" someone shouted.

All of a sudden they all began to sing the Mexican birthday song.

Estas son las mañanitas
que cantava el rey David
A las muchachas bonitas
se las cantamos así.

What was going on? Was it someone's birthday?

Socorro pushed her way to the front of the ladies and threw her arms around her. "*Feliz cumpleaños, mi amor!*"

Consuelo still didn't get it. Then it hit her. These weren't customers. It was a birthday party. *Her* birthday! Consuelo made no effort to hide the tears that were now streaming down both cheeks. Each guest came to her to give her a warm *abrazo* and say "*felicidades!*" There was Anita from the flower shop, Mila from the pharmacy, others from the local shops—and Rosita from Rosita's. It was a ruse! She'd been sent out to see if the sow had piglets! A card table was set up with a huge yellow cake with white roses. "Consuelo" was written across the top in pink icing. Eighteen candles flickered gaily.

"Make a wish! Make a wish!" the ladies all cried.

Like a ten-year-old, Consuelo closed her eyes tight, looked toward the ceiling then blew all eighteen candles out in one pass. There was a roar of applause. The whole store smelled like melting wax.

Consuelo threw her arms around Socorro and whispered through her tears, "*Ay,* Socorro, I've never had a birthday party. You are your name, *succor!*" Then she spoke words she had never spoken to anyone. "I love you."

Socorro held her tight. "And you, Consuelo, live up to your name, *comfort.*" Tears of joy filled her eyes and she said something she never thought she'd speak again in her life. "I love you too, *mi amor.* You fill all the empty places in my heart."

It was a happy little party. While Consuelo had been sent out to see about the piglets the ladies helped Socorro festoon the store with birthday serpentines and banners—everything but a piñata. Consuelo opened the first gifts she ever received within her young memory. There was a bottle of cologne, an exquisite ceramic bowl for her dresser, a blue silk scarf, a box of chocolates, dangly earrings, and from Socorro, a gold watch. Everyone filled up on miniature tacos, hot sausages, coffee and cake, and chattered like school girls until late.

That night, physically exhausted but emotionally high, Socorro sat alone by the fire in her bedroom. It wasn't cold but Navidad had laid the fire for her earlier. She'd already tucked Consuelo into bed with a kiss and now, wrapped in her favorite burgundy silk dressing gown, she began playing back the birthday party. Consuelo looked so young, so pretty. The look of surprise on her face when she walked in the door was priceless! Eighteen. She remembered what it was like to be eighteen. She could still feel the teary kiss Consuelo put on her face. She thought about their names, *succor* and *comfort*. Her breast swelled with a euphoria she didn't fully understand. *God, it feels good to feel good*! Where have I been?

It was quiet in the big house, the only sounds the crackling of an oak fire in the hearth and the steady drumming of an early rain. Without realizing she was doing it, once again, Socorro found herself in the attic of her memories sifting through all her old yesterdays. It's amazing, she told herself, how the memory can hold the heart hostage for so many years. Socorro didn't hold those old memories very long. One by one she tossed them all into the fire. "I don't need these old yesterdays anymore. I have todays, and I have tomorrows," she told herself. With a quick tug she pulled the gold chain from around her neck that imprisoned her for eighteen years. And the medallion went into the fire. "I have my daughter."

It didn't take but a few weeks for word to get around that there was a very pretty girl working at El Emporio and the *gallos* began to saunter in pretending to browse until they could talk to Consuelo. They came in every afternoon and the routine was the same.

"*Hola.*"

"*Hola.* What can I do for you?"

"I need a pair of white socks. What's your name?"

"Consuelo. We have athletic socks in packs of six."

"Maybe we could go out when you get off work."

Consuelo felt immensely flattered but she was also aware she had a job to do. Boys were a new experience for her and she wasn't quite sure how to handle so much attention. She had no snappy comebacks. She never learned to flirt and she was relieved when Socorro would live up to her name and come to the rescue.

"Consuelo dear, would you help that woman find what she's looking for?" Then she would turn to the young rooster. "Now, let me show you the socks." More often than not the young hopefuls said they would be back later.

One evening at home when they were reviewing their day, Consuelo said, "Why did you chase off that beautiful boy who wanted to look at shirts?"

"He's not for you. These young flirts that come in here aren't looking for someone to go have an ice cream with or to a movie or dinner."

"No?"

Socorro looked at her. My girl might be eighteen, she thought, but she has no experience whatever with boys. A fourteen-year-old *gallo* could seduce her before she knew it. She's vulnerable as a ten-year-old.

"No, *mi amor.* You have to be very careful of the friends you make. The boys that buzz around here are not seeking your friendship. And that particular boy is twenty-four and he's been plucking flowers since he was fourteen. As women we have to learn to take a close look at the men who want to date us."

"But it must be fun to be popular."

"Oh, it is, believe me. And it's easy to be popular. We've got what men want. Some men will bribe you for it with flowers, flattering *pirópos,* and gifts. Others with vows of eternal love and marriage. They are perjurers, felons, thieves, and blackmailers—worse than some *cabrón* who steals your purse—they'll steal your life! They're willing to destroy you for momentary pleasure."

One afternoon a few days later a young man oozing with confidence came into the store and made his way to Consuelo like a rooster in a henhouse.

"*Buenas tardes,* señorita. I need a couple of tank tops like the kind you have in the window."

He was an attractive individual, at least a head taller, thick wavy hair and a neat mustache. "They're over here." She led him to another counter. "Any special color?"

"Black."

He had a pleasant voice and a rather cute smile. "Anything else?"

"Yes."

She waited.

"What time do you get off work?"

Consuelo was not prepared for the question and didn't answer.

"I'd like to invite you out to get some dinner. We could walk around the plaza and get acquainted."

Consuelo felt a little electric tickle in her stomach. What fun! Socorro was busy with some ladies and before she could come over and chase him out she answered. "You can come by for me at five."

It was a busy afternoon but by four o'clock the place was empty. "You were too fast for me, Consuelo, you'd better go home and get ready for your *novio* to pick you up at five."

"You knew all the time didn't you?"

"Of course." They both laughed. "Now go make yourself pretty."

"I still have to wash my hair."

"You can't wash your hair now."

"Why not?"

"It won't dry by the time you're out and night air is bad for you. You don't want to come down with a fever."

Consuelo was back in half an hour in a blue denim skirt and off-white sweater. "I didn't get my head wet. How do I look?"

"You look beautiful, *mi amor*. Now, where are you going?"

"He just said out to dinner."

Poor child, she'll have to learn sometime. "It's almost five. Have a good time and knock on my door as you go by when you get home. I just want to know that you're home." Socorro walked back into the storeroom just as the front door opened and Fernando walked in.

It was well after ten when Consuelo let herself in very quietly so as not to disturb Socorro. She found her in a big leather easy chair wrapped in a silk robe the color of aged burgundy trimmed with white lace. She was leafing through a fashion magazine under the light of tiffany lamp.

"Socorro! What are you doing up?"

"Oh, I wasn't waiting up for you, *mi amor*," she lied. "I never get a chance to look at the clothing magazines. I didn't realize it was late. Did you have a good time?"

"Well, yes and no."

"Tell me about the yes."

"We walked to La Palapa for fish tacos. It was a nice walk. He held my hand the whole way. I didn't mind. On the way back he put my arm through his and we walked back to the plaza for coffee at the little *panaderia*. And that was nice too. Then we just sat in the plaza and talked. Got acquainted." Consuelo stopped her narrative in an embarrassed pause. "He kissed me here." She tapped her cheek. "It felt nice."

Socorro already knew how nice it felt to be kissed. "Then where does the 'no' come in?"

"*Ay!* All of a sudden I feel a hand going up my skirt and another trying to get under my blouse—he was like an *octópodo*. It was *horrible!*"

"You've got the wrong animal—he's known here as *el gavilán pollero*."

"Chicken hawk! A chicken hawk doesn't have eight hands!"

They had a good laugh. "Now get to bed, it's late." Consuelo kissed her cheek and ran off to her room. It wasn't until she got undressed that she realized she couldn't remember ever kissing anyone good night. She was barely under the covers when Socorro came in with a cup of hot chocolate.

By now two or three young *gallos* were coming in every day. In only took Consuelo a short time to become skillful at discouraging their solicitations while she sold them what they wanted. Occasionally she would palm one off on Socorro for pure amusement.

"I'm looking for *calzones*," a *gallo* said to her one afternoon, the double meaning dripping from his grin.

She'd never seen this boy before, but he was obvious. "Right this way."

The boy followed Consuelo until they reached Socorro. "This young man is looking for underwear. I'll look in back but maybe you can show him what we have out here," she said, and left him.

"Of course," Socorro obliged. "*Calzones* for men or for women?"

"*Ay!* I'm not sure. I'll be back later."

"I don't think that one will bother to come back," Consuelo laughed. "I hope he wasn't one of your better customers."

"Well, you said it was fun to be popular! Look, I've got a number of errands to run. You can manage the store while I'm gone?"

"Of course." She watched Socorro pick up her briefcase. "What on earth do you need that raincoat for? Look outside. It must be eighty degrees out there and there isn't a cloud in the sky."

"You haven't lived in Tecate long enough." Socorro walked to the door. "And when Navidad says it's going to rain you wear a raincoat no matter how silly it looks. It's kind of like Noah building his *barque* during a drought."

"I'll mind the store."

"And don't run off with the first good looking *gavilán* that comes in here!"

Consuelo watched her cross the street in her long black raincoat and laughed. There was nothing to do at the moment. She got busy rearranging the stock and dusting counters with a soft damp cloth. Suddenly it got very dark. She looked up to see if the ceiling fixtures had gone out but they were on. A sudden explosion of thunder made her jump. Now the lights did go out and Consuelo stood in the dark. She went to the window and looked out. The sky had turned to slate and a downpour of warm tropical rain came down in torrents. It sounded like rolling timpani. The water came down so fast it seemed a curtain had been drawn between heaven and earth. She couldn't even see the shops across the street. There was a quick flash, another roll of thunder, and she made out a blurred figure running along the sidewalk making its way toward the door.

The figure reached the door and pushed in. "*Qué bárbaro!* I wasn't ready for this." It was a young man in white chinos and yellow summer shirt. He stamped his feet and a puddle began to form around his shoes. "I'm so sorry, I do apologize. But I had no other place to run." His explanation was not intended for anyone in particular. The store was dark as a cave and he couldn't see anything.

"No bother."

The refugee shook himself like a wet dog, pushed the hair out of his eyes and noticed for the first time that someone was standing in front of him. It looked like a girl. A very pretty girl! She was smiling at him. "Señorita, if you have a mop I'll clean up the mess I made."

Señorita. "There's hot coffee in the pot, would you like a cup?"

"*Dios la bendigue!* God bless you!"

It did not escape Consuelo's notice that he spoke to her in the courteous third person. "I'll bring one." She went to the coffee machine and back.

"*Gracias, muy amable.*"

"I don't know how you'll ever get dry. Do you have far to go?"

"No, I work at the brewery. I'm an accountant. I just ran out to do some errands — and look!"

Consuelo left him drinking his coffee, made a trip to the utility room and came back with a mop and a towel over her arm. She began to dry the floor. "Oh no, señorita! Give me that." He took the mop away from her. "Please forgive my bad manners." He extended a soggy hand. "I'm Rafael Acevedo Beltran, your *servidor.*"

"Consuelo Hernandez," she answered to custom, and accepted the cold wet hand into her own. They were now properly introduced. He was about twenty, she figured, a head taller, and very slim. The wet shirt clinging to his skin detailed a broad, firm chest with two little peaks. His hair was a fright but he had nice eyes, and a pleasant voice. No mustache. He did not have the demeanor of a *gavilán.* Water poured off his ears. She had to laugh.

"Everyone calls me Rafa." The good looking stranger did the best he could on the puddle and handed back the mop. She handed him the towel.

"*Gracias,* señorita, *muchas gracias.*" He dried his hair and face. "Maybe I should buy all new clothes as long as I'm here."

He must be wet down to his underwear, Consuelo thought. She took it as a joke and answered him with a friendly laugh. "Look!"

The deluge stopped with the same suddenness as it came. The sun was bright, the sky innocent and blue. The streets were wet and shiny. "I can never repay your kindness, señorita." He hesitated. "Unless you let me take you out to dinner."

"Oh, there's no need for that."

"I am forever in your debt, señorita." He clutched his breast with both hands. "I owe you my life!" Such exaggerated gallantry tickled Consuelo but she wasn't prepared to answer. Rafa saw the hesitation. "Look, there's an art exhibit of local artists at the Centro de Cultura. There'll be work by Alvaro Blancarte, Lorena Brambila and an exciting new series by Laura Castaneda. Would you like to see it?"

"Yes!"

"Should I pick you up here?"

"At five o'clock if you're dry by then."

Rafa Acevedo Beltran bowed and made for the door. Consuelo followed him with her eyes as he walked across the street, turned the corner, and was lost from sight.

Consuelo was just ringing up the purchase of a blue baby blanket when Socorro returned from her errands with her raincoat over her arm. Socorro exchanged courtesies with her customer and walked her to the door. "Is there any coffee left?" she asked when the customer was gone.

"There is." Consuelo brought her a cup.

"Just what I needed." Socorro watched Consuelo return the mop and the towel to the utility room. "*Ay, Dios mio!*"

"What is it?"

"You're in love."

"*Yo, enamorada*? Certainly not!"

"You can't fool a woman old enough to be your mo — a woman twice your age. You're walking on air and humming a little tune, whether you realize it or not. Who is he?"

"Rafael Acevedo Beltran. He came into to get out of the rain just as you left."

"Rafa?"

"You know him?"

"Tecate is a small town. There are no strangers. He works as an accountant at the brewery. He's been in the store before, his mother too. Nice young man, nice family."

"He's taking me to the art exhibit at the Centro de Cultura this afternoon."

At a few minutes before five Consuelo was back in the store in white cotton pants and a rayon blouse the color of ripe strawberries. Her hair was obedient to the brush today and she felt pretty.

"You look delicious, *mi amor*."

'Thank you."

"Now go change your blouse."

"What!"

"It's cut a little too low for a first date."

She exchanged the low-cut strawberry frappé for a plum-colored turtleneck. "Is the neckline high enough?"

It was obvious to Socorro that she was beginning to fill out here and there over the last few months. Mostly *there*. "You're blossoming out in all the right places, so please be careful."

"I don't think I'm at high risk in the art gallery."

"It's not the art gallery I'm worried about."

"Then what?"

"The stroll through the plaza."

"*Ay!*"

She kissed her and Socorro disappeared just seconds before Rafa pushed through the door. He was in dressy black chinos and a black silk shirt. His hair was the same as it was earlier in the day, a mass of whiffles, whorls, and cowlicks. The only difference now was that it was dry.

They walked across the plaza to the CECUT. It was a warm afternoon scented with the rich smell of wet earth provided by the recent shower. The gardens looked bright and recently bathed. There was a line at the entrance. As they waited Consuelo scanned all the posters in the window announcing upcoming events. The headline on one read: OBRA DE TEATRO.

"Oh look! There's a play at the university next Sat—" Then she read the next line: MONOLÓGO DE UNA VAGINA.

Consuelo turned scarlet. Rafa saved the moment. "Oh look! Hot *churros*. I can't pass up a hot *churro*." A wave of his hand brought the pushcart over and their mouths were now too occupied with cinnamon and sugar for further comment.

And it was thus that two young hearts, two tender souls, began the gradual process of becoming one. Consuelo was like no other girl Rafa had ever known. She seemed fragile as a soap bubble, as though if he weren't careful she would vanish. She avoided the usual questions a boy and a girl exchange in the early part of their acquaintance. When he inquired as to her provenance her only answer was Sonora. Sonora is a big state, Rafa thought, but he let it go. She never talked about her family, or if indeed she had any. When he invited her to his house she would decline graciously and put him off with so much charm that he took her reticence as shyness and didn't press the issue. Consuelo told him she preferred to have him call for her at El Emporio. When he brought her back he delivered her to the gate at No. 26. There, under the soft glow of the lamp, the two lovers came together for that final good night kiss that is so hard to end, and the evening ended with a final clank as the big iron gate closed behind her.

They went out two or three times a week. There isn't much to do in Tecate. Sometimes it was an elegant dinner at Rancho Tecate Country Club, or La Fonda for pure fun, mariachis, and margaritas. If they wanted to see a movie they would have to travel to Tijuana. Other times it would be something as simple as tacos at Los Amigos. They always ended up snuggled on a secluded bench in the plaza. Here they emptied their hearts in whispers. They moved from little kisses light as the flutter of a butterfly to deep kisses confessing passion and desire. Their caresses could only be described as intimate and yet so filled with reverence as to render them chaste.

September, jealous of the praises gushed on summer, was now slowly pushing the fertile season from its place. The lush and verdant foliage of the *alamo* and *piocha* and *sauco* in the plaza were now tinged with a little red, tea roses in the gardens were gradually losing their blush and fragrance, and for good measure, the cold breath of autumn put a chill on Tecate in the early evening. Consuelo and Rafa left La Fonda earlier than usual and now sat in the plaza wrapped in each other's arms.

"I love you more now than the day I met you."

"You were soaking wet."

"And I know I'll never stop loving you. Consuelo, *mi corazón*. I want to marry you."

Consuelo dreamed of hearing these words and now she was terrified for having heard them. "*Ay, mi amor.*"

"I'm not like most men. I need you in my life because I love you. I don't love you because I need you."

"And I love you *mi amor*, body and soul."

"You've never mentioned your mother or your father. I don't know much about you. And I don't need to. I know all I want to know. But it's time I meet them so I can get their permission to make you my wife."

Consuelo panicked. She was ashamed of her sordid past. She felt guilty. When she first met Rafa she was careful never to mention anything about her past, not to deceive, but to help her believe it didn't exist. If Consuelo hadn't been in Rafa's arms she would have fled at that moment.

"Say yes, *corazón*."

"Yes." It was a low whisper Rafa perceived rather than heard.

"Now, tonight. I can ask your mother tonight. It's still early."

Consuelo and Rafa rushed into the store arm in arm, breathless from the run and excitement. It was nearly seven and Socorro was preparing to close up. Consuelo abandoned Rafa at the door and ran to her.

"Guess what, guess what!" she gushed like a child.

"What is it, *mi amor*?"

"Rafa wants to ask you something!" Consuelo turned to face him "Well, here she is. Ask her!"

Rafa stood paralyzed with confusion. He'd known Doña Socorro long before he met Consuelo. He'd been in her store. But he had no idea she had a daughter. Maybe they lived apart for some reason. Maybe she just recently arrived, maybe— He couldn't deal with it right now. He could hear his heart pounding in his head.

He looked at Consuelo. "You never told me Doña Socorro was your mother."

"The only mother I ever had!"

"Doña, I—I—I want to—I mean, I want your permission to marry Consuelo. I—"

Consuelo and Socorro fell into each other's arms. Neither knew exactly why they were laughing and crying at the same time.

Rafa tried to regain his composure. "I—I didn't know you were her mother."

"I am!"

Socorro and Consuelo opened their arms to Rafa who ran to join them.

"And the answer to your question is...yes!"

The Doughnut Man

I often sit in the plaza with no other motive beyond that of listening to the sounds of Tecate. Even with my eyes closed I can clearly see the human pageant as it unfolds with sound track alone; children, skipping and giggling and running up and down the stairs of the kiosk; the pretty mini-skirted office girls clicking along in high platform shoes, flashing colored stockings; teenagers with spiked hair and exposed bellybuttons laughing and flirting like noisy birds; I can hear the rusty laughter of the old-timer rancheros perched like crows in a row on the iron benches and concrete planters, gossiping in low voices about life and death, and telling romantic tales of questionable veracity of La Revolución that was over before they were born. Delicious little whiffs of onions browning and meat sizzling over a bed of mesquite coals float in from Tacos Los Amigos across the street. Without benefit of sight I know Don Ramon is roasting corn over an open brazier and all the good smells are now waking that hungry dragon that inhabits the stomach and can only be appeased with tacos *de carne asada* dripping with salsa and guacamole.

I open my eyes. Reality confirms imagination.

The warm air is embroidered with the lilting voices of the madrigal singers, the hawkers, and vendors, who sell everything from fake snakes to tamales. Some are ambulatory, others push their rustic carts, each voice coming in and going out in turn. The round usually begins with the bright tenor voice of the Doughnut Man.

"*Donas...aquí están las donas...donas calientitas!*"

Ching-ching-ching! "Ice cream...*chocolate, vainilla, mango!*"

"Leather! Genuine leather... purses, wallets, belts...*hua-raa-ches!*"
Talán, talán! "Sno-Cones...strawberry, lemon and lime!"
"Balloons, balloons! Every color, every shape...Shamu...Porky Peeg...Meeky Mouse!"

Then the canon begins all over again from the top, each clear voice fading in and fading out, sometimes homophonic, sometimes contrapuntal, reminiscent of the madrigals and canons of the Renaissance.

I've heard the street vendors hawking their wares in the plaza with song and rhyme forever. Six or eight months ago the voice of the Doughnut Man was not among them. His lilting tenor was a new addition to the chorale. Where did he come from? What brought him to Tecate to go into the doughnut business? There was a story here, I told myself. I was sure, I could sense it. It was palpable. But I was not going to invent it. His story, if there was one, had to be real.

"Donas...aquí están las donas...donas calientitas!"

I realized I was hearing the Doughnut Man long before he made his appearance from behind the tiled kiosk. I watched him enter center stage balancing an enormous tray on his head with his right hand. He moved like a dancer, taking long fluid strides with a rhythmic gait that seemed almost graceful. In his left hand he carried one of those folding luggage racks with straps you see in hotels. He flipped open the rack, set down the large tray heaped with fresh doughnuts, and sang his final line.

"Aquí están las donas!"

He was an interesting man to watch, lean, taller than most Mexican men. He was dressed in clean but rumpled black Dockers and a dazzling white T-shirt. When he turned I noticed his face, the color of chamois cloth, had deep grooves along both cheeks, and his dark eyes were intense. His hair was a wild black mane that lay flattened against his scalp owing to the weight of the heavy tray. The absence of a matching mustache gave the man a youthful aspect. I couldn't guess at his age but he wasn't young.

"Aquí están las donas!"

Men, women, the young, the old, converged on the doughnuts like piranhas. Though well beyond my hearing, I could observe an exchange of highly animated gesticulation of hands in pantomime and his big generous smile that insinuated friendly conversation was in progress with each customer. If someone tendered his hand the Doughnut Man was quick to reciprocate. Frequently someone would place a friendly hand on his shoulder before they turned and left with their doughnuts. What a congenial man of business! In a matter of a few minutes there was nothing left on the tray save a few crumbs and a scattering of sugar. This man could conduct seminars on direct selling!

One day while watching the matinee performance I found myself hankering for a doughnut. Tecate is a long way from Krispy Kreme. My palate tingled with the anticipation of a soft, warm, glazed doughnut freshly made. I worked my way through the piranhas.

"*Cuántas,* señor?" he said to me. "*Tres por diez.*" That felicitous smile again.

"*Tres,*" I answered. I paid him ten pesos in one fat coin. I found the only remaining shady bench in the square, confident I could make short work of three glazed doughnuts with minimum effort.

I closed my eyes, inhaled the fragrance. I was in doughnut heaven! I teased myself a few seconds before I took the first bite. Gag! I nearly lost my breakfast. It was like biting into a dirty gym sock covered with cinnamon and sugar. My face screwed up like that of a young child who, betrayed by his greedy eyes, puts something in his mouth offensive to his expectations and bursts into tears.

This defies all logic, I thought. I looked over at the Doughnut Man. The thick crowd of patrons was thinning out now, and when the last one withdrew, I saw that once again his large tray was empty! A little Chiclets boy, with high hopes for an easy sale in his smile and big soulful eyes, came by. I passed on the Chiclets but I gave him the two untouched doughnuts. "*Gracias,*" he said in that sweet soprano voice of little boys, and skipped off in childish ecstasy. By law they should have been marked KEEP OUT OF REACH OF CHILDREN. I felt I should register as a child abuser.

Now, I made it a point to come into the square every day at the same time in hopes of finding some explanation to what to me was now an undisclosed mystery. I would find a bench and sit at a distance and watch. It was the same scene every day.

"Aquí están las donas...donas calientitas!"

Ching-ching-ching "Ice cream...*chocolate, vainilla, mango!*"

"Leather! Genuine leather...purses, wallets, belts... *hua-raa-ches!*"

Talán, talán! "Sno-Cones...strawberry, lemon and lime!"

"Balloons, balloons! Every color, every shape...Shamu...Porky Peeg...Meeky Mouse!"

As soon as he placed the tray down on the rack he was mobbed and when the crowd withdrew, once again, every disgusting doughnut on that enormous tray was gone! The great minds of the ancients tell us there's a reason for everything. I'm okay with that. I can accept this as an eternal truth with a QED and all that. But this defied every equation you could advance. Even Descartes himself couldn't solve this one with all his funny triangles and analytic geometry.

More puzzled than ever, I gave up and left the square. Early the next morning I headed for La Fonda where I knew I would find the Cafeteros assembled around a coffee pot. If you need information, and you don't mind investing a good part of the morning to get it, there is no more fertile source than Tecate's unrecognized upper Chamber of Deputies. This august body convenes daily to write legislation for the Presidente Municipal, draft emergency legislation for economic reform for Vicente Fox, or rush a report to El Boosh to assure him that the VW Beetles produced in Mexico are no threat to the American wheat farmers. Los Cafeteros do not confine themselves to world affairs. They are just as quick to cover other vital issues such as grilling and barbecuing techniques, the best tequila and how to drink it, why any woman would wear Jockey *calzones*, or, does Life have meaning? All you need is a high capacity-bladder and an agile mind to follow the sudden changes in theme and theory.

The friendly smell of good coffee came to me as I walked through the door of La Fonda. Sssh! They were in session. I found an empty seat and slipped in unobtrusively. I scanned the table. They were all there, the doctor, the dentist, affectionately referred to as *sacamuelas*, the *licenciado*, the rancher, the dentist, a merchant, and a factory owner. The late arrival of our poet/accountant from the door marked CABALLEROS completed the quorum this morning. I found them in heated debate and I knew they must be dealing with a sensitive subject. I listened.

"A fish is not a pig!"

This remark was advanced by the ranchero and it seemed reasonable enough to me. The answer came from the merchant.

"My estimable friend, it would be hard to dispute your astute observation, but—"

"With all respect due you, you cannot use the same batter on a fish taco that you would on a pork chop!"

"The death penalty is barbaric," the doctor intoned and the fish/pig issue was tabled.

"We don't have a death penalty in Mexico," the *licenciado* was quick to point out.

"I'm referring to this article in the San Diego paper." They always have the morning papers spread around the table, *El Mexicano* and the *San Diego Union-Tribune*. "The convicted murderer dies tomorrow by lethal injection."

The ranchero put down his black coffee. "At least it's humane—I sometimes have to put down one of my animals."

"It's an improvement. In Europe it was popular to chop off heads." The dentist, or *sacamuelas* if you prefer, made a quick slash across his neck.

"I'm not referring to the method of execution, señores. Chop off his head, throw him in the ocean with all the other garbage. But don't order a doctor to commit murder!" El Médico pounded his fist on the newspaper. "How can a doctor, a man under solemn oath to preserve life, kill another human being? How does he reconcile the act with himself? How can he go home and face his family?" He pushed away his cup. "I can just see it," El Médico said, and affected what his ear must have told him was an American accent.

"Hi honey, I'm home."

He switched to a falsetto and fluttered his eyes to represent the wife as he thought would be appropriate. "Hi, sweetheart."

"Where are the keeds?

"They are playing weeth their friends. How was your day?"

"Okay, I guess. I keelled a man today."

"Oh, I'm sorry."

"Oh, it was perfectly legal. The jury found the man guilty of murder, the judge sentenced him to death by lethal injection and I got the call." El Médico paused for a beat then added. "What's for deener, honey?" The doctor had everyone's attention at the same moment in time. I haven't seen that happen too often among the Cafeteros. El Médico stopped his narrative here. Everyone got his point. Nobody spoke.

The merchant broke the silence. "We need a higher fence along the border. Are you gentlemen aware of the social changes that come across our borders illegally? I saw a young woman at the *supermercado* yesterday."

I told you you have to be quick of mind to follow the sudden shifts in topic of the Cafeteros.

"That's not unusual," observed our poet/accountant, stirring his coffee with a stick of cinnamon. "I see young women in the *supermercado* all the time."

"This one had a tattoo on her lower back almost reaching her *nalgas*!"

"You saw her *nalgas*?" the dentist asked. "*Caballeros* don't do that in the *supermercado*."

"It couldn't be avoided. She bent over to get a can of coffee, her shirt pulled up, her pants pulled down, and there it was, red and green scrolls and flowers and some kind of fancy belt."

"It's called thong underwear," the *licenciado* enlightened the assembly.

"What's happening to our young women!"

There was a short break as they all sipped or doctored their coffee to their individual taste with milk or sugar from the Gerber baby food jar with holes punched in the lid. This was my chance to open a new line of conversation on the subject of doughnuts. I wasn't fast enough. The factory owner beat me to it and they were off exploring new territory.

"I just don't understand it," he said. In front of him was Ruben Navarette's column from the *San Diego Union-Tribune*. His finger stabbed the columnist's face several times. This *cabrón* always makes a lot of sense, he does not beat around the *nopal*. He calls bread bread, and wine wine!"

"What is it you don't understand?" I think it was the ranchero who spoke. I was looking at my watch. I had to get them on the subject of doughnuts, and soon. They adjourn promptly at noon.

"Why does everything on the Other Side have to be a racial issue? The United States is a nation founded by traitors. Together, immigrants from all over the world — every color, every faith — shaped it into the great nation it is today."

"And your question?" the *licenciado* asked.

"Why do they all hate each other?"

"Have you seen the posters all over town?" our poet/accountant said and introduced a whole new theme. "The new play, *Monólogo de una Vagina* is coming to Tecate."

At this rate I knew I would never get a chance to swing the subject in the direction of doughnuts. If I didn't do something quick the Cafeteros would adjourn before I could get anything out of them vis-á-vis doughnuts. I excused myself but it hardly mattered. They were totally absorbed in the new play presented by the Universidad Autónoma de Baja California.

I wasn't gone five minutes. The conversation was now movies and they were talking about *Los Piratas del Caribe* and Johnny Depp. Beto, the waiter was removing an empty coffee pot and replacing it with a new one. I put a plastic bag with a half-dozen doughnuts on the table. "Beto, would you bring a few plates for the doughnuts?"

"Never mind the plates, Beto," the doctor broke in. "Place the whole bag in the trash barrel in the alley or the pharmacies will run out of Imodium before noon."

"Should I call the bomb squad?" Beto didn't wait for an answer. Holding the bag of doughnuts at arm's length, he cautiously headed for the back door.

"What are you talking about!" I cried. "They're fresh, still warm, I just bought them."

The *licenciado* held up his index finger, an indication he was about to speak. "It is obvious our guest this morning is not acquainted with the tragedy. Perhaps one of you should enlighten him."

My ears went up like my sorrel gelding when he hears me rattle the grain can in the morning. At last! The mystery would be solved, my burning curiosity assuaged. The ranchero on my left refilled my cup and I listened.

"*Pobrecito*, poor old man. His name is Alfredo Vasquez," El Médico began, "he's an electrical engineer. He used to work in an assembly factory."

"In Tijuana. He was there for fifteen years," the *licenciado* who cherished details added.

"Earned enough to live decently, a modest house, a nice car."

"He lost his young wife to breast cancer some years ago," the dentist added. "They had no children. His mother immediately left her home in Mexico City and came to look after the poor man. She's been a comfort to him ever since."

El Médico resumed. "About a year ago his old mother, she's eighty-something, became terminally ill. *Pobrecita viejita*, the poor old woman can do nothing for herself. Sometimes she even slips into a coma. Narcolepsia. It's just the two of them, no other family."

The banker had something to add. "He could easily have hired someone to come and attend her—but no—he quit his job to look after her just as the old woman had looked after him when he needed her. He told me once. 'She was there for me, I will be there for her. To the end.' What a noble man!"

El Médico nodded and continued his thought. "He now makes doughnuts at home and sells them in the plaza to buy some very expensive medicines."

The dentist cut in. "What we all know, and El Médico would never tell you, is that he has taken the old woman as a patient, and of course, he won't charge Alfredo *un cinco*."

"It wouldn't be right," El Médico said. "He's used up all his money and the doughnut business doesn't bring him enough to cover everything she needs."

The merchant came into the conversation. "They look like doughnuts, they smell like doughnuts, but eat one and you'll be calling El Médico." This remark brought a flurry of nervous laughter.

"But I see him in the square every day and in a few minutes he's completely sold out," I insisted.

Our poet/accountant explained. "Here in Tecate we're all family, we all help each other. So we all buy his doughnuts as fast as we can so he can get back to his ailing mother. A neighbor comes in when he's in the plaza but he doesn't like to leave her alone for very long."

What a tragic story, I thought, the mystery explained. I declined a refill from the *licenciado*.

"Gentlemen," the merchant began. "I'm glad the subject of commerce has come before us. Selling a few doughnuts in the plaza is a rather limited enterprise. He has to move product in large quantities if he's going to survive."

The banker saw the problem. "The market is very limited for lethal doughnuts."

"How about exporting them!" the merchant suggested.

The factory owner nearly choked on his coffee. "El Boosh would probably cancel the Free Trade Agreement!"

The *licenciado* addressed the merchant. "What do you suggest?"

"I move that we form a secret consortium."

"To overthrow Vicente Fox?"

"No, I'm still talking about doughnuts," the merchant insisted. "We give Alfredo an order for one gross of doughnuts every day.

He would be selling in wholesale quantities. That's the only way he's going to be able to afford the medications without selling his house." He pushed away his cup. "It costs money to die."

"He's got a point," El Médico agreed. "But he'd never be able to sell that many."

"He doesn't have to *sell* them. He only has to *make* them."

"That makes no sense!" the banker cried. "What good is making them if he can't sell them?"

The merchant explained. "Don't you see? The secret consortium picks them up every day and pays for them."

"And?" asked the *licenciado*.

"Details! Take them somewhere and dump them. What's the difference?"

"Wait!" the *licenciado* held up his index finger. "Since NAFTA our government has passed some very stringent laws about hazardous waste disposal. What do we do with one hundred and forty-four toxic doughnuts?"

There was a long spell of silence, something that occurs about as regularly as a total solar eclipse.

"I have it! I have it!"

Everyone turned to face the ranchero.

"Bring the whole load to my rancho and I'll feed them to my pigs." He licked his spoon. "They'll think they're in porcine heaven."

A cheer of brotherly spirit rose from the long table.

"A formidable plan," said the banker. "But who's going to negotiate the deal? It can't be any of us. It has to be a total stranger. Someone he's never seen before or the scheme will never work."

"That's a problem."

It got quiet again.

The *licenciado* came to his feet. I thought he was headed for the CABALLEROS. I was wrong. He had a plan. "We're going to hold a Mexican election right now."

"An election for president?" *sacamuelas* asked.

"No, no," the *licenciado* answered impatiently. "We had presidential elections four months ago."

"Oh yes, I remember, who won?"

"We don't know yet," the *licenciado* said. "Now, let's get back to my proposal. I nominate the gentleman in the blue and white shirt to be the emissary. Those agreed?"

"*Sí! Sí!*"

"It appears to be unanimous. Our secret consortium will finance the scheme. Our new elected emissary can go to work immediately."

I sat wondering where they were going with this then realized I was the only one at the table in a blue and white shirt. I should have worn a Cancun T-shirt that morning. I've joined the Cafeteros for coffee for many years. I've seen them write ludicrous legislation for heads of state, I've watched them draft new city ordinances and deliver them to the Presidente Municipal by special messenger. I've heard heated debates on carne asada, tequila, morals, nose rings and women's underwear. I have never really taken them seriously. This morning it filled my heart to watch this wacky, zany Chamber of Deputies mastermind an ingenious rescue operation for a friend without the embarrassment or injury to his personal dignity so often inherent in charity.

The next day I sat at a concrete table in the plaza not far from where the Doughnut Man sets up. A checkerboard was stenciled on the top and there were still a few Oreo cookies and some bottle caps the previous occupants must have used for a game prior to my arrival. I sat and waited. A few weeks ago the Doughnut Man was a nameless stranger to me, just another anonymous street vendor. Today he was Alfredo Vasquez, a man with a heart, and a soul, and a problem. And when the day came that his daily struggle came to an end, the real pain would begin.

"*Aquí están las donas!...donas calientitas!*"

I was his first customer. I bought three for ten pesos and returned to my place at the concrete table. I waited. Again, he was mobbed. As soon as the last doughnut went off his tray the DM closed up shop. He left his tray and his luggage rack with El Cepillos the shoeshine man, and headed for Farmacia El Parque. He was in there a good half hour. This gave me time to sneak unseen and dispose of two of the doughnuts in a trash can. When he came out he was carrying a white paper bag of pharmaceuticals that I expect set him back the entire proceeds from this morning's work.

I tore off a bite-size piece from my doughnut, tossed it to the pigeons, and stepped up to him. "You make a truly remarkable product, señor."

"*Gracias,*" He gave me a cordial smile but didn't appear to want to stay and talk so I followed him to Cepillo's shoeshine stand.

I waved my doughnut with a chunk missing in front of my nose. "You won't find doughnuts like this anywhere in Tecate. Do you sell these in the other *colonias*?"

"Oh no, señor, I work alone. Just here in the plaza."

"How many do you sell here in a day?"

"I make five dozen every morning and I sell them all."

I crunched numbers. Sixty doughnuts at three for ten pesos, he makes two hundred pesos or twenty dollars a day. "I know where there are customers just waiting for your doughnuts."

"Really! Where?"

"In the outlying *colonias*. Too far for them to come to you, too far for you to go to them. But I know that once they smell your fragrant glazed doughnuts they'll gobble them up by the dozen!" I didn't think it necessary to mention the species of the customers. After all, a consumer is a consumer.

"Are you in the business, señor?"

"Oh no, but a friend of mine is a food distributor and he's always looking for a new item to round out his product line." Better not say any more than that. I'd be in over my head. "Can you produce a gross of doughnuts every day?"

"A gross! I start at five in the morning to make what I sell here." He gathered his stuff and began to move away. He obviously didn't take me seriously and he didn't have time to waste.

"My friend told me he can go five U.S. dollars a dozen. Does that work for you?"

He stopped walking. "Five dollars a dozen!" He did the math. "That would be too wonderful. Are you serious?"

"Serious as the tax collector."

He put down his rack and tray. "I suppose if I started at two or three in the morning I could have twelve dozen ready by nine o'clock." He thought about it. His tired face broke into a wide grin. "*Sí*, señor, I could do it. *Absolutamente!*"

"Give me your address and you can begin tomorrow."

The D M looked embarrassed. "I would have to have some kind of deposit, señor."

"Of course!" I found two twenties and a ten and a piece of an old envelope in my wallet. I handed him my Cerveza Tecate ballpoint pen and he carefully wrote down his address and phone number. "A young *chavalo* will be at your door every morning at nine with the cash. His name is Alfonso."

We shook hands on the deal. "*Gracias*, señor, *muchas gracias!*"

There was a definite spring in his step when he collected his tray and luggage rack and started across the plaza.

The scheme was now in full operation. The Secret Consortium collected the funds every morning at coffee and Alfonso picked up the hazardous waste material, COD. By ten, the gross gross, still warm and fragrant, was delivered and the ranchero had some happy oinkers.

Every day as soon as I heard the cry of the Doughnut Man I would step up, buy the usual three doughnuts and make conversation. "How's the wholesale doughnut business?"

"Oh, señor, you were so right!" His whole face smiled at me. "I had no idea so many people wanted doughnuts. I can't thank you enough!"

"I told you!"

It must have been a couple days later when I paid a call on Cuchuma Feed and Granary, Zeferino Gonzales, prop., for a can of leather cleaner. There's a good reason for patronizing Cuchuma Feed and Granary. It's the only feed store in Tecate. The wood plank front porch is crowded with wire cages imprisoning live quail, chickens, geese, ducks, rabbits, and turkeys. A goose honked at me as I walked into the cavernous warehouse, always in a state of dusk in December. It smelled of freshly baled alfalfa, mixed grains, and harness leather. "*Buenas tardes*," I called into the darkness.

"*Buenas tardes, buenas tardes,*" the sonar echoed back. I recognized the voices of Don Zeferino, prop., and the Cafetero ranchero before they came into focus.

"Give me one kilo of rat poison," the ranchero said. "*Pinche* rats nested in my tractor and ate all the wiring!"

Don Zeferino began scooping the lethal pellets onto the scale. "Be careful with this stuff," he warned. "One bite, and it's permanent death."

"Why don't you just put out the doughnuts?" I suggested.

"Oh no! I have the happiest pigs in Tanama. By the third day the big fat *cabrónes* were coming out to meet the pickup like it was a catering truck driving into a factory. You should see them! They come snorting and squealing and pushing and shoving, they've got the pickup surrounded before Alfonso can park!"

"What's going to happen when there are no more doughnuts?"

"I hope they're sausage by then," the ranchero laughed. "I saw El Médico a little while ago and he told me Alfredo has rented a crank-up bed and some other hospital equipment to make the poor old woman more comfortable. He could never afford it before."

"The Secret Consortium came up with the perfect plan," I said. "I'm glad to see your scheme is working."

Don Zeferino turned to me. "What can we do for you, Don?"

Suddenly the C-drive in my head went blank. What did I come in here for? My mind was still on doughnuts and pigs. I hate it when that happens. "Would you throw a hundred pound bag of laying mash in the car?" I would think of it later, of course, as soon as I got back to my rancho.

The Doughnuts-For-Pigs plan was all we talked about at coffee for days. It was what you call on the Other Side a win-win situation. The Cafeteros were so jubilant they didn't even pass a new immigration law for El Boosh. A week or so later I had a shooting assignment on the Other Side to direct a few TV commercials. Back in those days I was still doing some work in Hollywood. I didn't expect to be gone very long, but almost everything went wrong.

The first big problem was a product called M'Lady's Eau de Lilac Bubblebath.

It was simple enough. The sexy model hands her cover-up to Laurie, our able production assistant, sinks into the bubbles, and holds a dreamy expression for thirty seconds. Cut—it's done. Music and voice-over would be mixed in a sound studio later. Simple.

"We have a problem," I said to the suit from the advertising agency.

"Camera problems?"

"No."

"Lighting?"

"No. The product."

"The product! Impossible! M'Lady's Eau de Lilac Bubblebath is the finest in the market. We make it from real lilacs freshly gathered. The eau we use isn't just any old eau out of a tap. We—"

"Look through the lens," I said. "We see more of the model than the FCC thinks is appropriate for family viewing."

The suit looked through the lens and stayed there.

"Enjoying yourself?" the model in the bubbles inquired.

"Well!" he sniffed. "For your information, I haven't the slightest interest in you, darling, but your cameraman is gorgeous."

I wasn't sure whether he was putting the girl on or what. I was grateful the cameraman didn't react. Chuck is cool. He's seen it all. But then the suit became hysterical. "What are we going to do?" he wailed. "We can't stop shooting, we have TV spots already scheduled."

"Is there anyone you can call?"

"That way madness lies! I can't call New York, they'll probably fire me on the spot!"

There's a lot of insecurity in this business. "Look," I said calmly. "Go have a nice lunch at the Brown Derby, a couple of Tanqueray martinis. We'll have the problem solved when you get back."

"Like what!"

"We'll do some camera magic."

As soon as he left the studio I sent Bunky, our gofer, to the grocery store for a bottle of Joy liquid detergent that claims it will make your dishes shine! When the suit, properly lunched and martinied came back on the set, the model was up to her chin in

M'Lady's Eau with the appropriate dreamy expression. Once again, I invited him to look through the camera.

"Oh, you're fabulous! How did you do it?"

"Camera magic."

"You're fantastic!"

We wrapped.

The dog food commercial was a disaster. It should have been simple. This time the talent was a really cute beagle called Snoopy. What else? I looked at the script: *Today's dog needs today's food. Kanine Kibble is low in salt, low in cholesterol, high in flavor!* Only in America, I thought.

Laurie set out a big bowl of Kanine Kibble and arranged the package alongside for product identification. The account executive, a young kid from the advertising agency, came with a prerecorded tag line that was supposed to play while the dog was munching. "Kanine Kibble...your dog will eat it up! Bark, bark!" I explained we were shooting MOS and sound would be laid in later.

We got set up. "Action," I called.

The account man released Snoopy who probably hadn't seen food for a week. He streaked in, stuck his nose in the bowl, and his exuberant tail sent the product identification flying out of camera range.

"Cut."

Bunky adhered the box of low cholesterol Kanine Kibble securely to the floor with gaffer's tape. It would stay there for several years.

"Take two."

"Camera rolling," I called out to the young agency guy and he released the talent. Once again Snoopy streaked in, and in his effort to slurp up all the Kanine Kibble before anyone could interrupt him again, he began to cough and choke and convulse on-camera.

"Cut."

In an instant our production assistant was on the set administering the Heimlich maneuver. She cuddled Snoopy, Snoopy licked Laurie's face. They bonded. A new Hollywood romance will make tomorrow's *Variety*. We had it wrapped by take six including a few tight shots of Snoopy barking.

I won't even tell you about the problems we had with the FeminX commercial, instant relief for feminine itch. Laurie saved the day. She called the local musician's union and found us a guy who played synthesizer and we got some really itchy music.

I was gone for nearly three weeks.

Next morning I strolled into the plaza. The first thing I wanted to see was that noble Doughnut Man, who already had a place in my heart, in action once again. Today I would buy my usual *tres por diez* then go in and congratulate the members of the Secret Consortium. It felt good to be back in my little pueblo. The scene that played before my eyes looked the same as ever. Nothing had changed in my brief absence. It seemed like any other day, as though I had never been away. That's what I like about Tecate. It's always there for you. The delicious smells of Mexican soul food were teasing the restless dragon. The unseen stage director cued the usual crowds and they threaded their way through the plaza in all directions. As expected, nearly all the tables at the sidewalk cafe were full. There was Miguel on guitar just as he was three weeks ago along with his companions, the accordion and the bass viol, playing a gay little polka for a group of tourists. Miguel tossed over a smile as I passed by.

I shared a sunny bench with an ancient vaquero in high-rise sombrero scattering little bits of tortilla to a flock of colored pigeons pecking and cooing at our feet. I listened to the sounds of Tecate, the music from the sidewalk cafe, the madrigal of the street vendors, the steam whistle at the brewery, noisy children playing *roña*. Presently I felt a strange sense of incompleteness creep over me. What was I missing? I closed my eyes and listened again.

Ching-ching-ching!...ice cream...*chocolate, vainilla, mango!*

Leather! Genuine leather...purses, wallets, belts...*hua-raa-ches!*

Talán, talán! Sno-Cones...strawberry, lemon and lime!

Balloons, balloons, every color, every shape...Shamu...Porky Peeg...Meeky Mouse!

Then it hit me.

The first tenor part of the madrigal was missing. Where was he? In my absence the Doughnut Man must have completed his consecrated mission of devotion to his ailing mother to the very end. My eyes felt like I was chopping onions.

I knew we would never hear the song of the Doughnut Man in the plaza again.

I kicked the pigeons out of my way and headed for La Fonda. I needed that palliative cup with the Cafeteros.

Jesus Rosencranz

I first met Jesus Rosencranz at a big fiesta at Rancho San Ignacio. My hosts and dear friends were Payo and Edmundo Guajardo. There must have been close to a hundred guests sitting, sipping, visiting or dancing under enormous oak trees. Mariachis filled the ranch with that special music for dancing, singing, reminiscing.

Jesus Rosencranz and I were both perusing the vast array of bottles spread out like a buffet on a hay wagon. His name alone intrigued me. There was a disparity between physiognomy and patronym. He looked more Mexican than I do. You could have cast him as a farm worker in *A Day without a Mexican*.

I can always spot a man, or a woman, for that matter, who's got a good story to tell. I'm going to let him tell it in his own words just as he told it to me over a tequila, lemon, and salt on that balmy June evening under a strawberry moon.

I will make every effort not to interrupt his narrative except maybe to clear up a point or two.

It was a number of years ago (Jesus began) before I could speak more than two words in Spanish. The whole thing started on a Monday, I remember that. I leaned there with my elbows flat on the table, my nose practically touching the paper covering. At that distance, even with my nearsighted optical equipment I could see every wrinkle, every crease on the white tissue covering the table. I didn't utter a sound. I didn't want to be there. I tried to think myself someplace else. Ooh! I winced suddenly and tried to concentrate on the music coming from the speakers. It didn't help. I still felt like a pervert but I recognized Jean Pierre Rampal playing Bach's Siciliana on his gold flute. I don't mean to imply that I have a vast knowledge of the world's great music but as it happens I have the same CD at home. I really wanted to get out of here. I was starting to feel strange, somehow indecent.

"OK, Mr. Rosencranz," the pleasant voice behind me said, pulling his finger out of my rectum. "You can put your clothes on now."

I do the physical exam thing every year. I'm not a hypochondriac, really, it all started with all those birthday cards you get when you turn forty. You know the kind I mean.

5 simple adjustments you'll make at 40

1. DENIAL
2. DENIAL
3. DENIAL
4. DENIAL
5. DENIAL

Life at 40 is like flying a plane —
put down your landing gear
YOU'RE ON FINAL APPROACH!

That kind of thing starts you thinking. And I've read all the pharmaceutical ads that warn you about all those silent killers that sneak up on a man when you're in top form and you least expect it. And that can ruin a perfectly good life.

ANGRY? DEPRESSED? NOW THERE'S SSRI.

NO ERECTION LAST NIGHT?

Here's all the help you'll need.

PROSTATE CANCER KILLS 20 MILLION AMERICANS EVERY YEAR. YOU COULD BE DYING WHILE YOU READ THIS!

"Well, you're in excellent condition," Dr. Rabin went on. "Your weight is excellent, your blood pressure is ideal."

"What about the other thing?"

His voice was reassuring. "Hardening of the prostate begins in the early forties. But I didn't find your prostate any harder or any larger than it should be for a man of forty-two."

"Can I do anything about it?"

"Not really, it's a normal process. But eminent members of the medical community have now confirmed that two or three ejaculations a week keep the prostate healthy and supple."

It was practically the same story Dr. Rabin gave me last year. I finished getting dressed, stopped by Krispy Kreme, and made it back to my office by half past ten. I won't have to suffer the recent indecency for another year. For a single guy I'm pretty good about following doctor's orders. I eat right, and try to limit my intake of trans fats and cholesterol. I get plenty of cardiovascular exercise at the gym, and I endeavor to take my prostate treatment two or three times a week as prescribed by Dr. Rabin.

I'm being treated by Jackie. We've been together for over two years and she's thinking seriously of moving into my place. My mother thinks it's time for me to find a nice girl and get married. I'll admit I'm a little late getting into the marriage thing. My first name scares off some nice Jewish girls and my last name turns off the Catholic girls. Jackie and I haven't found The Answer yet. She's a copywriter at Wilkins, Blanchard, and Knott, a major advertising agency in San Diego. We met in the frozen food section at Ralph's. She was struggling to make a decision over a frozen pizza. It didn't require genius to perceive that here was a working girl who didn't have time to eat properly. I suggested she scrap the pizza and let me take her out to dinner. The suggestion appealed to her. We went to a place in Little Italy and have been significant ever since.

Now at my desk I opened the Krispy Kreme box and ogled the contents, two each, glazed, buttermilk, and old fashioned. They were warm and soft and fragrant. I made my decision. The buttermilk! My door opened at that moment and Hoover, a veteran licensed private investigator up on the fifth floor, walked in. Let me amend that. Hoover never walked in through any door in his life—he burst in. He filled the open space from lintel to threshold and from side to side.

"Hey! Krispy Kreme!"

That's another annoying thing about Hoover, he is incapable of talking below a shout that has been known to crack plaster in the building across the street. I should also explain that Hoover is not his real name. The appellation came as a result of a remarkable resemblance to the upright model of that well-known household appliance. His mouth extends the full width of his face. The row of tough heavy-duty bristles on his upper lip is standard equipment and the bag is industrial capacity. With that nozzle this Hoover can scoop up anything in its path!

He was in the doughnut box before I could stash it in a drawer. He put the suction setting on TURBO and I watched my buttermilk doughnut disappear. *Ssssfftt*! My buttermilk!

It's not hard to tell I can't stand the sight of the man. There was no "*good morning, Rosie*," no, "*how are you, guy*?" No! Just comes in and vacuums up my buttermilk under the assumed rights of tenancy. I grabbed for the glazed just in case he was intending to suck that up too.

"Got a hot assignment for you, Rosie," he yelled when my buttermilk cleared his throat and started the long trip down.

I had to fight back a sudden impulse to go over and throw my arms around the repulsive man and crush him to my bosom in a tight embrace. Okay, so I'm a hypocrite. I admit it. I was a little down at the Rosencranz treasury at the moment and desperately needed the gig. "Here, have an old fashioned," I offered. "Or would you prefer the other buttermilk? Can I get you some coffee? Regular, decaf?" I got us each a coffee from the pot.

Hoover parked his ample butt on a chair and nosed into the Krispy Kreme box. *Ssssfftt*! The second buttermilk was on its way down to join the first one. "We're lookin' for a guy named Lopez. Been missing a while." He switched the vac to "High" and the coffee disappeared.

"I don't know if I can squeeze the job in," I said. "I'm buried in work right now."

So now you know, I'm not only a hypocrite, I'm a liar too. But you have to understand, you have to play hard to get with Hoover. If he sniffs out that you need to make the rent or a car payment, he pays you in peanuts and popcorn. "I'm afraid I can't take on anything new right now." I got up from my desk to sort of imply with body language that he was wasting his time. I think actors refer to this as method acting.

"You gotta do this one, Rosie. My client can go two hundred a day plus expenses. Maybe even a bonus!" he pleaded.

See how the system works? He's begging me. I've been a bounty hunter for ten years. I don't want to raise clarion to lips and sound my own praise, but I have a pretty good track record. And Hoover knows my minimum fee is five hundred a day. He's being cute. I shook my head for effect. "Look, let me get my present assignments cleaned up and I'll get back to you." That remark is sheer torture for a man like Hoover who demands everything NOW.

"Well, get back to me later today. I'm a subcontractor on this one but maybe we can do a little better."

I flipped open my desk organizer and made a note. *Call Hoover back at five o'clock and tell him I'll take the case.* It cost me my two buttermilk doughnuts but I'd have some work—and at my usual fee.

By two in the afternoon I was listening to some grumbling and growling emanating from somewhere under my shirt and began to give some thought to a bit of lunch. "What'll it be today?" I asked the concierge who dwells in my stomach. "There's Charlie's for a succulent, high cholesterol filet mignon medium rare with baked potato dripping with melted butter, and topped with chives. Or, we could put in at Garden of Eden for an infinite choice of wholesome salads, tender hedge clippings, bamboo shoots, and maybe some foliage." I never heard the answer. The door blew open full width and two of the most disagreeable-looking men I'd ever seen in my life stood there. Two Anglo-Saxon types with painfully blue eyes. It's amazing with what speed our animal instincts can get a message to the brain. *These are not people you want to know.*

"Mr. Rosencranz?" This from a pale-faced monolith in a black shirt I took to be silk and black pants. If people were cars this guy was a Brinks armored truck. That's as far as he got. His companion, a Hummer, flat across top and sides, equipped with four-wheel drive, rolled up to my desk unbidden.

"Yes, I'm Rosencranz." *Don't let them see your legs are shaking.* "What can I do for you?"

"Rosencranz, the bounty hunter, right?" the Hummer inquired in a voice that could drown out a moose call.

"Yes." There was no other answer. They obviously knew who I was.

"We came to do some business," the Hummer explained.

Maybe you can give them the same routine you just gave Hoover and they'll walk out. I cleared the phlegm of fear caught in my throat. "I'm a simple one-man operation and I'm presently under assignment to Hoover upstairs." I thought the answer sounded very professional and would preclude the need for further inquiry.

I was wrong.

The Hummer helped himself to a chair. The Brinks armored truck took a standing position behind him. The Hummer did all the talking. He leaned his face into mine close enough for me to see a black nose hair peeking out from its dark dwelling looking for daylight. His words exploded into the room like an AK 47.

"Forget the vacuum cleaner upstairs. We tried him and now we're going direct to the source. This is a really simple assignment, Mr. Rosencranz. Lemme give you the details." So, I thought, Hoover *was* being cute. Subcontractor, my enchilada! Maybe my oversize visitor's hearing was impaired and didn't hear me say I was presently under assignment and not available. There was a teeny little chirp like you might expect from a hamster who's down with flu and doing some chirping from under heavy blankets. "Shut the thing off!" the Hummer barked. The Brinks brought out a cell phone, pushed a button, and the hamster died on the spot. There was nothing wrong with the Hummer's auditory equipment. He was here to get what he wanted.

"We're looking for a guy."

"Most people who come to me are. Can you be a little more specific? You have pictures?"

"Well, no pitchers."

"Address, phone, place of employment?"

"Not exactly."

I was getting annoyed. "How about a name?" I put as much sarcasm in my voice as I could.

"Oh yeah, we got that. Juan Lopez."

"Sure."

"Look, lemme level with you."

"That would be a great start."

Frankly, and without the slightest indication of embarrassment, he told his sordid story. "Five years ago we did a bank, my buddy and me. Well, I been in banking a long time and I never had to kill nobody while I'm makin' a withdrawal. I do a clean job. But it wasn't my deal, see, it was my buddy Curly's gig. He invited me and I went in. Well, the guy panics and he knocks off two tellers. One was a pretty little thing."

I think my mouth was hanging wide open while he's telling of a robbery and murder as calmly as if he just went in to make a deposit.

"Financial institutions are different from your regular jobs. You can't panic. Anyways, Curly's on the Row waitin' for a miracle. My only part was just to take the cash and throw it in the car that was waitin' outside. I got five. Just got out."

"Oh, that's nice." I didn't say that, but I wanted to. I can also be ironic when I'm so inclined.

"Anyways, I take the bag, throw it in the getaway car parked out front and walk off nonchalant like, you know, just like I'm s'posed to. Curly was s'posed to go out the same door but stay in the building like he was shoppin' and stuff. It was a good plan until he panicked. There's no place for panic in this business, you know. A couple minutes later the place is swarming with black and whites. Nobody bothered with me. I'm just a guy on the street gettin' in the way. That was the plan, see?"

"So what went wrong?"

"The driver took off and we ain't seen 'im since. All he had to do was drive up this parking structure, park, sit there and wait for one of us, and collect two grand. That's the guy we're looking for. Name's Juan Lopez."

"And you have no pictures, no address, and you want me to find him for you. What does he look like?" I don't know why I asked the question. This wasn't my kind of job, but by now he had my curiosity fired up.

"Young Mexican guy, probably twenty-one, twenty-two, in there. It's been five years. He'd be late twenties now. He was drivin' a '89 Honda Civic. Blue."

"A vintage Honda Civic for a getaway car?"

"With handicap plates."

I couldn't think of this as business anymore, it was like being in a Danny Devito movie and I'm talking with the bad guys. He must have seen the incredulity in my face.

"It was the perfect plan. Who's going to stop a poor cripple in a beat up Honda Civic with a wheelchair strapped to the back who just happens to be parked in a handicap zone when the shit hits the fan?"

No comment.

"We were careful on this. We did interviews. It was like we were Central Casting looking for a guy who fit the part just right. Juan Lopez had a face like a thousand other Mexicans. He was just like one tortilla in a whole package. You couldn't ID him, you know? And he wasn't a loud macho type, neither. He was a quiet kinda guy, shy as a bunny."

"Let me see if I understand this. Juan Lopez, if that's his name, drove off with the proceeds from your transaction at the bank and never achieved the rendezvous. Is that right?"

"He never showed up, if that's what you mean."

"And, if I'm still following your train of thought, he's somewhere unknown in possession of a bag full of money."

"Fifty-eight grand."

He must have seen me blanch. "And you'd like me to find him."

"Yeh."

"But you've got no useful information about him, nothing but a name that's about as real as John Doe."

"I kinda remember he had a nickname. Everybody called him Patti, or Patta, or Patino or something like—"

"Forget it." I cut him off. "The nickname's as meaningless as Juan Lopez. Was he handicapped?"

"Naw, the handicap plates and the wheelchair was just props. He did walk kinda funny, though."

"Never mind. What kind of work did he do when he wasn't in banking?"

"Oh, he never done banks. This kid was clean, we made sure of that. Never even had a traffic ticket. Did odd jobs. Worked in a car wash or sometimes he parked cars, that sorta thing."

"And you have no idea in the world where he took off to."

"Well, it's been five years, but now we got reliable information to think he's in Tecate."

"Like the beer?"

"It's in Baja."

It was time to throw this guy out. I was wasting time.

"Hoover said it would be a natural for you."

"Well, it's not."

This has always been a problem for me which I should explain. I'm the fruit of a legal union between Jacob Rosencranz (now deceased) and Mariaelena Martinez (very much alive). All the Rosencranz I possess is on the inside, the liver, the spleen, the heart, the prostate, things like that. On the outside I'm all Martinez. Skin the color of a clay pot, thick black hair. That's me. I look so Mexican I can't even take a pleasant walk in the country. If I come within a mile of a cornfield the Border Patrol is all over me. I nearly got deported once. People look at me and assume I speak the Españolish. I don't. I was born and raised in L.A. I've never even been out of the country—not even Tijuana. When I take my mother to lunch on Olvera Street, the oldest part of downtown L.A., *dos tacos* and *adios amigos* is as far as I can go with it.

"Look, why don't you run down there yourself? You at least would recognize the guy when you saw him."

"I got too many irons in the fire right now, business you know, otherwise I would be down there right now."

"And then there's a language problem, you see."

"Hoover said—"

"He's wrong. I don't work outside the United States," I said with a tone fraught with finality. "Working as a bounty hunter in another country is against the laws of both countries. It can also be hazardous to your health. If you get caught by your prey, you're dead. If you're caught by the authorities you don't pass GO, you go directly to prison." I started to do my fake getting out of my chair routine that works so well with Hoover. It didn't work here.

"Look, I'll pay you a grand up front just to go down and scout out the town. You're talkin' an hour's drive and a day or two of snoopin' around. If you come back with nothin' I'll understand. You keep the grand. We're still friends, see?" This was a friendship I didn't really want to see blossom. "But if you do locate Juan and bring him in, twenty grand is yours right off the top."

"What if I find him and he doesn't have the money?"

"Not a problem. You bring 'im in, the twenty's yours. I'll take it from there. The deal stands. You can't lose."

I was incapable of speech for a minute. A thousand for a day's work and twenty thousand in one lump sum. I couldn't lose even if I came back empty handed. We'd still be friends, he'd said. The numbers justified thought. I saw the Hummer slip his big hand inside his jacket. I thought he was reaching for heat, as they say in the popular detective/mystery genre. He slowly withdrew ten one-hundred dollar bills and put them in front of me. I felt a sudden tightness in the vicinity of my heart. Here it comes, I thought, the silent killer! Just as I was about to make twenty thousand and live happily ever after, a chunk of cholesterol would choose this moment to lodge itself in my left ventricle. My heart would cease to function and I would expire right here at my desk clutching a thousand dollars. Life can be so unfair. I took in a long slow breath. The uncomfortable tightness in my chest began to subside.

"I can be in Tecate on Wednesday, the day after tomorrow."

He wrote something on the Krispy Kreme box. "That's my cell phone. Call me when you got somethin'. I'll do the rest."

He walked to the door just as the Brinks truck got there and opened it for him. The mouth on the Hummer, larger than the radiator grill on the vehicle that inspired my description, opened, and he spoke. "Is that your real name, Jesus?"

"Yes."

"Christ!"
"No, Rosencranz."

"How long will you be gone?" Jackie asked when I gave her the news. She didn't sound too pleased. We were having dinner at my place. I fixed a raw spinach salad with balsamic vinegar, bacon bits, a little prepared mustard, a pinch of sugar and a touch of Worcestershire. When it was properly tossed, I ignited the cognac, poured it over the salad, and served it to her in flames. There was a fresh baguette on the table and a chilled bottle of Chardonnay.

I was going all-out to please her and this supper was one of her favorites. "I can't imagine it's going to take more than a day, two tops. But I'll be keeping in touch."

She fought unsuccessfully against a smile of ecstasy when she presented the salad to her palate. "Couldn't you take up some other kind of work?" Now she sounded like my mother who lives under the illusion that I'm in the portable toilet business.

"I should've kept up the violin lessons." There was no reply so I thought I would sweep her off her feet. I raised my wineglass theatrically. "This job means we'll have enough money to get married."

"Oh? Oh. Oh! Oh!!!" She got all the inflections and modulations possible out of the simple monosyllable. "Promise me you'll be careful, darling. I love you!" We had an artery-clogging creme brulee for dessert. She gave me a prostate treatment and the next day I was on my way to Mexico.

I stopped at a gas station out in the boonies that still had attendants. "Fill 'er up?"

"Naw, just a couple hundred bucks of unleaded ought to do it."

I found a pay phone. "Hi, Mom."

"*Muchacho*! How are you dear?"

"Fine, Mom. Listen, I can't make it up to L.A. this weekend. Business, you know."

"Well, *hijo*, I'll miss our visit but it comforts a mother to know you'll never run out of customers. Everybody needs to go to the toilet. Are you taking care of yourself?"

"Sure."

"Are you eating right? You were always a fussy eater. I used to go to the *botanica* and get *hierba de manzanilla* to encourage appetite. I used to put it in your cocoa when you were little. I'll have some for you when you get here."

I'm just now beginning to understand my aversion to cocoa. "I have a good appetite."

"Are you still constipated? I used to buy *linaza* and grind it up fine so you couldn't taste it in your Coca-Cola. It always worked."

I'd often wondered why I never cared for Coke. "I'm fine, Mom, really. I've got to see a man who needs twenty-four toilets."

"Twenty-four! My mother used to tell me, '*no salgas a casa ajena con la vejiga llena.*' In other words, don't leave your house with a full bladder."

I forgot to mention. My mother always speaks in proverbs. "Take good care of yourself, Mom, I'll get up to see you next week."

"*Muchacho?*"

"Yes?"

"Did you send a thank-you note to your Tia Lupe for the shirt she sent you for your birthday?"

The shirt was a kind of paisley print swirled with creamy yellow and white. It looked like baby vomit. "Yes I did, Mom," I lied. "See you next week, Mom."

It must have been close to nine in the morning when I went through the gate and entered Mexico. Two very official-looking officers in smart blue uniforms flashed me a smile.

"*Buenos dias, que lleva en la cajuela?*"

The language difficulty had begun! Maybe I should have gotten a George W. mask for this gig. The alert officer saw the problem. "What are you bringing in to Mexico?"

"Just my clothes. Is there a good hotel in this town?"

"La Siesta," he answered. "Go straight ahead and turn right at the third pothole."

"You can't miss it," his partner assured me and handed me a printed flyer.

WELCOME TO MEXICO
Obey the law—drive carefully.

It is against the law in Mexico to drive
while using a cellular telephone.
It is against the law in Mexico to drive without a security belt.
Insurance is recommended.
ENJOY YOUR VISIT!

A strange feeling came over me as I passed through the huge
iron gates. My country was now behind me. I was now on foreign
soil, under another flag, different laws, another president, another
language. Everything looked different, the buildings, the streets,
the people—even the sounds were different. I came to my first
stop sign and had to look twice; it read ALTO. I made my stop and
suddenly felt a little reassurance. A huge bronze bust mounted on
a brick monument under the ALTO sign looked familiar to me.
The face was out of place here in Mexico, but John F. Kennedy was
smiling at me. What was he doing in Mexico?

I continued straight ahead to the third pothole. The officer
was right; I couldn't miss it. I think it twisted the tie rods on the
Explorer. I turned right. I didn't see anything that looked like a
motel. There were a number of stores on one side of the street. On
my side was Botanica La Hortencia, one of those spooky little shops
like the kind my mother likes to go into where they sell snake oil,
charms, mysterious herbs, love potions, and magic waters. Next to
that was a body shop where some guy was pounding out a fender. I
never saw anything that could pass for a motel. Okay, I figured, I'd
scout out the town a little then find accommodations later.

I drove west for a few blocks and saw more stores, taco shops, a
couple gas stations, then started back. When I stopped at a light I
could see the top of a Ferris wheel and the highest peak of a roller
coaster sticking out over the treetops. No doubt some kind of fair
was going on. Just as the light turned green a woman with a kid
gripped in one hand and a baby over her shoulder stepped right in
front of me. I hit the brakes. She was immediately followed by an
old woman swaying from side to side with a heavy shopping bag in
each hand. I started to move when I saw an old man on crutches
step off the curb and deliberate his chances of survival. He drew a
hasty sign of the cross and took the leap. I sat through another red

light. I took a left and drove a mile or so south and saw a sign for the airport, a big blue plane painted on a white field with an arrow indicating the airport was two kilometers east. I didn't bother with that. On the way back I came to the town square. It looked inviting so I dumped the car and walked back.

It was a pleasant little plaza, one square block of green lawns, a profusion of roses and geraniums and flowering bougainvillea climbing up towering ash trees. At one end was an enormous fountain splashing and singing with unrestrained joy. On the opposite side was a very pleasant looking sidewalk cafe with metal tables under red and white Cerveza Tecate umbrellas. Music was coming to me from somewhere. In the center of the plaza stood a large kiosk of blue and yellow tile with wrought iron railings and a red tile roof. I took a bench in the dense shade and watched the action.

Dark, macho-looking rancheros in tall sombreros straight out of a Cisco Kid movie sat in groups talking in low voices. Pretty secretaries in hermetically sealed pants and spike heels clip-clopped across the pavement. Young mothers pushing strollers and old women under bright summer parasols promenaded around the plaza. Teenage boys and girls flirted and stole kisses over near the fountain. Everyone seemed to have some kind of mission and the plaza was apparently the central point everyone had to walk through to get to where they needed to be. Every table at the sidewalk cafe was taken. I found the source of the music. A guitar, a festive accordion, and a big bass viol provided background music for the scene.

I watched the show for a while. It wasn't long before I was the target of every vendor and pushcart hawker in the plaza.

"*Bola*, señor?"

"*Chiclets*?"

I passed on the shoe shine and the chewing gum. A giant mass of colored balloons came floating slowly towards me. When it came closer I could see there was a live man hiding inside. He carried balloons of every color, round, heart-shaped, and star shaped. I recognized Mickey Mouse, Spider Man, and Snoopy.

The balloon man was followed by a guy selling plastic snakes and iguanas. I caught a whiff of onions browning and carne asada sizzling over mesquite coals and the concierge sent up a message from the stomach that I couldn't ignore for long. I listened to the caroling pushcarts.

"*Tamales… tamales calientitos...de carne, de puerco, de queso!*"

"*Elotes...ricos elotes!*"

"*Raspados!*"

"*Nieve...nieve de chocolate, sandia, limon y mango!*"

This last cry required no translation. All that was needed was a little sign language. The mango Popsicle appeased that large, saclike organ under my belt. It was just what I needed. Sweet and cold and wet and zero cholesterol. I turned my thoughts to my purpose. How do I start? I was looking for an American male subject of Mexican parentage twenty-eight to thirty years old, who came to Tecate about five years ago when he was twenty-two or -three.

Yeah, right. Now what? I didn't even know what he looked like. He could have been the guy that sold me the Popsicle.

I did what I always do. I tried to put myself inside my quarry's skin. It's a pretty reliable system. I came on it by accident once when I chased a convicted felon to Austin, Texas, and hit a dead end. Well, it turned out that the guy's last two jobs in California were in commissaries and restaurants on campus. So now I climb into my target's skin. I hit town, I need a job. Where do I go? I found him whipping up a short stack and sausage biscuit heavy on the gravy at the cafeteria at U.T. Austin. The Great Rosencranz gets his man!

So, here I am in Mexico. Put the system to work, I told myself. Okay. First, is he still here? Did he go back into the U.S.? I carried my second Popsicle three blocks back to the border. There was a lineup of cars entering the U.S. I stood just outside the gates on the Mexican side and watched the procedure. The officer looks at the license plates and punches something into his computer then goes to the driver side, and while I couldn't hear him, he was obviously asking questions. He inspected the car, looked in through the windows and knocked on the fenders with his fist. This gave another officer with a dog on a leash time to let his goofy yellow lab sniff for drugs. Sometimes the guy in the car would have to get out and pop the hood or open the trunk, sometimes both. I was pretty sure my man didn't come out through here. The license plate on his Honda had to be hot and I could safely assume it would be the same procedure at any border.

Congratulations, Jesus, you're a genius. He could *walk* across!

It was possible, I thought. No car, no plates, just saunter across, walk into the little American Market in Tecate, U.S.A. and get lost. Off to one side I saw a lineup of people doing just that. It was a squeeze but I got into my suspect's skin and got in line. There were four people in front of me, two Mexican women and an American couple. I couldn't hear the exchange of dialogue because you have to stand behind a red line until it's your turn.

It only took a brief eternity and I was facing a grim-looking officer who may have had pickles and thumbtacks for breakfast. There was little doubt that his scowl was sincere, the frown, straight from the heart. Joy did *not* rule his day. He was sitting at a computer but it was a safe bet he was eight-foot-two or -three when he stood up. The uniform was a serious navy blue, a shiny badge proclaimed Federal Authority, and his nameplate said JOHNSON. An embroidered patch on his shoulder read U.S. BORDER PROTECTION.

I stepped up to the plate.

"ID?"

I pulled out my driver's license and handed it over. He entered all the information into his computer.

"Citizenship?"

"American."

He scrutinized my face. "And how did you acquire your American citizenship?"

"By virtue of a natural vaginal delivery."

Stone face did not react. "What are you bringing back from Mexico?"

"Not a thing."

"What were you doing in Mexico?"

"I'm a tourist—shopping, stuff like that."

"And where are you going now?"

I was sure he was going to ask me if I brushed my teeth this morning. "I'm going to pick up a paper."

His expression never changed throughout the entire procedure. He could have been a wax figure from the Chamber of Horrors exhibit. He swiped my license through a scanner like the kind you see at the supermarket and handed it back. "Have a nice day."

I went to the little store, picked up the *San Diego Union-Tribune* to lend truth to my declaration and walked back into Mexico convinced my guy didn't leave as a pedestrian. He might not even be in Tecate anymore, he could be anywhere in Mexico, but he wasn't back in the U.S. He was locked out.

I walked the three blocks back to the plaza, found another bench, and pressed START on the brain mechanism.

Well, every town usually has a favorite restaurant or bar that seems to be the center of society. So, my first assignment would be to scout out the restaurants and bars, become something of a regular, and follow up from there. The hard drive in the brain shot back REJECT. That plan would require a couple of weeks for people to begin to accept you as a regular. And I wanted to wrap this up in a day, two at the most. I didn't want to skip my prostate treatment. Doctor's orders.

Then I realized I had an even bigger problem. Language.

Get real, I told myself, you don't know enough Spanish to buy a piñata. More time isn't going to help you. I abandoned the bench and wandered around the little town for the remainder of the day studying every guy who looked in his late twenties. I saw lots of them. Any one of them could have been Juan Lopez. Later that evening I ate at a place called Tacos Los Amigos. This required no language skills. All I had to do was hold up two fingers. Two little kids, one with a violin under his chin, the bigger one with a guitar, walked in and sang a song. They sounded like a cat fight in the alley. I gave them a buck. After dark I found accommodations at the Hotel Tecate a few blocks away. This transaction only required the use of only one finger and twenty American dollars. I turned in early.

I was up and out early the next morning. I found some place for breakfast and realized I didn't know any more Spanish today than I did yesterday. I had to play charades with a very pleasant Indian woman swathed in shawls and long black braids to get a coffee and a sweet roll. No lox and bagels here.

Time to go home. I gave it an honest shot. The Hummer said we'd still be friends.

I took another walking tour of the town and grabbed a bench in the plaza. It was a quaint little town, I had a thousand bucks in my pocket, and a shot at twenty more. It would be fun if I could overcome the obstacles and somehow make it work. But this called for a miracle. I've never been much good at supplicating prayers to a higher order. My father was in the rag business but made it to temple twice a year. My dear old mother used to light his menorah on Friday evenings. On Sundays she still lights candles to the Blessed Virgen de Guadalupe. She also has a squad of divine special teams she deploys as needed; San Lazaro, the healer, El Niño Divino for heavy duty problems, Juan Lumbrero for retrieval of lost articles, and others I can't remember. She still believes in magic and miracles and she is not ashamed to admit she employs the services of fortune tellers and seers. (And I strongly suspect *brujas* and *curanderas*). Personally, I just wish a lot.

"*Bola*, señor, *shine*?"

"*Churros...ricos churros...!*"

I passed on the shoe shine and the churros. It was time to think! I looked up to see an interesting man ambling leisurely across the plaza with no apparent destination in mind. He wore more white than a June bride, white shirt, white jacket, white pants, white shoes and socks. He wore a white Panama hat. I followed him with my eyes and realized he was setting a direct course for my bench.

"*Con su permiso*, señor, *vengo a la sombra si no es molestia*," he said as he took the other half of my shady bench.

Now what do I do? If I say *buenos dias* I've exhausted my vocabulary. He didn't resemble any Mexican I'd ever seen before.

The face was dark Mediterranean, the smile, cryptic and sinister. No mustache. He looked at me through hooded eyes that bulged when he spoke. I was looking at a Peter Lorre clone! He was probably a Corsican citizen traveling on a forged French passport on his way to Casablanca to meet with Humphrey Bogart.

When I didn't answer he spoke in thick accented English. "A day of extraordinary beauty," he said in a pharyngeal whisper. "Eef you don't find eet a great eemposeetion, may I share your shady bench?" My God, he was a Peter Lorre sound-alike too!

He extended his hand, whether to pass me a secret document or in friendship, I still wasn't sure. "Trinidad Contreras, your *servidor*," he whispered as though his throat was sore. "Everybody calls me Treenie."

"Rosencranz," I answered with enthusiastic indifference, and shook the outstretched hand. I wasn't looking for conversation. I had a problem to solve.

"You are new here een Tecate, Meester Rosie?" he rasped.

Damn! He wants to be chatty. Probably wants to sell me a solid gold Rolex for ten bucks. I didn't have time to waste. I didn't bother to answer. Maybe Peter Lorre would walk.

"There are no strangers een Tecate," he hissed, "I know every face, the handsome, the homely, the beautiful, the young, the old, and I have never had the pleasure of meeting you before today."

Suddenly my sensors were beeping. My miracle? If this strange man knows *every face in town* he could save me a lot of time. I could use him.

"Perhaps you would be eenterested een making the acquaintance of a beautiful and charming young lady." The eyes enlarged and seemed about to loll out into my lap. "Satisfaction guaranteed."

Geez! A pimp!

He must have read my mind. "Oh, eet ees not what you theenk, Meester Rosie. I am a legeetimate matchmaker licensed by the state of Baja California." From an inner pocket he withdrew a document with a lot of scrollwork and swirly signatures. It looked like the American Constitution I saw in my social studies book in school when I was a kid.

"I came down to see about investment opportunities."

"An excellent deceesion, Meester Rosie, Tecate teems with possibilities. Perhaps I can be of some useful service een your endeavor." His eyes seemed to enlarge. "Eef your beezness should require the movement of materials across the border I am a licensed eemport/export agent." From another pocket of his white jacket he withdrew a small card with a purple seal.

"The first thing I have to find is some industrial building suitable for a small factory," I improvised.

Peter Lorre—I mean—Treenie, reached into his back pocket and came up with his wallet. Through a window I saw an official looking card with more calligraphy and more stamps than a visa for Morocco. I couldn't read any of it, of course, it could have been his Costco card in disguise.

"What a happy coincidence that we ran eento each other! I am also an authorized leasing agent. I am at your service."

The concierge was complaining audibly. Treenie, in his white suit and raspy voice, did not fill me with a great deal of confidence but there was no doubt he could be useful. "Why don't you join me for lunch, Treenie?"

"An excellent suggestion, Meester Rosie."

"Where's a good place?"

"La Fonda without a doubt. Eet ees just across the plaza. Shall we go?"

We passed the sidewalk cafe. Every table was still full. I noticed a group of men with a pitcher of margaritas in front of them. The musicians were now playing at their table.

"Everyone here seems to enjoy a leisurely lunch and it isn't even Friday." I observed.

"Oh, that ees not a casual lunch, Meester Rosie. No one een Tecate does beezness een the office. Eet ees Moises from the bank across the street closing a deal with some investors who are erecting a new industrial park."

I noticed two of the men gave Treenie a friendly wave of recognition. This guy might be the best thing I've got so far. Certainly worth a lunch.

La Fonda was smoky and crowded. A dark man with a guitar cradled in his arms was singing a love song to a young couple obviosuly very much in love at a table against the wall. Nearly everyone gave Treenie a nod of recognition. He led us directly to a table shielded by a potted palm and a waiter appeared out of the smoke.

"*Adelante, señores. Bienvenidos. Van a comer?*"

I was glad I didn't have to answer.

"*Sí*, Beto. Eet ees my friend's first visit to Tecate so you better breeng menus."

Apparently we were already friends. "Bring us two margaritas and we'll scope out the menu," I said.

"You are the *cabellero quintaesencial*, Meester Rosie."

Treenie ordered chiles rellenos. I get enough soul food when I visit my mother. I ordered a plain steak. I surreptitiously studied the men at the tables and every man who left and entered. I was subtle, of course. No one could possibly know what I was doing.

"*Salud.*"

I knew that one. "*Salud.*"

Treenie took a couple of long sips before he spoke. "Are you expecting someone for lunch, Meester Rosie?"

"Huh? No, I'm not."

"Perhaps if you told me who it is you are looking for I could be of some meaningful assistance."

Now how did he know? "What on earth gave you a wild idea like that, Treenie? I'm here to look into some form of investment."

His answer was a sardonic snicker. "Oh, Meester Rosie, you might as well wear a sign that says 'Bounty Hunter' een beeg red letters." Lunch arrived and I tried to hide my humiliation by attacking the steak.

"You see, Meester Rosie eef you were here on beezness the first place you would go would be our cordial but useless Chamber of

Commerce. No one wastes hees time with Treenie Contreras unless he has a secret." He ate with appetite. "You were carefully studying every man that passed our bench een the plaza this morning and you are studying all the male patrons here. Some of Tecate's most beautiful women have crossed our line of vision and your organs of sight have not registered even the mildest eenterest. So either you are here to find someone or you are..."

"No, no, Treenie. I'm straight hetero."

I've always worked solo and I've done okay but here in Tecate language was going to be a major challenge. I might as well be in Katmandu. If this spooky character is that sharp, I figured, he might serve my purpose, save me a lot of time, and I wanted to wrap it up as quickly as possible. But how far could I trust him? The guy obviously read minds.

"You can trust me with complete *confianza*, Meester Rosie and I am loyal as a Rottweiler to my clients."

"Okay, Treenie, what's your fee for your trust and Rottweiler loyalty?"

"A nominal daily stipend, Meester Rosie, and I am at your disposal day or night."

I pushed a twenty across the table that instantly disappeared in one of the pockets of his white suit. "Is that nominal enough?"

"Most satisfactory. Now, let us begin. Who are we looking for?"

"We are searching for a Mexican male born and raised in the U.S. Probably late twenties. He would have come to Tecate five years ago."

"Eet ees a tragedy, Meester Rosie, but Tecate has grown since the advent of NAFTA. We can blame globalization for McDonald's and their abominable McBurrito, Domino's Pizza, graffiti, and at least five thousand new faces."

"His name is Juan Lopez."

Peter Lorre sneered. "Real names are meaningless."

"I should also tell you we don't know what he looks like and we don't have pictures."

"Ah! You see what trust can do? We don't need either, Meester Rosie! Where there's been fire ash remains." Geez, more proverbs. "We can already eliminate La Fonda. The man you want won't be here."

I felt I already got my twenty bucks worth. We finished lunch and left La Fonda.

"Do you mind if we drive a bit? It would help me to know the layout of the town."

"Of course, Meester Rosie."

We got in the Explorer. "Which way, Treenie?"

"Eet does not matter, Meester Rosie. To the left we end up in Tijuana, to the right we end up in Mexicali."

I took a left. "Driving down here takes some adjustment. I don't want to end up with a traffic ticket and jail would be an inconvenience."

"Oh, that ees not a problema, Meester Rosie. You are immune to any eenterference from local police."

"Immune!"

"You are with Treenie Contreras."

I was starting to enjoy his company. We passed a number of shoe stores, a bank, and a movie theatre. "Do they run American movies, or just Mexican movies?

"Neither, Meester Rosie."

"Oh, I thought it was a movie theatre."

"Eet ees but eet has been converted eento a clothing factory. NAFTA, you know."

Two minutes later we were out in open country, little farms and cornfields, an occasional Mini Mercado. Suddenly I slammed on the brakes. The scream of Michelin radials on pavement gave me goose flesh but I stopped in time to avoid slamming into a herd of goats loping across the road followed by their herder, a dark man with a leather rope. He held a cell phone clamped to his ear!

There was nothing of interest out this far and as I turned to come back I saw a huge prison complex, high-voltage fence, thick brick walls, and twenty-foot guard towers.

"That prison looks pretty new. Is it full?"

"Eet ees empty, Meester Rosie."

"Of course! Why not? It's only logical. Why build a penitentiary and fill it up with undesirable tenants?"

"There ees a very logical explanation, Meester Rosie. Eet was nearly completed when it was decided that Tecate needed a new municipal dump more than a penitentiary. A matter of priorities."

I didn't say anything. This whole town is a mirage, I thought, nothing is real. In two minutes we were back in the heart of town. I parked. A leisurely migration brought us back to the plaza where a shady bench waited for us and I slipped in beside him. "Now what? How do we find Juan Lopez?"

"But there ees a first priority."

"First priority! Finding this guy is what I'm here for, Treenie!"

"If eendeed Juan Lopez ees een Tecate, how deed he get here?"

"He drove in, of course, or he could have flown."

"We do not have an airport."

"Wait a minute! Just yesterday I saw a sign for the airport. It had a plane on it."

"*Si*, Meester Rosie. There ees a *sign* for the airport but no airport exists. Eet was the idea of our government but eet was abandoned half way through the project. They have not bothered to remove the sign. We also have a railroad depot but no train."

Another logical explanation. "All right, then he came by car. A Honda."

"*Bien*, Meester Rosie. What became of the vehicle?"

"Well, I suppose..." This strange man was on to something. "He probably unloaded it and bought something else down here." The guy wasn't short on funds.

"A doubtful contingency, Meester Rosie."

"Explain."

"Eef the car had California plates they have expired by now, *ergo* he could not sell eet or drive eet on the street. The police would confiscate the car until he renewed the license plates and paid the fine."

"Well, then he got a Mexican driver's license and drives a car with current California plates."

"*Imposíble!*"

"Why?"

"Getting the license would not be a problem. But he could not drive the car."

Treenie wasn't making sense. "Why the hell not?"

"Because, Meester Rosie, eet ees against the law to drive a car with American plates with a Mexican driving license."

Every time this mysterious man opened his mouth I learned something useful.

"So maybe he sold the car and now he's a pedestrian."

"Perhaps. But he could not sell it without eemporting it first."

And, I thought, he wouldn't want his name on any documents. Treenie had a point. Juan Lopez would have had to ditch the car. "Okay, so how do we find the car?"

"I would suggest we migrate toward the Diana Bar."

"To find a car?"

"The Diana ees not just a bar, Meester Rosie, eet ees a landmark, an eensteetution. Eet has been the social epicenter of Tecate for fifty years."

"And so?"

"And so, Meester Rosie, every man, young or old, ambulatory, or confined to a wheelchair, deaf or blind or mute, comes to the Diana to *convivir*—how you say?—to share together the life."

I couldn't imagine a bank robber hanging out and sharing together the life in a local bar.

"You see, Meester Rosie, we Mexicans are a very warm and cordial people. We must find human companionship. We are eensecure when by ourselves. A Mexican cannot be a loner as you say on the Other Side. Have you ever seen a dispassionate Mexican, who cannot laugh, and sing, and weep with his *compadres* when the music of the mariachis gets too close to hees heart? Never! Eet ees een our blood!"

Treenie had just described all my relatives on my mother's side. "Okay Treenie, you're saying at some point the man must cross the threshold of the Diana."

"*Exacto*, we shall gather eentelligence over a margarita." He folded his copy of *El Mexicano* and we walked a short distance to the Diana on the other side of the plaza. When we got to the door he turned to me. "Can you provide me with a few cash funds, Meester Rosie?"

Back on my side of the border we would have parted at this juncture. But here in Tecate I felt like Alice in Wonderland. I gave the Mad Hatter five twenties.

I interrupt this fascinating documentary to address what the alert reader will quickly perceive; Jesus Rosencranz could not possibly have understood and interpreted all the dialogue overheard at the Diana. What we have here is pure conjecture; however, as a certified denizen of the naked Diana's realm, I think he's in the general vicinity of Truth. And now...back to Jesus!

The Diana is long, dark, and narrow. A tunnel. The back bar is dominated by a huge painting of the huntress Diana with bow in hand, her back arched, the right arm pulled back ready to release her arrow swift and true. The deity of the hunt was stark naked. The arc of the bow, the strained bowstring and the straight arrow were hardly adequate cover.

We found at least a dozen patrons, all men, leaning on the bar. All but one, I noticed, greeted Treenie by name. Music, thin and unbalanced, came from a frilly accordion and a thumping bass viol. Treenie made introductions as we walked the length of the bar looking for a parking place. I shook hands with El Flaco, El Conejo, Chispas, El Negro, El Güero, and El Pollero. Then came El Pelon, and El Tweenkie. Everyone here had a nickname just like my Uncle Gordo in L.A. The names disappeared from my mind as fast as they were introduced. I let my eyes travel to the far end of the bar near the *baños* and saw a huge Great Dane sitting on a barstool with his long black tongue lolling out. He had a beer in front of him. It made me think of those old jokes that always start out with *this dog walks into a bar...*

We found leaning space somewhere near the middle. A giant panda with a cinnamon complexion appeared before us. "Señores," said the panda with a congenial smile. "What is your pleasure?"

Treenie answered. "Mario, thees ees my very good friend, Meester Rosie. He ees new een town."

The perceptive panda knew I didn't do Spanish. He offered his hand and spoke in English. "Welcome to Mexico. What can I get for you?"

I let Treenie order. "Bring us one of your renowned margaritas that have made you famous on both sides of the border."

Keeping one eye on the giant dog, I casually surveyed the patrons I had just been introduced to. I heard a toilet flush in the back and a man with a guitar came out of the gloom. He joined the accordion and the bass and the trio burst into a happy tune I think I've heard my Uncle Gordo play on his guitar.

At the far end were three men in animated conversation that I took to be of a political nature because I could make out the words PAN and PRI. I disqualified two on grounds of age but the third was definitely in the ballpark. At the other end were two young men, both viable candidates. They nursed their drinks and spoke little. Next to Treenie were two Americans in shorts and T-shirts, on my right was El Flaco, a handsome solitary drinker of the appropriate age. He was shedding big tears into his Cuervo straight up. "Rosita, my Rosita," he wept in obvious pain. "You have left me for another and my heart is in pieces!" He shot back the Cuervo and slammed the glass down on the bar. "Mario, another cup to ease the pain, *cabrón*!" He paid the trio. They sang *Amor Tracionero*, a tragic song of a lost love, and El Flaco surrendered himself to a chubasco of new tears. "*Ay, ay, ay! My Rosita!*"

I could see it was going to be an impossible task to meet them all and sort out the ones who came to Tecate from the U.S. within the last five years without arousing suspicion and blowing the whole enterprise. It was totally absurd, time to get out of here and come up with Plan B. I finished my drink and made my move to leave when one of the men at the other end shouted to the giant panda.

"Another round, Mario, it's Tweenkie's birthday."

Mario served two tequila shooters and two beers. "How many, Tweenkie?"

"Thirty-eight," El Tweenkie answered.

"Thirty-eight! You were thirty-eight five years ago, *cabrón!*"

One of his amigos said, "El Tweenkie's afraid of hitting forty." Then he faced El Tweenkie. "Forty is when you start popping Viagra." This was followed by big chunks of masculine laughter.

A big macho voice broke in "Look at me, I'm fifty-two and I don't need no candy for my *pajarraco!*"

"You were fifty-two when the Spaniards landed, *cabrón!*"

Another voice joined the fun. "Tweenkie, we celebrated your fortieth birthday two years ago. You were too drunk to remember!"

Treenie's raspy voice got everyone's attention. "It is useless to lie about one's years in this world. Our hands reveal our true age. "

"Hands! What are you talking about, Treenie?"

"*Sí*, Chispas, *las manos*, those extremities of the arm with twenty-seven little bones and a complicated arrangement of phalanges that provide us with infinite dexterity; the hands that can grip each other in agreement to a deal or as a promise of friendship. Hands strong enough to throw a steer to the ground or gentle enough to caress the woman we love. The hands cannot lie!"

"That's impossible!"

Treenie's sandpaper voice could be heard throughout the bar. "I will bet anyone here that I can guess your birthday just by examining your hands. I buy a drink if I'm wrong!"

Everyone at the bar had a good laugh including the panda behind the bar. "You can never guess my birthday." This from El Negro, a swarthy man in a red embroidered cowboy shirt and a Pancho Villa sombrero the color of butter.

Treenie passed him a cocktail napkin. "Come over here, Negro, and write your birthday on the napkin. Don't let me see it. Put it in your pocket, just let me see your hands."

El Negro scribbled numbers on the napkin and shoved it in his pocket. He put out both hands. Treenie inspected both sides carefully. "You were born July seventh, 1960."

"Wrong!" The man gave the napkin back to Treenie. Treenie looked at it, furrowed his brow, and put it in his pocket. "I wonder what I did wrong? What are you drinking? It's on me." The place burst into laughter and Mario put another Tecate in front of El Negro.

What the hell was Treenie doing?

"All right, Treenie, guess my age, *cabrón*." This from one of the men with a fair complexion who was talking politics. El Something.

Treenie handed him a cocktail napkin. The man scribbled something and put it in his pocket. "Now, let me see your hands, Güero." Treenie took both hands and examined first one side then the other. El Güero was laughing. Treenie palpated and examined each finger meticulously then answered. "You were born on November eleventh 1968."

"You're wrong, Treenie, wrong, wrong, wrong!" El Güero shouted in triumph.

"Mario, give the man anything he wants, I'm buying," Treenie said, and put one of my twenties on the bar.

Mario served up another drink. "Hey Treenie, the answer is not in the hands. Maybe you should inspect feet instead!"

"They take off their shoes and I leave!" someone cried.

There came a burst of macho laughter. Now every man in the bar wanted to play Treenie's ridiculous game. I'm next! Me, me, me! My turn, *cabrón*! The guitar and accordion and the bass viol suspended providing live entertainment to watch in fascination.

I watched my twenties hit the bar and finally realized what Treenie was trying to achieve. But this was an awfully small sampling. We'd have to do every man in town and I would go broke. Still, I gave him an A-plus for ingenuity.

EL Flaco seemed to have forgotten about his beloved Rosita. He sniffled, dried his tears, wrote his birth date on a napkin and put it in his pocket. He put his hands out for Treenie. Not unexpectedly, Treenie struck out. El Flaco ordered another tequila shooter with a Dos Equis on the side, and resumed his torrent of tears for his Rosita who dumped him for another.

One by one they came to Treenie, El Negro, El Conejo, a guy they called Chispas, and several others I couldn't remember, waited their turn. In a half an hour everyone with the exception of the two Americans and the Great Dane were sipping drinks on Treenie. Make that, on me! Closer examination proved the giant dog to be a fiberglass replica. Who bought him the beer I'll never know.

I nudged Treenie, and indicated we were leaving. The friendly giant panda lumbered to the cash register at the end of the bar near the Great Dane and did the numbers. Treenie walked back to make payment.

"Forget about guessing age from hands, Treenie," Mario advised. "You'd have done better examining *nalgas*." This observation was followed by another all-male chorus of laughter. We said adios to all our amigos, and we returned to the laser-bright daylight outside. I could hear them all still laughing inside.

"We had a most successful afternoon. We have our suspect identified," he rasped with a sneer that I knew was intended to be a smile of triumph. He handed me the cocktail napkins. I didn't bother to look at them.

"Did we? All we've got is a bunch of birthdays, a dozen, maybe. We're going to need more than that."

"Oh, we got much more than birthdays, Meester Rosie, we have *names!*"

"Yeah, right. Names like El Flaco, El Gordo, El Pelon, El Negro, El Tweenkie. What good are nicknames? They're as good as aliases."

"Oh no, Señor Rosie. Een Mexico neecknames are more reliable than baptismal names. Neecknames identify an eendividual like fingerprints. Today you met people like El Tweenkie who delivers cakes and bread for Hostess on the Other Side, you met Chispas which means sparks. He ees an electrician. A neeckname ees as permanent as a brand burned eento the hide of a steer. We can change the way we look. We can shave off a mustache, or grow one, but we can never hide from our neeckname. Eet ees positive identification—like DNA!"

I thought of my Uncle Gordo and my cousin El Pollo, the youngest in my mother's family who got saddled with El Pollo for the rest of his life although he could no longer be considered a baby chick. Maybe Treenie had a point.

"Now, Meester Rosie, let us address the matter at hand."

This whole thing was unreal. I was in La La Land where the laws of Logic didn't apply, where they had a sign for an airport that didn't exist, a depot for a train that didn't run, and a city dump with twenty-foot guard towers. I guess when you're in La La Land you do as the La Las do.

"Meester Rosie...?"

"Wait a sec, Treenie, I'm making a psychological adjustment, here." I shuffled through the rumpled napkins.

8/3/70
16/4/55
6/12/72
10/15/60
11/21/57
29/2/56
13/3/48
22/7/55
28/2/56
20/1/54
20/6/58
14/11/56

"I just don't get it, Treenie. There are only twelve months in the year and some of these numbers are too high. There's a 14 and a 20, and look at this, a 29! What do they use down here, the Aztec calendar? We're wasting time, Treenie, I think maybe we'd better—"

"Please, let me explain you something. Anyone who went to school een Mexico has been taught since first grade to put the *day* first, followed by the *month*, then the *year*. We are also taught to cross the number seven. Een your country you put the month first and you do not cross the seven. We have two starting with a low number, under twelve. One ees much too old. And look at the sevens! That leaves only one man who ees the right age, born 6/12/72. And look at the seven — no cross. Our suspect ees twenty-eight years old and he obviously came to Tecate from the United States."

"Do you remember who it was?"

"Of course."

"You collected a dozen cocktail napkins with birthdays and no names and you remember who's who?"

"*Todo se me grava.* My brain records everything I see and hear."

"Incredible, Treenie, who was it?"

"El Conejo."

"El what?"

"El Conejo, the rabbit."

"Now that's a big help — the rabbit!"

"Oh, but eet ees a very important piece of intelligence."

"Yeah, sure, we got a guy who eats carrots, wiggles his nose, and has the DNA of Bugs Bunny." How much more twilight zone can I take? "I don't know, Treenie, you can't expect me to just suspend reality."

"Reality ees a major cause of stress, Meester Rosie. Theenk, Meester Rosie. Why deed the people in Tecate baptize heem El Conejo? Because he ees a quiet individual who, like hees namesake, ees shy and talks leettle. Deed you not notice?"

I ran the tape back to the scene in the Diana. Treenie was right. The guy hardly opened his mouth. Even when all the boisterous fun was going on around him. "Okay, El Conejo is the right age. He writes the month first and doesn't cross his sevens. He was obviously raised in the U.S. and entered Tecate later. But how long ago?"

"Ah! I have more good news, Meester Rosie. While I was paying the bill I casually asked Mario how long he has been serving El Conejo."

"How long?"

"About five years."

"Treenie, you're a genius!"

"*Gracias* for your *confianza*, Meester Rosie."

"You did it, Treenie, you hit the jackpot! El Conejo is the right age, he was raised in the United States, and he came to Tecate at the right time."

I'd been in this business long enough to know you didn't hit a hole-in-one on your first shot. But I didn't want to rain on Treenie's fiesta. The guy definitely lived in his own reality, but he was a good ferret. If I kept him sniffing he might turn up something useful. "Now how do we isolate El Conejo?"

"I have to do some further investigating. Have you geeven any thought to how you are going to transport heem across the border?"

He had a point. If my man didn't have proper ID I'd never get him across and I wouldn't be comfortable stuffing a body in a trunk. I realized then that finding him was useless if I couldn't bring him back. This required some thought. "Look Treenie, I have things to do. I'll meet you back here in an hour."

"An excellent idea, Meester Rosie. I will be here."

I didn't really have anything to do. I just needed to step back through the looking glass, get out of Wonderland for a while, and back into the real world. In my room, alone with my thoughts and a giant scorpion on the curtain, I began to think of ways we could get El Conejo to put one toe across the border. Even if we were wrong, nothing would be lost. He would simply walk back. But if we were right, I could fill out a deposit slip for twenty grand!

An hour or so later I found Treenie hiding behind the front page of *El Mexicano*. I slipped in next to him. He put down his paper.

"So, Treenie, you've had time to investigate further?"

"Yes, Meester Rosie."

"Well, give me the good news."

"I regret to say, Meester Rosie that for the first time een my long career of walking on water, changing base metals eento gold, and performing other miracles for which I am renowned in Tecate, Treenie Contreras has failed."

"What happened?"

"To reduce a long epic and condense eet eento a short story, Meester Rosie, El Conejo came to Tecate from the United States five years ago. From El Paso, Texas. El Conejo has never been een California."

We sat in silence, the miracle worker in disgrace, myself discouraged although I wasn't too optimistic to begin with. The only thing to do was accept defeat. I had to admit it was an entertaining experience, I still had most of the grand in my pocket and the Hummer said we'd still be friends. Time to pack up and go.

"Here's a little bonus, Treenie, you did your best." I started digging out twenties.

He didn't reach for the money in front of him. "I feel we are close, Meester Rosie, but close does not count een my beezness. A tiny detail ees escaping us. A tiny detail, that ees all."

I couldn't be much help to Treenie. He knew the town, he knew the people, the customs, he was full of tricks. All I had was my recent conversation with the Hummer. I ran the tape back in my head.

"*But you've got no useful information about him, nothing but a name that's about as real as John Doe.*"

"*I kinda remember he had a nickname. Everybody called him Patti, or Patta, or Patino or—*"

"*Forget it. That's as meaningless as Juan Lopez. Was he handicapped?*"

"*Naw, that was just part of the scam. He did walk kinda funny, though.*"

Treenie brought out the handful of cocktail napkins he'd gathered at the Diana and studied them like they were the Dead Sea scrolls, looking for the answer that might be hiding there.

"Yes!!" I shouted with double exclamation points. Treenie nearly dropped his collection of cocktail napkins. "Treenie, sometimes I get so impatient I blow things off that are significant. You gave me a comprehensive lecture on the nickname and its importance and significance in the fabric of Mexican culture and customs—and I paid no attention."

"How so, Meester Rosie?"

"The guy DID have a nickname!"

"*Sí?*"

"But I rudely dismissed our only clue. And now I can't remember it. It started with a P."

"There's El Perico, El Pompas, El Pinole, El Pajaro, El Prieto..."

"You're stimulating the mind, Treenie. Let me think a minute."

"I shall do nothing to deestract you."

"It's not coming to me, but it started with a P. I'm sure of it. Let's go through all the vowels. El Pato?"

"The Duck?"

"It's coming back, Treenie! The Hummer—I mean my client—said he had a funny way of walking."

"We could begin by looking for someone who walks like a duck."

"Except it wasn't Pato. I'll run through all the vowels and you tell me what they mean."

"Very good, Meester Rosie."

"El Peto."

"That ees not a word."

"El Pito?"

"I hardly theenk so, Meester Rosie. That is the vulgar form of the male member."

"El Pota?"

"That ees not a word."

"El Puto."

"Not unless he ees a prostitoot."

"El Patio, El Pata, El Popo—I give up Treenie. That's all the vowels. But I know I'm close."

"Perhaps eef we were to stroll around the plaza the mild exercise and diversion might stimulate the *neurotransmitores.*"

We started to stroll like all the locals, no specific destination, just ambling along. The balloon man floated by in silence as did the guy selling plastic snakes and iguanas.

We passed a barefoot Indian dressed in brilliant blue, yellow, green and red feathers pounding on a small drum and hopping up and down like the pavement was burning his feet. Anyone who dropped a coin got an extra boom-boom for his generosity. A good looking guy with a guitar in his arms sang a love song to a young couple cuddling on a wrought iron bench.

"Treenie, I'm catching on to the language. That cart that says RASPADOS is the Sno-Cone cart, right?"

"Yes, Meester Rosie, *raspado* means to scrape—the ice, you know?"

"I thought that would be mostly for kids, but I see he's got a crowd of men."

"There ees a good reason for thees, Meester Rosie. Eef you know the secret password he weel make you a Sno-Cone margarita."

This pleasant idea was interrupted by some very loud and excited shouting coming from twin loudspeakers mounted on a pickup truck. "What's all the shouting about, Treenie? It sounds like the revolution has broken out and they're telling us to grab our belongings and flee."

"That ees Tecate's form of mass marketing, Meester Rosie, cheaper and better than radio. Hee ees advertising a beeg sale at El Rubí, thirty percent off on everything!"

I didn't need help translating the sign that said FARMACIA. It struck me that the plaza was the heart and soul of Tecate. I saw at least three generations, grandparents, parents, kids, and babies sleeping in strollers wandering around sharing the day with each other. No one could feel lonely or left out or forgotten in the plaza. The only place we have to hang out is the mall and the mall is sterile. It lacks heart. No Sno-Cone margaritas, no balloon man, and nobody with a guitar crooning a tender love song to a couple in love. I began to think I could get to like it down here. I wouldn't need an office. I could do business from a table at the sidewalk cafe surrounded by musicians. I wondered how Jackie would go for it.

It felt good not to be straining both hemispheres of the brain with my problem even if only for a couple of minutes. It was like taking a sharp pebble out of my shoe. "Hey, Treenie, what does that sign across the street mean, RETACERIA?"

"Oh, that is a fabric shop."

"Hey, are we doing something that's illegal?'

"I hardly theenk so, Meester Rosie."

"I'm looking at that sign nailed to a tree and I can figure out the first word."

PROHIBIDO
USAR
PATINES

"I can see the first word means prohibited. What are we prohibited from doing, are we doing it, and will they throw us in jail?"

Treenie gave me his sinister laugh again. "No, Meester Rosie, that simply means that eet ees prohibited to use rollerskates in the plaza. And neither of us is presently occupied with that form of recreation. So, we are probably—"

"Treenie, that's it! That's it!"

"That's eet?"

"Okay, that's eet if you want me to say it that way. Treenie, that *must* be the nickname, Patines!"

"Patines?"

"Yes! I remember now. The Humm—I mean, the client said everybody called him Patino and that he had a funny way of walking."

"Ah! You see the eemportance of neecknames? I know exactly what I have to do."

I had to face facts, Treenie had all the moves. On my own here in Fantasy Land I couldn't find Arnold Swartzenegger in the ladies room. "Look Treenie, it's almost dark. I'll meet you back here for breakfast tomorrow at nine sharp."

I went back to my room to find the scorpion on the window curtain had taken a wife and they were walking the kids. I checked my voice mail.

"Hi Mom, I got your message."

"*Muchacho!* How are you *mi hijo?*"

"Just fine. What's happening?"

"Am I going to see you this weekend?"

"You can count on it."

"Good! I have the most wonderful girl I want you to meet."

"Mom."

"She's a friend of your cousin El Chino. Listen *muchacho*, take it from me, the future doesn't come riding in on a burro, it comes racing in on a Thoroughbred!"

My mother never runs out of proverbs. "Mom."

"She is *muy simpatica*, beautiful personality. She's a little on the heavy side, but her smile is luminous."

"Mom."

"Listen to your mother, *muchacho*, the sooner you put the kettle on, the sooner the water boils."

"Mom, I have someone."

"Why haven't you brought her to meet me? Look, *muchacho*, I'll be frank. You're forty-two, not married, no *novia*. All the cousins are starting to make little jokes. Are you, you know, different? You can trust your mother. A mother always loves her children."

I had to laugh. "Mom, relax, I have someone."

"You do?"

"Yes, name's Jackie."

"I understand *muchacho*, that's your choice. There's nothing to be ashamed of. Bring him with you. Your mother will always love you."

"Mom, Mom, Jackie is a girl."

"A girl!"

"Yes, Mom, a real *muchacha*. I'll bring her up this weekend. "

"Oh *muchacho*, you've made me so happy! I'll have all your favorite food, *menudo, pozole*, tamales, *champurrado, nopales,* and *sopa de flore de calabaza...*"

"I love you, Mom. I have to run. See you this weekend."

I rang up Jackie. "Hi sweetheart."

"I'll call you right back. I'm naked."

"A party?"

"I just got home from work. I was in the shower. I'll ring you back in two minutes."

It was more like fifteen before she called back. "How was the party?"

"Don't be silly. When are you getting back? I miss you terribly."

"Me too, sweetheart. The business looks good. I hope I can wrap it up by tomorrow or the next day."

"Are you okay? How's your prostate?"

"I haven't had a treatment since I left but I seem to be doing okay."

"I'm glad to hear that."

"See you soon."

We rang off and I thought of running down to the plaza for a Sno-Cone margarita, but then I realized I didn't know the secret password. I called it a day.

Friday morning at nine I strolled into the plaza. An old ranchero wished me *buenos dias* and the man pushing the churro cart gave me a friendly wave. I felt like a local. I found Peter Lorre exactly as I had found him yesterday. He was hiding behind the open newspaper sipping a cup of black coffee.

"*Buenos dias*, Meester Rosie."

"*Buenos dias*," I answered. I wished my mother could have heard me.

"I have made good use of my time, Meester Rosie. I have just had a long interview with El Cepillos."

"El Cepillos, don't tell me, let me guess. A nickname."

"*Exacto!* A neeckname, Meester Rosie."

"I have a new respect for nicknames, Treenie, and trucks that shout, and movie theaters with no movies, and signs prohibiting rollerskating in the plaza."

"*Cepillo* means brush, and almost anywhere you go in Mexico the man who shines shoes is soon known as El Cepillos. Look at my shoes. I just had them cleaned and shined."

I looked at his white shoes. They looked brand new. "That's really terrific, Treenie, but I fail to see where that's going to contribute anything to the matter at hand."

"Ah but you see, Meester Rosie, El Cepillos knows the men of Tecate intimately!"

"Intimately?"

"By their shoes."

Oh, boy!

"El Cepillos claims there ees no better way to know a person. He knows their gait, whether they toe-in or toe-out, where they've been. El Cepillos says the only one who can tell you more about that person ees probably hees mother."

"El Cepillos."

"Yes! He shines El Patines's shoes regularly. He does not own a car. He walks everywhere. And—thees ees the most eemportant—he wears out the soles of both shoes on the eenside edge."

"Like skating."

"*Exacto.*"

"Bingo!"

"*Loteria!*"

"Any more?"

"Yes, Meester Rosie. Soap scum on his brown shoes, always brown, would indicate he works at a car wash. Salsa stains reveal the fact that he takes his meals at taco stands. And the thick red dust implies that he works or leeves near where bricks are made."

I was back in La La Land. "Okay Treenie, when does my fairy godmother show up with her magic wand?"

"You make a joke, *sí*?"

"El Cepillos can tell us what he had for breakfast. So what?"

"Cepillos is sure he has been shining his shoes for at least five years."

"I'm impressed, Treenie, I really am."

"Cepillos charged me fifty pesos."

I slipped him five American and took the loss of half a buck. "Treenie, this calls for a celebration. Big time!"

"An excellent idea, Meester Rosie."

"Run over to the Sno-Cone cart and get us a couple refreshers. All the brain work has left me parched." Treenie began to move toward the pushcart. "And Treenie—use the secret password!"

Parched throat relieved, palate refreshed, and stress subdued, we were ready to return to business. "Okay, Treenie, what's next?"

"A drive to where they make the breeck would not be a waste of time. Eenstinct tells me we might find something eenteresting."

This business is more guts and luck than science so I went along with the idea. "Which way do we go?" I asked as we got in the car.

"Let us take Highway 3 into the Valley of Tanama. That is where all the breeckyards are located."

Town quickly disappeared and we were in open country. Highway 3 is a narrow, twisty, windy strip of buckled asphalt pocked with potholes deep enough to swallow a wheel. Wild sunflowers, toxic Jimson weed, and assorted cacti grow on both sides of the road, occasionally punctuated with little white crosses, constant reminders that Death waits in ambush around every curve for the careless and the cautious alike. I saw farms with row crops and scruffy looking cattle, lush vineyards. A couple miles down the road we started to see brickyards with adobe kilns the size of a house belching black smoke. The earth was red with brick dust. Our man must walk home along this road on his way to and from town, I thought. Things were starting to look good.

It was not a laid back drive. I swerved sharply to avoid tangling with a couple of black and white bovines who insisted on the right of way, and nearly ditched the car in a gully to avoid a head-on collision with a kamikaze eighteen-wheeler coming right at me in an effort to pass another car on a blind curve.

As we came around another bend I saw a huge mushroom cloud of white steam rising a hundred feet into the air. This could only mean some suicide terrorist dropped a bomb on Tecate, or natural subterranean thermal activity on the order of Yellowstone. I concluded it was the latter. I remarked to Treenie, "Now, if you could harness that energy Mexico could produce a lot of low-cost power for home and industry."

"That thermal geyser, Meester Rosie, ees not a natural phenomenon. Eef you would be good enough to pull een."

"I don't mind. I'd like a better look at this myself." I pulled off the highway. We got out and walked toward the geyser. I could feel the intense heat as the huge funnel of live steam roiled upward. When it thinned out a faint image began to take form. The figure of a lone man came into focus. He stood there dressed like a field hand in a loose-fitting guayabera blouse, white chinos, and a broad sombrero. The terrorist? The cloud began to thin out and that's when I saw the source of the thermal explosion, a Chevrolet pickup that left Detroit about the time the pilgrims landed. It may have been green in those days.

Treenie hurried toward the man. "Father! Are you all right?" he inquired in English.

"Perfectly fine, my son."

"Thank God! Let me eentroduce you to my friend, Meester Rosie."

The rumpled field hand thrust out a firm, warm hand in the company of a cordial smile. If this was Treenie's father he was not what I would have imagined. I saw no physical characteristics that would imply they shared the same gene pool. The man was not thin as a breadstick like Treenie, he was round but trim, his face smooth as chamois. And his beautiful robust voice was nothing like Treenie's laryngitic rasp, either.

"A pleasure to meet you, señor," the man said. "A burning bush at the side of the road could be no greater proof of God's existence than your arrival at this moment." He held up a Motorola. "I tried to call, but God was away on business. I got His answering machine and left a voice mail—and here you are!"

I liked the man immediately. He was my kinda guy. "So, you're Treenie's dad. I am at your complete disposal."

"Ah, Meester Rosie, thees ees Father Ruben our local Padre."

Oops! "Can we give you a lift?" I offered. "We could bring back a jug of water while this thing cools off."

"May God repay my debt to you, señor. I was just on my way to Casa Los Encinos to deliver a box of tomatoes. It isn't far."

"No problem, Padre, I'll put them in the trunk and we'll be on our way."

Father Ruben beat me to it. He lifted the heavy crate of ripe tomatoes out of his pickup, I opened the back of my Explorer, and he tossed it in. "There is one more thing I must do before we go, Señor Rosie."

"Of course." I watched the good father reach into the front seat of the spewing dragon and withdraw a large plastic bowl filled with fresh brown eggs badly cracked. "I'm afraid those are totaled, Father, an omelet is about all they're good for now."

Father Ruben looked down at his bowl of fresh eggs with a beatific smile as though bestowing a blessing. "Like God's children, we are fragile perhaps, but endowed with noble purpose and hidden virtue."

I watched the Padre begin to separate eggs with all the skill and speed of a fry cook at Denny's on a busy morning. One by one he discarded the yoke and dropped the white into the radiator.

Treenie must have seen the undisguised perplexity on my face. "For some chemical reason I do not fully understand, egg whites are an efficient sealant."

"I guess we learn something new every day."

"Oh, eet ees hardly new, Meester Rosie, eet has been in use in Mexico since the appearance of the automobile."

Now I've seen everything; an organic, all-natural, eco-friendly Stop Leak. And cholesterol free! We got into my vehicle and we were off.

"Father Ruben supervises the vineyards of San Lorenzo we passed a few kilometers back," Treenie explained as we rolled along.

"You must come and sample our product, señor."

"Thank you, Father, I'd love to."

"It is still in an early stage this time of year."

"Reposing in oaken casks?"

"Hanging on the vines."

The padre had a sense of humor.

"I wonder if I could impose further on our brief friendship, señor."

"Of course, Father."

"I have been on the road for over twenty minutes without food or water."

"I could use a little sustenance myself. Is there a cafe on this road?"

"See that group of cows cropping grass at the side of the road? Pull in there."

Two brown cows the size of a locomotive and one black and white glared at me, switching their tails in annoyance as I drove between them into a bare dirt lot. Under a grove of towering poplars I saw a small adobe dwelling surrounded by a few pickups and several horses dozing at a hitching rail. I parked between a bright red F-150 and a sleepy palomino. The delicious aroma, an amalgam of refried beans and sausage and eggs and coffee and wood smoke reminded me of my mother's kitchen and summoned appetite. A half-dozen colored chickens scratching in the dirt, and a big red rooster determined to have his way with a white leghorn, scattered as we approached the front stoop.

Inside, Cafe Los Alamos seemed to get smaller. Three or four small tables and a half-dozen hungry men crowded the little room to the walls. A newsman babbled on a television set mounted high on one wall. No one paid attention. We were greeted by a chorus of *buenas tardes* which we all acknowledged. Treenie and I took the only available table by the front window while Father Ruben went to shake hands with someone called Amador, and Francisco, and Carlos, and a bunch of others. He chatted with Chola in the tiny kitchen who was stirring a steaming kettle while her husband Tito threw more wood in the big iron stove.

"Let us place our orders before I pass out," the Padre said as he came back to join us.

Father Ruben ordered *machaca* and eggs with potatoes and beans and a "little side of cactus." Treenie went for the green *chilaquiles* smothered in a tart tomatillo sauce and a side of sausage. I stayed with plain scrambled eggs and politely declined chile, *carnitas*, *chicharrones*, *machaca*, and other add-ins. Chola looked crestfallen so I added a side of fried potatoes only to win her smile.

"I'm glad we made this stop," Father Ruben said as Chola put down our food and a basket of hot flour tortillas. "I never would have made it alive to Casa Los Encinos."

"A house in the oaks?" I asked, showing off my growing vocabulary in my mother's tongue.

"Oh, more than a house," the priest said. "Casa Los Encinos is an orphanage administrated with love and devotion by Ramon and Simona." He anointed everything on his plate with hot red salsa and took a tortilla. "They were sent by God."

"Eet ees something beautiful wrought of tragedy, Meester Rosie."

"They lost their two children when a school bus on a field trip went over the cliff on the Rumorosa about ten years ago," Father Ruben explained. "Ramon and Simona were inconsolable." He subtracted another tortilla from the basket. "Then one day they both heard God's voice, *give everything to the poor and follow me.*"

"*Café?*" Chola asked and poured three coffees.

"They sold their house, gave away all their possessions, and made a home for those unfortunate leftover children who need everything and have nothing and no one."

One of the *vaqueros* jumped up suddenly and ran for the door. "I think those are my cows on the road. I better get them out before the *judiciales* show up!"

I watched Father Ruben kidnap a little piece of Treenie's sausage while he was momentarily absorbed in a news brief on Vicente Fox.

I didn't realize how hungry I was. I left nothing of the scrambled eggs and while I dug around in the basket for the last tortilla I saw Father Ruben spear a potato off my plate. I hid a smile.

We all made short work of the food. I didn't think we'd left a crumb behind but Father Ruben rooted through the tortilla basket and came up with a small scrap just large enough to scoop up a little dab of green tomatillo salsa from Treenie's *chilaquiles*. While he was occupied in this endeavor I grabbed the check.

Four kilometers along the same pitted highway brought us to Casa Los Encinos. Two huge Fruehauf trailers, once part of a big rig, sat on blocks under a deep pool of shade cast by ancient oak trees. Although someone who was a fair hand at carpentry had cut out a door and several windows I could still see remnants of

TRANSPORTES GONZALEZ S.A. in big orange lettering on the pale blue sides. Young children scampered like mice playing you-can't-catch-me games. A group of little girls jumped rope while waiting their turn on the swings. Boys along with the girls were playing a form of hopscotch. Off to one side two of the older boys and a girl in clean but mismatched clothes were raking leaves in slow motion. There was a washing machine set up out in front, and two clotheslines where wet clothes of every color hung like holiday bunting.

We were barely out of the car when a man and a woman came running to meet us. This must be Ramon and Simona, I thought. They looked about my age.

"Padre! *Buenas tardes. Que tal*, Treenie!" There was a lot of hand shaking including mine and I had yet to be introduced.

"I would like you to meet the man who saved my life on the highway." Father Ruben made it sound like a valiant helicopter rescue at sea. This announcement brought on another round of hand clasping from Simona and Ramon. They said what I thought were a lot of nice things about me. But they must have seen the lost look on my face because they quickly switched to serviceable English with little trace of an accent.

"So nice to meet you, Señor Rosie. Please come in and have a refreshment."

They led us to some old kitchen chairs near one of the trailers. Ramon was thin as a rake with a mop of black hair and an untamed mustache to match. Simona, short, and plump, moved with the vivacity of a dancer. Both had smooth terra cotta skin, and their gleaming smiles never left their faces. I couldn't perceive a trace of their tragedy. A light of love shone in their eyes.

We sat in a circle enjoying the shade while Ramon and Simona ran into the trailer. They were back in minutes with a huge pitcher of ice-cold orangeade and plastic cups.

I could hear the churning and sloshing of the washing machine, birds peeping in the branches above, the rustle of dry leaves being gathered, and that sweet innocent giggle and laughter of children at play.

Simona put a plastic plate in Father Ruben's hands. It held a fat bean burrito and a dollop of guacamole. "*Andele* Padre, breakfast was a long time ago!"

"*Dios te bendiga, hija.*"

Simona turned to Treenie and me with that look that implied more food was coming. I've seen that same look on my mother's face. We quickly declined her kind offer and I watched fascinated as Father Ruben disposed of the bean burrito, and with the remaining bit of tortilla, scooped up the last of the guacamole. We'd just had a heavy lunch not twenty minutes ago! How could this man consume so much food and not look like a Sumo wrestler?

"How many children do you have here?" I asked to avoid sitting there like a stump.

"We have twenty-six children from three to nine. Four are in *primaria*. Ramon takes them to school every day. They're on vacation now, of course."

"It has to be hard depending on donations."

Father Ruben answered for them. "These two perform miracles."

A little girl of eight or so in a blue dress that she would grow into next year came up with a smaller girl in tow. "Sonia fell down." Sonia wasn't crying but she looked unhappy.

In one fluid movement Simona pulled out her handkerchief, wiped a smudge of dirt, put a kiss on the little face, and popped a yellow candy ball in her mouth. "Now go see if the big children will let you play in the leaves."

I watched them scamper off like squirrels.

With a residual smile still on her face Simona went on. "We grow a few crops, keep some chickens, we have a cow. We get a lot of help from our friends and neighbors." She turned her smile up toward the filigreed sky. "But God does most of it."

"And we have a tenant," Ramon added. "And that's a big help."

"He's a nice *muchacho*. He was looking for a place to put his camper so we rented him a space in the back."

"He's a very quiet young man. Gathers wood for us when he gathers for himself, draws his own water. Never asks for anything."

"And he's always bringing little treats for the children, candy, small toys, things like that. He brought them that swing set last year."

"And he's very punctual. We don't go look for him. On the last day of each month he comes here to us and puts five hundred pesos in my hand. We hardly see him otherwise. He's very shy."

"He never misses a Mass," Father Ruben observed.

"He's been here about three years, I'd say."

"Closer to five, *mi amor*." Simona corrected.

A blip appeared on my radar screen.

"I guess you're right. How time flies! But, you watch, tomorrow is the last day of the month. At four o'clock he'll be here with the rent money and candy for all the *muchachos*."

"I think Juan has been telling them about the fair because they ask me every day if they can go."

"*Pobrecitos*, of course they want to go—but there are so many of them!"

We visited a little while longer. Then, while Father Ruben and I unloaded the tomatoes, Ramon filled a couple of gallon jugs with water. "Come on, Padre, I'll drive you back. Your truck should be cooled off by now. I'll just get some eggs."

"Not necessary, I've already administered first aid."

I was glad to see the party was breaking up. It was time to disappear. Treenie and I gave our thanks for their warm hospitality and went to the car. Simona brought Father Ruben a paper cup of flan. "Just a little something for the road, Padre."

Back in the plaza, Treenie and I went into conference under an umbrella at the sidewalk cafe. We ordered a beer. The trio that had been playing in the Diana was now playing *Cuando Calienta El Sol* for a group of tourists at another table. The ching-ding-a-ling and jingle of little bells came from the brightly painted ice cream cart pushed along by an old man who used it for a walker.

"Well, Treenie, we had a very productive afternoon."

"With God's help."

"Yeah, I guess you're right. Nothing would have happened if we hadn't rescued Father Ruben."

"How do you want to proceed, Meester Rosie?"

"You have tomorrow off. I'm making a solo trip back to Casa Los Encinos."

"You want to be present when Juan comes to pay his rent and distribute treats to the children, yes?"

"*Exacto.*" I was picking up vocabulary from Treenie. "The operation gets very delicate from here on. If the tenant turns out to be Juan Lopez, and he sees us together, he'll sniff it out."

"I am een total accord, Meester Rosie. Have you geeven more thought as to how you eentend to get heem across the border?"

"I haven't thought of anything else."

"And what ees the plan, eef I am not being eendiscreet?"

"I wish I knew."

"Very well, Meester Rosie, I shall occupy myself een other endeavors tomorrow until I hear from you."

"Five o'clock tomorrow at this same table."

At a quarter to three the next day I pulled into Casa Los Encinos with two big crates of fresh peaches.

"God bless you, Señor Rosie."

"*Que Dios se lo pague.*"

Ramon and I unloaded the boxes and I was soon sitting under a canopy of oaks sipping icy orangeade with Ramon and Simona.

"*Ay* Señor Rosie, these are beautiful peaches. *Gracias!*"

"Well, I would have brought you another cow but I couldn't get the beast in the car." This lousy line brought me some laughs and a refill. "How did you ever find such a beautiful setting for your children?"

"Oh, we could never afford to buy it. The property belongs to an old relative of Simona's and he lets us use it."

"He lives on the Other Side and he never comes down here."

"Well, I've never seen anything as beautiful."

"There's even a little stream in back," Ramon said, "and it runs all year."

"That is where we collect our water," Simona said. "Would you like to see it?"

I was just waiting to be asked. "I'd love to!"

"Take him out back and show him around," Simona said to her husband and he led me away.

I followed Ramon past a small garden with rows of green squash, cucumbers, and beans and some strange foliage I didn't recognize. Two boys and two girls were picking the vegetables and placing them in a cardboard carton. Beyond them was a stand of yellow corn.

"We just chased out a rabbit, Don Ramon!" one of the girls called over in triumph.

"Good for you!" Ramon called out to the girl then turned to me. "The wild animals get most of it, I'm afraid. The only thing the gophers and the rabbits and squirrels and the raccoons don't steal is Margarita. That's the cow." The cow, an enormous Holstein with huge black patches scattered over pure white hide, acknowledged us with a loud moo and ran her long red tongue up her nose. Her udder was pink and full.

"Come, I'll show you the little stream."

Ramon led me to a beautiful creek of sparkling crystalline water gurgling happily over rocks then tumbling into a deeper pool. "It would be easy to stay here all day and forget the world outside," I said.

"Yes, it is beautiful. The children beg to come here and play in the water. But we don't allow them near here, poor little things. It is much too dangerous."

"What is that old building over there? I've never seen such beautiful stone work!" I walked toward the outbuilding knowing Ramon would follow. "I suppose you store your crops here in the winter."

"Oh no," he laughed. "Rain pours in through the roof, the doors are gone. We let our tenant store his things in here. He has his camper parked in back."

I poked my head in. It smelled wet and musty. There was an old sofa, providing equal opportunity housing for rats, spiders, and other vermin without regard for social preference or biological origin. A couple of rusted bedsprings leaned against the wall, on the earth floor, a pile of tires, stacks of wooden fruit crates, and a half-dozen bales of sorry-looking hay. My curiosity was satisfied. There was no point in wasting any more time here. I turned back and Ramon followed.

Partially hidden under all the junk, and a heavy coat of brown dust, was a blue Honda with handicap plates. A wheelchair was strapped to the back.

Simona offered us another round of orangeade when we got back and we chatted easily until we heard children screaming, "It's Juanito, Juanito!" I looked up to see the subject walking toward us with a dozen children hanging on either side. He scooped up one of the little ones and held her in one arm. I tried to study his gait but it was impossible. By the time he reached where we were sitting, more kids came running and soon he had swarms of boys and girls climbing all over him. Then I looked down at Juan's shoes. They were covered with red brick dust. I immediately thought of Cepillos.

"Children! Children! Leave poor Juanito alone."

The loving reprimand had no effect. The shy young man worked his way to a chair and began to empty his pockets of chocolates, marzipan, cactus candy, and butterscotch balls. He filled their little hands as fast as he could move. They smothered him with hugs and kisses. I actually felt a lump in my throat as I watched the spontaneous burst of affection.

"Now, children off you go! Beto, you help bring in the vegetables. Maria and Sara, take the little ones in and get them cleaned up. I'll be starting dinner pretty soon. Magi, Tere, you can help." The gaggle of kids disappeared as fast as they had formed.

"*Ay que muchachos!*" Simona sighed.

"You have them spoiled, Juanito." She spoke to him in English. Interesting.

"I like to see children when they're happy." He unbuttoned the pocket on his shirt and withdrew a bill. I could tell by the color it was a five hundred peso note. He folded it several times and tucked it into Ramon's hand as though it was a secret message.

Ramon introduced us. "This is Señor Rosie from the Other Side. He doesn't speak Spanish."

I began talking before Juanito had a chance to speculate and form an opinion. "I'm considering the possibility of opening a factory down here."

I was lucky that before he could think, *then what are you doing here?* Simona added, "Señor Rosie rescued Father Ruben on the highway yesterday and brought him here."

"Oh, I thought you looked familiar," the young man said in English. "I've seen you in the plaza."

"You two make yourselves comfortable and get acquainted,"' Simona said. "It's time for Ramon to milk the cow and I better start on dinner."

"You need help?" Juanito asked.

"No, no, thank you. Enjoy a visit. We'll be back shortly."

Juanito had to be in his late twenties but he had the face and voice of a child. There was an endearing aura of innocence about him.

"What kind of industry are you in?"

I could see "rescuing Father Ruben" had a reassuring effect. He was totally at ease with me. "I'm planning a *maquiladora* factory. Essentially it will be an assembly works for clients on the Other Side."

"How soon do you expect to be in operation?"

"Well, that depends on Treenie. But if we can find something suitable on this trip I hope to be operating in six or seven months at the most."

"You will be hiring people from here?"

"Are you interested?"

"Very much! I want to get married but I told my *novia* it would have to wait until I had reliable employment."

"Do you have experience in any phase of manufacturing?"

"Oh no, I was born and grew up in the lettuce fields of Fresno. I never knew my parents. I was abandoned as a child—like the kids you see here." His voice was soft as a girl's. "Only not so lucky."

I could hear dishes clattering inside the Fruehauf and the lowing of Margarita as she saw Ramon arrive with his pail.

"I was raised by aunts and uncles who worked in the fields following the crops from farm to farm. They were rough on me. My uncles were heavy drinkers, one went to jail for stealing a car, another uncle was dealing drugs to the farm workers."

What a horrible way to grow up, I thought. "You don't look like you do either."

"No. Fortunately, they had to put me in school. That's when I got my first pair of shoes. I stayed there where it was safe as long as I could."

"What about when you turned sixteen?"

"The uncles wanted me back in the fields or selling their *drogas*. I told them I was going to stay in school and they were afraid to go to the administrators. Some of them were illegal, you know."

"How far did you get in school?"

"When I graduated from high school I ran away. I found a place to stay in a warehouse where they needed a night watchman. I did odd jobs here and there, put myself into a community college and learned accounting. I wanted to be an accountant."

I noticed we'd both drained our glass of orangeade.

"I couldn't get work up there so I came to San Diego. But it was the same thing here. I found a job in another warehouse. They let me stay at night in exchange for janitor work. During the day I picked up odd jobs here and there. But it wasn't enough to live on."

The next logical question in a conversation like this would be, and what brought you to Mexico? But I didn't ask it. I could see how driving half a mile to a parking garage and collecting two thousand dollars was like winning the Lotto jackpot. Under the same circumstances would I have done the same thing? In a heartbeat!

"I can definitely use you in the new factory." I've lied before but when I saw that innocent face brighten with hope I felt like a rat.

"Doing what?"

"Oh, inventory control is just like accounting. You have to keep track of everything. "

"And you can use me?" He sounded just like a kid when he says, "Can I play?"

"You're already hired!" I gave myself another black mark.

I stood just as Simona came back to her chair. "Well, Simona, I've got to be heading back. Treenie has some man from Tijuana who has a building to show me."

"Thank you for all your kindness," Simona said, taking my hand. "Come and see us soon."

The shy boy who drove the getaway car for a murderer offered his hand. "It was nice to meet you, señor. Good luck with your project."

"Thanks, you'll be hearing from me."

I found Treenie at the same table in the sidewalk cafe. He had a beer in front of him. The place was packed. A handsome dark man with a seamless tenor voice cradled a guitar in his arms and sang old love songs to a group of men and women at the next table.

"I am anxious to hear about your day, Meester Rosie."

I sat across from Treenie and gave him a complete and detailed report. An attractive young woman with bright red highlights in her naturally black hair came up to our table to take my order. She wore a yellow T-shirt with a message silk-screened in pink. I tried to read the lettering but the topography made it impossible without getting unacceptably close to the text.

"Bring me a straight shot of Clorox," I ordered. "Ammonia chaser!"

"Señor?"

"*Ponle un tequila al* señor," Treenie instructed the girl. "Do I perceive a loss of spirit, Meester Rosie? A fading of resolve? You have been eminently successful and een such a short time."

I hardly ever touch tequila but under the present circumstances I shot it down and sucked a lemon before I could put the problem into words. "Yes, Treenie, we've got our man. So what? If I can't get him across the border this whole business has been a waste of time."

"Perhaps he could be tempted with parties and pretty girls. I can supply a number of—"

"Not this kid."

Treenie sat in silence, his inscrutable face, void of expression. A total blank. He either went comatose on me or he was into transcendental meditation. Neither of us spoke. The music from the next table wafted over us and I began to wish Jackie and I were sitting at that table drinking margaritas and listening to romantic music. If human thoughts produced sound we would have sounded like two freight trains highballing in the night. Treenie's uncharacteristic display of emotion brought me back to the moment.

"An epiphany!" He threw both hands toward the umbrella above us.

"What are you talking about, Treenie?"

"Yes!"

"Yes what?"

"Eet ees early yet, Meester Rosie, I suggest we spend the rest of the afternoon at the fair."

"The fair! This whole endeavor is about to crash and burn if we don't solve the problem. We're sitting in the dark and you want to spend the rest of the afternoon at the fair? Riding the loop the loop, I suppose, swinging round and round on the Ferris wheel, the roller coaster maybe, eating cotton candy and tacos and tamales and *churros*?"

"The best thing to do when we are in the dark is to light a candle, Meester Rosie."

Geez, a philosopher.

"Eet ees a commonly accepted theory that solutions to the most deefeecult problems lie dormant een the subconscious mind until they are set free."

"And just how do we accomplish setting them free?"

"Very easily, Meester Rosie, we simply get out of the way."

"You'll have to explain that one."

"The conscious mind ees an obstruction, Meester Rosie."

"So you're suggesting we go off and play like we didn't have a care in the world."

"*Exacto*. Eet ees well known that recreation stimulates the *neurotransmitores* to the brain."

"And while we eat and play and entertain ourselves with whirling rides and silly games, the subconscious mind does all the work and by the time we leave the fair with our arms full of kewpie dolls and stuffed bears, the answer comes to us in one cosmic moment of revelation."

"*Exacto.*"

"Finish your beer, Treenie, we're going to the fair."

An hour later we entered the fairgrounds. It was a typical small town fair. Everything was decorated with the vivid colors of the Mexican flag. Green, white, and red streamers and garlands hung from high wires. Fluttering pennants snapped and popped in the breeze. The whole place smelled like popcorn and cotton candy. Music blared from the merry-go-round where brightly painted horses went round and round, up and down in a frozen prance. There were bumper cars, a roller coaster, two Ferris wheels, and a hot air balloon also in the colors of the Mexican flag sponsored by the brewery with huge lettering:

CERVEZA TECATE
¡ La Mejor!

There were games too, ring toss, a shooting gallery, a baseball batting cage, dunk the clown, and a giant roulette wheel. We couldn't have been there more than five minutes when Treenie was already asking for money like a kid.

"I wonder eef you could provide me with a few cash funds, Meester Rosie."

"Like how much?"

"A hundred American should be ample."

"Treenie, you couldn't spend that much if you rode every ride and ate everything they've got." I peeled off five twenties. "Here, go loosen up your neurotransmitters."

I must have wandered around for over an hour. I think my conscious mind was overpowering the subconscious because it gave me nothing but tired feet and a pressing need to find a portable toilet. I found a whole row of them marked HOMBRES and felt a lot better when I stepped out. Maybe portable toilets weren't such a bad business. I walked over to the roulette wheel to watch the action.

It was a huge red and black wheel about three feet across with numbers painted in white all along the outside edge. Next to every number was a small round hole.

The croupier spun the wheel. "Place your bets, señores, today you may win a fortune!"

I was waiting to see the little white ball come bouncing out. Nothing happened. The croupier put his hand over what looked to me like a plastic salad bowl sitting upside down in the center of the wheel. "Now watch the numbers, señoras y señores. One of you is going to be a winner!" He lifted the plastic bowl and a big ugly rat came scrambling out.

The crowd screamed out their numbers, "Here little rat, here, here!" But the rat kept running around the wheel. "*Aquí, aquí, ratoncito aquí!*" Suddenly the frantic rat found one of the numbered holes, dropped in, and disappeared.

"*Veinticinco!*" called out the croupier. "*Veinticinco* is our winner!"

The crowd groaned, all except for the woman who had her money on number twenty-five. The croupier paid her off, scooped up the bets, and prepared for another spin. "Place your bets, señores!"

I don't know what became of the big ugly rat, but there was no way you could rig this wheel.

I remained there watching the crowd place their bets on the numbers. I could hear the clickety-clackety of the roller coaster as it climbed to the top, followed by the screams as it plunged down with a roar and a rumble that shook the ground. The air was heavy with the smell of greasy hot dogs. I'd had enough recreation. As I turned to go Treenie mysteriously appeared.

"I've given my subconscious all the recreation and diversion I can handle in one day, Treenie. My neurotransmitters are dead. I got nothing. Let's get out of here."

"Of course, Meester Rosie, but on our way out I would like to eentroduce you to a very good friend of mine."

"Sure, okay, Treenie, as long as it's on our way out."

Treenie led me to a dark, slim man standing near the brewery balloon with a face like a Belgian waffle. He was dressed in a blue United States Marines tunic with red trimming and a regulation white-visored cap. He wore plain Levis.

"Meester Rosie, allow me to introduce you to Capitan Vargas." I shook hands with the guy only to avoid being rude. I was in no mood to be sociable.

Waffleface said, "*Mucho gusto*, Señor Rosie. We can start your lessons now if you like."

The neurotransmitters delivered. "Treenie, you really are a genius!"

"*Gracias* for your *confianza*."

The next day just before four o'clock I paid another visit to Ramon and Simona.

I found them at a sawhorse. Simona was holding a two-by-four while Ramon lopped it off with a handsaw. As soon as they saw me they stopped what they were doing and came to greet me like a favored guest. I received a warm embrace from both of them. Simona went into the Fruehauf and, as I expected she would, returned with a pitcher of orangeade. I waited until we were all sitting under the oaks to announce the purpose of my visit.

"I hope you have strong lungs, Ramon, I think it's going to require two of us." It was fun to watch their smiling faces register confusion. I went to the back of the Explorer and pulled out a large carton. Ramon was there to help me. We laid it on the ground and were instantly surrounded by a crowd of curious kids.

"What on earth is it?" Simona squealed like a little girl.

Ramon opened the carton. "A wading pool! A wading pool for the *muchachos*!"

More warm embraces and a shower of thank you's. "The kids can play in the water now without going near the creek."

The effusive thanks that followed was almost embarrassing. More hugs from Ramon and Simona and now the kids were throwing their arms around me. I felt my eyes sting. It could have been some pollen in the air, but it wasn't. We had the thing put together and we were just about to blow it up when Juanito aka El Patines showed up.

"I could hear the *muchachos* screaming even before I got here."

"*El* señor brought us a swimming pool!" they all screamed at once.

We had to take turns blowing the damn thing up but it wasn't long before we had it set up in the yard. Ramon hooked up a garden hose and we started to fill it. But the kids couldn't wait.

"Can we go in, can we go in!"

"Go get changed." Simona said.

The gang disappeared into the Fruehauf like a shot. They were back in minutes and started climbing in even before we had it full. The little ones were in their underpants, the bigger boys in their boxers, the grade school girls who had nothing to hide came out in shorts and T-shirts.

We sat and watched the kids splash and frolic. "It doesn't take much to make kids happy." I thought it was my own thought but I must have said it out loud because Juanito answered.

"No, it doesn't. It just takes somebody to do it."

One of the bigger boys jumped out, picked up a big red plastic ball, and plopped back in. Another game started.

"Just look at those *muchachos*," Juanito said to Ramon and Simona. "They are so happy in their ignorance of life. They're splashing and playing and have no idea that they are poor, or that the world is bad and ugly. Thank God they have *you*." I watched the children squealing with innocent delight, paddling, jumping, splashing each other and pretending to swim. "I wonder what lies ahead for them," Juanito continued. "We have some difficult choices to make while we're growing up."

I looked over at Juanito. I knew what he was feeling. He could have ended up like the rough uncles who raised him, selling drugs, robbing gas stations, stealing cars. These little kids were human discards but here with Ramon and Simona they had as much emotional security as any rich kid back in town. Ramon's and Simona's love healed the scars of the past. The future didn't yet exist for them. They were living in the present moment, a *now* where they knew only love and security.

I couldn't understand a word the kids were saying but I didn't have to to know they were playing water tag, splashing each other, and running from the 'shark.' They spoke a common language spoken by children anywhere in the world. I looked over at Ramon and Simona, their faces beaming with pride. I think Juanito was wishing he was a kid again so he could start life over.

Usually, the people I get hired to bring back are scumbags, people you don't even want to know exist. But business is business. Hey, I came here to do a job and I'm doing exactly what I'm being paid to do, I told myself. Further thought vanished when our hosts went into the Fruehauf.

They were back in less than a minute with another pitcher of orangeade and a huge plate of sweetbread. Simona poured, Ramon passed the plate around. "The sisters at the convent came by today and brought us a basket of their cookies and fruit tarts. We'd better have some before the piranhas smell them!"

"I just got a brilliant idea," I said as I took a fruit tart. "I would like to invite all your children to the fair."

Simona clapped her hands with delight. "What a generous offer!"

"And expensive! There are a lot of *muchachos*, Señor Rosie, and once inside they will want everything they see—rides, food, ice cream—everything!"

"That's the whole point and the invitation stands."

Simona clapped her hands again. "*Ay!* Señor Rosie! How can you manage so many *muchachos*?"

"I was thinking maybe I could get Juanito to come along and help me."

The naive Juanito snapped at the bait. "Yes! We could take a small group of, say, six *muchachos* every day."

My brief moment of conscience passed. I had him! Now I was congratulating myself. I'd have this job wrapped up tomorrow. I'd only invested about four hundred of the thousand the Hummer gave me and missed only one prostate treatment. By the day after tomorrow I'll have twenty thousand bucks in my hand, Jackie in my arms, and a happy prostate! It was an effort not to get up and celebrate like a running back jiving in the end zone.

"I'll pick you up here in the morning then you and I can scout it out before we bring the kids."

"I'll be ready."

The Baja air was sweet and pleasantly cool at nine in the morning when Juanito and I walked into the fairgrounds. The gates didn't open until ten but ever resourceful Treenie had provided me with a very official-looking pass supposedly issued to important guests by the Presidente Municipal. I expect Treenie had it made where he had all his other credentials made. I could see my quarry was impressed when the guard waved me in with a flamboyant salute. The place was silent, nearly deserted. It smelled of wet concrete, the pavement having recently been hosed down. The concessionaires were just setting up their rides and their games. The croupier kept his stable of big ugly rats in a small wire cage while he set up his wheel. The food stalls were just taking down their wooden shutters. I knew Treenie was somewhere on the grounds. He would remain invisible until his moment came but I could sense his presence.

"Well, what do you think, Juanito?" I said to give some verisimilitude to our mission. "No roller coaster, no bumper cars, no twister. We don't want to get them sick."

"I think you're right. There are plenty of little rides."

"Think we can escort as many as eight or ten kids at one time?" I asked his opinion. That's what all the how-to books advise for climbing the career ladder.

"I'm sure of it. They are better behaved than most kids who have home and parents."

"Hey, look the coffee wagon appears to be open. You ready for a cup?"

"*Magnífico!*"

I ordered two cups from the fat lady with a beautiful smile and paid her twenty pesos I found rattling around in my pocket. We had a good view of the Cerveza Tecate hot air balloon but I kept my mouth shut. I wanted him to react to it first.

Two sips into his coffee he obliged. "I think the hot air balloon ride is out for our *muchachos*."

I laughed. "I think you're right, Juanito. First of all, we couldn't get that many kids into the basket."

He looked wistfully at the green, white, and red balloon. "It's got to be a thrill, though."

"Have you ever been up in one?" I asked, knowing the answer.

"No, have you?"

"Would you like to go up?"

"Yes! Could we?" He was a little kid again.

"Sure. Finish your coffee and I'll take you up myself."

"You mean it, really? You mean you can actually fly one of those things?" He was eight years old.

"Many times. It requires a high degree of skill, of course, but it's a simple principle." I tried to sound modest.

We threw our empty coffee cups in a trash barrel. "Wait for me, I'll be right back. The coffee, you know."

I found a portable toilet marked HOMBRES, went inside and took out my cell phone. The Hummer answered on the first ring.

"I've got your man."

"Jesus, you really are slick!"

"He doesn't have the proceeds on him but you hired me to bring back the man."

"That's right, Jesus. You just get me the man, believe me, I'll get the bread. I've got a lot of experience with this sorta thing." It was stifling in the toilet. "I'm a man of my word, Jesus. You done your job, I got your twenty right here."

"Okay, drive east on Highway 94. Get as close to the border as you can and wait. We should be there by ten or so. What are you driving?"

"A yellow Hummer."

I nearly dropped my Nokia in the toilet.

"How will I find you?"

"Look up in the sky."

"Whaddja say?"

"We're coming in on a hot air balloon."

"Holy Jesus!"

I found Juan Lopez waiting for me where I left him. Together we walked over to meet Capitan Waffleface, my flying instructor of the previous day. I was able to study Juan's walk for the first time. As his feet went out he swung his arms out from side to side. He was skating! "Good morning, Capitan Vargas."

"*Buenos dias*, Meester Rosie. We going up this morning?"

"My friend here has never been up."

"You're in for a thrill of a lifetime," the Capitan said to my guest. "Most people never get enough. It's a beautiful sensation. But the rope will keep you from going around the world in eighty days." The captain laughed at his own cleverness and indicated a huge hawser coiled like a giant python under the balloon that held it fast. Waffleface opened the gate and we stepped into the wicker basket. My guest was almost giddy. The burner was set on low, just enough heat to keep the balloon filled but nothing more.

"Okay Juanito, ready?"

"Yes!"

"Here we go, then." The burner roared impressively as I opened the valve and the balloon began to climb. "You see," I said to my passenger, "it's simply a case of keeping the air inside the balloon at a higher temperature than the ambient temperature. The greater the difference in the two temperatures the higher you go. But of course, we can only go up the length of the rope. About a hundred feet." I thought I sounded pretty knowledgeable but I was only repeating everything El Capitan had told me yesterday when he gave me balloon lessons. Treenie had to pay him another hundred U.S. dollars of my money but it would have been a bargain at any price. Of course, Waffleface didn't know Part II of the scheme.

Slowly the craft ascended. Juanito's eyeballs nearly dropped out of his head, his hands gripping the rail. He was speechless. So was I but for a different reason. I didn't have to touch the burner. We continued to float gently upward. Juanito was mesmerized. In a few minutes we felt a bump and a gentle lurch. Juanito looked startled.

"That's as far as we can go. We've reached the end of the rope. So get your fill. It's a great view, right?"

Juanito relaxed visibly. He removed his death grip from the edge of the basket and took in a view as awesome as the Grand Canyon. I could see he was thrilled but totally at ease. We could see all of Tecate: the plaza, the surrounding buildings, I recognized the church and the brewery. It looked like a toy town. I could see the actual border fence that separates the two countries. I was hoping my passenger was too enthralled with the experience to give the sight any significance. Farther out on the American side I could easily make out U.S. Highway 94, a black snake bordering small farms, green fields that from here looked smooth as gabardine. Beyond that, rugged mountains studded with granite boulders and draped with wispy shreds of morning clouds. I was not relaxed, however. I tried to look it but I was tense, waiting, watching, feeling really, for the sign that Treenie had managed to complete his assignment on the ground.

I felt it.

An almost imperceptible tug and the balloon began to rise. We'd lost our tether. I turned up the heat. The burner began to roar. We were climbing!

It took Juan Lopez several seconds to react to the increased roar of the burner. He watched me adjusting the valve, things on the ground were getting farther away. And farther!

"What's happening?" It wasn't a question. It was a moment of raw terror.

I didn't answer.

"We're climbing! We're going higher. Have we lost our tether?" There was a quaver in his voice.

I didn't want him to panic. "It's okay, Juanito, we're perfectly safe. See that green belt on the other side of that little stream? We're coming down there."

Then it hit him.

He drew the sign of the cross in the air and spoke in a soft, low voice. It was the voice of someone accepting his inevitable execution. "So that's why you're here. Of course. It's been so many years that I put it out of my mind. You came here to take me to them, didn't you?"

"Him. They killed a couple of people in the bank. One's on death row, the other one is out. He's the one that wants you."

"Dear God! They killed people. I never knew that. I came straight here to Tecate to disappear. They'll kill me too."

"Not if you give them back the money." I kept my hand on the gas valve. "If you haven't spent it by now. You're sitting on nearly sixty thousand dollars."

"I've never touched their filthy money! It's theirs any time they want it. It's still sitting in the car. I never even counted it. They hired me for two thousand dollars. I took out a thousand to buy my camper and get by until I found a job."

"They think you ran off with their money."

"That's not the way it happened. I waited at the curb outside the bank like I was supposed to. The big man threw the bag in the car and kept on walking. Just as I started the car the whole place was surrounded by police, in cars, on motorcycles, on foot. They were getting everybody out of the way so they could cordon off the area. They waved me through to get me out of their way."

I'd never heard this part. I listened.

"I couldn't get to where I was supposed to go. The police had that street roped off too and they pushed all the traffic into another street. I panicked. I drove and drove without knowing where I was going or what I was going to do. I just had to get as far away as I could. I don't know how long or how far I went. The next thing I remember seeing was the sign on the highway that said, International Border 2 Miles. I'd never been in Mexico before in my life. I drove through the gates. Nobody bothered with me, they just waved me through. As soon as I was in Mexico I thought of the money in the car. If they'd found it I'd still be in jail. And then I realized I could never get back across to the United States."

"I want you to know I have no personal hard feelings toward you at all. I was hired to do a job and I'm doing it, that's all."

"Then all your acts of friendship, your generosity, were all false, a betrayal for money."

I felt like dirt.

"Your gifts to the children were not gifts at all. They were bribes to win their trust and friendship. You did an excellent job of deceiving all of us, Señor Rosie. Ramon and Simona never stopped praising you last night after you left." He stopped for breath. I thought he was going to cry. "You even fooled Father Ruben. I went to Mass last night and he said God had a reason for sending you to us." Juan Lopez began to cry like a child with a broken heart.

Now I felt like shit.

He wiped his eyes on his sleeve and caught his breath. "Here I am condemning you and I'm just as guilty as you are. In one way or another I guess we're all for sale if the price is right."

I couldn't find words.

"Please, don't take me to them." His voice trembled. "They'll kill me. Just tell them to come and get it. Their filthy money has blood on it. I don't want any of it. It's theirs—all of it."

That's when I realized why the Hummer couldn't go after it himself. He wasn't out on parole. In all probability he was an escaped con. He'd be on the hot sheet. They'd nail his ass as soon as he returned across the border.

"Who else knows about this?"

"No one."

"Father Ruben?"

"No one."

He obviously hadn't been to confession. He'd been carrying his own baggage. A steady breeze was taking us in the direction of the green field. I turned down the burner and we began to come down. I didn't want to drop too fast but I didn't want to slam into the mountains either so I kept adjusting the heat. Juan Lopez watched the ground coming closer. Then at me. He looked sick.

I couldn't worry about the kid now, I had to concentrate on what I was doing.

I had no skill at steering this thing. All I knew was how to make it go up and down.

For the first time I felt genuine panic. What if I wrapped this thing up on electric wires? We'd both get fried.

We came down so slowly and yet it seemed we were coming down so fast. It's a difficult illusion to describe. I figured we were only a couple of minutes from the ground.

I could see the cars traveling on Highway 94. A big yellow vehicle was parked at the side of the road. The Hummer.

Damn it all! We were coming down too fast! I cracked the valve and we started up again. That's not what I wanted. I reduced the heat slightly. The balloon hovered for a few seconds then began to come down slower. I kept adjusting the heat to keep the downward speed constant. We were nearly on the ground, maybe twenty, thirty feet to touchdown.

I knew the Border Patrol would be all over us but I wasn't worried about that. We were both American-born U.S. citizens. They had no reason to bother us. They would check the balloon for drugs, of course, but we were clean. I would simply explain that our tether broke and we had to put it down here.

Five feet to touchdown! In a few minutes I'd be on my way home with twenty thousand dollars in my jeans. Another successful case for the Great Rosencranz!

We hit the ground!

I killed the burner and started to open the gate. Juan Lopez just stood there, silent, defeated, accepting the end.

"Juanito, do you trust me?"

"No."

"I don't blame you."

Juanito almost sobbed. "Please do me a favor?" He didn't wait for my reply. "If I don't get back please don't give the money to the killers. Give it all to Ramon and Simona."

I let us out of the basket. "I want you to get out and help me gather up the balloon. Don't start running. And don't open your mouth." He didn't respond. "Do you understand me?"

"But they'll—"

"Under no circumstances do you open your mouth!"

We both ran out and started gathering up the balloon before it dragged off. It wasn't quite dead yet and it looked like an enormous monster spread out on the ground. A border patrol Jeep was already coming at us across the meadow leaving a wake of dirt and gravel. They were in a hurry. Two men got out.

"It's one for the books, Mike, I thought I'd seen everything!"

Just as the two officers reached us a second car came tearing up and two more armed agents came out. One was a woman.

"Now I've seen it all," I heard the woman say.

The four officers reached us from two angles. Juanito and I dropped what we were doing and stood there waiting.

One of the Border Patrol agents stepped closer. "You tango passaporty?" he said to us in bad Spanish, worse than mine. Even I recognized the wrong conjugation of the transitive verb.

If Juan Lopez opened his mouth now we were both done. We stared blankly at the border agents. Then at each other. Then at our feet. I thought we both did a good job of looking dumb. And we looked scared too. But that wasn't an act.

"Awright, Mary, load 'em up. Give 'em a free ride back to Me-hee-co."

By the time Jesus finished telling me his story it wasn't just the two of us standing around the hay wagon/bar. We were surrounded by twenty or thirty guests who came for refreshment and stayed for the tale. Father Ruben had joined us. He was holding a beer. Jesus was a good story teller and he had the voice for it, smooth, sonorous, full of color.

"So you got deported," someone said. "How did it all end?"

"Well, we got processed first, then driven back to the border. We walked back into Mexico without incident. Capitan Waffleface and a few men from the brewery brought back the balloon."

"Did they throw you in jail?"

"They must have been ready to prosecute. Hijacking a hot air balloon!"

Jesus raised his glass in tribute to the Padre. "Like a career diplomat, Father Ruben mediated the peace conference. He invited all parties to his vineyard and we all walked away friends."

"He is well satisfied who is well wined," Father Ruben said. It had the ring of a proverb.

"I'm sorry but the whole thing is just too fantastic," one of the guests said and approached Father Ruben. "Padre, did all this really happen?"

I looked over at Father Ruben. He seemed astounded by the question.

"Well, I'm a native Tecatense," the Padre answered. "And I see nothing extraordinary in the story. But yes, it's all true, the beautiful and the tragic. Are you going to leave that sausage?"

"What about the fifty-eight thousand dollars?" another voice inquired.

Jesus answered. "Next time you travel south on Highway 3 stop in at the orphanage. It is now called Orfanatorio Juan Lopez. The Fruehauf trailers are gone. They've been replaced with two modern buildings. There's a swimming pool for the kids, new playground equipment, and an indoor gym. And the entrance is no longer a cow pasture. You now enter through a massive stone arch with lacy wrought iron gates."

"Ramon and Simona still there?"

"Oh yes! They're there, still depending on donations. And God."

"And Juan Lopez?"

All the color went out of our storyteller's voice. "A drunk driver ended his life on that sharp curve at kilometer 10."

"I thought I'd find you here!"

It was Jackie, a vivacious young woman in a pretty turquoise dancing dress. "No wonder no one's dancing, you have all the men over here! The mariachis are playing to the squirrels!"

Jesus gave me stewardship of his Jimador and lemon and led Jackie away toward that festive mariachi music that can fill the eyes and wring the heart.

One Cappuccino and a Kiss to Go

"*J*ust answer the question! Do you love him or don't you?"

"I don't think so."

"You don't *think* so! What kind of answer is that?"

Carolina stood under the shower where a conversation was in progress between her heart and her head.

"I'm—I'm not sure, okay? I like him, yes, we have a good time together." Carolina bent down and began to lather her legs. "He's lots of fun to go out with."

"If you're not going to be honest," her mind snapped, "there's no point to this conversation."

"All right, all right. Mayolo is always so serious and sometimes he's rather intense. He's not *fun*. Satisfied?"

"You still haven't answered the question."

"Okay, okay, I'm not in love with him."

Carolina's heart and her mind had this same conversation at least twice a week. The shower was where she did most of her heavy thinking. The hot water, the enclosure, the assurance of privacy, were all conducive to self-communion.

But the mind nagged on. "If you don't love Mayolo, why do you go out with him, why do you let him kiss you and touch you?"

Carolina faced the spray and lathered her underarms. "Because I'm nineteen and no one else seems interested. And it's better than staying home and listening to The Colonel telling me how to live my life. She gave it to me, yes, but it's mine now."

"What about Eduardo and Gabi at work? They're kind of cute."

"They're nice *muchachos* but they've never asked me out."

"Then what about Adrian? He's nice."

"He's beautiful. No—Mayolo is beautiful, Adrian is *gallant*! When he smiles at me it feels like a warm *abrazo* and my knees turn to *gelatina*. Even his eyes give off little sparks that ignite feelings I didn't even know I possessed. I see him every day in his father's coffee bar. He takes my order, makes my cappuccino, he's very pleasant and friendly, but no more than he would be to any customer." The stinging spray was cutting into her breasts like tiny needles. She turned her back to the water. "And you have to go out *once* in a while. You have to kiss *someone*. And yes, I do like Mayolo's hands on me. It feels nice."

"Are you going to give him what he wants?"

"No!" Carolina could hear The Gorilla moaning in the closet. The Gorilla was the household's appellation for the cantankerous hot water heater that gurgled and belched and groaned and retched like Godzilla with stomach cramps. She turned off the shower. "It's just dinner at La Fonda and maybe a movie."

"And some kisses."

"And some kisses," she admitted. "I just wish it was somebody else."

"And some feelies?" the mind taunted.

"That's enough!"

"You must have *chorizo* for brains. As long as you're seen together everyone is going to think you're *novios* and no one is going to ask you out."

"We're not *novios*!"

"Maybe you don't think so, but Mayolo thinks so."

"Okay, okay, you're right. I have to break with him if I expect someone else to ask me out. I wish I could talk to Olga about it, but that'll have to wait till Monday."

"Olga will tell you the same thing."

"Okay, I'll tell him tonight."

"Tell him what?"

"I'll define the relationship. Friends and no more."

"That means no more kisses."

"I know that."

"No more feel—"

"Shut up!"

Carolina stepped out of the enclosure. The whole room was hot and steamy like a tropical night in Cancun. The damn toilet was still running! She jiggled the handle, took a towel from the bar, and wiped the moisture from the mirror before drying herself. First her back from nape to *nalgas*, then her arms. With one foot up on the toilet she ran the towel down each leg from its point of origin to the toes then vigorously toweled off chest and stomach. She looked at the fuzzy image in the wet mirror. There's my whole problem, she told herself. My nose is too big, my breasts are too small and, turning her back to the mirror, twisted her head around. And my *nalgas* are too broad!

Her other self came back. "You've been told you have beautiful dark eyes."

"*Por favór!*"

Carolina's physiognomical self-assessment was not only overly severe, it was an affront to truth. She was a perfect size seven. Nothing about her was too big or too small. The features of her classical face were in complete harmony with each other. And you could put her smile to music. She did have a dark round mole three inches below and to the left of her belly button but it was too sexy to be considered a blemish. And only her mother ever saw it.

In the small living room Carolina's mother, aka The Colonel, sat deep in her big overstuffed armchair covered with a green chenille spread the color of cooked spinach. She was a rather large and lumpy woman of fifty-five. The jasmine fragrance emanated from a scented candle placed before a color print of the Blessed Virgin in memory of her husband who succeeded in drinking himself to death before he was fifty. Doña Raquel was presently employed stuffing her face with marzipan as she watched the *telenovela*.

"*No me dejes, mi amor. Me haces pedasos mi corazón!*" It was a woman's voice, a voice filled with desperation.

"*Mataste mi cariño, mujer, ya no siento por ti lo que sentía,*" a strong masculine voice with undertones of previous injuries.

A gush of stage tears. "*Voy—voy—voy a tener tu hijo!*" Followed by another flood of heart-rending sobs.

An incredulous "*Qué!*"

"*Tu hijo!*" This confession was immediately followed by a dramatic D major ninth with a flatted fifth which ended the segment for a quarter-hour break of wall to wall commercials.

Carolina walked into the room smelling like a bouquet of freshly-gathered lilacs. She wore black pants and a black knitted top with pink and blue rhinestones scattered across the front. For once, her raven hair yielded to the cajoling and wheedling of comb and brush, grazing her shoulders in thick gentle waves and making her tiny onyx earrings redundant. She felt almost pretty.

"Don't you look nice, *mi amor*," her mother sang.

"*Gracias!*" Carolina answered in a little six-year-old voice and affected a curtsy.

"I could hear The Gorilla all the way in here. I'm afraid that boiler is about to die."

"Then you'd better light a candle, Mamá. If the boiler quits it means a new one and we don't have the money."

Doña Raquel came to her point. "Don't stay out too late. You know I can't get to sleep until you're safely home in bed. You're going out with Mayolo, *sí*?"

Here we go again, Carolina thought. "*Sí* Mamá, it's Mayolo."

"I guess it's all right for dinner, but I don't like your choice of *novios*. He's not right for you."

"Mamá, do you realize you've said that about *every muchacho* I have brought home since I was fifteen?"

"Mayolo is much too old for you."

"He's only twenty-six this year."

"A man of twenty-six has too much experience for a young girl of nineteen. I just don't want to see you make a mistake, some mistake that could ruin your life." She tossed her head toward the house next door. Carolina understood.

"You mean," Carolina held her hands out six inches away from her belly and waddled a few steps. "I don't think they would allow anyone to do that in the restaurant."

"*Ay, muchacha!* Go now, don't stay out too late."

Carolina bent down, kissed her mother's cheek and went out the door. Doña Raquel listened to the whiny sound of the vintage Nissan as Carolina pulled away. With some effort she pushed out of her overstuffed chair, abandoning the *telenovela* and the hysterical woman who was about to have someone's baby. Today's outfit was an orange pantsuit and this gave her the appearance of a large baked yam endowed with arms and legs. She was lumbering her way over to visit Mariquita, her next door neighbor. It was time to trade fresh gossip, far more salacious than the *telenovela*. She found Mariquita watering her container plants behind the low wall that separated their houses.

"*Hola*, Mariquita your plants look lovely."

"It's my only chance to water them. The little one is asleep and Didi is still at work. Have you heard any more about the Chavez boy? With Carolina working at the courthouse you probably get all the latest news."

"Of course! In her position Caro is always well informed." Carolina was only a file clerk but it provided Doña Raquel with a measure of prestige. "She saw the boy enter the courthouse with his father two days ago."

"You know what that means. Don Arturo will pay his way out and the boy will go out and do it again. Stealing beer when they have enough money to buy the brewery!" Mariquita began to pour water into the hanging basket with the fuchsia. "I saw Caro leave a little while ago. She looked so grown up. A proper señorita."

"She makes me very nervous. Caro is too young for a serious *novio*."

"The heart rules, Raquel. And nineteen isn't too young. Sooner or later she's going to fall in love, get married, and leave home."

"Bite your tongue! I discourage her young men as soon as I meet them. That usually puts an end to it until a new one comes along. All men are a threat. I make sure they don't last too long. It's the only way."

"But you can't rein them in too close, Raquelita, look what happened to my Didi. She was just seventeen when she came home pregnant."

"But look how happy you are now. You have a darling baby in the house and a loyal daughter who needs you and must depend on you. You'll always have her at home. You won't end up old and abandoned by your children." Raquel didn't say 'like me' but it was understood. "I'll need Caro here when I'm old."

"I hope God is listening. If it weren't for Didi I would be all alone in this world."

"All I have left of Rafa is that white cross on Highway 3."

"Believe me, I know. Caro is all I have left. My two sons don't even remember they have a mother." Her oldest son moved to Tijuana before The Colonel could do further damage to his marriage. Her second son moved to Chihuahua so he didn't have to come any closer than the telephone. "But once a mother, always a mother. Our children grow up and marry but they will always need us to advise and guide."

"But they never appreciate our help."

"Ma, ma, mama—a"

"He's awake!" Mariquita threw the hose down, turned off the faucet, and hurried toward the house. "I'm coming, *mi amor, sí, mi rey*, I'm coming!"

Mayolo was next in line at the *cajero automatico* on the wall of the Serfin bank. When the old man walked out, they exchanged a nod of recognition and Mayolo dipped his card into the slot. In less than two seconds the heavy bullet-proof glass door slid open with a hiss and he walked into a small room. The only thing in it was a small counter for the customer's convenience and an ATM. He kept a bank account on the Other Side but he didn't like using American ATMs. They provided no privacy, they were wide open, and they didn't offer the security of an Open Sesame entry system. An easy mark for a thief. He got his cash, touched a button, the door obeyed his command and he walked out into the warm evening.

His handsome face could have been silk-screened on a sheet of brown fabric any time in the past five years. Mayolo's features never changed. He looked the same today as he did five years ago and would in all probability look the same five years from today. Mayolo would remain handsome in perpetuity. Under perfectly formed eyebrows that might have been stenciled, he looked at life through hard ebony eyes. They were as bright and alert as those of a fox. He didn't look at people so much as he looked *into* them. A thin black mustache formed an arch over his mouth, the ends connected to an equally black chin beard, meticulously trimmed. The effect was that of a padlock placed over dark thick lips. His maintenance manager was Lucila at Lucila's Salon Unisex. He had a standing appointment with her every Wednesday at three for the personal grooming that kept him looking the same day after day, year after year.

He started out across the central plaza. He was a lean young man, thin as a shadow at sundown. While he wasn't particularly tall, his legs were long, his movements fluid and precise like that of a cat walking on a rail.

"*Buenas tardes*, Mayolo."

Mayolo looked up to see one of his lady clients. "*Buenas tardes*, Paulina. How nice to see you—and how nice you look!"

Paulina squirmed with joy and a smile lit up her entire face. She was barely starting her forty-second year of life and already feared the ravages of aging. She felt it was time to bribe nature. "I need a new jar of anti-aging cream."

"I'll deliver it first thing Monday."

Mayolo was a distributor for VITAVIDA, purveyor of miracles: food supplements that eliminated all known diseases and some not yet identified, cosmetics that could reverse the aging process, weight loss pills with the warning to discontinue use when you were wearing Barbie clothing. The company was headquartered in Atlanta. They were experiencing some problems with the FDA and the FTC who felt their claims exceeded the legal definition of truth and were already making inquiries. Before the ink was dry on the NAFTA documents VITAVIDA moved their operation to Mexico where miracles are accepted as a birthright guaranteed by the Constitution of 1917.

"I'm so glad to see it's working for you, Paulina, but it takes time, remember."

"Expensive but worth it. It's marvelous! I use it every night and I don't see a single dark spot."

Mayolo figured he had several years before she would demand her money back. "Keep it up, Paulina. Five years from now you'll look fifteen!"

Paulina giggled and resumed dancing her way across the plaza. Mayolo wanted to call on a few other clients before his date with Carolina. There was a young woman desperate to lose fifty kilos over the weekend, an older woman who regularly ordered Gel de Juventud to reclaim her youth, and a forty-year-old insurance salesman on a hair restoration program.

Mariachis filled La Fonda with *alegría*. They were playing *Tu Solo Tu* a few tables away from where Carolina sat with Mayolo. It was the usual Saturday night crowd, single men, single women, couples in love, the married, the divorced, a few tables of tourists from the Other Side. Carolina and Mayolo knew everybody in the restaurant but for a table of tourists and a long table where eight American women were getting hammered on margaritas. Everyone knew they were AWOL from Rancho La Puerta, the exclusive health spa where they'd just spent a week doing daily aerobics followed by a death march to the summit of Mount Cuchuma, and fed an all-natural diet of organically-grown twigs and sticks.

Carolina was glad the music was too loud for conversation. She was resolved. In the twenty minutes it took to coax her Nissan from home to La Fonda she'd made up her mind to cinch up her *calzones* and tell Mayolo that it was time to part, to go their separate ways. She became proleptic at once. I'll tell him he needs to find someone to give him what I can't. If he says it's all his fault, I'll tell him there is no one to blame. If he says, "what have I done?" I'll say, "you haven't done anything." She was well rehearsed by the time she got to La Fonda. As soon as the mariachis move to another table, she decided, I'll begin with something like, *we have to talk.*

"To us!" Mayolo toasted his date across the table as soon as the margaritas arrived.

Carolina looked over at the perfect digital image of the man she'd been kissing for six months. He was dressed in stonewashed blue jeans and a rather lavish embroidered crimson shirt under an expensive camel hair jacket. "*Salud,*" she answered. But the usual color in her voice that was so much a part of her charm wasn't there. The moment the last chord of the love song drifted away to join the smoke in the ceiling, Carolina seized opportunity.

"Mayolo, we have things to talk about."

"Yes Caro, my love. Let's talk about *us*!"

"There are things I have to tell you."

"I know, *mi amor*, me too. Have I told you lately that I love you? That my heart and my soul are yours to keep? That my life would turn to ashes if I didn't have you to love?"

Dear God! she exclaimed in thought. I have to say what I have to say *first*, before he falls over the edge. "What I mean is—" But she was too late. On Mayolo's almost imperceptible cue, the mariachis surrounded their table and her words were lost in the opening chords of *Toda Una Vida*.

Their food arrived just as the mariachis finished with a flourish of the trumpet. Damn! She would have to find another opportunity. To tell someone his one-way love affair was over while he was eating his dinner seemed unnecessarily cruel. It would have to wait.

Carolina smiled graciously as he paid the mariachis and they moved to a back table. "How is your lobster?" she said lamely.

"*Rico*! Would you like a taste?" Mayolo already had his fork in her direction.

"*No, no gracias*. I'm enjoying my Halibut Veracruzano very much."

"You know, Caro, I have something important to tell you too. Something very exciting. You can probably guess what it is, but you'll have to wait until after dinner and we're in the plaza."

Carolina felt jumping beans doing handsprings in her stomach. She could guess what he had to say. And she was terrified she would be right. Maybe they could forego the plaza tonight. Should I say something now, she thought, *before* he says what I know he's going to say and we're both embarassed? The thought was blown away by the appearance of Sujey, the flower girl, a darling little girl of ten or so who worked the tables at La Fonda every weekend.

Mayolo nodded to her, indicating she was to hand his date a bouquet of red roses. The little flower girl placed the fragrant arrangement in Carolina's hand.

"You look beautiful, *mi amor*."

"*Ay*, Mayolo! Gracias." Carolina did her best to sound gracious. She pressed them to her bosom and made a show of inhaling the fragrance. "They're beautiful, just beautiful."

"I hope you will take them to bed with you tonight and think of me. They'll fill your bedroom with their perfume and you'll dream of me all night."

The *sopa* was getting too thick for Carolina.

Following coffee and flan they stepped out of the cacophony of La Fonda and into the arms of a sensuous evening perfumed with jasmine and orange blossoms, an evening friendly to strollers. The crush of music, talking, the clatter of dishes, were all part of the festivities while you were buried alive under the landslide of sound. But now it felt good to listen to silence. They strolled once around the plaza under massive ash trees. Neither spoke. The sky was growing dark now. There was only a sliver of pale yellow moon. Heaven was just lighting her lamps and they twinkled at them through the tangle of branches above. A few couples strolled arm in arm. Two young lovers were hopelessly tangled in the dark corner of the kiosk. By unspoken mutual consent Carolina and Mayolo settled into a bench at the edge of the rose garden. They could just hear the hiss of the fountain.

Now was her moment! *Now!* Carolina spoke softly, almost whispered. "Mayolo, There are things I have to tell—" He clamped his mouth over hers. His arms came around, one hand found her breast and began to fondle. Quickly she turned away to remove the hand and break the kiss. "Mayolo, we have to talk."

"Of course, *mi amor*, let's talk of love and faith, and you and me."

Now that she'd begun Carolina was more determined than before. "What I'm trying to say is I think maybe we're going too fast. Maybe we'd better slow down." Too lame, she thought, but it was a start.

"But *mi amor*, what's come over you? We've always kissed like this."

"It's just that I don't feel right doing this."

"But don't you love me? Have I done something wrong?"

"You haven't done anything wrong, Mayolo."

"Well?"

"It's just that I can't give you what you want."

"It's all my fault."

"It's nobody's fault. Don't look for blame. It's no one's fault that I'm not what you want me to be."

"And after all this time together, I'm not what you want?"

"It isn't *you*. You must understand that. Don't you see, Mayolo? We're strangers."

"Strangers! How can you say that? We've been together for six months."

"Yes, we've kissed, we've touched but—"

"But what?"

"Our hearts are strangers."

"*Buenas noches*, Mayolo. *Buenas noches*, Carolina."

Both looked up to see Babalu, the local witch, shuffling across the plaza in her long black rags that dusted the pavement as she walked. She held the two large claws that served for hands as though in prayer and this gave her the look of a four-foot-tall praying mantis. Her face was a huge walnut, dark and deeply creased, the whites of her faded brown eyes were yellow. The troubled couple on the bench was so involved neither noticed the old hag until she spoke. Carolina mumbled something by reflex and Mayolo answered for both of them. "*Buenas noches*, Babalu."

Babalu stopped before them. She thrust her hideous face into theirs close enough to smother them with the smell of garlic, musty body odors, and other mysterious smells. She offered them a crooked smile and pointed a gnarled finger toward the sky. "A sickle moon bodes ill tonight."

Carolina could feel her flesh prickling as the witch crept away and got lost in the night. "What was she babbling about?"

"Pay no attention to her. The old witch is crazy."

"That awful woman has been here in Tecate as far back as I can remember. She always makes me so nervous. I've heard all sorts of terrible things about her. Do you actually know her? Do you sell the old hag your products?"

Mayolo laughed. "No, I rather think she makes her own secret potions under the full moon. I've seen her on market day telling fortunes, selling her potions and magic amulets to the superstitious. I've heard she even casts spells and curses for a price."

"I've heard the same thing."

"They're always supposed to come to pass on a full moon."

Carolina felt a chill and shuddered. "But how did she know your name?"

"I think she probably knows everybody in town. She knew your name too." The bells of the Church of Our Lady began their dissonant clanging. Carolina drew the cross in the air in front of her. Mayolo recovered from the incident that broke their dialogue of a moment ago. He was determined to say what he had to say now, while Carolina was momentarily in a state of awe. When the last gong melted away he turned to face her and took both her hands into his own. "*Mi amor*, I should have said this sooner. I've loved you since the day I first met you. I love you now. I will love you forever. And I'm asking you to marry me."

Ay Dios! Carolina pulled her hands away from his. This can't go on, she thought. I've got to do it! *I've got to do it!* "Mayolo, I can't marry you."

"You what! Carolina, look at me. You don't love me?"

"Not the way you want me to love you."

"What's wrong with me? Tell me what's wrong with me and I'll fix it."

"There's nothing *wrong* with you, Mayolo, you're a wonderful man. And you deserve a girl who can give you every-thing—everything I can't."

There came an eternity of profound silence. Mayolo choked back a sob. His voice came thick. "Is there, is there...somebody else?"

"No."

"Thank God!"

Ding-a-ling-ling! A lone ice cream cart rattled by. They ignored it.

Mayolo's face twisted with pain, as if she'd just plunged a dagger into his heart. She felt mean, heartless. Carolina allowed him to throw one arm around her, draw her close and cuddle her breast like a desperate child. Gently as a mother, Carolina spoke softly. "Listen to me." Out of custom she almost added *mi amor.* "There *is* nobody else. Not now, at least."

"I couldn't bear it if someone else held you in his arms. I would rather die than see you kissing another man, another man's hands where mine are now." It was Mayolo who was wiping away his tears now.

"You have to understand! There *is* no one else. But maybe some day you and I will find the other half of our heart."

Mayolo pulled back. "Period, new paragraph. You're saying this is the end, aren't you?"

"Something has to end in order for something new to begin. Don't you see, Mayolo? This is the *beginning*—for both of us!"

That night in bed Carolina couldn't sleep. She could smell the sweet perfume of the roses she'd laid on a chair when she came into her room and got undressed. She felt like she'd just killed her dog.

"One medium cappuccino and a large mocha, *por favor.*"

It was nine-thirty Monday morning. Olga had sent Carolina out to the Continental for coffee. Like almost everything else worthwhile in Tecate the coffee bar stands just across the plaza. It's one long and narrow room with a half dozen small "ice cream tables" and bentwood chairs once seen in American soda fountains. The dark walls are lined with original oils by local painters. The smell of coffee, cinnamon, nutmeg, and chocolate was somehow comforting to Carolina.

"You look beautiful this morning, Carolina! You give a gray Monday the joy of a Cinco de Mayo fiesta," Don Pancho, *propietario* of Café Continental sang out in his high tenor. His greeting was an aria. "But then every day becomes a holiday when you walk in that door!" Don Pancho always showered her with verbal confetti every day she came in, and he punctuated everything he said with an exclamation point.

"*Ay,* Don Pancho!" Carolina smiled her thanks.

Don Pancho was tall by Tecate standards. His head was a hopeless tangle of black curls and cowlicks, his happy face the color of kiln-dried adobe. There was always mischief in his fiery eyes. His face split into a grin exposing a full octave of ivories. "I'll get my lazy, good-for-nothing son on it immediately." Adrian, his good-for-nothing son, was pulling coffee, steaming milk as fast as his two hands could move. "Medium cappuccino and a large mocha to go!" he called out. "And Carolina wants them before the day after tomorrow!" Don Pancho never missed an opportunity to torture his son but it was all in good fun and he often got as good as he gave.

"I'm not in a hurry, Adrian, really."

"Oh, I pay no attention to my father, Caro. Tomorrow I start a new job at the municipality."

"*El municipio!* What can they pay you?" Don Pancho growled. "The city's broke! Have you seen the condition of our streets?"

"At least they won't pay me in coffee beans." Adrian put two coffees on the counter for another customer and kept working at nearly the speed of light.

"And you're not qualified to do anything."

Adrian's voice turned dark and dangerous. "Next time you see me, Papá, it will be as the city inspector. And you better have all those *cucarachas* out of the pantry." He got a few chuckles from the regulars.

"Aren't you worried, Don Pancho?" someone called out.

"Worried? My son is susceptible to *mordidas!*" Everyone in the coffee bar burst out laughing.

Adrian put lids on the cups and handed Carolina her order on a small tray borrowed but never returned from Tecate Brewery. "I know it isn't far to the courthouse but I would feel bad if you were to spill coffee on your pretty dress that blooms with summer flowers." She was wearing a navy skirt bordered with giant stylized zinnias and daisies. Adrian was a younger version of his father, same face, same whorls of disobedient black hair. Even the color of his voice was indistinguishable from that of his sire. "I could never forgive myself!"

"*Gracias*, Adrian, I'll manage just fine."

"Would you allow me to carry it for you? I would consider it an honor!" Adrian also had his father's flair for extravagant *pirópos*.

"Don't trust the *cabrón*," Don Pancho warned her with a grin. Carolina laughed at the lavish gallantry. "You can't trust him, Caro. He was once arrested for practicing medicine without a license."

"What!"

"His mother found his secret clinic behind the garage!" Don Pancho accused.

"Papá! I was only four."

"You were fourteen and don't deny it!"

The idea of Adrian "playing doctor" amused Carolina. She stifled a giggle.

"You can bring the tray back tomorrow, Caro, and bring sunshine and light into this miserable place."

"My son is hopelessly in love with you, Carolina."

"Papá!"

Carolina looked over at Adrian and realized they were both blushing. Other customers could not help but titter. Carolina recognized the voice of Don Pancho's wife from somewhere in the back. "Francisco, behave yourself. I'll come out there and pull your ears!"

"I hope you do, Mamá."

Still laughing to herself, Carolina made it back to the office without spilling and handed the large mocha to Olga.

"I might have to send you out again for a recharge. It's going to be one of those days." Olga took a sip of her mocha then reached in a desk drawer and brought out a small whisk broom. She began at once to sweep the top of her clean desk as though sweeping invisible bread crumbs left from breakfast onto the floor.

Carolina looked at her mentor. She was a slender woman, her Acapulco-bronze skin a gift of nature, the fleecy maple-tinted hair acquired by art at Lucila's Salon Unisex. "What on earth are you doing?"

"I'm sweeping away all the bad karma from yesterday. I want the day to start over after coffee." Olga was Judge Ramos's secretary. She got the job just as a bad relationship was breaking up that left her abandoned and jobless with two young children. At fourteen she was easily seduced by some *gallo* who promised love, home, and family. Fate wrote Olga a tragic book of betrayal, but she found the courage to plagiarize it and brought the story to a happy ending. Today, at twenty-nine, Olga had the love of a faithful husband, three beautiful children, and a home of her own. Her young face gave no evidence of the bitter adversities of life. She kept her scars hidden. Only her dark Mediterranean eyes revealed a calm wisdom. They had met while Carolina was working for the local stationer, Olga recognized ability and got her the job as a file clerk. They quickly became intimate friends. They could talk to each other about anything at all. Carolina listened and learned. By the time she was fifteen Carolina realized all mothers raise their daughters to meet their own needs. When it came to laying open your heart and your soul, Olga was better than her own mother.

Olga took another grateful sip. "Well, did you do it?" Her voice was low and sonorous for such a young woman, like the D-string on a violin.

"Yes, I told him last night."

"What did he say?"

"That life would be dark and hopeless without me."

"That's a standard line from emotionally insolvent men. They prey on women of generous heart, who would do anything to avoid hurting someone's feelings. Then they hook themselves up to her like an IV. Remember, I had one of those. I know the whole script."

"I know I did the right thing. I could never marry him."

"Then he wept unashamedly."

"How did you know?"

"It's on page ten of the script."

"It's just that I feel so bad, Olga, I just don't like to hurt anyone."

"And men know that. But you can't be somebody's life-support system."

Judge Ramos came out of his office and set a course for Olga's desk. Carolina got up and headed for the file room. "I'll bring you the Chavez file."

"You'll feel better tomorrow, *mi amor*," Olga called after her.

Apart from her job Carolina didn't go out for the next two weeks. She was terrified she would run into Mayolo at the coffee bar. He might say something and embarrass her in front of everyone. She didn't want a showdown. He was in there every day and had a friendly relationship with Adrian and Don Pancho. In fact, that's where she'd first met him. She stayed home weekends and got a lot of unsolicited advice from The Colonel. But, as usual, Olga had been right. The painful lump of lead in her heart was beginning to melt. Slowly, the guilt seeped out and Carolina felt a little lighter every day. The daily routine during the week remained the same. Her fear of running into Mayolo lay dormant until she left the courthouse. That's when her stomach would lurch with apprehension. She went into the coffee bar a couple of times a day as usual, ran the same errands, the stationers, delivered files to some of the lawyers, or went to the *comandancia* to pick up a police file that Judge Ramos requested. On one or two occasions they saw each other in the plaza at a distance too great for conversation. But still, she feared the unavoidable face to face encounter.

Then one afternoon the thing she most feared happened. Carolina was just leaving the Continental with two coffees in her hands just as Mayolo was coming in. They had to dance a quick *danzón* to avoid falling into each other.

"*Ay perdón!*" Mayolo cried.

"That's all right."

"I wasn't watching where I was going. Did you get hot coffee all over yourself?"

"No, I'm fine, really."

"*Gracias a Dios!*" He held the door open for her. "See you around."

There, it was over! The inevitable confrontation had occurred at last and it wasn't the nasty scene she feared it would be. He was apologetic, friendly. A total stranger, if there were any in Tecate, would have done the same thing. Carolina was relieved to know he wasn't mad at her. She returned to the courthouse feeling ten kilos lighter.

The following Friday afternoon Carolina was in the Continental picking up an emergency mocha for Olga and her own cappuccino. "*Buenos dias,* Caro!" Adrian flashed her a smile. "The usual?"

"*Buenos dias*, Adrian, yes, the usual. Where's Don Pancho?"

His tragic face darkened. Carolina expected bad news. "I had to fire him just yesterday," he answered in a gray voice. He hung his head. "He's been taking money from the till. Yesterday I caught him with his *manos en la masa.*"

"*Buenos dias, encantadora bonita!*" Don Pancho appeared from the back. "I've always wanted a beautiful daughter. All I got was three ugly sons. Tell your mother I'll trade Adrian for you."

"*Ay* Don Pancho!" Carolina gushed.

"Of course, I don't expect your mamá would go for the trade. What would she do with a lazy *cabrón* like him?" He tossed his cowlicks in the direction of his son.

"He's not lazy, Don, look at him!" Carolina said in his defense. Adrian was working like a whirligig.

"And then, he's mentally retarded. As soon as you leave all he talks about is Caro this, and Caro that. He's dying to take you out but he's too shy or too stupid to open his mouth." Don Pancho flashed her the full octave and growled at his progeny. "Ask her out, *cabrón!*"

Carolina could feel her face burning. Adrian turned to her with a grin to match his father's. He whispered loud enough to be heard throughout the bar. "Tonight I make my escape, Caro, tonight! Say you'll help me."

Carolina immediately fell in with the theatrical conspiracy. "Of course. But how?"

"You can help me get across the border. Meet me at the monument to Benito Juarez at five—and bring wire cutters!"

"Don't trust the *cabrón*, Carolina, he'll probably convince you to run away with him—*ay!*" Don Pancho's wife came up behind him at that moment and yanked on both his ears.

"Tonight at five!" Adrian whispered as he handed across her order.

"Tonight at five!" Carolina whispered back all in fun.

"And I want a grandson!" Don Pancho cried as Carolina made it to the door.

Carolina left laughing. The last thing she heard was, "*Ay*—my ears!"

The courthouse normally closed at three-thirty but Judge Ramos was in one of his moods today and asked Olga and Carolina and a few others to work late. It was nearly five when Carolina left the office. She'd better pick up a package of Ella at the Farmacia del Parque on her way home. This morning the box in her dresser was nearly empty. She walked across the plaza, admiring the brilliant reds of the bougainvillea, inhaling the scent of summer roses, watching little children eating *churros* as they skipped and jumped followed by hungry pigeons waiting for the inevitable crumb to fall.

"PSSSSSSST!"

Carolina nearly jumped out of her shoes when Adrian leaped out from behind the monument to Benito Juarez.

"I was afraid you wouldn't be here!"

"*Ay*, Adrian you stopped my heart!"

With a hand at her waist Adrian led her to a bench. "Oh, forgive me! We must get your circulation going immediately." He took her hand and massaged her wrist. "Better?"

Adrian whipped out his cell phone. "I'll call the Cruz Roja and send for the *ambulancia*. Try to hang on!"

Carolina was laughing too hard for someone in cardiac arrest. "Yes, Adrian, you clown, I'm over my fright. You can put the phone away."

"I'm so relieved! But we must get some food in you right away to elevate your blood sugar. At least that's what I've heard. How about La Palapa for fish tacos?"

Carolina abandoned her errand. "I would love it!"

They walked along Callejón Reforma, an alley too narrow to be called a street. At first they stayed on the sidewalk but there was hardly room for two people to walk abreast without becoming intimate. Whenever they came to a telephone pole or a fire hydrant growing out of the pavement one of them would have to step off. By mutual consent they walked down the middle of the street. There was little danger of tangling with a car. The road was so covered with potholes they could easily hear a car a block away rattling as it was being disassembled. The *callejon* was lined on both sides with Tecate's older houses in the style that was popular in the nineteen fifties; white stucco, red tile roof, lavish gardens behind fancy wrought iron grilles and the standard feral German shepherd on guard duty.

Together they entered La Palapa, exchanging *saludos* with people they knew. La Palapa is a huge umbrella of woven palm fronds providing the illusion that one is in Guaymas or Topolobampo looking out over the sparkling sea dappled with whitecaps, seagulls crying, fishing boats hooting their horns, though forty miles from the coast. Here the seagulls are painted on the blue walls and the only hoots come from local street traffic. Almost involuntarily Carolina swept the tables with her eyes. She realized she was looking to see if Mayolo could be at one of the tables. He wasn't. I'm still doing it, she thought. Carolina was on her first date, although rather spontaneously, with a *chico* she always wanted to know. And here they were. Just the two of them. She was determined to expunge past events from her mind and thoroughly enjoy herself.

Eating fish tacos at La Palapa approximates ritual. The man behind the counter handed them each a plastic yellow basket with two steaming fish filets dipped in their secret batter and tucked into corn tortillas. Together they moved to the next phase of the rite to baptize their tacos. They faced a long row of stainless steel bowls filled with fresh-cut limes, finely chopped tomatoes, white onions followed by red onions, a red chile sauce that looked and tasted like lava flow, and ended with minced cilantro and fresh cabbage shredded fine as angel hair. They helped themselves to a little of everything and found a table. Conversation flowed easily.

"You and your father enjoy working together, don't you?"

"We're best friends."

"I can tell."

"Mmm, can I get you more salsa?"

"No *gracias*, I'm fine."

"More lime?"

"I'll steal one of yours."

"Anyway, my father and mother worked hard to put us all through school."

"All?"

"I'm the youngest of three boys. The oldest one is an engineer, the next one is an architect. I'm the only one who wanted to go into business. When my father offered me a partnership, I grabbed it." Adrian put down his taco. "What about you? I know! You're the bossy older sister."

Carolina laughed. "No, I'm the youngest. I have two older brothers, one in Tijuana, the other in Chihuahua." She felt comfortable with Adrian and went on to tell him about The Colonel, and in a careless moment, even included The Gorilla.

"I think our parents knew each other in school."

"I'm sure they did, there was only one school back then."

"Can I get you anything more?"

"Heavens, no! I'm stuffed."

"Me, too. Shall we start back to the plaza?"

"A mí me dicen el feo porque sin gracia nací..."

A young boy, solemn of face and shy of eye, scarcely in his first decade of life, entered the palapa with a guitar in his arms and began to sing. His thin fingers traveled over the strings with all the virtuosity of a young Segovia, the chords and arpeggios clear and pure. He sang like a nightingale gargling broken glass. Young Segovia finished his number and walked among the tables in hopes his live concert might culminate in a small coin or two.

"Muchacho, come here!" Adrian called out.

Carolina watched the boy shyly approach the table. "Where did you learn to play, *muchacho?"*

The long face looked at the floor. *"Mi* papá."

"He taught you well."

"Gracias."

Adrian pulled out an American dollar and stuffed it in his hand. "See that man over in the corner with the white shirt?

"Sí, señor."

"I want you to go over to him and sing *Las Mañanitas*."

The young musician thanked him and worked his way among the tables to the man Adrian had indicated. Carolina followed him with her eyes. The man was in the company of a dark woman with black hair, straight as a shoelace, and highlighted with *lucecitas*, little streaks of blonde hair. They appeared to Carolina to be man and wife. The woman was sipping something red from a straw. The husband was just introducing the second fish taco to his palate.

"Why did you send that man the birthday song, is it his birthday?"

"I have no idea."

They watched the boy approach the table indicated and face the man in the white shirt. He strummed a nice intro and began to sing the traditional ode to birthdays, sounding very much like the nightingale mentioned earlier.

> "*Estas son las mañanitas*
> *que cantaba el rey David...*

The man, who now had a fish taco pushed into his mouth, put it down and looked up startled. His wife did the same thing. People from nearby tables looked around them to see who was having a birthday. One or two at a time they began to go over to him and give him the warm birthday *abrazo*. He was soon surrounded with effusive felicitations and caught in a hopeless tangle of embracing arms while his fish with all the fixings was getting cold.

As Adrian and Carolina stood to leave they glanced at the victim of his prank who was now scanning the palapa in search of an explanation to such an extraordinary event.

Together they began to stroll back toward the plaza. "Were you always so *travieso*?"

"Mischief maker? *Incorregible!*"

"I thought so."

"I was born on the first of April and my father tells me that my first words were 'April Fool'! But I don't believe him. That holiday doesn't exist in Mexico."

"Maybe Vicente Fox should declare it a new holiday."

They were nearly at the end of Callejon Reforma. The air was warm and languid and scented with roses, carnations, and alyssum growing in the front gardens. "*Ay* Adrian!" Carolina stopped in her tracks and pointed. "Did you ever see such a perfect white rose? It's exquisite!"

In one sudden leap that left Carolina without speech Adrian was scaling the wrought iron grille.

"Adrian! What are you doing?"

Adrian didn't answer.

"Adrian, no! Come back here!"

Adrian didn't appear to hear or care. He dropped to the other side like Cyrano de Bergerac storming a walled city and headed for the rosebush offering the perfect white rose. The standard-issue German shepherd got there about the same time. There was a terrible brawl.

"Adrian!" Carolina screamed. "Adrian!"

With the vicious animal still determined to rip off at least one of his legs, Adrian made it over the iron fence and landed on the narrow sidewalk in triumph. His arms were covered with bloody streaks, his clothes shredded. The dog was still throwing himself at the iron grille gnashing his large yellow fangs, and barking furiously. The man of the house came running out to see what it was all about. When he saw Adrian kneeling at Carolina's feet offering one of his wife's white roses, he burst out laughing, told the dog to shut up and went into the house.

"*Ay* Adrian! I didn't say I wanted it, I just said it was beautiful." Carolina pressed the rose to her bosom and inhaled the fragrance. "Just look at you! You look like Santo Cristo on the cross!"

"What does it matter? No thorn can pierce as deep as love. And besides, it was but a common rose, uncherished and unfulfilled until you held it to your heart."

"And your face is scratched." Carolina took a small handkerchief from her purse and began to gently blot the red rivulet that wended down his cheek.

"Caro, *mi amor*, I wear these wounds sustained in your service as I would a medal."

By the time they stepped into the plaza two people who hardly knew each other a few hours ago had become old friends. Carolina didn't even realize she had her arm through his until they stopped at the Benito Juarez monument where the evening's adventure had begun. It was June when the sun, like a naughty child, stays up much too late until the Divine Mother finally coaxes him off to bed behind the hills of Tanama and darkness falls. Neither spoke, as though if they spoke they would both wake up from a dream they didn't want to end.

If I say, "thank you for a nice time," Carolina thought, the date is over.

Adrian was the first to speak. "Caro, my Caro, you've given me an afternoon I'll treasure forever. But now," he continued in a half-whisper, "I'm afraid."

"Afraid! The man who just minutes ago risked his life to present me with the perfect white rose, who is still bleeding, his clothes in shreds, is afraid? Afraid of what? Certainly not afraid of being impaled on steel spikes. Certainly not afraid of being dismembered by a wild dog. What are you afraid of?"

"My father."

"Your father!"

"My father is going to ask me if I kissed you. And I'm afraid of what he'll say if I say I didn't. And then, I'm afraid of what you'll say if I do."

Carolina's heart did a little pirouette. She was prepared for a fleeting brotherly peck on the cheek. In matters of love, el corazán es capitan, she told herself, and offered her face. "There is only one way to find out."

His mouth touched hers, light and wispy as dandelion fluff, but Carolina felt the voltage course though her entire body.

What neither saw while two hearts became one at the touching of their lips, was the dark figure skulking in the deepest shadows within the *kiosko*. Anger seized him, he was livid, and his breath came in gasps. Inside the man was seething, tears streamed down his face like molten lava. His mouth filled with acid. *He'll never have her. No man will ever have my Caro. She's mine, mine! Her beautiful mouth, mine to kiss. Her perfect breasts, mine alone to touch. If she can't be mine, no man shall have her. Never!*

The two people on the cusp of love remained with their arms around each other, neither willing to break the warm embrace. Carolina was the first to sever the magic moment. "It's late. I'd better head home."

"Afraid?"

"Me, afraid! Of what, the dark?"

"No, The Colonel."

Mayolo watched them kiss again, then go off in the direction of their cars. He came down the stairs and started aimlessly across the plaza like a sleepwalker, blind to everything around him, deaf to the music of strolling musicians and the cries of street vendors. He wasn't even aware that he'd dropped heavily onto a bench. He sat alone in the darkness burning with white-hot fury, misery festering in his soul.

Mayolo ignored the pushcarts, the shoe shine boy, the tamale wagon, the ice cream man, the *churro* cart. His heart pounded in his head. He was blind with silent rage. Then he heard the unmistakable sound of leather-soled sandals shuffling across the flagstones.

"*Buenas noches*, Mayolo."

"*Buenas noches*, Babalu."

"Trouble is written on thy furrowed brow. I see sorrow in thy heart."

Carolina was lost in love by the time she got home. She pleaded a hard day at work, kissed her mother, and went to bed early. She fell asleep dreaming of Adrian.

Cuando calienta el sol....
Aqui en la playa...

La Fonda looked like a scene out of an old Ricardo Montalban movie. Smoke curled above the tables like calligraphy. Mariachis poured out their music, violins, guitars, the big bass guitarron, and a silvery trumpet put everyone under the spell of their alchemy.

Every table was full. There were married couples, young people out on a date, couples in love, a table or two of women in Tecate's social deep freeze: the divorced, the single mothers, those attractive unattached women who would never be invited to a party where susceptible husbands could succumb to temptation. A new group of escapees from Rancho La Puerta health spa was on their second pitcher of margaritas. Two older American couples were hopping and stomping and playing air castanets. La Fonda is the kind of place where Americans, doubtless aided by mariachis and margaritas, can release the spirit of their former youth in ways they wouldn't dare in a restaurant back home. There was a great deal of table hopping among the locals.

Against the back wall Carolina and Adrian were holding hands across the table. *Their* table, now. Beto kept it reserved for them any day they came in which was several times a week. It was September. Three months had unrolled like thread curling off a spool since that first kiss in the plaza in June. Hour by hour, day by day, two hearts grew together until they became one. Carolina and Adrian were inseparable. They couldn't go ten minutes without a kiss.

Beto put two margaritas before them. Their left hands remained clasped. Only the right hand picked up their drink. They said *salud*, formed a kiss with their lips, and whispered *I love you*. Carolina waved to Olga as she and her husband passed their table on their way to be seated. Olga gave her a subtle thumbs-up. She spotted Didi, with her new *novio*, a good looking *muchacho*, his dark beard gathered in a ponytail with a thin gold cord. He wore a large gold hoop in his left ear. It looked to her like there would soon be a new baby next door. Carolina hid a grin as she overheard the confusion of the waitress when one of the Americans ordered tortillas with his quesadilla. And there was Mayolo, obviously in very high spirits with a group of his friends. Two of the two girls were laughing and gesticulating about something. They appeared to be teasing the men. It pleased Carolina to see that everything was finally resolved without bruised feelings on either part. The strain was gone. Two *licenciados* from the courthouse walked in, exchanged *saludos* with Carolina and Adrian then gave Adrian a sly wink as they moved away.

The couple in love sipped their drinks. Adrian noticed Carolina's eyes had left him and were now focused on another table. "What are you looking at that seems to be so interesting?"

"See that woman having dinner with the man with the bushy mustache? I was admiring her shawl. It's two shades of blue, turquoise and cerulean, with silver threads running through it. I've never seen anything like it before. She must have had it made." Carolina took another sip and licked the salt from the rim of her glass with the tip of a tiny pink tongue.

She saw Adrian get up from the table. "Adrian! What are you doing? Sit down!"

"What's wrong?" He was already on his feet.

"I'm beginning to know your mind, that's what's wrong. You're going to go over there and buy that shawl right off that woman's back!"

"Honestly, I wasn't. I was just going to the you-know-where."

"Well, okay, but if I see you stop at their table, I won't be here when you get back!"

Carolina watched him enter the *caballeros* and relaxed. When next she looked up again Adrian was in animated conversation with the woman—and he was actually handing her money! Carolina was so embarrassed she turned her face to the wall. Adrian arrived back triumphant, the shawl draped over one arm, ready to accept praise.

"Adrian you are *incorregible!*" Carolina sat frozen to her chair unable to execute her recent threat.

Adrian looked like a little boy who had been naughty and was about to cry. "I'm sorry, Caro, really I am." He looked down at his feet. When he looked up again he saw the fire in her eyes. "Just kidding! In truth, she's my sister-in-law and she let me borrow it. The man with her is my older brother, the architect. I'll introduce you to them later."

Carolina looked over at the table. The woman who cooperated with the gag was in spasms of laughter. Adrian's older brother was laughing too, but he was shaking his head as though conveying to her that his little brother was a lunatic beyond help.

Carolina reached out for his hand and held it tight. "Don't ever change."

Beto brought them a second margarita then dinner. *Ensalada Cesar* and *chimichangas.*

"*Hola!*"

Both looked up to see Mayolo at their table. "Why are you leaving so early?" Carolina asked.

"Join us for a drink, Mayolo. I only see you at the coffee bar when I'm working."

"I wish I could."

"You can't be working at this hour, come on, sit down," Carolina coaxed.

"Believe it or not I really am working. But we'll definitely get together another time," and Mayolo threaded his way among the tables to the door.

"He's a very serious type, you know," Adrian observed. "But underneath I think he's really just shy."

"You're right. Underneath his shyness is a sincere heart." Carolina actually liked him more now than before.

Dinner over, the check paid, the generous tip carefully hidden among the little packets of artificial sugar, the couple in love walked out of the party and stepped into the quiet serenity of the plaza. Arm in arm they strolled their usual pattern. Once around the outside then toward the center and the kiosk. At this late hour there were plenty of benches available, but the two people in love did not welcome the intrusion of hawkers and even less the ramblings of the old witch Babalu. Together they took the stairs and sat on the top step of the kiosk where it was dark.

Neither spoke. After the din of La Fonda the absence of sound in the dark plaza under a sliver of moon was soothing, the only music, the pleasant splashing of the fountain. They spoke in sighs and kisses.

After a long interval of silent kisses and soft murmurs Adrian, as usual, whispered the first words. "Caro, *mi amor*, have you any idea how much I love you?"

"I love you more."

"Impossible. I'll love you until coffee trees become extinct and I have to push a taco cart through the plaza to earn a living."

"And I'll always love you more tomorrow than I do today."

Two hungry mouths found each other in the dark, one long kiss trembling with desire that neither was willing to end. Carolina ached for his touch. She'd been waiting three months for Adrian's caresses and could wait no longer. She found his hand and placed it over her heart.

"*Te amo, mi corazón,*" he whispered.

"*Eres mi vida,*" Carolina answered.

"And I'm so afraid."

"No, *mi amor,* you have nothing to be afraid of."

"But I am — I'm afraid of my father." Adrian dropped his hands and placed them on her lap.

"Your father!"

"Yes."

"Again? But why?"

"Because I know the man. He'll be waiting up for me when I get home and he's going to ask me if I proposed to you. I'm afraid of what he'll say if I say I didn't, and I'm afraid to hear what *you'll* say if I do."

Gently, tenderly, Carolina took his hands from her lap and replaced them on her breasts. "I would say yes."

Two steps forward, two steps back, promenade your partner, first to the left, then to the right. Carolina was dancing a vibrant ballet folklorico to the beat of a native orchestra, strings, wooden flutes, and percussion. Her dancing partner was an upright Eureka.

She repeated the pattern twice then turned off the radio, parked the vacuum cleaner, and grabbed a feather duster of brilliant plumage. It looked like an exotic South American parrot in flight as it flitted over tables, chairs, television, behind the sofa. Even the Blessed Virgin under golden crown of holy light received a vigorous dusting across her saintly face. Caro ripped away gossamer cobwebs draped in the corners of the windows that weren't there yesterday and would be back again tomorrow. Next she removed the ugly green chenille spread from her mother's big chair that appeared to be molting. For only a moment she assessed the two frayed arms worn down to the white cotton batting. She put it back. There was nothing to be done about the worn spot in the carpet near the door or the Z-shaped crack in the wall. The Colonel could be heard remodeling the kitchen.

"They'll be here in less than twenty minutes, Mamá. I'll finish in there, you go get dressed."

"Pancho had a terrible crush on me when we were in school, you know," her mother answered from the kitchen. "Put fresh towels in the bathroom then come help me with my hair."

Carolina assessed the rooms. The house was presentable, and anyway, nothing more could be done. She got rid of the Eureka and all other evidence of last minute housecleaning then went to help her mother. "I just hope The Gorilla doesn't start moaning and groaning while they're here."

In twenty minutes Don Pancho, consistent with social statutes, rang the bell. Carolina answered the summons. There stood her *novio*, his face the color of rice pudding, and next to him, her soon-to-be father-in-law. Don Pancho burst in with his usual affability, dark eyes flashing, piano keys grinning. He ran to Raquel with his arms wide open and wrapped her in a tight embrace. "Raquel! *Hermosa, bonita, luz de mi corazón!* Look at you! You're as beautiful now as you were in school. Tell me your secret — I'll buy a gallon!"

"*Ay* Pancho!"

He turned to Carolina. "Your mother was the most beautiful girl in school. We always knew where she was because there was always a mob of *muchachos* hanging around her like yellow jackets on a candy bar."

She watched her future *suegro* embrace her mother. It was no effort to imagine him a dashing high school *gallo*. She only had to look at his son. But she could not form an image of her mother, young, flirty, and sexy. It was too great a leap for the mind's eye.

Raquel covered her face with both hands, pretending to hide an embarrassed blush. "You haven't changed a bit, Pancho, still throwing *piropos* like confetti. The years are creeping up on me, I'm afraid. I'm starting to see little lines where there weren't any before — and a few more lumps."

"I don't see any lines and I like lumps."

Doña Raquel yielded to the praise. "And where's Alicia?"

"Somebody has to watch the business. She'll be over after closing. She sends you her love."

Raquel indicated chairs for the company, ran to the kitchen and returned with coffee and little *empanadas* filled with peach preserve. They prattled for a few minutes then Don Pancho came to his purpose.

"Raquel, I am come to ask you for the hand of your daughter Carolina."

His hand flew up as Raquel was getting ready to speak. "I know, we are getting the best of the bargain. Adrian is homely like his father, sometimes he shows signs of some mysterious brain disorder while Caro has inherited all your charm and beauty. Raquel, you are our only hope for beautiful grandchildren. It would be an honor to join our family with yours."

Before Raquel could summon words, Adrian, who had yet to speak, fell to his knees before Doña Raquel. "Señora, please do me the honor of becoming my mother-in-law. You will be my aegis against my father. And I can promise you a loyal and devoted son." He placed a box of marzipan on her lap.

There followed a free-for-all of hugs and kisses and the uncorking of a fine champagne Don Pancho had brought along with complete confidence.

The next day Caro was wearing a diamond ring, six months later Father Ruben posted the banns in the vestibule of the church of Nuestra Señora de Guadalupe. Don Pancho gave the young couple the house he and Alicia bought when they first got married twenty-eight years ago. By the time Adrian had been born they were in a position to buy a large comfortable house in the beautiful Colonia Downey and they rented out the little house. Now it would become Adrian and Carolina's first home.

Every moment they could spare, after work, weekends, Carolina and Adrian worked at getting their new home ready to move into when they were husband and wife. They only had three months to get it done. It was a small dwelling, living room, dining room, kitchen, two bedrooms, and a bath. They kept old clothes in the closet so they could change into work clothes at any given opportunity.

Carolina changed in the bathroom with the door closed, Adrian in one of the bedrooms. The decorum was a tableau of propriety and could not have been more chaste had The Colonel been sitting right there watching them, although there were opportunities for lots of kissing and mutual caressing that sometimes left an accusatory smudge of paint.

"Why don't you let me do that?" It was Saturday and the young couple in love planned on getting in a full day. They wanted to get it finished. The combined smells of latex, and enamel, and paint thinner, and linseed oil hung in the air like the smog in Tijuana. Carolina was in a pair of baggy white shorts and a threadbare white shirt, both so thin they never left the house. She covered her hair with a bandana. Adrian wore a pair of white, beige, green, blue and yellow twill pants and a matching shirt. He looked like an artist's palette.

"You just hold the ladder." Adrian did as he was told while Carolina climbed to the top and installed four flame-shaped bulbs in the ceiling fixture in the dining room. "You'd leave it for last."

"Well yes, I probably would wait until the electricity was turned on." He brushed away an ugly green fly crawling up her bare leg. "And what if we spatter paint on them?"

Carolina took out four plastic sandwich bags from her back pocket. "You see? I've thought of everything."

"Well, maybe not everything."

"What do you mean?"

"You're wearing a cute pair of red *calzones*."

"Shame on you! Nice boys don't look up a girl's shorts when she's at the top of a rickety ladder."

"I wasn't looking up your shorts, honest. The red shows through."

"Well, it's only the two of us."

"*Tan-tan!* Anybody home?"

Adrian looked toward the voice. "*Hola* Mayolo! Come any closer and we'll put you to work!" Suddenly aware of Adrian's recent remarks on her interesting wardrobe, Carolina scrambled down the ladder.

"Any closer and I'd be asphyxiated. I saw your front door wide open."

"It lets the flies in, but it was that or die of the fumes in here."

"I brought lunch!" Mayolo walked into the eye-stinging fog holding two plastic bags from Tacos Los Amigos.

"This is a surprise!" Carolina was obliged by centuries-old custom to go through the motions of the mandatory embrace. Anything less would have been inexcusably rude by Mexican standards. But Carolina had a legitimate reason to keep it brief and impersonal. "Be careful, I'm covered with paint and I don't want to get it all over you." She was still self-conscious of her see-through clothing but no one else seemed to perceive it.

"Hey, this is really coming along! It looks like you'll have it finished in a few days."

"There are just a couple more things to do," Adrian answered. "Come on, we'll show you around. Caro, you lead the way."

"Well, as you can see," Carolina began. "You're standing between the *sala* and the *comedor*. Come on, I'll show you what's finished." They entered the small kitchen glistening with high-gloss white enamel walls and recently-oiled natural wood cabinets. "I'm going to hang some cheery yellow cafe curtains in here and it's finished." They moved down the hall. "The enamel in the bathroom is still tacky so we better not go in there." Carolina led her tour to the small bedroom. "We couldn't decide whether to go with pink or blue so we left it white. This will be the baby's room."

Adrian led him to the next room. "And this is the factory." Carolina saw Mayolo's face wince with pain. The sudden slap on Adrian's shoulder, somewhat harder than playful, quickly took the form of a caress.

Mayolo covered his discomfort with a laugh Carolina recognized as counterfeit. She felt sorry for him, but Mayolo recovered quickly. "Well, come on, hand me a roller and I'll give you a hand."

"Oh no, Mayolo," Carolina objected. "You'll ruin your clothes."

"She's right. I thought you said you brought lunch."

Mayolo put the bags down on a stool. "We've got tacos *de carne asada*." The agonizing smell of grilled meat and onions and cilantro aroused the carnivore in two hungry stomachs. "A tub of guacamole, a heap of freshly made *chicharrones*, and flan!"

"Say no more!" Adrian went to the cooler and came back with three amber bottles of Corona.

They sat outside on the front stoop and devoured everything but the plastic bags. They chatted easily about anything that came to mind, Carolina so relaxed, she totally forgot about her disreputable shirt and shorts and the red *calzones*. Maybe she was never in love with Mayolo, but at this moment she had nothing but admiration for him. It took courage she knew she didn't possess to walk in here on his own and offer his friendship without conditions. She knew herself well enough to know she'd never do it. What a noble deed! Rather than blame him for his past behavior when they broke up, she realized you'd do *anything* to keep from losing the one you love. No one is to blame in these situations, she told herself. If the mortar doesn't set, the adobes won't stick. And the adobes didn't stick. It was just that simple, just that painful. She saw Mayolo's beer was one sip away from finished. She lost her silly self-consciousness, went inside to the cooler, and put a fresh Corona in his hand.

Mayolo smiled his thanks. "Well, come on, now, Adrian, get me an old shirt and we'll have this room finished in no time."

"You're on!" He didn't give Carolina time to protest. They went to the back bedroom. Carolina saw him come out in one of Adrian's old red and blue plaid shirts with long sleeves.

"But before we get started we have to have a picture of the two of you."

"Looking like this?" Caro cried.

"Come on, *mi amor*, one day we can show it to our kids."

Mayolo pulled out a disposable camera. "How about the two of you up on the ladder where you were when I walked in."

Carolina remembered her red underwear. "Okay, Adrian at the top and I'll hold the ladder," she said at once.

The models took their places, Mayolo snapped the shot and they all got to work.

Together they had the small dining room painted in half an hour. "That really went fast, Mayolo," Carolina praised and began to gather the newspapers she'd spread on the floor.

"You're a lifesaver!" Adrian said. "You should have come earlier in the week. We'd be finished." They all laughed. "We've been so busy here I haven't even had time to get a haircut."

"And just look at him!" Carolina exclaimed. "I may be marrying a man with rainbow hair like those *cholos* they call punks on the Other Side."

"Lucila takes appointments only on Saturday so it's going to have to wait for next week."

"Again?" Carolina turned to Mayolo. "That's what he says every week."

Mayolo came to the rescue. "Hey, I have an appointment for two o'clock today. You can have mine."

"Oh, I couldn't do that."

"Don't give me that. Make him be sensible, Caro. We can finish the living room when we get back."

He hadn't called her Caro since they broke up six months ago. "He's right, Adrian. You're talking twenty minutes. But I'm going to put a plastic bag over your hair when you get back."

The two young men ran off while Carolina picked up the remains of the lunch things. The bags and paper napkins in the trash barrel out back, the empty bottles back in the carton. She just had the living room floor papered when they were back. As promised she artfully arranged a plastic bag from Tacos Los Amigos around Adrian's beautiful hair and they started rolling paint. They chattered while they worked and in a short time the walls of the living room were transformed into a soft dusty rose to match the dining room. They couldn't stop thanking Mayolo.

"Why don't you join us for dinner and margaritas tonight?" Adrian suggested.

"Wish I could but I have a VITAVIDA meeting tonight."

"On a Saturday?" Carolina protested.

"They always have their awards dinners on Saturdays. But we can do it another time."

Adrian embraced Mayolo followed by Carolina who, forgetting her inhibitions, allowed her cheek to touch his. "Thanks for everything," she said. Together they walked Mayolo to his car and waved him off.

Owing to unexpected company and lunch and a haircut Adrian and Carolina had gone nearly two hours without a kiss. They made it as far as the front door when they fell into each other's arms and kissed ravenously.

When they came up for breath Adrian said, "That was nice of Mayolo to come by and give us a hand."

"I was just thinking the same thing." Carolina pulled the plastic bag from Adrian's head as they walked back into the house. "And he got you in for a haircut."

"Oh look, Mayolo left his shirt."

"Does that mean he'll show up at the awards wearing your old paint shirt?" Carolina giggled.

"Knowing Mayolo, he'll figure it out sooner than that. Hey, we're finished here, Caro. Let's get cleaned up and go to La Fonda for dinner. We can finish up here tomorrow."

"Good idea! I'll go straight home to shower and change. Pick me up when you're ready."

"We could save a lot of time if we showered here together, you know."

Carolina smacked his bottom. "Not until Father Ruben says it's okay." She kissed him hard on the mouth, pinched him where he'd never been pinched before, then flitted out the door.

It was mid-August now. Carolina and Adrian stood thrilled as the big truck from El Rubí pulled into their driveway. Two young men jumped out and began unloading the furniture they'd put on layaway months ago. It took nearly half a day but they placed everything for the living room and dining room reasonably close to where Carolina wanted it. There was only one place the bed and dresser and bureau could go. The baby's room would remain unfurnished for the time being. Stove and refrigerator were installed.

As soon as the delivery men left Carolina and Adrian caught up on kisses and set about placing the smaller items. "Wouldn't you like the floor lamp by the big *papi* chair, rather than next to the sofa?"

"That makes sense." Adrian dragged it over to the matching easy chair, plugged it in, and flopped down. "I think I'm going to like this. What are we going to do with that prissy little table you insisted on having?" He was referring to a tall occasional table with long curvy legs and a round leather top.

"It's not a prissy little table. I'll center it at the window or maybe in a corner of the dining room. What do you think?"

"Either one, I guess. It isn't big enough for a cup and saucer. What are you going to put on it?"

"I thought maybe a vase with flowers would be nice."

"Those gangly girl-legs wouldn't support a bud vase."

"Don't be smart."

"I still think a big vase of flowers would look better on the dining room table."

"*Tan-tan*...Anybody home?"

Both looked up at the voice. "Mayolo!" they cried in unison.

"Don't you ever close your front door?"

"We just had all our furniture delivered."

"I'll put up some coffee, Mayolo, you'll be our first guest." When Carolina went over to receive him, she stopped short. He carried what appeared to be a huge vase of vibrant colors she recognized as the typical work of the native artisans of Puebla who use full strength blue and yellow and orange. It only took her a second to see it wasn't a vase at all, it was a ceramic swan. The slender neck of brilliant cobalt blue swept gracefully to join the voluptuous breast of brilliant yellow like the curve of a concert harp. Big bold splashes of blue and orange covered the body, the ebony wings were delicately tipped with flecks of emerald, sapphire, and carmine red. Carolina stood mesmerized.

"Your wedding gift."

"But—" Adrian began.

"I know, I know, you're not married yet."

"Not till next Saturday."

"But I won't be here next Saturday."

"What!"

"I'm being transferred to VITAVIDA in Monterey. I leave in the morning so I wanted to bring you your wedding gift before I left."

Mayolo gently placed the swan in Carolina's arms. "I wish you both the best of everything."

"It's the most exquisite thing I've ever seen! Just look at the colors! I just love the ceramics from Puebla. And you just settled our first argument. I know exactly where this is going!" Carolina carried the swan to the prissy little table with the curvy girl-legs and set it down gently as she would a baby. "Oh, Mayolo, thank you!" She gave him a tight *abrazo* in the company of a warm kiss that said everything she was feeling better than words. She felt Mayolo's full mouth pressing firmly into her cheek. "It's gorgeous!" Carolina was well aware that she was gushing but she didn't care. She dried her eyes with her shirt tail.

Adrian opened his arms to Mayolo. "*Gracias*, Mayolo. It will be like having you here when you're far away from us in Monterey."

"I'll put up some coffee."

Adrian put Mayolo in his new easy chair and took the sofa. They talked a little bit about everything and nothing and soon Carolina came in with the coffee pot. "We haven't unpacked anything yet so it's going to be disposable cups and paper napkins for plates. I do have some *pan dulce* I picked up at the *panaderia* just this morning."

They settled down to coffee and conversation and sweet bread until Mayolo came to his feet. "I'm sorry I'll miss your wedding, *muchachos*, but I can promise you I'll be thinking of you down in Monterey." They walked Mayolo to his car and there followed another series of hugs, kisses of forgiveness, kisses of friendship, and good wishes. They waved until he was lost from view.

With their arms around each other Carolina and Adrian walked slowly back to their first house and their new furniture.

It was a beautiful wedding followed by a lavish reception at Rancho Tecate Resort and Country Club. One hundred guests ate and drank and danced to mariachis until daybreak. The bride and groom, however, could wait no longer and with the help of Ronnie Rosa, maitre d' at Rancho Tecate, they sneaked quietly away. Five days in Ensenada was all they could afford. The newlyweds were back now, cuddling on their new sofa in their new home. Adrian in sweats, Carolina in shorts and a souvenir T-shirt. Nothing else.

"Well, at least we had a beach-front cabaña for our honeymoon." Adrian moved his hand to Carolina's breast.

"A lot of good that did. We couldn't go dancing, we couldn't take romantic walks on the beach, we couldn't do anything *else* because I couldn't get too far from the cabaña." Carolina took his hand from her breast, kissed it, then put it back. "I'm sorry, *mi amor*. It wasn't much of a honeymoon."

Adrian stroked her cheek. "But one we'll always remember."

"One I'll never forget! Sick for the first three days then indisposed for the last two."

Adrian pulled her Las Brisas T-shirt away, kissed first one nipple, then the other. "The real honeymoon starts now."

"We didn't even get a full moon."

"We have one tonight."

"Really!"

"Really. Come on, we'll go outside and look." Adrian took her by the hand.

"Dressed like this?"

"Unless you want to take it off."

They stepped out the back door onto a small enclosed patio and stared up at huge golden disc suspended on a mantle of black organdy.

Carolina's voice was soft as the night. "What is it about a full moon that makes us talk in whispers, that can fill us with wonder, or abandon our vulnerability and confess the contents of our heart?"

"I never thought of it before, *corazón*, a big lifeless rock wandering around space like a lost soul and it makes me want to cry. I love you more than exist words to say it."

For a long interval they spoke only with kisses then Carolina pressed herself tight against him. "Maybe we better go back inside.

I think you're ready to start the honeymoon." She reached down and touched him. "And so am I." She gave her husband a breathy kiss on the ear and whispered, "Take me inside now, and make love to me."

Together they returned to the sofa where Adrian began feverishly to undress her.

"Wait for me. I'll just go put on my nightgown."

"Why bother?"

"Oh no, we're going to do this right. I want to wear my honeymoon nightgown and you're going to undress me." She kissed him and stood."Don't start without me. I'll only be a minute." She disappeared into the bedroom.

Carolina wasn't gone but a few minutes. She returned swathed in pink froth to find Adrian cradling his head between his hands. "What's wrong, *mi amor*, what is it?"

"Headache."

"Oh, I'm sorry. I'll get you some aspirin."

"No! Don't leave me, *mi amor*, oh God it hurts. It *hurts*!"

Carolina watched in horror as Adrian rolled off the sofa and collapsed in a heap on the floor.

The next half hour was a living nightmare. The ambulance arrived in minutes. She rode with him to the emergency clinic. Adrian was rolled into a room. His parents arrived minutes afterward. Together they paced the depressing dark green hall, they drank bitter coffee. They prayed. They wept.

In minutes uncounted Dr. Lopez-Macias came out. "Cerebral hemorrhage. He's gone. I'm so sorry. God, I'm sorry. It was so fast." He choked on his own words. "I've never seen anything like this in such a young person."

And that's when Carolina went numb and her mind went blank.

The events that followed were a surreal nightmare of horrors, a kaleidoscope of meaningless fragments of sounds and visions. Nothing registered in Carolina's mind. A Mass. Incense. A funeral. Tears. Candles burning. Bells ringing. People in the house. The noxious smell of food. Always food! Talking. Weeping. *Voices, voices, voices.*

When the nightmare subsided Carolina woke in her new home. Alone at last. She walked through the house she and Adrian shared for what, a day? She touched the furniture they chose together, the sofa, the easy chair, the brass bed where they never slept, the armoire. She looked into the empty baby's room. She surveyed the dining room, the cherry wood dining table and chairs where no one ever sat. The prissy table Adrian teased her about. Her eyes filled. Adrian's big *papi* chair. Empty. The swan. Adrian had been right. It would look better on the dining room table.

Carolina lifted the delicate ceramic figure as carefully as she would one day hold her own baby. She carried it to the table. Did she stumble on the rug? Did it just slip through her hands? With a sickening crash the elegant swan lay shattered on the mosaic floor in blue and yellow and orange shards.

Tears of anger, tears of frustration, tears of grief rained down Carolina's face. She bent to the floor and began to gather up the larger pieces. She wasn't even aware she was doing it. Her nerves were snapping like electric wires in the rain. It was hopeless. There, among the wreckage was a small bundle of fabric wrapped in twine. Where did *that* come from? She picked it up and looked at it through blurry eyes. Why did it look familiar? As she removed the twine she recognized Adrian's old red and blue plaid paint shirt. Tucked inside was a swatch of thick hair. Black hair with white paint on it. Hair? Whose hair? What on earth was it, she wondered? None of it made any sense. Then she saw the curled paper half hidden under the fabric. She unrolled it. A photograph. The photo Mayolo took the day he helped them paint. She saw herself in baggy shorts and shirt holding the ladder with a happy smile on her face. Adrian stood near the top grinning at the camera. Carolina wasn't sure she was seeing right. She brought the photo closer to her face to get a better look. Then she saw it. She understood. And her world ended.

A long, sharp cactus thorn was driven straight into Adrian's head.

Señor Frog He Would A-Wooing Go

I've known Paco Mendez for a number of years and yet I never learned the real story behind the courtship of his adorable young wife until just recently. A bunch of us were gathered in the courtyard at Villa Hermosa, Paco's stately home. Mariachis played and we all sang *Las Mañanitas*. We were celebrating Paco's fiftieth birthday. On the Other Side you could describe Paco in one simple idiomatic expression: drop-dead gorgeous. He was tall by Tecate standards, his skin smooth and dark as polished alder, the hair, black as C sharp on a Steinway. His mustache was always neatly groomed, and Paco was gentle and charming by his very nature. The pile of gifts on the table rivaled the Pyramid of the Warriors in Chichen Itza. After about an hour of opening gifts and receiving congratulatory kisses and *abrazos*, his best friend Federico handed him the last package. Paco removed the wide silver ribbon, opened the box, and a big green frog leaped out. *Rivet-rivet.* There followed a few screams from the ladies, riffles of laughter, and the *Rana esculenta* hopped away and quickly found a happy home in the darkest part of the garden. *Rivet-rivet.* A closed-circuit joke without a doubt, but what did it mean? There was a story here and I wasn't going home without it.

That same night, or maybe it was two or three in the morning of the following day, I was elected to drive Federico home and the whole story unfolded. If you think I'm being careless with the truth I can show you the "monument to everlasting love" that still stands (sort of) today. It all began one afternoon in Paco's courtyard.

"That's it for me!" Paco Mendez declared with a vehement passion. "*El fin!*"

Paco was in conversation with Federico, his best friend and *compa*, professor of classical literature at the university. The two men were performing the rites of tequila, lemon, and salt, seated in the pleasant shade provided by one of the arches in the courtyard of Villa Hermosa.

"*Salud.*"

"*Salud.*"

The pudgy bottle of Chinaco tequila *reposado* sat between them on a small wrought-iron table. The afternoon air was heavy with the scent of roses and jasmine and orange blossoms. Silvery braids of clear water tumbling down from a stone dolphin atop the tiled fountain spilled into three bowls of pink marble, gurgling and bubbling like laughing children.

"From this moment on I am having absolutely nothing whatever to do with women!"

"Nothing?"

"Nothing!"

"That leaves you only two options, *monje* or *maricón*."

"I'd never make it as a monk or a homosexual."

This conversation that looked like it was going to develop into something interesting was interrupted by Mavi, a pretty little maid of twenty Aprils, timid as a bunny sneaking tidbits in somebody's garden. "Excuse me, señor," she said in a tiny voice. "Do you need anything more?"

"*Sí*, Mavi, *gracias*," Paco answered. "Bring us a little guacamole and a few chips to play with."

"*Sí*, señor." Mavi twitched her little nose and scampered away.

"I don't understand the rotten luck I've had with women," Paco continued when Mavi returned into the house. "I'm honest with women, I'm generous, I'm faithful, and look what happens!"

"What happened now?"

"I came home unexpectedly and found Carmela in bed with a man not of my acquaintance."

"My God! What did you do?"

"I threw them both out just as they were."

"In union!"

"No, no, without their clothes."

"Did Carmela at least have an explanation?"

"Yes, she said the man was forcing her."

"Did you ever stop to consider that she might have been telling you the truth?"

"Carmela was on top."

"What happened to that pretty girl before Carmela, Liliana, wasn't it? She was nice."

"Very nice, to every man in Tecate while she was supposed to be my *novia*." Mavi entered here with a platter of guacamole and a bowl of warm tortilla chips. "*Gracias*, Mavi, we don't need anything more."

"Maria asked me to inquire if you have a preference for dinner."

"Veal chops, Italian salad, Asiago rolls, and a Pinot Blanc."

"*Sí*, señor. For two?"

"For one."

"Good tequila, this Chinaco." Federico smacked his lips in appreciation and refilled their glasses. "*Salud*."

"*Salud*."

"Maybe you're choosing your *novias* too young," Federico suggested. "You're what, fifty?"

"Forty-five and you know it. I won't hit fifty for a long time. All the women my age are already married, divorced or grandmothers."

"True enough."

Paco dipped into the guacamole. "What's my problem with women?"

"Well, you're a handsome *cabrón*."

"I can't help that, it's what God wanted! I'll go to a plastic surgeon and come out looking like Dorian Gray's portrait."

"And you're filthy rich."

"So? I hate money. Money is trash. I hate being filthy rich!"

"No, you don't."

"No, I don't."

"Don't you see the problem, Paco?" Federico took a chip and scooped up a dollop of guacamole. "Mmm, Mavi makes good guacamole! You attract the wrong kind of girl. They come here and see how you live in your grand villa, servants, the big Land Rover and the BMW." Federico dipped again. "You are the living illustration of the point Ovido was trying to convey when he said, *'Abundancia me tiene pobre.'*"

"*Plenty has made me poor*? Make sense, *cabrón*. Do I look poor?"

"Another form of poverty, Paco. Look at that shirt you're wearing. Four hundred pesos at least."

"Six hundred."

"You take your girlfriends to the very best places for fine dining in San Diego, you whisk them off to New York for dinner or to Europe for a new dress. The women fall in love with your lifestyle, not with Paco the man."

"And what do you suggest I do, take them to the taco carts for a dinner of calf-head tacos then treat them to a Popsicle? Please!"

"*Salud.*"

"*Salud.*"

The conversation drifted off in the direction of politics, corruption, graft, and quite naturally alighted on the coming presidential election. They talked, and drank, and said *salud* until the courtyard was bathed in shadow.

Presently Federico stood as best he could. "I'd better be getting back while I can still drive, *compa*."

Paco walked his best friend to his car, they exchanged the big macho *abrazo*, and he walked back into the courtyard. There was still a half bottle of Chinaco on the table. He filled his glass and performed the ritual by himself, a slug of Chinaco, a bite of lemon, and a lick of salt. There had to be an answer to his problem and he sat there thinking and sipping. Sipping and thinking.

As so often happens with good tequila, the answer to his problem was only waiting to be discovered somewhere near the bottom of the chubby bottle. Just as the last drop of *reposado* went down, and he bit down on the lemon, and licked the salt from the back of his hand, the idea fell out and hit him over the head as from a bursting piñata. And what an idea! It was the legendary *Epifanía del Chinaco*!

"Mavi!"

"*Sí*, señor?"

"Find Sancho and Pancho and send them in immediately. I'll be in my library."

"*Sí*, señor."

Paco's library was a pleasant room with big comfortable leather furniture. Open cases on either side of a stone fireplace were packed from pink mosaic floor to beamed ceiling with the books he loved to read; Oscar Wilde, Somerset Maugham, Thomas Wolfe, Garcia-Marquez, Carlos Fuentes. The dark paneled walls held his favorite prints, Goya, Renoir, Monet, and Whistler. A CD of one of Bruckner's epic symphonies sat on his side table. He'd been wanting to hear the eighth, and he promised himself he would just as soon as he could sit down for a day and a half to listen to it in its entirety. While the inspiration still burned within him, Paco took a notepad and pencil and got to work.

In a few minutes Sancho and Pancho walked into the room. Sancho was a short, fat *hombre* with the strength of a team of mules. In the State of California he would have been required to wear a sign reading WIDE LOAD. He was born and raised on a large hacienda in Durango sixty-some years ago, *mas o menos*, he wasn't sure. Sancho couldn't read the words on a pack of cigarettes but he could have taught a course in farrier science, orthopedic problems in horses, or diseases of feedlot cattle at Texas A & M. He even understood the John Deere which was more than Paco could do. Pancho, on the other hand, was skinny as a rawhide braided rope and just as tough. He earned his degree in agriculture on the farms in Mexicali at age ten. He did his post-graduate work in the Imperial Valley until he made an unexpected acquaintance with a Border Patrol officer in the Holtville General Store. Both Sancho and Pancho had the dark ocher face of the *campesino*, jet black hair, and an oversize macho mustache.

"You sent for us, *patrón*?"

"Yes, here's a list of materials I need. Take the big truck and have it all down by the twin oaks tomorrow."

Sancho took the list and passed it over to Pancho while he hitched up his Dickie work pants and secured the fly. Pancho studied the list. It produced a frown of confusion and a slight drooping of the mustache, but Pancho was not in the habit of asking questions when orders were given. The pair reminded Paco of Laurel and Hardy.

Paco pulled out his wallet. "Here's two thousand pesos. This should cover it. Tell me as soon as you have everything there and I'll give you further instructions.

"*Sí*, señor," Sancho and Pancho answered in unison and El Gordo and El Flaco left the library.

Paco wasn't through. "Maria, Mavi!" He was still scribbling.

"*Sí*, señor?" Maria said as she made her appearance in a huge white apron over a black dress and pink plastic sandals on her feet. Maria was sixty-something. There wasn't a gray strand in her black hair that framed a round face the color of terra cotta clay. She appeared to be made of down-filled sofa pillows carelessly arranged. Maria was in all probability the best cook in la Republica de Mexico. "Mavi is in the bathroom," she explained. "She'll be right in."

"*Sí*, señor?" Mavi said rushing into the room in answer to the summons that had caught her at an awkward moment.

Paco finished scribbling and handed the note to Maria. "I want you and Mavi to go into town tomorrow and get me everything on this list." He handed Maria a five hundred peso note. "You two know more about these things than I do. You think five hundred will cover it?"

Maria read the list carefully, and like Pancho, she furrowed her brow. There was, of course, no macho mustache to droop, but her full mouth sagged noticeably at the corners. "This is more than enough, señor, but..."

"But what, Maria?"

"But nothing, señor, it's just that..."

"Just that what?"

"Just that nothing, señor. We'll have everything here tomorrow afternoon."

"*Magnífico!*" Paco was pleased with his ingenious scheme. As soon as Maria and Mavi were out of the room he poured out two fingers of Chinaco *reposado* and grabbed the phone. He couldn't wait to tell Federico. "Hola, *compa!*"

"*Salud.*"

"How did you know I just poured out a sip?"

"I knew."

"It may be a few weeks before I see you, *compa.*"

"A new girl, a new disaster."

"No, no. I have a plan that's simply ingenious. You're not going to believe this." Paco told him of his new inspiration.

"*Ay* Paco!"

"What is it?"

"By the itching of my thumbs something *malo* this way comes."

"You can never stop quoting the classics, can you? No, *compa*, really, this is the best idea I ever had."

The master of Villa Hermosa was aware of a lot of whispered conversations among his domestic staff and his farmhands but it didn't bother him in the least. He knew exactly what he was doing, he knew it was right—and he knew it would work. The Epiphany of the Chinaco never fails! Early the following week he called them all together in his big library for another conference.

"I called you here together because you've all been with me for many years and I have complete *confianza* in every one of you," he began. "I have been commissioned by a large publishing house in Mexico City to write a book. To bring this endeavor to a successful end I must undertake an experimental project. It will be difficult for me, but I cannot do it without each of you doing your part."

"*Sí*, señor, what is it you need from us?" Maria asked.

"Maria, you will act as the señora of the house. And Mavi, you will continue to be Maria's niece. No aprons. If you see me on the grounds you are to ignore me." Paco looked into four blank faces. He knew they didn't know what he was talking about. But it didn't matter. An explanation would only confuse them further. His employees were unwavering sticklers about following orders and that was all he wanted of them "Now, Sancho and Pancho, until further notice you will be the *mayordomos*. You will give me work to do and address me as you would any hired hand. Does everybody understand their role?"

"*Sí*, señ—"

"Ah-ah-ah! The first one who calls me señor is fired. Understood?"

"*Sí*, señor!" Mavi threw both hands over her mouth.

This private conference precipitated a noticeable increase in the buzzing among the staff of Villa Hermosa. The very next day Sancho and Pancho pulled the big truck under the twin oaks as instructed and began to unload.

"What do you think El Patrón is going to do with all this stuff?" Sancho asked.

"You should know by now we don't ask questions," Pancho answered. "We just do what we're told. You heard him, it's all part of his project."

"What's a project?"

"About the book, *pendejo*!"

"His library is stuffed with books. Why does he need more—why not just go out and buy one?"

"Take the other end of this thing, *cabrón*, and stop asking questions."

A similar exchange was taking place in the villa. Maria and Mavi were in the master bedroom unpacking the things the master had ordered. "I think El Patrón is not right in the head," Maria confided. "It's all that tequila. He reminds me of his father. He too, had a few strings missing from his guitar. He kept carrier pigeons in his bedroom."

"Carrier pigeons! But why?" Mavi asked.

"He didn't trust the telephone and he was going to send all his messages by pigeon." Maria opened another carton. "The poor man didn't even know his own name when he died." She sketched the Holy Cross in the air.

"Do you really think El Patrón has cast a shoe?"

"It looks that way. Why would he send us to the *segunda* to buy all these old clothes. Look at these shirts! The collars are frayed, I'll have to sew buttons on most of them. And the pants! Even Sancho and Pancho wouldn't wear them."

"And the underwear!" Mavi cried. El Patrón has never worn anything but white Jockey *calzones*. Why would he want these atrocious *mata pasiones*?"

"They're called boxers."

"By any name you care to call them, they would still kill any woman's passion."

But Don Paco Mendez was neither concerned with his sanity or the poorly concealed rumbling among the servants. Doubt did not exist for him today. He took his place on a pleasant shady bench in the plaza near the rose garden. The curtain was going up for Act l! He felt perfect for the part in his rumpled clothes that had provided so much comfort and utility to other men before him. Maria had everything on his list neatly laid out, laundered and ironed. She was sure her master was displaying the early signs of his genetic mental illness when he had told her to wash everything again and throw the iron away. He pulled off a few buttons himself. The deformed sombrero, one of Pancho's discards, was a last-minute inspiration. He sipped black coffee from a plastic cup he bought at a stand. It wasn't the rich coffee from Chiapas Mavi served him every morning. In fact it was vile. But he wasn't here to enjoy himself.

He sipped the nasty stuff and watched the crowds go by. He came into this scheme with no preconceived requisites, no physiognomic conditions, no *sine qua non*. Paco delivered himself entirely to Fate. Doña Fortuna, always on the side of justice, would send the right girl to him; dark as a plum, plump as a goose, fair as porcelain, thin as a pin. Fate would make the choice. All he sought was a girl with an honest heart.

"*Bola! Bola!*"

The shoeshine man paused at his bench, assessed his torn and laceless work shoes, and passed him by.

"*Rosas... bellas rosas para la novia!*"

Long experience had taught the flower girl what kind of man buys roses for his *novia* and who doesn't. This man was an obvious stiff. She passed him by.

The offensive coffee finished, Paco sat holding the empty cup while he watched the human pageant in the plaza. A dignified old woman coiffed in gray walked past and dropped a coin in his cup. "*Dios lo acompañe*," she said, and continued on her way.

"*Gracias, gracias!*" Paco answered. This simple act of charity convinced Paco Mendez he was in character, his stage play would be a smash hit. And when the final curtain came down, the woman with an honest heart would be in his arms. He just had to give it time.

On the third day he sat on the same bench contemplating the mysteries of Life. Somewhere out there is the girl I am destined to fall in love with, the girl I will marry and live with happily ever after. Somewhere out there is a beautiful young woman for whom I am the answer to all her dreams and prayers. It is only a matter of mutual discovery.

Suddenly he leaped out of his bench with such a burst he frightened all the pigeons and they scattered in a clattering flight. "My God, there's an angel loose in the plaza!"

Indeed, the angel was walking across the far end of the plaza near city hall. She was dressed in a cream-colored summer frock covered with dainty little pink daisies with a matching belt. She carried a tiny white purse. Paco had to throw his arms around a huge tree for support as his heart leaped to his Adam's apple. The field of daisies was walking in his direction! She walked with a smooth, liquid rhythm, as though dancing to music that she alone could hear. Paco recognized the girl at once. It was Goya's "Nude Maja" that hung in his library, except this one had clothes on. The clothed Maja's face was pink as a seashell, her hair, a mass of waves and curls and ringlets of ebon silk. But the celestial apparition never made it as far as his bench. The field of daisies stepped across the plaza and entered Banco Serfin.

Paco followed.

The bank wasn't all that busy at this hour. The teller lines were short, the angel was fourth in line and Paco fell in behind her. He admired the life study in front of him while waiting his turn. She was holding a traveler's check. Obviously not a local, Paco thought. All the curls, waves, and ringlets were neatly arranged and lightly dancing on her shoulders. The thin summer dress caressed the gentle contours of the Maja's body right down to the hemline. The only mark on her smooth back was the little ridge of the hook and eye from the bra strap. He caught a whiff of fresh carnations.

"Señor Mendez!"

It was the effusive voice of Señor Romero the bank manager who, having experienced some difficulty recognizing his favored customer, was now rounding his desk and coming toward him at full throttle, teeth and gums bared in a gaping smile, cordial hand extended. Paco realized his ranchero image would be ruined in seconds if Señor Romero recognized him. He took his only option and fled Banco Serfin like a bank robber who'd just seen a flattering closeup of himself on the security video in full color.

Paco had to get back to see a man about a cattle deal but he was back at his post the following day.

"*Bola! Bola!*"

"*Sombreros!...sombreros de palma...*"

The shoeshine man ignored him as before, the old man selling hats did not view Paco as a hot prospect for a finely crafted palm leaf sombrero imported from Yucatan. Big Nalgas Machado, Tecate's fattest cop, passed his bench too busy stuffing a *churro* in his face to make recognition and waddled into the municipal offices.

Doña Fortuna was on the job today.

Stepping into frame from behind the *kiosko*, the mystery girl strolled languidly toward his bench in a white cotton skirt and an orange blouse worn on the outside. She reminded him of two scoops of ice cream, vanilla on the bottom, orange sherbet on top. Paco got up and ambled along with full intentions of following her until an acceptable means of getting acquainted presented itself. She led him around the bronze Benito Juarez, past the Sno-Cone cart, once around the fountain, then disappeared into the Centro de Cultura art gallery.

Paco was already on his way to follow her inside. They could share their views on light and color and composition while assessing Adame's new *Divas* collection, exchange their names, invite her to coffee, propose to her, and whisk her off to Rome to be married on the Spanish Steps.

Perfect!

Nearly at the door Paco skidded to a stop. He couldn't follow her in there. Maestro Brambila would recognize him at once, embrace him warmly and invite him to a glass of wine. His whole plan depended on being nobody. Paco retreated to a bench where he could watch the door. He sat there for nearly forty minutes before the two scoops of ice cream came out. She was smiling.

Her next stop was the *panaderia*. He'd never been in there so recognition would not be a problem. He would simply buy something while he made his observations and watch for opportunity. It could begin with a casual remark over the merits of strawberry tarts as opposed to cream-filled puff pastries. Then, if the thing got off to a good start, he could casually suggest marriage. He gave her a full minute head start then stepped inside.

It was hot in the small bake shop and smelled deliciously of yeast and fresh bread and cinnamon. There were half dozen people in the shop so he wouldn't be noticeable. There he found her with tray and tongs, browsing the long racks of *pan dulce* shaped into braids and twists and hearts sprinkled with pink and yellow sugar, gingerbread boys and gingerbread girls and gingerbread pigs. Paco took a tray and a pair of tongs, contemplated the French rolls, and watched. She was having difficulty making a choice. Her tongs gripped a palm leaf glistening with yellow sugar, then released it in favor of a chocolate cupcake covered with colored sprinkles. Almost at once a tart filled with pineapple preserve caught her attention. She abandoned the chocolate cupcake with colored sprinkles, gently put the fragile pineapple tart on her tray, and went to the counter to pay for her purchase.

Ahead of her was a young grade school girl in a Padre Kino uniform, maroon blouse and skirt with white knee socks. She had a giant cream horn on her tray.

"*Cinco pesos*," the woman behind the counter said, and counted the coins the girl put on the counter. "You only have *cuatro pesos* here, dear, would you like to take something else?"

The little girl's face crumpled like a paper napkin.

"Oh, here, I have an extra peso." It was Miss Two Scoops of Ice Cream! Her voice was sweet and warm as the air in the bake shop. She dug into her tiny white purse, put the extra coin on the counter, then paid for her pineapple tart.

"*Muchas gracias!*" The little school girl gushed and ravaged the cream horn.

The beautiful benefactor patted her cheek affectionately, gave her a rainbow smile, and left the shop nibbling her pineapple tart.

By the time Paco took his tray to the counter with a French roll he didn't want and couldn't return, and left the shop, there was no trace of the vanilla and orange confection. He walked several blocks in all directions. Not a trace. She was not a local girl, Paco remembered, and felt a heavy weight in his heart when he realized she could leave Tecate anytime and out of his life forever.

The following day Paco resumed his post with renewed optimism and faith, determined that nothing would stop him from making her acquaintance. Nothing! He recognized her the moment she rounded the rose garden. It was an effort not to run up to her, fold her into his arms, and confess love everlasting. She was dressed in tan chinos and a hot pink T-shirt. White pumps matched her tiny white purse, a plastic shopping bag hung over her arm. Authentically costumed for his present role, Paco knew he couldn't very well pop up off his bench when she walked by and shout, "*Hola!* Let's you and I get acquainted. We may be two hearts each searching for its other half. Our search is over!"

It is well known in Tecate that Fate spends a lot of her time in the plaza arranging people's lives for better or for worse. Doña Fortuna was right on cue. The grocery bag ripped and its entire contents scattered on the ground. Goya's Clothed Maja looked as though she was going to cry. Paco Mendez recognized opportunity. In less time than it takes to tell it, he was on the ground gathering everything up. He handed her two bright red Jonathon apples with a serious dent, four navel oranges that had rolled under a bench, three unscathed bananas, a little tube of some mysterious ointment from the pharmacy, and the unmistakable box of Ella, *servilletas femeninas.*

"*Gracias,*" she said breathlessly and blushed a deeper pink than the seashell mentioned earlier.

"Wait here. I'll run over to the shop across the plaza and get another bag. "

"*Ay, gracias!*"

In only minutes he was back and together they put everything in the new plastic bag. A caballero down to his toes, Paco Mendez found something of extraordinary interest in the sky to study with the intensity of a dedicated astronomer, while the young woman stuffed her intimate purchases from the pharmacy into the bottom of the bag.

"*Gracias,*" she repeated.

"I'm glad I was here to help. Paco Mendez, your *servidor.*"

"Lydia Lucero," she sang. "*Mucho gusto.*" They shook hands.

"*Lucero!* Yes, it makes sense, the heavenly light of the bright evening star." Lydia blushed like the evening star. "You have been through a terrible ordeal, Lydia. All your apples, oranges, bananas, and your—your—look, refreshment is available just across the plaza. Shall we go?"

They shared a small table for two under a red and white umbrella on the sidewalk in front of La Flor de Michoacan ice cream parlor. And thus the process of acquaintance began. Their first discovery of importance was that they were both mad for mango sherbet.

"You must be recent to Tecate."

"Yes, I only arrived a few days ago from Guadalajara."

"And what brought you to Tecate?"

"I'm twenty-eight and I feel I have never experienced life so I left my job as private secretary to the president of a major insurance company, and came here to put myself in the hands of Fate and let Doña Fortuna make all the decisions." She did not go on to say that she was totally disillusioned with the men she knew back home trying to make a statement with their designer clothes, their

Rolex, the flashy cars, their expensive macho cologne—all liars, hypocrites, cads, scoundrels, and unfaithful *sin vergüenzas*! A man must be measured from the inside, she told herself. All the men my age are either married or career adolescents. Maybe the kind of man I want no longer exists except in fairy tales.

"All alone, you're not staying with family?"

"This mango sherbet is incredible! All alone. I'm renting a room. There's no kitchen so I have to eat out. It gets expensive." Lydia pointed her spoon at him. "And you?"

"Native of Tecate," he said with obvious pride. "I work at Villa Hermosa, an old hacienda not far from here."

Lydia looked across the table at this handsome older man. He had that look of an honest man who worked close to the soil, hand in hand with Nature. She didn't know what kind of car he drove, but she could bet her package of Ella it wasn't a BMW. His clothes were hardly more than faded remnants, and if they made a statement at all, it was of sweat and toil in the fields. No Rolex, he didn't even wear a watch, and no cologne. The pleasant man in front of her smelled of the earth and fresh air. He had honest hands. Honest hands, honest heart, she thought. She admired his dark mild eyes, his innocent demeanor, and his gallantry.

Paco wanted to devote his entire day to the girl licking the last of the mango sherbet from the spoon, but he summoned his inner strength and forced himself back into character. "Well, I suppose I must get back to work or El Patrón will flail me with his leather belt."

"Oh, no!"

"With steel studs. My *mayordomo* is mean as a centipede with bunions."

They came to their feet and stood facing each other for a poignant moment. Paco wanted to smother her with kisses and invite her to a weekend in Paris. Lydia wanted to throw her arms around him and keep him there forever. Neither surrendered to their feelings.

"*Gracias*, Paco. You're the first friend I've made since my arrival," Lydia said with arms slightly apart as though prepared to be embraced.

Paco put his arms around her as though she were his sister. "It has been a joy to know you, Lydia Lucero, light of the evening star. Could we meet here again tomorrow?"

"I would love it!"

And, as mandated by Doña Fortuna, a beautiful friendship blossomed. They met every day on the same wrought-iron bench near the singing fountain and spoke in soft murmurs like the colored pigeons cooing and crooning at their feet. They strolled the plaza joined by the hands, and learned about each other. Paco wanted to crush her in his arms and kiss that beautiful laughing mouth but opportunity had not presented itself. Paco also wanted to whisk her off to La Fonda for a margarita followed by an elaborate dinner while mariachis played love songs around their table but, as we've seen, Paco was a disciplined man and remembered he was but an actor on the stage and could not allow his heart to make decisions for him. He mastered the impulse and escorted her instead to Tacos Los Amigos for tacos *de carne asada* smothered in guacamole sauce. They always ended up at the little sidewalk table at the Flor de Michoacan for a mango sherbet.

In a matter of a few days friendship ripened into true, but unspoken love. Paco was now sure he had found the love of his life, the woman he would spend the rest of his life loving, the mother of his children. Lydia looked at him and saw a man needful of love and understanding and all her maternal instincts, so strong in Mexican girls, unfurled like a rose in June.

By the first of the following week Doña Fortuna cast a dark shadow across Paco and Lydia. The roses in the plaza lost their perfume, the love song of the fountain became a dirge in A minor. Lydia was on the point of tears. "What is it, *mi amor*?" Paco asked, now dropping endearments like confetti at a fiesta. "Don't cry. Tell me all about it."

"I've only been here two weeks, I've met the love of my life and now I must lose you."

Paco's heart filled with joy. He wanted to celebrate, to shout *olé*. He was about to break the record presently held by the Tecate

Athletic League for the vertical high jump from a wrought iron bench, but he restrained himself just in time.

"Lose me? Lose me to what?" Gently, he wiped the tears from her face.

"I've run through my money. I have to go back to Guadalajara."

"Lydia, *mi amor, mi corazón*, I've only known you a little more than a week and I know I could never live without you. If you leave me I'll be dead by morning."

Lydia pressed her hand to his lips. "You mustn't say that. I love you, *corazón*. We have to be brave." Paco kissed her fingers. "I'll go back to my job and as soon as I put enough money together I'll be back in your arms."

"I have a better idea."

"You do?"

This is the moment, Paco said to himself, the curtain rings down on Act 1!

"I have a small house on the hacienda. It isn't much but you could come stay there." Paco instantly perceived a hemidemisemiquaver of hesitation appear on Lydia's face. "Oh! It isn't what you think. No, no! You'll have your own accommodations. Everything will be quite proper."

"Somehow, I have a feeling I can trust you." Lydia touched his arm. "I'll just go up to my room and get my things. I only brought one suitcase."

They gathered her few belongings and walked a couple of blocks to where Paco had left the car. One look at the car and Lydia knew that here was a man who was so self-contained he needed no affectations, no false image to cover his insecurities. Back in the year of its birth, circa 1989, it had been cheery yellow Volkswagen Rabbit with russet brown upholstery. But time was hard on the Rabbit. With the exception of the green hood that replaced the original after a fight with a Chevy pickup, the paint was worn past the primer, down to the bare metal and the Rabbit looked like it had a bad case of myxomatosis, so common to the species. The driver's door was crushed in owing to a confrontation with a utility pole and was now non-functional. An old Nike sock served as a gas cap. Anticipating the need for the perfect prop, Paco had found the car in a junkyard near the U.S. border. He bought it on the spot for cash. Seventy-five, American. He brought Lydia around to the passenger side, put his hand in where there used to be a window and opened the door from the inside. Always the caballero, he excused himself for preceding her.

The brown plastic upholstery never received the benediction of sun screen lotion with an adequate SPF rating to protect against UV damage and help prevent premature aging. The seats were stiff and cracked. It was like sitting on Fritos corn chips. But the little Rabbit had the zippy spirit of the genus *lepus californicus*. One turn of the key and it scampered away through town and into the countryside.

"That oak forest on your left is the entrance to the convent of Santa Brigida and up ahead on your right are the vineyards that Father Ruben looks after." Paco realized it was hard for her to see all the sights properly through the cracked spider web that spread over most of the windshield. The look on Lydia's face told him he had cast the right car for the part.

In only a few minutes they pulled up to a pair of enormous twelve-foot double gates flanked by a high brick wall and topped with gleaming brass lanterns. The wrought iron lettering across the archway read, VILLA HERMOSA. Paco heard Lydia's little gasp of awe when they drove through the imposing entrance and took the lower road. Paco was pleased.

Curtain going up on Act II!

"Here we are!" he announced with pride as they pulled up in front of the set. He helped Lydia put her shoulder to the door. It opened on the second push and they stood in a little meadow bathed in sunshine and birdsong. "*Estas en tu casa,*" he said with a wave of the hand.

Paco looked into Lydia's face for any sign she might suddenly decide to sprint the twelve kilometers back to town. "I told you it wasn't much, but it's home, and it's yours as long as you want it."

Lydia lost the ability to form words.

There, under the soothing shade of stately twin oaks stood a trashy little slum-shanty slapped together with old wooden pallets and corrugated sheet metal. The windows were framed with old tomato crates and had neither glass nor screens. A sheet of buckled fiberboard claimed to be the front door. There was no peephole, but there was a dark hole with a rope hanging out where you would reasonably expect to find a doorknob. Paco watched horrified as a squirrel leaped out. A black sheet metal stovepipe stuck out from the wall forming a Times Roman upper case L. The roof was an architectural inspiration. A bright blue plastic tarp held down with heavy rocks provided shelter from hostile elements. Red and yellow Honda Civic hoods, crumpled and creased and veined with orange rust, added bold color and texture to the structure providing an authentic image of an honorable man living in honest penury. A bunch of old tires stacked three-high formed a ring to make a raised planter for a few geraniums and sunflowers, tomatoes and some yellow squash. The only patio furniture was the front seat of an old Ford station wagon placed near the front door. This would never make *Better Homes and Gardens*, Paco thought, but as set designers Sancho and Pancho are beyond praise!

Inside, the humble abode proved to be even less imposing than the exterior. It was but a single room with a mattress on the floor, a small table, two perilous wooden chairs, and a cast-iron potbelly stove. A galvanized steel tub served as the kitchen sink. Paco nearly leaped into Lydia's arms when he saw a big black cockroach skittering its way across the floor in the direction of his foot. A white porcelain bathtub was conveniently placed just outside the back door and only a few short steps to the outhouse. Truth be told, Paco was more horrified than Lydia. He'd never stepped inside the wretched shack since it was slapped together by Sancho and Pancho and the thought of spending a single night in here made him shudder. *I can't do it!* he wailed in silence. *I just can't do it!*

Lydia, however, was endowed with the high spirits of adventure so common to the young. She took both his hands into her own.

"*Mi amor*, what do we care if it's a modest little dwelling? It's our cozy little nest and as long as we're together I'll be happy!"

Maybe I've gone too far with the charade, Paco thought. Should I confess the whole thing? No! Too soon. But standing so close to each other it was a natural thing that they would fall into each others arms. The kiss was long, wet and passionate, and would have lasted until dinner time had it not been for the sudden banging on the door.

"Hey, *cabrón*! Are you going to hoe the corn today or are you going to take a holiday?"

It was Sancho! Why of all the ner— Paco stopped himself before he could tell his fat, insolent hired hand to pack up, pick up his check, and leave. But his fat, insolent hired hand had already left. "Coming, *patrón*," he called out, remembering this was theater and turned to face the love of his life. "*Mi amor*, I must go back to work but I'll be back this evening."

"And I'll have your dinner waiting for you, my love." Lydia threw him a noisy kiss and watched him head across the meadow with a hoe slung over his shoulder.

Paco surveyed the vast field of tasseling corn. He counted forty rows, each thirty meters long, or if you prefer, a hundred feet. It was his intention to a hoe a couple of rows to give verisimilitude to the play he himself wrote and directed just in case Lydia decided to take a walk and find him idle, then slip into the barn for the afternoon. But he was in no condition for this kind of work and the moment he thought it was safe, slipped into the barn. It was shady here, cool, and with a wistful melancholy he began to dream of all the creature comforts available to him up in the villa, a hot shower, real food, good wine.

His spirits soared when he saw Pancho coming up the road. Paco wanted to throw his arms around him. He would send up him to Maria with instructions to come back with a tender chicken a la provençal and a chilled bottle of Corona to hold body and soul together until he returned to that wretched hovel under the twin oaks.

But Pancho saw him first and beat him to the draw. "*Oralé cabrón*! Is this how you intend to do your work when you're not being watched? Get your *nalgas* out there and start hoeing!"

The scathing words Paco was preparing to throw at this impertinent man died before they could burn the air. It wouldn't be fair, Paco realized. I wrote the script, after all, he's only reading his lines. Defeated by his own hand, Paco threw the hoe over his shoulder and headed for the field without a word.

That evening Paco came limping down the road toward his new home with a weary trudge that would have convinced the most demanding director in Hollywood. There isn't a part of me that doesn't hurt, he whimpered in silence, God, even my *nalgas* hurt! And I'm famished!

Smoke was curling out from the Times Roman upper case L and he smelled—beans!

Lydia met him at the door with a warm kiss. "Dinner is ready!" she announced proudly and returned to the potbelly stove where she began to stir the clay pots. "It's only beans and squash and tortillas, *corazón*. That was all I could find in here but who cares? For two people in love it's a banquet!"

Paco saw the dinner and took a different view. His feet hurt, his hands were blistered, his back was killing him. All he wanted now was to sink into his big leather chair in his library, pour himself two fingers of Chinaco *reposado* and listen to Bruckner while Maria prepared a succulent pork roast with black cherry sauce, a warm baguette, and a nice Cabernet. A full confession was about to roll off his tongue when that sweet voice spoke.

"Dinner time, *mi cielo!*"

They sat at the wobbly little table on splintered chairs that nipped your *nalgas* if you weren't careful how you sat. "What an alchemist you are, *mi amor*, I have never tasted anything so good!" Paco possessed a noble soul.

"Hunger is the best salsa, *mi amor*, and it's fun to cook for a man who appreciates good food."

"But you mustn't work too hard."

"Oh, I don't mind going to the well to draw water and carry it in here to wash the dishes. I'll haul enough water tomorrow to do the laundry in the bathtub. More beans, *mi amor?*"

Dinner over, Lydia sent him outside. "Now you go sit out front and relax while I wash up. I'll be out to join you in a minute and together we can watch the sunset!"

Paco was glad to get out of the shack. He sat on the car seat and asked himself how much more of this could he take? And this was only day one! Presently, Lydia joined him with a cup of hot chocolate made with water. They watched the sun go down in flames and when the insects got too agressive they decided to go inside. Paco lit some candles and they enjoyed each other's company until Paco yawned. That was a lot of corn to hoe, he thought, I think I'm ready for bed.

"You've put in a hard day," he said to Lydia. "You take the mattress."

"And where will you sleep, *mi cielo*?"

"I'll camp outside under the stars."

"I can't let you do that—I'm driving you out of your own house!"

"Oh, I do it all the time. I'm a ranchero!"

"And I'm afraid to be all alone."

"Afraid?"

"La Llorona, you know."

"You mustn't let that silly legend of La Llorona frighten you. The old hag rises out of the arroyo every night screaming and wailing, but you're quite safe in here."

"Please stay."

"Okay, I'll sleep right here on the floor next to you."

Paco turned his face to the wall while Lydia undressed and slipped into a skimpy T-shirt. They kissed goodnight, he blew out the candle, and tried to make himself comfortable on two blankets spread out on the plywood floor, trying not to think of the whereabouts of the big black cockroach. It was quiet. The only sound in the room was the beating of two hearts in love and the whining of a mosquito. I'll be dead in the morning, he thought.

But the next morning Paco knew he wasn't dead. A Zapatista terrorist pounding on the door startled them awake before dawn. Lydia gave him a breakfast of eggs and kisses and watched him head for the fields with a hoe over his shoulder.

The days went by slowly and painfully for Paco, but as we've come to know him better, we can see he was made of good clay, and Paco endured the living hell for several days. Like all couples who play house, Paco and Lydia fell into a routine. Every afternoon when no one was about, Lydia drew water from the well, heated it on the iron stove, and poured it in the outdoor bathtub for her bath. She prepared the tub for Paco every day when he got home from the fields and with respect for his privacy kept herself busy in the house.

One afternoon Lydia met Paco at the door as he stumbled home sore and achy. "You poor thing! I just finished filling the tub with hot water. Go soak away the aches and pains. I'll give you a back rub when you come out."

Paco did as he was told and came in wearing the atrocious *mata pasiones* boxer underwear that had provided the servants with so much mirth and laughter earlier in the week. He was too tired to care.

"Lie down on the mattress, *mi cielo*, I'm heating up some ointment."

Paco collapsed on the mattress and moaned while Lydia rubbed away all the aches and pains. She started at his neck and shoulders where the muscles were knotted like shoelaces, worked over the dorsal area, then slowly worked her way down to the lower lumbar region. She pulled his boxers down a few inches and kneaded his lower back. Paco lay still enjoying the relief. Her hands felt nice, too nice, and now he was feeling good all over. He was thankful he was lying in a prone position.

"Finished!" she slapped his *nalgas*. "Better?"

"Oh yes! All the aches and pains have disappeared."

"Tonight you get the mattress."

"Oh no," he protested.

"I insist on it! You work hard in the fields all day. You can't come home and sleep on a hard wooden floor. I won't allow it!"

"But then *you'll* be sleeping on the hard wooden floor."

"No, I won't."

The next morning Lydia was up while Paco played dead. It was still dark outside and even darker in the shack. The smell of hot chocolate lured Paco out of an erotic dream he was reluctant to leave. He cracked his eyes and in the faint glow of the stove saw Lydia, still in her sleep shirt, stoking the fire. Hot coals cast a rosy light over her sleepy face, soft as antique satin, her dark hair artfully disarranged from sleep. Paco watched her with melting heart as she poured two cups of chocolate. She was humming a little tune. Paco closed his eyes and and tried to retrieve the dream. Minutes later he felt a warm kiss on his cheek.

"*Buenos dias*," she sang softly in the dark, put a chipped cup of chocolate in his waiting hands and slipped in beside him on the mattress. Paco smiled his thanks and put a feathery kiss on her mouth. "I'll have your breakfast ready by the time you wash up."

"All right, *cabrón*, the cows are out! Get them back in and fix the fence. You're not on vacation, you know!" It was the Zapatista.

This has to end soon, Paco thought. Lydia served him a quesadilla and a kiss for breakfast and he headed for the fields. At the pasture he found a break in the barbed wire fence and some ten or twelve cows of various colors and personalities happily grazing in the beans. First, the fence.

Back in the barn he found what was needed. The posts were the size of railroad ties, heavy, and much too long to carry. He wrapped his arms around one and dragged it back as thought it were his Cross. With pick, shovel, and steel digging bar, Paco replaced the rotted post. He returned to the barn and came back with a short roll of heavy gauge barbed wire. As he pulled each strand tight the wire seemed determined to assume its original configuration and coiled painfully around his head. When he had it all done he was left with several splinters embedded in the soft flesh of his hands, and bleeding stigmata on arms and face. It put him in mind of the events at Calvary he'd read about in the Scriptures. Now to get the cows back in.

Paco swung the gate open wide and looked at the problem. It was a simple matter of walking them back through the opening. He'd seen Sancho and Pancho do it any number of times without even breaking a sweat. This was not high science. What Paco didn't understand from lack of practical experience was that bovines, as a species, are *non compos mentis* and most are demented or deranged or both. Paco approached the group. They were monstrous beasts averaging a half ton apiece, black and white Holsteins, black Angus, a couple short horns, and a giant Hereford. The cows stopped their feeding and stared back at him with malevolent eyes, shaking their enormous horns, like a street gang guarding its territory. The leader seemed to be the sullen red Hereford the size of a C & NW freight car. One of the gang members let out a warning moo much like the lowest B flat on a bassoon. Paco took it as a racial slur. But he held his ground. With arms outstretched like he'd seen Sancho and Pancho do, he got behind the group and walked toward them. The cows turned and plodded along in front of him without enthusiasm. Piece of cake, Paco thought. He had them nearly to the open gate when a half dozen veered off to the right and another five made a similar maneuver to the left.

I'll deal with each group individually, Paco thought. He took his position behind the ones nearest the gate and started the slow march. The animals moved along until they reached the opening. They stopped. Now they turned to face him with big dangerous eyes. There came a couple more of those threatening B flat moos. It was a tense moment. A sudden "hayaa!" and they loped in. Highly pleased with himself, Paco went after the others who by this time were back grazing in the beans.

With a stick in one hand, his hat in the other, Paco got behind the group and slowly, calmly began to walk them out of the beans and toward the open gate. Of all God's creatures great and small, cows are the dumbest of them all. To begin with, their proportions are all wrong. Four stomachs to one brain and they're not noted for taking directions. You'll never see a cow performing at a circus. Just as the first beast, the big red Hereford with an attitude, was about to enter, she wheeled around and they all scattered in every direction. They reconvened in the beans.

But Paco persevered. Employing the same technique of stick and hat, once again he got them as far as the gate only to have them scramble and return to the beans. He felt like Sisyphus must have felt when the heavy boulder came rolling down the hill and he had to start over.

On the sixty-fourth try he finally succeeded in getting the first cow to go through the gate. The rest followed peaceably. All but a playful Angus calf that suddenly decided she was having more fun in the beans. She did a quick one hundred and eighty degree turn and flattened Paco. Lying there in a squishy blanket of fresh pasture pies he thought of Federico's classical quotation and lost his patience. "All right Ovido, my flesh is torn, my bones are bruised, and I'm covered in cow shit. Am I poor enough, *cabrón*?"

That evening Lydia could smell him several minutes before he arrived. *"Dios mio!* You look like you tangled with a jaguar!"

"There were ten of them."

"What happened to you?"

"You don't want to know."

"Get out of your clothes."

"Here?"

"Here!"

"But — "

"This is no time to be shy." Lydia stripped him bare, washed him down with a bucket, helped him into the bathtub, and handed him one of her scented soaps. Paco felt there was little left of his dignity but he had no other choice. "I'm afraid your clothes will have to be burned. You'll never be able to wear them again."

"That is the best piece of news I've heard in a week. The answer to my daily prayer." He came out smelling better than when he went in. Lydia gently patted him dry with a towel and led him inside. Paco put on his *mata pasiones* underwear, sat on a chair, and leaped into the air. "That chair just bit me on the *nalgas!*"

"I'm sorry, *mi cielo*." She draped the chair with a towel. "There."

Paco relaxed and submitted peacefully until he saw something in her hand. "What's that?"

"Ay! It's simply a tube of arnica first aid cream."

"The one I saw fall out of your grocery bag?"

"No, that was something else. Now, stop asking questions and behave."

He watched Lydia take a pair of her white cotton *calzones* and tenderly clean the angry gashes that were still oozing blood from arms and face. "I hope that's not your last pair."

"Hush!"

Paco relaxed and allowed her to attend to all his wounds. He was beginning to like it.

They had an early dinner and went straight to bed. Early the next morning Lydia was teasing him with a cup of chocolate under his nose.

"Feeling better, *corazón*?"

"All restored. What are you going to do today, *mi cielo*?"

"I thought I'd clean house, bring a few buckets of water up from the well and do the laundry. I can heat it on the stove. Then, I want to gather some sweet potatoes and make you *empanadas*."

Paco didn't have to hear any more, see any more, or think any more. At last my search is ended. She loves *me*! I'll have the joy of a woman in the house, a faithful *compañera* at my side in times of onions and times of sweet cakes. His eyes welled up and Paco knew. He *knew*! He put down his cup, gently put his arms around her, drew her tight to his chest and crushed her mouth with his. "Lydia, *mi amor, mi corazón, mi cielo, la luz de mi vida*, there's something I have to tell you this morn—"

This tender moment was interrupted by the return of the Zapatista terrorist tearing the door down. "Hey, *cabrón*! Where do you think you are, at some resort? Get your *nalgas* out here! The cows need milking, the melons need picking, and the corn needs hoeing!"

"Then milk the cows, pick the melons and shove the hoe—"

"Sssh!" Lydia's hand covered his mouth before he could finish expressing the idea in fuller detail. "You'll get fired—then where can we go, what can we do?" A little baby tear appeared in the corner of her right eye.

With gentle hand Paco wiped away the tear. "We're sleeping late this morning."

"We can't! You have to go to work, I have to do laundry and —"

Paco cut her sentence short with a kiss. "You won't be cleaning house today, or lugging water in buckets up from the well, or doing laundry."

"But —"

"Let's get dressed."

Paco washed up and shaved outdoors and got into his shabby work clothes. Lydia pulled on a pair of blue jeans with a few soot smudges and a clean but rumpled white shirt. "I must do laundry today, we're out of clean clothes. Your *patrón* will probably kick us out today. But I want you to know it doesn't matter to me. I'll go anywhere, do anything, as long as I have you to love."

Now it was Lydia's turn to wipe away a tear trickling down Paco's cheek. He put out his arms. "Come here."

They held tight for a few minutes and Paco led her outside. "I'm taking you for a walk."

"A walk! When we've lost everything we have?"

"There's something I want you to know." Paco took her hand and led her away.

Hand in hand, like two sweethearts without a care in the world, they ambled along the road. It was nearly June and they walked among wild flowers, paintbrush, lupin, baby blue eyes, and poppies all showing their pretty faces of yellow, red, orange, and blue. Finches trilled a happy little tune, quail peeped and fluttered, gold-breasted tanagers sang to them from the branches of the highest trees, colored butterflies flitted across their path.

As they came around the bend Lydia froze where she stood. "Look at that! My God, we're at the Gates of Heaven!"

Rising from a gentle knoll in front of them was Prince Charming's castle from the pages of a fairy tale. It was guarded on all sides by a regiment of tall Italian cypress. Villa Hermosa looked like a huge vanilla cream cake decorated with graceful arches, fluted columns and finials. There was no tower but the crenellated parapet could easily shield any number of archers shooting flaming arrows and pouring boiling oil on hostile invaders. The only thing missing was the drawbridge and a moat infested with ravenous alligators.

"We'd better turn back," she said with a little panic in her voice, but Paco held her hand in his and continued toward the villa as though he hadn't heard. "Paco, Paco, my love, *please*, let's start back. We don't belong here!" Paco didn't answer. He tightened his grip on Lydia's hand and continued toward his objective. They were nearly at the massive double doors, deeply carved with swirls and scrolls and cherubs. "Surely, you don't intend to ring the bell! You'll say something you shouldn't and they'll throw us out on the street. Darling, *please*, we can't go in there dressed like this! Oh, my darling Paco, that mean and overbearing *mayordomo* has driven you mad. Let's pack our things and leave!"

Paco scooped her up, kicked the front door open, and stomped into the foyer with his prize in his arms. Lydia screamed. When they reached the *estancia* he put her down and kissed her.

"Welcome to your home."

Lydia was sure than man she loved was insane. She was mortified when she saw a large formidable-looking señora all in black with a young girl at her side, enter the *estancia* and stare at them in cold silence. "Oh, señora, please forgive him. Paco is just a little—"

"Master!" cried Maria.

"Master!" cried Mavi.

"Master?" inquired Lydia.

"Meet your new mistress," Paco announced to his domestic staff. Lydia stood numb. "Now, we're famished for real food. Maria, bring us a huge mushroom omelet with plenty of Gruyere, a big basket of warm French rolls. Mavi, go to the cellar and bring up a bottle of champagne."

"*Sí*, señor!"

"*Sí*, señor!"

"We'll be in the rose garden."

"*Sí*, señor!"

"*Sí*, señor!"

Paco put his arm around Lydia's waist and walked her through the courtyard and stepped into the rose garden. There he found

Sancho and Pancho with rakes and trash bags grooming the rose beds. Good, he thought, it saves me the trouble of sending for them. But before he could open his mouth Sancho and Pancho dropped what they were doing and stood as though rooted to the ground. Lydia took one look at El Gordo and El Flaco and drew herself closer to Paco.

Sancho was the first to come to life. "Hey, *cabrón*, who do you think you are, sauntering in here, Maximiliano and Carlota?" he cried. "You didn't do a very good job on the fence. The cows are in the corn."

"The project is finished, Sancho," Paco explained in a calm even voice.

"Finished! Go look at that fence. And get those cows out of the corn!"

Pancho stepped up beside his coworker, then elbowed him sharply in the vicinity of his spleen. "Sancho, the master just said the project is over. Just say *sí* señor."

"Are you crazy? I don't want to get fired!"

"Say, '*Sí*, señor,' *pendejo*!"

A dim light came on in the dark bone enclosure of Sancho's brain. "*Sí*, señor," he answered but he wasn't taking chances with a *patrón* who was probably losing his stirrups. "Please don't fire me, I was only obeying orders." He removed his sombrero.

Paco smiled at the pair. "No one is getting fired, you both proved you can be trusted with a difficult assignment." Sancho and Pancho looked relieved. "Everything is back the way it was. This is your new mistress."

"Doña," they answered in unison, sombreros held respectfully over the heart. Lydia offered them a fragile smile which was all she could summon under the circumstances.

While Sancho was making a slow recovery Pancho had a question. "What do you want us to do with the shack?"

"Burn it to the ground!"

"*Sí*, señor!"

"Then haul away the ashes. Don't leave anything behind—not even a nail."

"*Sí,* señor!"

"I never want to see it again. I want it to disappear without a trace. Understood?"

"*Sí,* señor!" They turned to go.

"Oh, darling." These were the first words spoken by the new mistress of the estate. "Please, Paco. You mustn't destroy it. That little house is so full of beautiful memories for me. That little shanty is where I discovered an honest man, where I fell in love with you, where we, uh, uh, for the first time..."

Paco drew her into his arms. "Of course, *mi cielo*," he reassured. "Villa Hermosa is your realm to govern with your infinite wisdom." He turned to Sancho and Pancho. "I want that miserable little shack preserved, every plank, every nail—every rat and cockroach! It shall stand forever as a monument to everlasting love!"

Mavi padded into the garden soundless as a bunny. "Your breakfast is served in the courtyard, señor."

Paco escorted the new mistress to a table under a grapevine. The mushroom omelet was pure perfection, the French rolls were warm from the oven, and the champagne properly chilled.

And the chairs didn't bite.

"Is everything all right, señor?" Maria asked.

"Everything is perfect, Maria. Call my travel agent and tell him to book a flight to Rome."

"*Sí,* señor!"

"Rome!" exclaimed Lydia.

"We're getting married there—unless, of course, you would prefer Venice. Venice is exquisite in June."

"Rome! Venice! Married! I don't have any clothes."

"Maria, tell the travel agent to schedule a stopover in Paris."

"*Sí,* señor!"

"Paris!"

"We'll pick up some clothes for you there and continue on to Venice. Oh, *mi corazán*, I love you, I love you, I love you. I never want to be without you!"

"I love you too, *mi amor.*"

"I know you do." Paco went around to her chair, lifted her like a ballerina and spun her around the courtyard. "Poverty has made me rich!"

The very next day Paco and Federico were once again seated in the courtyard at Villa Hermosa taking the sacrament of tequila, lemon, and salt. The chubby vessel of Chinaco *reposado* sat between them.

"*Salud.*"

"*Salud.* I'm so glad you're here, *compa*, I've met the most wonderful girl in the world and I wanted you to meet her before we leave for Paris to get married."

"*Felicidades*, Paco, no one deserves it more."

"The only thing that could make me happier is if you could come along with us."

"On the honeymoon?"

"No, no! As official witness, best friend, and best man. I'll put you on a plane back to Mexico as soon as we say 'I do.'"

"I would be happy to go with the two of you."

"*Magnífico! Salud.*"

"*Salud*," answered Federico who couldn't take his eyes off the bloody scabs all over Paco's arms and face. "*Dios mío!* What happened to you?"

"God alone knows the pain, the deprivation, the suffering I've endured. But at last, I've found the girl with an honest heart who loves *me*, Paco, the man!"

"Remarkable."

"You won't believe it! This heavenly creature is the Graces all rolled into one — beauty, charm, poetry, music, art — she's perfect!"

"And when do I get to meet this heavenly creature so full of charm and beauty and grace?

"Any minute. She's taking a shower." Paco refilled their glasses.

A door opened at that moment and Lydia bounced into the courtyard barefoot, hair wet, looking very much like a frozen dessert in butterscotch jeans and a chocolate brown cotton shirt covered with big swirls of whipped cream. She ran the full length of the courtyard, flew into Federico's arms, and kissed him.

"Uncle Rico!"

"Uncle Rico?" Paco looked startled.

Federico held her tight. "Well, little one, I'm glad to see everything worked out as planned."

"I'm sorry I was so skeptical. All you said was you wanted me to meet a poor man of the soil with an honest heart. You didn't tell me the rest of it."

"Would someone explain it all to me?"

"It's like this, *compa*, Lydia has been dreaming of marrying a prince since she was ten. When you told me your absurd plan to turn yourself into the celebrated frog of fable, I knew you would only get yourself into more trouble. So I made a plan of my own and sent for my niece in Guadalajara."

"So!" cried Paco. "I am the victim of a dark conspiracy."

"And I made love to a frog!" Lydia charged. "You deliberately misled me!"

"But you got your prince," Federico answered.

Lydia left him and ran to cuddle up with Paco. "But I forgive you, Uncle Rico, I'm the happiest girl in the world!"

Federico picked up his *reposado*. "Better the end of a thing than the beginning thereof."

"Ovido?"

"Ecclesiastes, ch. 7. v 8."

"*Salud.*"

"*Salud.*"

El Secreto

I was sitting right here at my corner table at La Fonda listening to the mariachis, that unique musical form that fills your heart with joy, or awakens a forgotten memory that moistens the eyes. They do it all with three violins, two guitars, the big bass guitarrón and a silvery trumpet that talks to the soul. I was watching the effects of the music on the sippers and the diners. Mariachis sang *Guadalajara* followed with *Cuando Calienta El Sol*, both big favorites with visitors from the Other Side. Then they thunked out *La Bamba*. That got everybody out on the floor hopping and stomping to the infectious beat. But I thought the vigorous dance lost some of its color. Americans and locals alike were all dressed either in shorts or pants and a big part of the charm of *La Bamba* is the rustle and swirl of colored skirts and flashes of lacy petticoats. Then they played Carrasco's *Adios*, and nearly all the men and women in La Fonda were wiping their eyes.

It was Saturday night. The place was packed and alive with voices, talking, laughing. Smoke curled around the chandeliers like serpentines. There were two tables of Americans eminently qualified for AARP, and the usual refugees from Rancho La Puerta. I couldn't believe it! There was Comandante Big Caca. I hadn't seen him in La Fonda since Big Nalgas Machado busted him for driving a car with California plates with a Mexican driving license. The gorgeous young woman feeding the Comandante tortilla chips dipped in salsa was Lizette. You might remember they met when Lizette was trying to sneak about four hundred dollars worth of intimate apparel into Mexico duty free. Big Caca needed entertainment usually excluded from most conjugal contracts and Lizette needed a friend in the customs office. Mutual need blossomed into romance. Isn't love wonderful?

Beto showed up at my table with two perfectly blended margaritas. I touched glasses and exchanged a warm *salud* with my companion. My dinner partner was Polly Sveda, an entrancing medley of natural beauty, grace, and talent. Polly is a broadcast journalist in San Francisco and expressed a desire to know Tecate. Three tables away I waved to Carlos, the *profesór*, and his beautiful wife Anita. They were holding hands across the table. At the very next table I nodded to Ignacio, the *ingeniero* and his wife Linda. Ignacio and Linda were sending little kisses to each other. Both couples were handsome in appearance, in their mid-forties, would be my guess.

"It lifts my heart to see middle-aged married couples who aren't afraid of showing their love and affection for each other. This is what I love about Mexico," my companion said.

"I would have to agree," I answered, "were it not for the fact that I knew Carlos back when he was married to Linda and I was present at Ignacio and Anita's wedding. They haven't exchanged a word since the bitter divorce."

My companion gasped. Her margarita stopped short of its objective. "You mean, you mean those two couples are sitting next to their exes?"

I understood her gasp perfectly. You'd never believe it to look at them. No one seemed in the least uncomfortable with the seating arrangement, and while they weren't exchanging waves and smiles with their exes, they certainly didn't look strained. They didn't even appear to be obvious about trying to ignore each other. Tecate is a small town. You just can't avoid bumping into people you never want to see again. It's *inevitáble*. I've often wondered why Tecate doesn't simply explode with the tension that results when a relationship ends in harsh words and bitter tears, when the one you loved becomes the one you loathe, and you run into them every day in the plaza, at the bank, or sipping margaritas with their new sweethearts at La Fonda.

I remember when the men and women in Tecate got married and stayed married. Do those couples who stay together have a special secret to a long and happy marriage? Is it genetic, something in the water, maybe? I thought for a moment of the oldest married couple of my acquaintance in Tecate. Don Florentino and Doña Elvia Torreon. If anyone had the Rosetta Stone that would disclose the secret, they would. Don Florentino and Doña Elvia have been married for nearly sixty years. And not just years of living under the same roof—fifty-eight years and still in love! I would give anything to know their secret.

Dinner over, we reluctantly left La Fonda and stepped into the plaza followed by the haunting strains of *La Llorona*.

Two days later I decided it was time to pay a call on Don Florentino and Doña Elvia and see if I could glean the secret of everlasting love. Knowing of Don Florentino's disdain for anything with a motor on it, I saddled up El Alazan and headed for their little rancho tucked away in the back country near Rancho Viejo. An hour or so at an easy jog, and I was opening the gate at Rancho El Porvenir. It was about eleven in the morning. I could see the house well before I got to it. It was a white adobe structure with a roof of red tiles and a long front porch. The air was sweet, spiced with chaparral and wild sage and wood smoke I could only hope was coming from the kitchen.

I found them sitting out on the front porch with mugs of hot *champurrado*—and holding hands! I looked at Don Florentino, eighty-three years old now, dressed in slim fitting Levis, black cowboy shirt and a very macho black felt sombrero. Doña Elvia wore a printed brown dress that put me in mind of autumn leaves, and a white cobbler's apron. She was seventy-eight. Their hair, snowy white, their beautiful faces, creased and crinkled with age and wisdom.

"*Buenos dias!*" I stepped onto the porch and unloaded a sack of Elberta peaches I'd picked off the trees earlier that morning. There was a festive exchange of *abrazos*. They fussed over the peaches like grandparents fuss over a new baby. I noticed Florentino's guitar lying across an empty chair.

"Still playing the guitar?"

"He'd leave me before he'd part with his guitar," Doña Elvia laughed.

"My godfather gave it to me on my twentieth birthday."

"He still plays love songs for me every day."

They led me to a chair. At the appearance of a guest Doña Elvia quietly disappeared into the house and returned with a *champurrado* for me. She went behind her husband's chair, put her arms around him, and pressed her cheek to his. "You're sitting there holding an empty cup, Tino."

Tino petted her hand on his arm, surrendered his mug and, giving me an exaggerated wink, said, "Nobody in the world can make love or *champurrado* like my Elvia!" He tickled her ribs. Nearly sixty years of marriage and still flirting. Their love was palpable. This is what I came for!

Doña Elvia returned with a refill for her husband. It's amazing to me how conversation flows without thought or effort over a hot cup of *champurrado*. I disguised my questions as casual conversation and their story flowed. It took most of the day. But sometimes a story just doesn't turn out the way you expected, or wanted it to. I have to admit the chronicle I'm about to offer my readers is that kind of story. It wasn't until some weeks later sitting in the plaza that I learned the story has a coda.

I'll begin my documentary at Rancho Las Tunas in 1938 when Tecate had about eight thousand head of people and an unknown number of livestock.

Benito watched Florentino clinch the last nail, release the big sorrel's hoof gripped between his knees, then stand up and straighten the kinks in his back. "Try not to wear them out so fast," he told the old sorrel who wasn't paying a whole lot of attention. He threw a hand-tooled saddle across the noble beast's broad back.

Florentino and Benito worked as all-around vaqueros at Rancho Las Tunas, one of the largest cattle ranches some fifteen kilometers south of Tecate. The two were friends since infancy. But they climbed out of the cradle twenty-two years ago and were now full grown machos with their fair allotment of testosterone. Florentino was hopelessly in love with the girl of his dreams. He saw Elvia's pretty face in the languid summer sky, her smile was reflected in the clear water of the Arroyo Verde that sang all day, her image took form in the fluffy clouds at sunset. Benito was also in love beyond anyone's help save the Lord Himself. The girl he wanted desperately to marry lived in his heart all day and appeared in his dreams every night and he'd wake up whispering her name—*Elvia!*

The alert reader can quickly see there's going to be a problem here. Two good-looking young men in love with the same beautiful girl. There simply won't be enough Elvia to go around.

"It's my turn to court Elvia," Florentino said, cinching up the latigo. "What are you going to do with yourself all day?"

"Eat my heart out."

"Hey, it was your idea, remember? You had your turn last Saturday. You should have asked her to marry you right there, and the contest would be over."

"She loved the flowers and the chocolates. I got a very tight *abrazo* and a kiss. I came that close to proposing." He brought his thumb and forefinger a hair apart to make his point.

"Well, it's my turn today and I'm coming back engaged to Elvia."

"Just don't forget the rules," Benito reminded him. "We made a solemn covenant. We take turns fair and square every Saturday. We can shower her with gifts, kiss her passionately in the moonlight, serenade her at her window—anything we think will work. The one who wins her heart can ask her hand in marriage. But absolutely no hard feelings between us. We've been friends since we were weaned from our mother's breast. Love is dependable as a loose calf, friendship is forever."

"The winner wins, the loser loses, all with a good face."

"And the loser gets to be godfather of the firstborn." They shook hands to reaffirm their agreement. Florentino gave Benito temporary custody of his guitar while he got into the saddle. He was dressed in black ducks trimmed with enough silver conchos to make a trip to the assayer's office worthwhile.

"Aren't you taking a gift?"

"It's in the saddlebag."

"Flowers?"

"No."

"Candy?"

"No."

"What then?"

"A wheel of *queso fresco*."

"Cheese! Cheese? That's customary for any visit to any house. What about a gift for *her*?"

"I don't need to bribe her," Florentino answered. "I want to win her heart without strings. The day I ask Elvia to marry me she'll say yes because she loves me, not for a box of chocolates."

"If that's your approach I'll have a ring on her finger before you can buy another wheel of *queso fresco*." Benito slapped the sorrel on the rump and watched his friend lope out the gate of Rancho Las Tunas. "Give Elvia a kiss for me!"

"Sure!"

Florentino moved down the road at a steady walk singing *Amor Mio* in the company of his guitar. He didn't need reins. The old sorrel knew the way blindfolded. Back in 1938 the road to Tecate wasn't paved. And it wasn't called Highway 3 as it is today. It was simply referred to as *el camino a Tecate*. For lack of engineers it was left to the cattle to survey and construct the road as they wandered following the succulent grass that grew wild from Ensenada to Tecate. It was a dusty road with more twists and turns than a rattlesnake with an itchy belly. In those days box wagons loaded with dirt pulled by a pair of gray mules brought a road crew to fill the big potholes in the road that appeared after every rain. And back then, both sides of the road weren't lined with little white crosses to mark a fatal accident. No one ever heard of two horses colliding. Not too much has changed since 1938. By 1965 the road was paved and baptized Highway 3. They painted a yellow line down the middle but even today no one seems to understand its purpose. The biggest difference is that the picturesque mule-drawn box wagon has disappeared from the scene forever. Today the road crew arrives in a late model pickup truck loaded with dirt to fill in the potholes that appear after every rain.

Every verse he sang brought Florentino closer to his betrothed who wasn't aware of her commitment. He was desperately in love and he was courting the prettiest girl in Tecate. One day when the time is right I'll ask her to marry me, he thought. But I have to make my move pretty soon or Benito will have a ring on her finger. Day or night his only thoughts were of Elvia.

Elvia lived with Tata Pancho, her aging grandfather, on a small patch of ground called Rancho Los Girasoles where the Manuel Ceceña soccer stadium stands today. The little rancho lived up to its name. That whole part of town was overgrown with wild sunflowers. To the west, where the Church of Our Lady of Guadalupe now stands, was nothing more than a huge *cienega* teeming with fish and home to the blue heron, ibis, and wild geese.

The sun was at its zenith when Florentino opened the gate at Rancho Los Girasoles and jogged on up to the house. It was a small frame house with a steep tile roof and a covered porch. Fragrant smoke curling out of the black stove pipe promised there was something good sitting on the cast iron wood range in the kitchen. Clothes were fluttering on a long clothesline strung between two large eucalyptus trees. A yellow dog was the first to greet him with a happy bark. The comely Elvia appeared on the front porch with Tata Pancho. Everyone called him Tata out of affection for the venerable old man but Florentino always spoke to him respectfully as *usted*.

Florentino looked at Elvia. He knew her back when she was a twelve-year-old bundle of sticks that could ride anything with hair on it and tucked her dress into her *calzones* when she did somersaults. Somehow, nature saw to it that now there was more of her to look at.

It's something of a strain on the chronicler to describe a young woman like Elvia. Poets can do it better. The Elvia standing on the porch this afternoon to welcome Florentino was a willowy young girl of seventeen. Her skin was the color of Cuervo Gold, hair straight as the A-string on his guitar, black and shiny as the tail feathers of a crow. Her smile was a rose unfurling. She was dressed in a blue cotton frock with bright yellow trimming. Florentino looked at the apparition before him with reverence, convinced Elvia was descended from Our Lady Queen of Angels.

Tata Pancho was a stout, short-coupled vaquero with a round face of deep russet and a huge mound of snow-white hair on top of his head. He had snowy eyebrows and an extravagant mustache to match. Tata looked like a pumpkin left out in the field overnight with a dollop of snow on its head. Within all the deep ridges and creases in his dark face was a two-volume anthology of romantic tales of yore.

"Tino! *Buenas tardes!*" the Queen of Angels and the old vaquero called out in unison.

"*Buenas tardes*! How is everyone?" They all exchanged a filial embrace. "Something smells awfully good!"

"Elvia has a big kettle of pozole on the stove, " the old man said and gimped ahead to show the way.

"Put up your horse, Tino, and come in! You must be hungry," Elvia said.

Florentino returned and presented his hosts with the soft white cheese. "What a beautiful *queso fresco*," they both exclaimed as though they had never seen cheese before. Tata Pancho indicated a chair and the two men sat at a round table covered with white oilcloth printed with little clusters of faded red cherries. Elvia worked her alchemy at a big cast-iron stove the size of a cathedral pipe organ and ladled out big bowls of steaming pozole. The beautiful smell of pasilla and California chiles combined with white hominy enveloped the room. Little cups containing chopped onions, fragrant cilantro and lemon wedges were already on the table. Elvia brought a stack of hot flour tortillas she made by hand. Tecate didn't have a *tortilleria* until 1950 when the Contreras family opened La Victoria on Avenida Juarez. She set out cold beer, and joined the men.

"Tecate is growing too fast," the old man complained. "They're talking about paving Avenida Juarez to make it easier for the *automóvil*."

"Things change, Tata," the Queen of Angels said.

"Then let them change for the better not the worst! There must be two dozen *automóviles* in Tecate now. We don't need any more!"

"*Ay*, Tata!" she said sweetly and put another tortilla on his plate.

Tata's grumbling was never serious, it was simply cynical observations spoken with a gruff voice rusty from age. And Elvia adored him. She couldn't remember her mother or her father. Tata Pancho and her Nana raised her until her Nana died and now she looked after her Tata as much as her Tata always looked after her.

Everyone's hunger sated, the men stood, and Elvia began to clear plates. Florentino started to help when a soft hand tapped the back of his hand with mock severity and a sweet voice that pretended to scold, said, "Leave that, Tino, take Tata out on the porch and talk to him. I'll be out in a few minutes with coffee."

Talking to Tata was easier than swallowing spit. The falling of a leaf, the lowing of the cows, the cries of the crows could induce a tale of high adventure from the old days. "You were right, Tata, Tecate is growing."

"Growing in the wrong direction, Tino. I fought for this town during the big war. Got hit in the leg, but we never gave up."

"You mean La Revolución?"

"In 1910 a young Francisco Madero went to see Presidente Don Porfirio Diaz and told him that his four year term as president of Mexico was now in its thirtieth year and that maybe it was time to hold a new election. El Presidente did not like that. Don Porfirio took offense and that started the Revolucion." Tata pulled a little sack of La Morena tobacco from his shirt pocket, a small pad of cigarette paper the color of tanbark, and began to roll a cigarette. "Providence brought us the right man to lead the Revolucion. Francisco Madero was not an illiterate *cabrón* who killed for pleasure like Pancho Villa or Emiliano Zapata. He was an educated man. Madero studied at a University called Berkeley in Alta California, but here in Baja California it was a different war at the same time."

"You mean the *filibusteros*."

"*Sí*, I mean that *cabrón* Ricardo Magon and his gang. Ricardo Magon thought he could seize Baja California while the rest of Mexico was busy with the Revolucion and declare himself president." Tata put out his tongue, licked along the edge of the paper, and put the completed cigarette between his lips. "Magon organized a good size army. Mostly from the Other Side. The *cabrónes* had all the modern equipment. They got financial support from a bunch of rich gringos and some evil Mexicans. They all wanted a piece of the enchilada!" The yellow dog came up the porch and plopped at Tata's feet to better hear the story. "In January of 1911 Tecate fell to the Magon forces. It was cold. We'd had some snow, I remember.

"I heard we almost lost all of Baja California."

"Almost, but we fought back with every finger and toe! We sent the *cabrónes* running for the border into Alta California. It was in that battle that I got hit right here." He indicated his right ankle.

"What became of Don Porfirio Diaz?"

Tata paused, took a wax match from his box of Clasicos and ignited the end of the product he had so laboriously produced. He was in the habit of using one of Elvia's flower pots where she grew a few annuals as an ashtray. She could never break of him of the habit. She even bought him an ashtray but Tata Pancho preferred snuffing out his cigarette in the soft soil. It was something of a nuisance for Elvia who had to clean out the pots every day, but certainly not of enough importance to make an issue of it.

"In 1911 his loyal troops smuggled Don Porfirio to Veracruz. A boat was waiting for him and he fled Mexico with all the gold bars in the treasury."

Elvia came out on the porch with three steaming mugs of coffee and *pan dulce*. When nothing remained of either, Elvia said to her Tata, "You look tired, why don't you go in and rest?"

Tata snuffed out his homemade in the flower pot. "It's my ear, I got air in it yesterday. It's been hurting me all day."

"*Ay* Tata! Why didn't you tell me? Stay here, I'll be right back to fix you up." Elvia went in the house and returned with a page from an old newspaper. "Which ear is it?" The old man indicated his left.

With a new sense of wonderment Florentino watched the girl he loved a little bit more each day take the newspaper and fashion it into a cone. Gently she inserted the cone into Tata's left ear. "Can you hold it for me like this?"

"*Sí.*"

Elvia struck a match and lit the wide part of the cone. The air in the cone began to heat up. In a few seconds they all heard the loud poof as the cold air trapped in the ear canal was forced out.

"You did it *mi amor*, what a relief!" Tata took the flaming cone from his ear and crushed it out on the concrete floor. He kissed her forehead. "I think I'll take a little siesta now." He limped into the house, arms flailing like a wounded chicken, and they were left alone on the porch, if you don't count the yellow dog.

"Play something for me," Elvia said.

Florentino picked up his guitar, twisted a couple of pegs and sang...

Cuatro milpas tan solas quedadas
en el rancho que era mio, ay
Ay, ay, ay...

Elvia joined him in the next line.

Y aquella casita
tan blanca y bonita
tan triste que esta!

"I love the way you play."

"I love the way you sing. Remember this one?" Florentino strummed a couple of bars.

"Yes, I love it! Play it for me?"

"If you sing it with me." Florentino began,

Porque no han de saber
que te amo todavia...

Elvia's voice came in,

porque no he de decirlo
si fundes tu alma
con el alma mia...

When the song ended Elvia's eyes were wet. "Come, let's take a walk around the rancho."

"Yes! That would be nice. I haven't seen your new calf."

Florentino thought of reaching for her hand but he mastered the urge so Elvia took his, and they walked hand in hand to the far end of the rancho. They stood, shoulders touching, at the old wood rail fence and admired the new calves, looked at some pigs, and visited with Elvia's two palomino mares. Suddenly Florentino pulled back his hand.

"What is it?"

"*Nada.*"

"Let me see." She took his hand in hers. "It's a nasty sliver!"

"It's nothing, really."

"Let me look. Nothing! It's big and it's deep." It was a huge splinter buried into the soft heel of his hand. Florentino didn't really care how big or how deep as long as she continued to hold his hand. He allowed her to pull it out. "There!" She took her little handkerchief, cleaned the puncture, and Florentino got his first kiss on his hand. "All better," she said and they started back.

"Look!" Florentino said. "Your old swing is still under that big oak tree."

"I remember when you and Benito climbed up there to tie the rope." She ran to the swing like a little girl. "Push me, push me!"

"You haven't changed." He got behind her and began to push her.

"Not so high! Not so high! The rope is probably rotten."

"Girls never know what they want," he said, giving her one last push then seated himself against the trunk of the giant oak to watch.

Elvia jumped off the swing, scooped up a huge handful of dry leaves, threw them in his hair and fled. She was no match for the young vaquero. He caught her before she could gain the barn and now it was his turn to drop a bushel of leaves in her silky hair. They laughed like children then helped each other get the leaves out of their hair. Her face was so close to his he contemplated placing a light kiss on her cheek but somewhere between thought and deed his nerve abandoned him like an orphan on the steps of the convent.

"Look at your quince trees, they're loaded with fruit!"

"Aren't they beautiful? I want to make quince marmalade. Would you help me take some back to the house?"

Florentino, who was two heads taller than Elvia, reached up and brought down a half dozen. He watched Elvia raise her dress to make a basket of her skirt. He tried not to stare at her white slip with a lacy hem. He kept his eyes firmly on the harvest cradled in her dress.

"That's enough, Tino, I can't carry any more. *Ay, Dios mio!*"

"What is it?"

A fresh breeze from the east was picking up. "Oh, how I hate the Evil East Wind! The clothes are flying off the line. They'll get dirty!"

Elvia was helpless. Both hands were holding on to her skirt with a load of quinces. Florentino ran over, quickly gathered up the laundry scattered on the ground, and bundled it up in his arms. "At least the wind served a purpose. Everything's dry."

They returned to the house. Florentino dumped the laundry on the sofa, then took the fruit from her skirt and put it on the table. They sat out on the porch a little longer. They sang a few more songs until the declination of the sun declared it was time to go.

Florentino didn't want the day to end. Elvia walked with him while he bridled his horse, handed up his guitar, and watched him as he loped out the gate.

The following Saturday was Benito's turn to court and he was getting himself ready to deliver the contents of his heart at the feet of the girl he worshipped. His bay mare was bathed, curried, mane and tail shampooed. Florentino watched as he saddled and bridled. "You look fully armed to conquer the heart of a beautiful señorita. One dozen long-stemmed roses. What else?"

"A half kilo of marzipan. She loves marzipan."

"No cheese?"

"No cheese. I'm out to make love to a lady not a mouse."

"What happens when Doña Maria discovers she's missing a dozen red roses from her garden?"

"She'll blame it on her milk goat. She's always getting out." Benito was decked out in chocolate brown pants with white embroidery. He looked like a *charro* at a fiesta on Sunday afternoon. He leaped up into the saddle. "I'd like so much to spend the day with you, Tino, you're my best friend and you always make good conversation, but I'm getting engaged today—*hasta luego!*"

With big macho tears welling up in his eyes, Florentino watched him gallop out the gate of Rancho Las Tunas then walked away to eat his heart out in the dark privacy of the barn.

An hour later the yellow dog met Benito at the gate and followed him up to the house. There Benito saw the girl who made his heart ache. Elvia was sitting out on the porch shelling peas into a bowl on her lap. Tata was busy fumbling with his brown cigarette paper and his little sack of La Morena tobacco. Elvia put the bowl aside, Tata finished fabricating his cigarette, and they went to exchange warm *abrazos* as Benito came up on the porch, spurs ringing. The old mare didn't require spurs but Benito liked the ching-jing-ring of the rowels that he perceived gave him an aura of a macho vaquero.

"Oh, Benito they're beautiful!" This was the young vaquero's reward for a dozen red long-stemmed roses acquired by cunning and blamed on an innocent milk goat. It brought him another *abrazo*.

"Oh, Benito, I can hardly wait to open it!" This was in regard to the box of marzipan that changed hands and it brought the bestower still another *abrazo*. *Pan comido*, Benito thought. This expression loosely translates to, I'm on a roll.

As soon as the hugs and the cheek-kissing ended Benito got a whiff of something good to eat. "I could smell the menudo all the way down at the gate."

"We were just waiting for you to show up, *muchacho*. Put up your mare and let's slurp menudo!" Tata said.

Benito simply removed saddle and bridle, let the mare go, and headed for the table like a steer that had smelled water.

"Tata and I haven't seen you in two weeks, Benito, what have you been doing?"

"The work never ends on a rancho. Last week we drove some cows all the way to Las Palmas."

Elvia set big bowls of steaming menudo and cold beers in front of the men. She had tortillas spread out all over the top of the wood range. With quick and nimble fingers to avoid singeing fingertips, she turned them over once or twice, wrapped them in a towel, and joined the men.

"I sold a few steers last week," Tata said, squeezing a lemon wedge over his soup. "The price wasn't right, but what could I do? Elvia wants to start her trousseau."

"*Ay* Tata!" Elvia's Cuervo Gold cheeks turned a beautiful rosy copper. No one ever knew what Tata was going to say. But then, she playfully turned the tortilla on him. "The truth is, Benito, Tata wants to buy an *automóvil*!" Elvia knew that would send him off in another direction.

"An *automóvil*! Never!"

Benito played along. "I see them in town on occasion. You have to admit it would be fun to have one."

"Never!" the old soldier repeated. "I think there are fifteen or twenty of the monsters in Tecate now. They're noisy, they smell bad and they scare the horses." He quenched his thirst. "I can remember when there were only two cars in Tecate."

"Really! When was that?"

"Twenty years ago—1918, 1920, in there. Don Tibursio who owned the warehouse had to have one. He bought a Ford in Tijuana. It was black and the ugliest thing you ever saw."

"Who had the other one?" Benito asked. Elvia had heard the story a thousand times.

"Some big *delegado* brought back a new Pierce Arrow. It was even bigger and uglier than Don Tibursio's little Forito. It looked like a hearse and had more brass fittings than that iron cook stove." He accepted a fresh beer from his pretty ward. "For a long time the Ford and the Pierce Arrow were the only cars in Tecate—and they crashed on the corner in front of the feed store!"

Benito had never heard the story and paid the narrator in nuggets of golden laughter then tipped him lavishly with a slap on the knee. Elvia laughed as though she'd just heard the story for the first time and put another beer in front of Benito.

Tata grew serious. "The *automóvil* shouldn't be allowed in Tecate. One of these days one of those things is going to kill someone. A group of us from the Cattleman's Association are going to stage a protest. They're pointless. These roads aren't meant for rubber tires, there are no gasoline stations, you have to cross the border for that, and nobody knows how to fix them." He emptied the remainder of his beer. "And you can go more places on a horse than you can in an *automóvil*!"

Elvia began to gather up empty bowls. "You men go out on the porch. I'll be out with coffee and flan in a few minutes."

"Can I help?" Benito offered.

"You're sweet. I won't be long."

"I can wash dishes."

"*Gracias, no.*"

"Wash the windows?"

"No, please."

"Sweep the floor, do the laundry..."

Tata put an arm over his shoulder and walked him out to the front porch. He took out his little bag of La Morena, a book of papers, and began to construct his postprandial cigarette. Benito offered him one from his own pack, but old Tata declined.

"You shouldn't smoke those things."

"Everybody says cigarettes make you cough, but they don't seem to bother me."

"I mean you shouldn't smoke manufactured cigarettes. You never know what they put in them in those big modern factories. I had a *compadre* who found a *cucaracha* in his cigarette. I prefer to make my own. It's safer that way." He lit his cigarette and tossed the expired match into a flower pot where a little daisy lived. It bounced out.

"So you don't think you'll be buying an *automóvil* any time soon."

"Never!"

"Do you think you'll ever buy a radio, Tata?"

Tata laughed so hard he choked on his homemade. "Radio! Now, what would I want with a radio? What would I hook it up to, a kerosene lamp? We have no radio stations in Tecate and the ones in Tijuana don't reach this far."

"Our *patrón* once took us to work at his rancho in Tijuana. He had a radio. It's a big wooden box, looks like a chapel with knobs, and we heard music and they announced the inauguration of the new bullring in Tijuana. Armillita was on the bill." Benito came into the world too soon. He loved anything new. He was born for high technology. "They even have a *teléfono* at the ranch."

"*Teléfono*! Things are getting ridiculous. You'll never see one in Tecate."

"Have you ever ridden in an *automóvil*, Tata?" The two dozen cars in Tecate fascinated Benito. They made such a nice sound, like a purring tiger, and he liked the way they floated over the dirt roads.

"Never!"

"I have to admit I would like to ride in one some day. I heard the army is using them now instead of horses."

"In 1911 we fought the *filibusteros* with horses and we won the war. We didn't need motors. Our garrison was just east of here. Of course, there's not much left of it today. But the people who live near there claim they can still hear the horse-drawn cannon coming down the hill on the night of a new moon."

Benito had heard the rumors and he was not about to disbelieve it.

"All the men in my family were military men. We overthrew Don Porfirio Diaz with horses and brave men."

"You fought in the Revolucion?"

Tata's cigarette was going limp. He crushed it under the daisy. "I fought here in Tecate against Magon. That's how I hurt my leg." Tata put a hand on his right ankle. "I was thinking of my uncles and cousins who fought in the south. My godfather was a hero at the famous battle of San Angel de la Cueva."

Benito never tired of stories of the Revolucion. He heard them from his parents, his grandparents. The war was over and the new Constitution proclaimed by the time he was born in 1918 and he always felt he missed some high adventure. "What happened?"

"It was a fierce and bloody battle. My godfather had killed their colonel, a man they called La Escoba, the broom, because when he attacked he made a clean sweep. No one, soldier, woman or child was left alive. Don Porfirio's men captured my godfather along with his corporal who was just a boy of fourteen. 'I'll spare the boy, but you prepare to die, *cabrón*.' The young boy wept openly for his commander."

"Did they execute him in front of the boy?"

"No. Before they tied his hands behind his back, he picked a wild *girasol* and called the boy over. 'Take this flower to Mirasol,' he said to him. That was my godmother's name. 'And tell her not to weep for me. It doesn't matter that you die, it's *how* you die. In killing me they give me immortality. *Viva la Revolucion!*' The boy ran off and heard the shot."

Benito said nothing. He was awestruck.

"Well, the young boy wept all the way back to the house and put the golden flower in my godmother's hand. She was heavy with child. The old *curandera* who attended her told her she was carrying a boy and he would be born with a birthmark to honor his father's memory."

"And did she have a son?"

"Yes."

"And was he born with a birthmark like the old *curandera* said?"

"That boy is my cousin. And yes, he was born with a *girasol* plainly printed on his back."

Benito and Tata Pancho were the perfect go-togethers, like saddle and bridle or harness and traces. Benito never tired of hearing about the Revolucion and Tata Pancho never tired of talking about it. Tata took his little bag of La Morena from his shirt pocket and began the manufacturing process. "Those were bad and bloody times for Mexico. Presidente Madero was executed in 1911. Then came Carranza who legalized divorce and gave us the Constitution."

"My papá said he was a good president."

"He was, but then he was assassinated in 1920. Presidents didn't last long in those days. Then came Elias Calles and the Cristiada, the bloody war against the Catholic Church. The Cristeros had a big army. Fifty thousand soldiers. That war lasted five years." Tata Pancho was just warming up to his favorite subject. He cleared his throat preparatory to a smooth segue into the looting of churches and convents, shootouts in the streets, public executions of priests, when Elvia arrived with flan and coffee.

The conversation drifted off in the direction of weather and farm prices until old Tata began to nod.

"You look tired, Tata" Elvia said.

"I am, a little, *mi amor.* It may have been the second beer."

"Why don't you go in and take a little siesta?"

"I think I will." Tata straightened himself out and, arms flapping, gimped into the house.

"If I don't move around I'll fall asleep too," Benito confessed. "Are you up to a little walk around the rancho?"

They took the tour, admired the stock, and ended up in the barn. The smell of fresh hay was strong and pleasant. "Hey, look, there's your little red wagon."

"I remember when you and Florentino used to pull me."

The sound of Florentino's name was as pleasant to Benito as a razor cut. And besides, he did most of the pulling. "That old door is coming off its hinges. If you've got a screwdriver I'll fix it right now."

"Tata keeps some tools here in this box." Elvia rummaged through the junk and came up with a screwdriver. She watched him tighten the rusty screws on all three hinges.

"Next time I come out I'll bring new screws."

Elvia expressed her thanks for his thoughtfulness with a warm hand on his arm. He felt her lean in closer and would have bet his new hand-tooled leather boots a kiss was coming. Benito would have ridden home in his socks. The kiss didn't make the payroll. They put the tools away and walked back toward the house. When they passed the big oak tree with the swing Benito slid to the ground and sat with his back against the gnarled trunk. Elvia sat beside him.

"You've got hay in your hair. Come here."

Benito put his head on her lap and Elvia began to pick strands of hay out of his hair.

Her lap was soft and warm like a feather pillow, her gentle hands going through his hair felt like caresses. Neither talked. The only conversation came from a passing group of young quail gossiping in that high chippity-chippity language of their own. Benito could feel her soft breasts on his head as she bent forward to swish a fly crawling on her ankle. This is the moment, he told himself, this is the moment. Propose to her *now*!

"You'll never guess what I'm about to say," he said in a voice husky with emotion.

"Tell me," she murmured. Then suddenly, "*Ay, Dios*! Look!"

Benito's view was restricted to a soft bosom, a pretty face, and a squirrel up in the oak tree. "What?"

"The calf is out!"

Betrayed by a dumb calf! The spell was broken like a soap bubble. Instantly, they both jumped to their feet and began the pursuit of a little red Hereford calf that could zig and zag with the best ziggers and zaggers in the herd. With arms outstretched Elvia got behind the little fugitive and guided him toward the barn. Benito made all the moves of a blue ribbon cutting horse. It took a while. When the rodeo was over and a refreshment was served it was on the late side, and Benito had to save his proposal of marriage for his next turn.

"Well," Benito said as he entered Rancho Las Tunas, "I'm a man of my word. You can be best man."

"You asked her?" Florentino felt his heart hit the ground.

"And as agreed by our oath of allegiance you are designated godfather to our firstborn."

It was evening and they had some meat browning over manzanita coals on the grill, a pot of beans and a bowl of guacamole. Florentino was crushed. He was almost there! "You really asked her and she said yes? You're engaged? Really, truly?"

"Almost."

"Almost! What's almost engaged?"

"I came close. You couldn't have slipped a horse hair between my lips and the words that would make her mine."

New hope burst in Floretino's bosom. He retrieved his heart from the ground still intact. "What happened? I've never seen you miss with a rope."

"Lost my nerve. Threw short, didn't pitch my slack, and she got away."

"Well, next Saturday is my turn and you can be sure I'll be officially engaged when I ride in here next week."

"That's what I'd like to talk to you about. I'd like to modify the terms of our agreement."

"Just what does that mean?"

"Well, my turn is two Saturdays away. A lot could happen in two weeks."

"So, what are you suggesting?"

"How about I get a bonus day?"

"Bonus!"

"Yes, you let me make an extra trip during the middle of the week, say next Tuesday."

"So you get in an extra turn." The two cow punchers were saddle brothers at Rancho Las Tunas and that was a sacred trust. Florentino listened.

"But then you can have an extra bonus day on Wednesday." Benito saw that Florentino stopped his taco midway between hand and mouth. "So you get to see her before your regular turn, too."

Miracle! thought Florentino without revealing that the idea fitted perfectly with his own secret plan. "*Chócala!* You have a deal." They shook hands to bind the agreement and resumed heating tortillas on the grill.

Benito rode out early Tuesday morning with high hopes and fancy dreams. He was back in a couple of hours with a face so long he could have used his lower lip to clean furrows in a cornfield. The yellow dog wasn't even there to meet him. Later he saw him with his nose coated with dirt, digging into a squirrel hole. When Benito got to the porch the only one there was Tata rolling a cigarette.

"Elvia is not here, *muchacho*, she's gone to market. No telling when she'll be back." Tata gave life to his cigarette with one of his Clasicos. "Sit down and play me a game of checkers." Benito went through the motions and left at a belly-dragging gallop.

Florentino's bonus day wasn't that much better. He was met at the gate by an escaped inmate of the Hereford variety. Florentino dropped a noose over the red calf and led him jumping and frolicking back to his pen. Tata met him on the way back to the house.

"Elvia's not here, *muchacho*, she took the surrey early this morning. She didn't say when she'd be back but she put an extra stick in the fire and left lunch on the stove." He fumbled around with his tobacco pouch. "Women are as predictable as the weather in March."

"I brought her a little climbing rose. I might as well put it in the ground while I'm here."

Tata brought a spade from the shed and between the two of them and the yellow dog, the hole was prepared. Florentino dropped the plant in the hole, covered it up, and threw a bucket of water on it. He headed home as soon as the game of checkers was finished.

The following Saturday was Florentino's regular turn. He rode through the gate at Los Girasoles as bold and confident as the Conquistadores when they rode into Moctezuma's capital a while back. The yellow dog stayed with him all the way to the porch where old Tata Pancho and the beautiful Elvia sat drinking orangeade.

Elvia met him at the porch steps. "*Hola* Tino! I'll take your guitar while you put up your horse."

There were the usual *abrazos* and sisterly cheek kisses, big bowls of pozole, then coffee on the porch. Predictably Tata expressed his opinion as to *el radio, el teléfono, el automóvil,* played a couple of reruns of La Revolucion, and toddled off to his siesta. That left only Elvia and Florentino with his guitar, and a yellow dog that was developing an ear for music, on the porch.

"Play for me, Tino."

"If you sing for me."

Florentino picked up his guitar, fingered the strings, and they sang together.

> *Porque no han de saber*
> *que te amo todavia...*
> *porque no he de decirlo*
> *si fundes tu alma*
> *con el alma mia...*

Then Florentinno sang the last line alone...

> *quiero gozar esta vida*
> *teniendo cerca de mi*
> *hasta que muera.*

There could be no doubt that he loved Elvia with all his heart and soul and that love would burn forever. With misty eyes Florentino put aside the guitar and said, "Elvia, *mi amor,* I love you. I love you as I've never loved before and never will love again." He drank from her deep black eyes and said, "Elvia, *alma de mi vida,* will you marry me?"

Then Elvia spoke the words all men loathe and fear to hear, those words that are intended to be a gentle rejection. "*Ay,* Tino," she laid her soft hand upon his. "I've loved you and Benito like brothers, the brothers I never had, since I was ten years old."

Florentino's heart got another bruising. He felt it drop into his yellow boots. "That's what I was afraid of."

"It's the strangest thing. I didn't realize it until just recently. Now I know it's you I love, and not like a brother. I love you, Florentino, as a woman loves a man!"

The warm air on the front porch smelled of an impending summer shower. I looked over at my hosts. Don Florentino placed his hand over his wife's. I could feel the love coursing from one hand to the other. "We got married the next year, 1939," Don Florentino recalled.

"The following year Tata Pancho went to be with my Nana in Heaven. I think Tata was just waiting for me to marry Tino to be sure I'd be all right." Doña Elvia brushed away a tear with her hand.

We could hear the vroom vroom and the angry roar and whining of dirt bikes scrabbling up the hill behind the rancho. "I remember when all we could hear out here on your porch was the loony call of the quailcock, the road runners, and the cooing of palomas."

"It's the times," Doña Elvia lamented.

"If Tata Pancho, God rest him, heard that, he'd go out there and shoot them all," Don Florentino laughed.

"Did Tata Pancho ever ride in an *automóvil*?"

"No," Don Florentino said. "And he never heard the radio or saw a *teléfono*, and continued to keep his money under the kitchen floor. We didn't have a bank in Tecate until 1948. The old Banco del Pacifico."

"And was Benito your best man?" I asked.

"Oh, yes. We're *compadres*. Benito and Clarita are *padrinos* to Florentino *chico*, our first son. We had six more children and didn't get another boy."

"And we're godparents to their first, a girl."

"Do you still see Benito and Clarita?"

"Oh yes! Especially at Christmas time," Doña Elvia answered. "They all come here and we celebrate *posadas* with them and the grandchildren and the great-grandchildren."

"Benito always liked cars. He used to drive a bright red pickup. A Chevrolet." Like all Mexicans, Don Florentino pronounced the "t" in Chevrolet. "But he crashed it into the barn. His *muchachos* do most of the driving now."

"What a beautiful life! What is your secret?"

"What secret?"

"The secret of a love that lasts forever."

"Oh, there is no secret, Don," Doña Elvia answered. "Real love is forever. Today's young people just don't understand. Love is lust but lust isn't love. They don't know the difference."

Don Florentino put down his empty cup. "I don't understand it. Today these young people stay in school until they're adults. They have television, they have *el eenternet*. My grandchildren have their nose in that thing like it was a feed bin full of oats. But they never learn anything about life."

"When we were young the schools out here didn't go beyond the third grade," Doña Elvia said. "You don't need school to learn to be happy. The young just don't seem to know the difference between pleasure and happiness."

"When we bought or sold stock we did the arithmetic in the dirt with a stick and a few pebbles," Don Florentino recalled. "It's good to learn things, Don, but knowledge isn't wisdom."

"I can tell by the smell the tamales are done," Doña Elvia said, getting up. Her sudden move was too fast for Don Florentino and she easily escaped the hand intended to pat her bottom. "Don't get your hopes up, Tino!" she laughed, and went inside.

"Love like this is no accident, Don Florentino," I said, "what is the secret to a long and happy marriage."

"Three simple rules."

Here it comes!

"When it's important, let her have her way. When she's swinging a lariat and you need to cut yourself some slack, stay in the barn. And never let the sun set on an argument."

I was disappointed. I don't know what I expected, but this was not what I came for. I've heard that a thousand times. Maybe there was no answer. Was it ranch life that kept them so close to each other? I've known a lot of rancheros over the years and they all have one beautiful thing in common—they're uncomplicated. When they're happy they laugh, when they're sad they cry. Their idea of strength isn't to clench your teeth and deny your feelings, it's to learn to live among your feelings. I've seen the rustics handle life and death better than I can. And most of them can't read a newspaper! What makes these simple people so wise and emotionally solvent? I realized Don Florentino couldn't give me an explanation of something he didn't understand himself. Life is what you make it, there is no "secret" as such. I'd been looking for something that didn't exist.

"You can have no idea, Don Florentino, how this visit fills my heart. Fifty-eight years and still in love. Doña Elvia loves you totally. I can see it on her face, in her eyes when she looks at you. You have total possession of her heart."

"I know, she can't help herself."

I laughed at the stale macho humor just to join my mirth with his. But my laugh hung naked in the air. Don Florentino wasn't laughing.

"I've known you for many years," Don Florentino continued. "I think I know what you're thinking."

I wasn't really thinking anything, I was watching a tiny hummingbird zooming, and thrumming as he dipped into a red hibiscus, the little body changing colors from copper to green to blue to copper again as his feathers diffracted the sunlight. I could see I wasn't going to come away with a story but I was thoroughly enjoying the visit.

"You came to learn *El Secreto*!"

I wasn't sure what he was talking about, but it sounded like the prelude to something interesting. There is a Mexican proverb that says, *he hears more who doesn't talk*. I took the advice, said nothing, and waited to hear more.

"Elvia is under a *bruja's* magic spell." Dead serious.

Now it did get quiet. Very quiet. Did he say what I thought he said?

"Many times over the years I've started to tell her, but my courage turns to bread pudding. I've kept *El Secreto* hidden in here for sixty years." He tapped his shirt in the region of his heart. "Even my best friend and *compadre* Benito doesn't know *El Secreto*."

I wanted to hear this. All of it. I didn't open my mouth. He tapped a Raleigh out of the pack, took a wax match from the box of Clasicos and lit up.

"There is no one I can tell. But I can't count on being around here much longer and I don't want to go to my grave with that worm in my heart." He tossed the expired match into a chipped saucer on the floor. "Follow me."

Don Florentino got up and started down the porch steps with an agility I never expected to see in an eighty-three-year-old vaquero. He was thin as a hay rake, all sinew and muscle. With no idea of what he was going to show me, I followed him to the side of the house.

"There's the secret," he said.

I didn't see anything in particular. There were a couple of quince trees near the house, some geraniums, and a climbing rose fragrant with pink blossoms that reached almost to the roof tiles. "Where, Don?"

"Right in front of you. The whole secret is in that rosebush." He could tell I still didn't understand what he was talking about. "When Benito and I were taking turns courting Elvia, I wasn't taking any chances. One day I rode out to Cuca La Loca, the ugly old witch up in Canyon Manteca. She must have been a hundred years old in 1938. I told her to prepare me a love *talisman*—a magic spell that would make a pretty girl fall in love with me. She told me to bring her the girl's undergarment and a hundred pesos. That was all the money in the world in those days."

"And you did it?"

"*Sí*, señor!"

"But how?"

"Doña Fortuna kissed my hand that day. One day when it was my turn to court her, a wind came up and blew all the clothes off the line. I'll never forget. She couldn't do anything about it, she was loaded down with quinces in the skirt of her dress. When I gathered up the laundry I slipped a pair of pink *calzones* in my pocket and galloped all the way to Cuca La Loca. It took the old witch several days. They have to do these things according to the moon, you know. When I came back with a hundred pesos she gave me the little plant. 'I've done my magic,' she said in that creaky voice of hers. 'The young lady will love you and you alone for as long as that rosebush continues to grow.' "

I, of course, was not in the least incredulous. Over the years in Tecate I've known any number of people who lived or died as decreed by *brujeria*.

"Did you believe it?"

"How much more proof could I want?"

Then I thought he was having a joke with me. "But that house was torn down when they went to build the stadium."

"I wasn't taking any chances. I transplanted the rosebush when we moved here.And just like the ugly old witch said, Elvia has loved me faithfully for nearly sixty years. It was the best hundred pesos I ever spent." He tossed his head toward the climber. "That's *El Secreto*."

Doña Elvia called us back to the porch for tamales hot from the kettle, and we ate and talked until the lower edges of the sky burst into flames against the hills of Tanama. I embraced Don Florentino and Doña Elvia and headed for my rancho. I rode home in triumph. I got what I came for. I had my story!

CODA

A couple of months later I was sitting in the plaza trolling for a new story, watching the live show of human drama unfold before me. I saw the banker come out of the coffee shop with a gorgeous creature I'd never seen before. His sister, his cousin? I hoped so. He has a charming wife in Tijuana. A young couple with faces too serious for teenagers were having their fortune told by a little yellow canary. They held hands while the bird pecked around in a big wooden bowl filled with paper scrolls, each one containing the voice of destiny. The little winged psychic finally picked up a scroll, delivered it, and fluttered back onto its perch in a yellow flash. I wanted to see their faces as they opened it but I was momentarily interrupted.

"*Quien es?*" I felt a pair of warm soft hands cover my eyes.

"Cuca La Loca, Britney Spears, La Cucha..."

The hands yanked on my ears, their owner came around and pressed a kiss on my face. It was Señorita X. She's one of the rare young women in Tecate who prefer dresses to pants. This afternoon she was in a dotted pink sundress with a charming white pique collar that tied behind her neck. Her head was covered with auburn plumage. Señorita X is not unattractive.

She slid in beside me. "Well, are you still subsisting on a diet of bread and wine and kisses?"

"I have simple needs," I answered.

"What are you working on?"

"I was sitting here thinking about love and friendship."

"Is there a difference?"

"I mean the secret of a love that doesn't end because she burned the tortillas or he doesn't pick up his clothes." Señorita X remained quiet as though looking for the answer to come from the pigeons that were now crooning around our bench. "Where does old love go?" I said. "Does it simply melt and disappear from the crucible we call our heart? Or does it just lie dormant like a banked fire, waiting for a special piece of music, a sound, a familiar smell, the touch of a hand to burst into flames again?"

"Why don't you ask Don Florentino and Doña Elvia? They're probably Tecate's oldest married couple."

"You know them?" I couldn't believe she knew as many people as I do—and they're my neighbors! I met Señorita X when she first arrived here, ten or twelve years ago. She was a beautiful young woman in full flower. She still is, for that matter. It was one of those things that could have been, should have been, but just never happened.

I told her of my visit to their rancho. I told her the whole story. When I got to the end she had the nerve to say to me, "You didn't get the whole story!"

"What!" I was annoyed and I think it showed. I have never presented my readers with an incomplete story. Was it possible there was a piece missing? But what? Don Florentino told me *El Secreto* and that was the whole point to the story. "I'm perfectly satisfied with the denouement. There is no more." So there!

Señorita X stood. "Come with me." I didn't like the smirk on her face that chanted, *I know something you don't know.*

I was still annoyed. The first thing I knew I didn't want was a case of bird flu. The second thing I knew I didn't want was to go anywhere with Señorita X. But she took my reluctant hand, gave it a determined tug, and I came to my feet. She kept my hand in hers, whether as a gesture of friendship or to prevent my bolting for the Diana, I didn't know. She towed me to El Jardin, a sidewalk cafe and bar at the south end of the plaza, an open garden of white tables under red umbrellas in a permanent state of festivities. Every table was full. I could hear the hum of beautiful noise, happy voices, flutters of gay laughter, bursts of music. Little frills from Chemo's accordion decorated the warm air and over near the planter José Machuca was singing *La Malagueña* in the company of his guitar. Señorita X escorted me directly to a table where an old woman sat alone. I recognized her at once.

"Doña Elvia, *buenas tardes!*" I greeted as I embraced her.

"*Buenas tardes*, Don."

"Where's Don Florentino? Are you here all by yourself?"

"I might as well be. Tino is on the ranch, my daughter parked me here while she's doing some shopping, and my dear friend, pink as a sunrise, has been keeping me company."

I saw the big platter of guacamole they were sharing with tall drinks and realized the poor woman had been sitting here by herself while I was resisting Señorita X.

"Sit down and dip," Señorita X said like a hostess at a party, and turned to Doña Elvia. "He's writing a story that reveals the secret to a beautiful long and happy marriage like you and Don Florentino."

I sat, but I had to overcome a strong urge to stuff her mouth with guacamole. I felt like I was on the spot. I couldn't reveal Don

Florentino's secret. Maybe Doña Elvia didn't know she's been under the magic spell of a *brujeria* for fifty-eight years. It wouldn't be right that she should learn it from me. But the moment of embarrassment passed quickly.

"*Ay!* There is no secret!" Doña Elvia laughed. "All men and all women are made like those bed quilts we used to make at home."

I shook my head at a kid who came by with a shoeshine box over his shoulder and pointed at my shoes accusingly. "I don't understand."

"Look at a bed quilt. Is it one piece? No! It's little scraps of everything, a little square from an old blanket, a snip from a worn out flannel shirt, an odd piece cut from an old shawl, or an old skirt, all colors, all patterns, different threads and knotted yarns of every color and thickness run through it." Doña turned to face Señorita X. "That's the way we're made, *mi amor.*" She turned to me again. "And if there's a little stitch or patch you don't like, you don't throw the coverlet away. The rest of it is beautiful! There's still plenty there to bring you warmth and comfort for many years. That's the only secret."

Señorita X got up and went into the bar. "She's such a lovely girl," Doña Elvia said to me.

"Yes, yes she is."

We watched the crowds passing our table. There was a long pause before Doña Elvia spoke. "You really came for *El Secreto*, didn't you?" I answered with a smile. She seemed to think about it then nodded her head toward where Señorita X had gone. "Of course, *she* knows. She's like a granddaughter to me. But we've been friends and neighbors for many years, Don." Doña Elvia placed her old wrinkled hand over mine. "We have *confianza.* Why shouldn't I tell you?"

Chemo moved to another table and squeezed out *Cielito Lindo* for a group of Americans. Doña Elvia continued.

"I knew Tino loved me. But a young good-looking vaquero is the devil's troubadour and I wanted Tino's love forever. My Tata Pancho approved of Tino and told me I shouldn't let him get away."

"Well, one day at the ranch he got a splinter in his hand. I removed the sliver and cleaned his hand with my handkerchief. I saw opportunity. My Nana used to say 'better one risk in time than two regrets too late.' Tino wasn't out the gate when I saddled my mare and took the bloody handkerchief to Doña Lala, an old witch my Nana went to see on occasion and said could do remarkable magic. The old witch stuck a needle in my hand, drew a drop of blood, and put my blood on his. Then she told me to kiss it. A few days later she handed me a tiny *amuleta de amor*. 'He will love you and you alone for as long as he has this magic amulet.' "

I know I gasped because Doña Elvia put her hand over mine. "Where did you put it?"

"In his guitar."

A double whammy! I sat there inert, dumb as the Sphinx with a bad case of dysphasia.

I can't say how long my labial incapacity lasted. My first moment of awareness came when Señorita X put a frothy margarita in my hands.

"*Salud*," I managed to babble when I regained the ability to form words. I put the frosty drink to my lips—and stopped! *Brujeria*?

Stolen Property

"Whatever it is the women are doing in the kitchen, it sure smells good!"

"Talking," Octavio senior answered. "Women! Their hands and tongues are on the same circuit." He was having a beer with his *compadre* Julian at the dining room table.

Julian put his cold bottle of Corona down just long enough to ask, "Have you talked to Manuel?" As soon as his voice rose to imply the question mark the Corona returned to its purpose.

"No, but I talked to Carmen. They're going through with the divorce."

"What about the store?"

"Carmen said they're going to build a wall down the middle. She gets the souvenir and trinkets half, Manuel gets the leather goods." Octavio opened another beer for Julian.

"*Salud*! Hey, where's your handsome son? When is the wedding?" Julian inquired.

"He's in his room getting himself beautiful for his *novia*."

The wives came in at that moment and the luscious smells of chopped cilantro and onions followed them into the room. They carried a big plate of hot-from-the skillet tortilla chips, a bowl of spicy red salsa, and a deep oval platter covered with molten Oaxaca cheese, still bubbling, over strips of jalapeño chiles.

"What are you men gossiping about?" Faustina, Octavio's lawful wedded wife accused, and put down the platter of *queso fundido*. "It just came out of the oven so be careful."

"Leave men alone for one minute and they chatter *chismes* worse than women!" Julian's wife Perla said, adding another charge to the indictment.

"We weren't gossiping. Men may sometimes trade intelligence, but we *don't* gossip. My *compadre* was just asking about Octavio *chico*," answered Octavio senior. "He'd better put a ring on Delia's finger before some *cabrón* comes along and steals her away in the night."

"Don't be silly," his wife answered. "They've been *novios* since they were children." She turned to Perla. "I still have a picture of Delia and Octavio *chico* together in the bathtub."

"You can probably get a good price for it now," Julian laughed.

"It's the cutest *foto* you've ever seen! They had been playing in the dirt and Delia's mother and I put them in the tub. Little Octavio was petting Delia's little *nalgas*!"

"He's probably doing that now!" Octavio senior said and all the *compadres* collapsed with laughter.

Octavio *chico*, who was at this moment getting himself ready to go out with Delia, heard the laughter and knew that in some way, he was grain for their gossip mill. They always teased him without mercy. Had there been a back way out he would have employed it. But he had no option but to walk through the dining room and face some good natured torture. Octavio *chico* was a handsome young man of imposing height, bronze of face, a dense thatching of wavy black hair. Two untrimmed black shrubs grew wild over his dark eyes. His thin-line mustache was cultivated at fifteen in an effort to appear older, suave, maybe debonair. It did all three. Young Octavio drew a breath, and bracing himself for the onslaught of adult humor, walked in wearing a burgundy suede blazer over a white shirt and pearl gray slacks. He greeted the company.

"*Buenas tardes.*" He embraced Doña Perla.

"*Ay que muchacho tan guapo!*" she gushed when her kiss cleared his cheek.

"*Gracias.*"

Doña Perla turned to Faustina. "You have such a gorgeous son. If I had daughters I'd be a grandmother!"

"When is the wedding?" Julian asked the young man.

"I ask him the same question!" his mother said. "I go out every week to find the right dress."

"Well, Octavio, when are you going to make an announcement?" Doña Perla insisted. "Delia is the sweetest girl you'll ever know."

"Oh, she's already family," answered Faustina. "She's like a daughter to us. We're just waiting for Señor Shy to make it official."

Octavio senior spoke to his son. "I was just telling Don Julian you'd better put a ring on Delia's finger soon. Some *cabrón* will steal her away and you'll never find another like her."

"La Cucha told me she saw you in Oscar's jewelry shop just the other day," his mother said. "So we know you've been shopping for the ring."

La Cucha! Octavio *chico* blanched. That evil dwarf probably knows the color of my *calzones*, he thought.

"If it's money I can help you out—just do it!" Octavio senior said.

Living in Tecate is like living in an aquarium, Octavio *chico* sighed in silence. "I just haven't seen the right one. He'll have more rings for me to look at first of the week."

"And there's so much to do!" exclaimed his mother. "The caterers, Tito Rios is the best, and he's always booked, and then there are the flowers, and the music, and finding a hall and hiring waiters—it's endless!"

"Your mother was hoping for a June wedding, but June is half over so that's out. Are you thinking December? We need to know, *cabrón*." Octavio *grande's* voice dropped to a lower register. "And listen, *hijo*, don't do like you always do and leave everything for the last minute."

It rankled Octavio *chico* to be spoken to like a ten-year-old. High color rose to his face. His comeback was already taking form on his lips when he realized words were under quarantine in the presence of company. All he could say was, "*Sí, Papá.*" He reciprocated with a counterfeit smile. "I'd better be on my way. We're going to the Other Side."

"Don't forget to kiss her!" he heard somebody shout followed by a flutter of laughter as he got into his car.

Not far away from the *compadres*, Delia was at her dressing table, still in her underwear. Her mother, Doña Anita, was doing her hair.

"You are so fortunate to have your father's hair. It has such body you can actually do anything you want with it." Delia was well aware of nature's best gift to a girl and maybe even a little vain. Well, maybe nature's second-best gift. "My own hair has always been thin and wispy. Even if I just walk down to the corner I come back looking like I've been through a tornado. Your Nana used to accuse me of rolling in the grass when your father brought me home." She brushed and shaped the shoulder-length strands of black silk like a sculptor creating a masterpiece. "You're going to make a beautiful bride."

"He hasn't asked me yet, Mamá."

"Oh, he will! Don't despair, *mi amor*, he will! Octavio has always been a little shy. But I heard he's been seen at Oscar's jewelry shop. The only possible business he has there is to choose your ring. Oh, it's so exciting!"

"Oh? I had no idea."

"Don't say anything. I'm not even supposed to know." Doña Anita teased the ends into saucy little wisps. Mother and daughter's eyes met in the big mirror and she burst out laughing. Delia's lips looked like she was trying to turn them inside out. "What on earth are you doing to your mouth!"

"I thought I felt something stuck between my teeth."

"It looks *terríble*," she laughed again because it was something of a funny face. "Be sure to brush again before you leave."

Doña Anita smoothed the sides of her daughter's hair with the aid of her hands. She put down the brush and comb. "There! I've already talked to Doña Eva about making your wedding gown. She showed me some absolutely adorable pictures. I thought you and I might drop in on her on Monday so you can see the gowns."

"Of course. We can go as soon as I get off work."

"You're so lucky to be marrying such a fine young man like Octavio. He's already like family. Your father and I love him like a son."

"Well, yes, of course, you've known him since he was born."

"Yours is truly a marriage made in heaven! The two of you have loved each other since you were little." Doña Perla trotted to the bedroom door. "I have a *foto* you just have to see. Wait."

Delia was already rummaging through her wardrobe when her mother returned and put the blackmail snapshot in her hand. "Is this cute or what!"

Delia's mouth fell open when she recognized herself and Octavio, age four or five, standing stark naked in the bathtub, his hand cupping her *nalgas*. "Ay, Mamá! You have to get rid of this!"

"Not on your life!" She snatched it back. "Come let's find you something sexy to wear."

"Sexy?"

"Men all over the world are the same, *mi amor*. Whether they admit it or not, men want their women to look seductive."

"I was thinking maybe I could just go like this."

"In your under—! *Ay, muchacha!*"

They heard the rasp of the doorbell and knew Octavio was in the living room watching the soccer game between Guadalajara and Mexico City with her father.

It was after midnight when Octavio and Delia entered La Fonda. Only a few late diners remained, mostly dreamy couples, hands across the table, speaking their own silent language. A few toyed drowsily with after-dinner brandy and coffee. The mariachis were gone now, leaving behind only faint echoes of their musical alchemy.

They'd been to San Diego to see a movie and barely squeaked back across the border before American border officers slammed the gate shut at twelve. Delia tried to tell him several times that they were running late, but so characteristic of the male sex, Octavio didn't listen. Maybe selective deafness is a common disorder in men, she thought, a kind of hormonal imbalance.

Beto showed them to their favorite table. Beto was a standard fixture at La Fonda whose fun-loving charm and graciousness never waned however late the hour. "The hour is never late for either a margarita or a kiss when a man and a woman are in love!" He held a chair for Delia.

"*Gracias,*" Delia answered as she sat. Her mother had chosen a swirly white skirt and a lime sherbet blouse that was not only off-the-shoulder, it was nearly off the torso! A gold cross resting on her throat pointed the way for the fertile male mind.

"Beto, I've always suspected you can divine human thought," Octavio said with a friendly grin.

In minutes Beto was back with two perfectly blended margaritas. "I'll leave you to your dreams, Octavio. Give me the *ojo* when you're ready for menus."

"*Salud.*"

"*Salud,*" Delia answered and began at once to scratch her head. Her hair, so recently arranged to form an abundant bouffant of fine black silk, became disarranged as busy fingers scrabbled around in a vigorous effort to locate the point of her discomfort.

An ant bite? Octavio thought. She hasn't stopped scratching all evening! Mange, maybe. They sipped and chatted sporadically. Octavio was relieved to see Delia finally abandon the activity in her hair having apparently located and satisfied the itch on her scalp.

Crack, crack!

The pretty girl in front of him was now cracking her knuckles! It sounded like she was cracking walnuts. Why am I here? he thought. Octavio gave Beto the *ojo* and they turned to studying the menu. "What are you in the mood for?" he asked his dinner date.

"I'm going for something light. That was a heavy dinner." Delia curled her lower lip down and extended her upper lip, exposing the tips of pearly white central incisors as she studied the menu.

Octavio couldn't watch. That can't be easy to do, he thought. "How about a simple omelet?"

"Perfect choice!" Having to employ the oral muscles to form words the grotesque labial distortion ceased, and Delia's velvety mouth returned to its usual sweet and kissable state. She reached across and patted his cheek. "*Mi chulito chulito!*" and excused herself to go the *damas*.

Octavio's mind was reeling. How could I possibly have fallen in love with this girl in high school? How have we remained *novios* for so many years? I should have dated other girls. Especially Lorena. She looked so sexy even in her school uniform—intended to make girls as attractive and interesting to the male eye as a dead cat. He could still remember Lorena's big dark eyes, the hills and peaks hidden under her sweater, her virginal face, smooth as satin, the color of almond candy. All the *muchachos* called her Lorena Morena, the walking dream.

Hee-hee-hee haw! Hee-hee-hee-haaawww!

The sudden braying snapped Octavio out of his thoughts and back to his table at La Fonda. How did a donkey get into the restaurant! It was a wheezing intake of breath followed by a series of strident gasps and screeching similar to that heard when a dull hacksaw is drawn across sheet metal. He looked in the direction of the sound. It was not a burro.

It was Delia!

She apparently stopped at a friend's table on her way back from the *damas* to exchange a joke that now had her braying like an ass! With traces of a smile still lingering on her pretty face Delia returned to the table. They consumed their late supper with little conversation and were soon in the car on their way to her house. There was little conversation as she never stopped biting and gnawing her fingernails. Octavio pulled up to her door.

"It's late. I better get right in." Delia put a sloppy kiss, half on his mouth, half on his nose, and patted his cheek. "*Mi chulito chulito!*" And she ran into the dark house.

What perversity of mind made me think I was ever in love with that girl? Octavio asked himself, and drove the rest of the way home thinking of Lorena.

"Love can be so depressing!"
"Love is delightful!"
"Bitter!"

"Sweet!"

"Exasperating."

"Exquisite!"

"Foolish."

"Fun!"

"Love is nothing more than a state of insanity."

"Oh, to be crazy in love!"

"A sickness."

"May they never find a cure!"

"Another Cuervo, Mario!" Octavio demanded.

"Another Cuervo won't help us," Kikki said. "But it's okay with me."

The two young men, who'd known each other since they were in diapers, sat at the bar in the dusky Diana. They were both twenty-five now. Octavio was plant manager at a large American factory in Tecate, Kikki was in his second year of law practice. Mario, the bartender put a Cuervo shooter, a plate of lemon wedges, and a salt shaker in front of them.

"There's got to be an answer," Octavio went on. "I'm not in the least in love with Delia. Why should we continue to be *novios* and I run the risk of having to marry the girl?"

"Have you asked her?" Kikki asked, incredulous.

"No, thank God! But I'm on thin ice. Her parents and mine have taken our marriage for granted."

"Mexican parents haven't arranged marriages since the social liberation following La Revolucion of 1910."

"*Salud.*"

"*Salud.*"

"No, no. Not arranged in that sense, but parents fall in love with the idea when you're three or four and susceptible and now they have their hearts set on it. The only thing they haven't done is take a picture of us naked together. They love Delia like a daughter. They're on my *nalgas* three times a day. You can't imagine the pressure. I've even been to Oscar's a couple of times."

"To buy the ring?"

"Yes, but I always get cold feet at the last minute and run out of the shop. They've been pushing us together since we were kids. They're just waiting for me to put a ring on her finger so they can throw a big fiesta."

"Can I be best man?"

"Don't be smart!"

"I don't know what you find so objectionable about Delia. She's a beautiful girl, an angel carved from antique ivory, her voice, a sonnet. And a body that leaves men breathless since seventh grade. None of the rest of us could get near her. You always had your arm around her or under her sweater."

"What good is beauty if I have to close my eyes when I kiss her?"

"Oh, it can't be that bad."

"You don't take her out, to the movies, to dinner, to a dance, or some fiesta. She's forever scratching her head, she cracks her knuckles in the movies and constantly gnaws at her fingernails. When she's deciding what to order for dinner she has that detestable way of deforming her mouth. She looks like a ferret. I'd rather kiss a ferret!" Octavio sucked a lemon wedge and licked the salt from the back of his hand. "Then she has that obnoxious habit of patting my cheek and saying, *mi chulito chulito*. It's odious!"

"I can remember when you were hopelessly in love with her."

"I can, too. I can also remember when I was crazy about bread pudding with raisins. People change, Kikki, you outgrow things. Over time you get used to each other. You become a little careless with your appearance, or maybe a yawn goes uncovered, or you allow a little gas to escape, things like that. Delia used to have the voice of a nightingale. Lately she sounds more like a crow in a cornfield. And her laugh that once tinkled like silver wind chimes in a summer breeze, now rents the air like the braying of an ass!"

"So you really want to break up with her?"

"Desperately! If I could just unload Delia I could start going out with the girl I really love."

"Who?"

"Lorena."

"Lorena Morena! She was so beautiful we were all afraid of her. She didn't have a *novio* all through school—and what a gorgeous creature she was!"

"And still is!"

"I kissed her once," Kikki recalled. "El Feo dared me, but she wouldn't let anyone near her sweater."

"I think maybe I've always loved her, I was just too tangled up with Delia to know it. I wonder if she's still available? I hope I'm not too late."

"I don't think she's ever had a great deal of interest in anyone special. I see her almost every day at city hall. She'll go out with some of the *muchachos* there, but one date and it's over."

"That's what I mean. I have to make my move on Lorena now, before she finds a *novio* and I'm forever saddled with the ferret. I can't imagine waking up with her every morning and watch her scratching, cracking, chewing, and braying like an ass in heat." Octavio took a slug of his Cuervo. "I'd rather eat a toad!"

Kikki licked the salt from his hand. "If Delia is that bad," he suggested, "why don't you just end it?"

"Just dump her *como un saco de frijol*?"

"*Exacto.* Like a sack of beans."

"I don't want to hurt the poor girl. And it wouldn't work anyway. That's the problem with a small pueblo like Tecate. We're all family. Her parents and my parents are friends from way back in their school days. If I started going out with someone else it would strain all the family friendships. Her parents would immediately want to talk to me. My parents would badger me—there would be even more pressure. And she's so emotional about everything. If I tell her it's over she's capable of throwing herself in the river."

"There's no water in it."

"Then she'd lie on the train tracks."

"The train doesn't run anymore."

"It wouldn't matter. Delia is also a *masoquista*."

The two friends sat at the bar in silence, grinding gears in the organ of thought. They paid no attention to Miguel, El Guacha, when he strolled in with a guitar in his arms and his two friends on accordion and bass viol.

"*Una canción, muchachos?*"

"Play a love song and I'll shoot the three of you! The guitar first."

"Why the guitar first?" asked Miguel more startled than offended.

"Because you sing better than the other two *cabrónes.*"

The trio struck up *Te Fuiste Con Otro*, a song about a faithless woman who ran off with another man. They sang and strummed and squeezed and thumped all three verses.

The song ended with a thunk of the bass and Octavio nearly dropped his Cuervo on the floor. "I have it! I have it!" he shouted.

"You do?"

"Yes!" he handed the trio a hundred pesos. "Now run off somewhere else, Kikki and I have business to discuss."

"Business?" Kikki watched the trio slowly file out of the bar.

"Yes! I have the perfect plan."

"Inspired by the song the trio just sang."

"*Exacto!*"

"And?"

"Delia is going to run away with another man—just like in the song!"

"You're crazy."

"Don't you see? It's the perfect plan. *She* dumps *me!*"

Mario removed the two empty shot glasses and the sucked-out lemon wedges from in front of them. "*Otro?*"

"Might as well have another. We're celebrating!"

"I still don't get it," Kikki answered.

"Don't you see? I don't have to do anything. Delia pins the horns on *me*. That leaves me the wounded party. I've been *betrayed*—I'm innocent!" Octavio took a slug of the new Cuervo and bit ferociously into a lemon. "Auuuugh! Everybody will feel sorry for me and I'll drown my sorrows in Lorena's arms. It's perfect!" He slammed the glass down on the bar as an exclamation point.

"Just like in the song."

"Just like in the song."

"The only problem I see with that plan is you'll need someone to steal her away."

"I have him!"

"Who?"

"You!"

"You're drunk."

"I confess it! But it's still the perfect plan because nobody gets hurt. All you have to do is take her out. Nothing more. When the gossip in this town begins, I can say *aha*! and it's over. It's beautiful!" Octavio shot back the remaining Cuervo. "You don't have a *novia* right now so it can't do anyone any harm."

It was true, Kikki thought, he didn't have a *novia*. While Octavio played and partied, he worked day and night to get his *licenciado* degree and open his own law office. And now that he had a measure of stability all his old girlfriends were either engaged or married. Love and romance passed me by, he thought.

Kikki put down his glass. "Look, there's an easier way. Go to the *botanica* and ask Doña Lala to give you a girl repellent and your problem is solved."

"Won't work."

"Her potions never fail."

"That's the problem. Her girl repellent is a broad spectrum potion. It would repel all *muchachas*."

"But there's one thing you haven't thought of."

"What haven't I thought of?"

"If Delia discovers you're going out with Lorena you have given her just cause to prosecute and you'll precipitate the very *escándalo* with the families you're trying to avoid."

"Stop talking like a *licenciado*. I am an honorable man. I will court Lorena with passion, but I will not soil her velvet lips with mine, nor hold her silken hand, nor stroke her ebon hair. Her virgin body will remain innocent of my touch."

"Then how do you propose to court her, *cabrón*?"

"*Por teléfono.*"

"On the phone!"

"*Exacto.* I will call her twice a day and confess my secret passion. I will send her kisses of fire. I will tune my guitar and bring her a *serenata* over the wires every night."

"*Salud.*"

"*Salud.*"

"A love affair without leaving a shred of evidence. It's ingenious! Come on, *cabrón*, all you have to do is ask her out."

It wasn't that Kikki didn't like Delia. He saw her at Copitec several times a week. She was a lovely girl in high school, he remembered. But the whole scheme sounded just a little too convoluted to his logical legal mind. "What if she says no?"

"She might at first, but you're *simpatico*, you're *guapo*. Sooner or later, she'll go out with you—and I'm free. Free!"

"It's not a good plan."

"Why not?"

"It could get expensive."

"Oh, that's the least of my worries. I'm fully prepared to finance her act of betrayal!"

"What if she falls in love with me? Then I get stuck with the ferret."

"Not a chance. You're okay, but you're just not her type."

"It could happen, though."

"Tell you what. You know me as *hombre de palabra*. For all my faults I am a man of my word. If you have to end up with Delia I'll eat a toad!"

Kikki began to think it over. It could be fun—and what the hell—it wouldn't cost him anything. By the time the two lifelong friends left the Diana, the scheme, aided in large part by tequila, lemon, and salt, looked as viable to them as the legendary wooden horse must have appeared to Ulysses when he ordered Epios to build it.

"I'll call Delia today and tell her we're going to be working late at the factory and I won't get to see her this week. That gives you plenty of opportunity."

The next day at quarter to three in the afternoon Kikki left his law office upstairs in the Guajardo Building, strolled across the plaza, and walked into Copitec. There was Delia, her back to him, squirming and bending in her effort to load the printer. Kikki couldn't take his eyes off the pseudo frayed spots legislated by fashion on the seat of her jeans of blue indigo. Kikki was a practical man. He never quite understood the tyranny of fashion. He was convinced that if Britney Spears wore a fried egg on her head today, every girl in Tecate would be wearing an egg sunny-side up tomorrow. The only difference would be that in Tecate there might be a dollop of refried beans on the side.

She turned as soon as she felt his presence and came to the counter. "*Hola* Kikki!" Her voice was warm and gay.

"*Que onda?*" he answered. "I brought work for you."

"You're just in time. I'm off at three. How many copies do you need?"

"Two each." Kikki was overcome by a sudden attack of acute stage fright and the invitation to dinner stayed lodged in his throat.

Delia enjoyed it when Kikki came into the shop which was several times a week. She'd known him since kindergarten. They had played tag, and hide-and-seek, and all the other games with the rest of the kids in the *colonia*. In only a couple of minutes Delia handed him his copies and rang up the sale.

"What a beastly hot day," Delia said, fanning her face with a sheet of copy paper. "We might as well be living in Mexicali!"

"I was just headed for the ice cream parlor for a lemon ice. Want to come along?"

"I'd love it!" She went back to the desk and took her purse. "I'm off, Don Luis," she called to her boss who was working at a paper cutter. "See you in the morning."

It was a short walk to La Flor de Michoacan, the ice cream store at the north end of the plaza. Kikki surveyed the pretty girl at his side. He admired her loose and carefree gait. She stepped out as though she were walking to music. Delia looked the same to him now as she did in high school, the bouncy black hair, the deep dark eyes that touched his soul, and a mouth that put him in mind of ripe strawberries. He was careful not to let his eyes wander into the vicinity of her pink jersey sprayed with little white pearls.

They found an empty table on the sidewalk facing the plaza and both ordered a lemon ice. Delia looked over at Kikki. He'd never bothered to nourish a mustache and didn't look much different here eating a lemon ice than he did in high school. She remembered kissing him once. It was during a game of penalty at Octavio's house. Half dozen kids sat around in a circle. The boys were usually the ones who started the game. One would light a match, say "penalty," and hand it to the next kid. The flaming match would get passed around the circle from hand to hand. The one who had to blow it out or drop it to avoid scorching his fingers paid the penalty. Delia dropped the match and sucked her fingers. El Feo ordered her to kiss Kikki—on the mouth! The faded memory brought her a smile.

They watched the perpetual pageant in the plaza; old rancheros in tall sombreros gossiping in the shade, women coming and going from market under colored parasols, the balloon man, the doughnut man, the brush and broom man in his wheelchair. Offstage someone was playing a love song on a guitar—Antonio, without a doubt.

"My God! There goes La Cucha, Tecate's twenty-four-hour news satellite," Delia said. "She's been orbiting around the plaza since we were kids."

They stared at La Cucha the rumormonger. The withered old gnome, lumpy as a peanut shell, came trudging along near the kiosk. Her raiment never changed, a long black shawl over heavy skirts that ended at a pair of thick red leggings and tattered black shoes. Her mouth was loose, and too large for the shrunken face covered with bumps, wrinkles and warts. Her millinery was a cone-shaped knitted cap of red wool. La Cucha looked like the evil troll of myth that lurks under a bridge and steals little children.

"I've seen her out as late as midnight and early as six in the morning," Kikki observed.

"She's better than Channel 2."

"Let's hope she doesn't come this way. We'll be on the evening news."

Delia laughed. "Look at the kids flirting and stealing kisses over by the fountain! Remember when we used to do that every afternoon after school?"

Kikki watched the uniformed teenagers sitting on the edge of the fountain like pigeons. The girls were in white knee-socks and plaid skirts rolled up at the waistband to shorten the skirt far in excess of parental statutes. The boys wore navy blue pants and white shirts. Kikki remembered the scene from years ago. Lorena would hike her skirt to the upper limit and sit giggling with her girlfriends. He tried to sit near Delia but it was impossible. Octavio and Delia sat nearly on top each other, holding hands or linking arms.

"They make me feel old at twenty-five," Kikki said.

Delia sighed. "Life gets so serious as soon as we're out of school. We get busy or we get married and pretty soon we lose touch with all our friends."

"You're right. I haven't seen El Feo or Marisol or Sandra in a long time."

"Marisol and Sandra are both married and stay home. El Feo moved to Tijuana."

"I see Octavio all the time, of course. And I see you every time I need copies." He watched her lick a little fleck of sherbet off her spoon. Remember why you're here, he told himself. "Why don't we go out for dinner one day? That would be great fun!"

Going out with Kikki had long been a cherished dream for Delia. To appear over eager however, went against all her feminine instincts. "I'm with Octavio now. Don't tell me you didn't know."

"Oh God, I'm sorry! Of course. It just slipped out."

Delia reached across the little ice cream table and took both his hands into her own. She squeezed affectionately. "I'm sorry! I didn't mean it to sound the way it did."

"I understand. It's just that I get so busy I don't know what's going on around me."

Kikki felt the cool air as Delia took her warm hands back. "Besides, I don't think Octavio would object and he's the only one I would worry about."

Delia put down her lemon ice. "You know, you're right. I was being silly. Look, Octavio is going to be busy all week. I don't think two old school friends out to dinner would raise eyebrows."

"Unless La Cucha sees us."

Delia laughed in little ripples. "Saturday?"

"Are you sure?" Suddenly Kikki found himself reviewing his case before the tribunal that now presided in the chamber of his mind; if Delia declined, the deal was obviously off. The curtain would come down and that would be the end of his role in the play. On the other hand, it could be a lot of fun to go out.

"Of course I am! It's not a secret or anything. Pick me up at Copitec."

At eight o'clock in the evening the following Saturday Kikki walked into La Fonda with Delia at his side. Not on his arm. The place was packed as it usually is on a weekend. The restaurant was thrumming with music, voices talking, laughing, the clatter of dishes. At least half the patrons were Americans over-dosing on margaritas. Mariachis filled La Fonda with their festive music, guitars, violins, and a silvery trumpet with a soul of its own.

Beto led them to a table that was just being vacated. "*Hola* Delia, *hola* Kikki! I'll have your table cleared for you in an instant. Your margaritas are at this moment being prepared."

It was a table for four and they sat at opposite ends. They could have been brother and sister. They exchanged a smile and a wave with people they knew at the other tables which was everyone. Both Delia and Kikki were relieved to see no one looked at them in any special way. They aroused no curiosity. Margaritas arrived, they said *salud*, and their voices joined the others, talking and laughing over their old school days.

Delia ordered enchiladas, rice, and beans, Kikki went for chiles rellenos. They dallied leisurely over flan and coffee. By ten o'clock they waved adios to friends and walked into the soothing silence of the plaza, the only sound at this hour, the hissing of the sprinklers. The air was scented with roses, the lazy moon, waiting backstage on the other side of darkness to make her grand entrance in a gown of gold at a later hour.

Together they walked the short distance to Delia's car. Kikki did not offer his arm. At her car Delia brought out her keys, unlocked the driver's side, and slid in. They said *buenas noches* through the open door. He stepped back and she was gone into the night.

On the way across the darkened plaza to collect his car Kikki dropped into a bench, and, as he so often did before a court appearance, fell into a conversation with himself. I have to admit that was a fun evening. I should go out more often. I'd forgotten how much fun Delia can be. I couldn't take my eyes off of her in high school. God, I can still feel that kiss on the mouth she gave me when we were playing penalty at Octavio's. She still has the same dancing eyes, the same melodic voice.

The sudden scream of an ambulance flashing red lights along Avenida Juarez cut into his pleasant daydream. In a few seconds silence returned to the plaza and Kikki resumed his sweet remembrance of things past. Wait a minute! I didn't see any of those obnoxious mannerisms Octavio was complaining about. On the contrary, she was utterly charming tonight. Kikki left his bench and started across the plaza. The voice in his head followed him to his car.

Know what I think, Kikki?

What?

I think you're in love with her.

No, I'm not!

Yes, you are!

Well, maybe.

"Two Cuervos, Mario," Octavio called out. The two friends were back at headquarters.

"Well, did you make love to Lorena?"

"Yes! I sang *Toda Una Vida* and *Morir Soñando*. But I think it was the last line of *Júrame* that clinched it...*bésame, bésame hasta la locura... y sabras la amargúra que estoy sufriendo por tiiii...!* We're officially engaged!"

"*Por teléfono.*"

"*Por teléfono.*"

Mario served up the two shooters, lemon wedges, and the salt shaker. Octavio turned to Kikki. "*Salud.*"

"*Salud.*"

"Well, I'm anxious to hear your first report."

Kikki handed him a note. "Two lemon ices, two dinners at La Fonda. Four margaritas before dinner, two plates of flan, four coffees. Forty-six-fifty American."

"That's not what I want to know!" He pulled out his wallet and happily paid his debt of honor. "How did it go?"

"It went."

"Well? Did you kiss her?"

"No."

"Did you hold her in your arms?"

"No."

"Did she talk about me?"

"No."

"You see? Just as I told you. Beauty on the outside, ice crystals on the inside. Passionless! I won't be eating a toad!"

"But it isn't over. Everybody saw us, no one thought anything about it. So you can't say *aha*! You still don't have grounds to accuse her of pinning the horns on you." He sounded like a *licenciado* again.

"You're right. Take another shot at it next week. I'll let her know we're still working late at the plant."

This whole thing may have started out as a sham but Kikki recognized that today he had feelings for Delia that weren't there yesterday. It just didn't seem an honorable thing to do. He would be playing a part written by someone else. "I don't think I want to play anymore."

"Look, you're just in this until Delia is off my back. You have no further obligation of friendship. You never have to see her again.

The moment I say *aha!* and it's all over between us you're as free as the proverbial *golondrina* on the wing."

"I don't think so."

"Oh, come on! We're almost there. You can't let me down now. You're my best friend."

Mario put two more Cuervos in front of them. "Hey, how did you know I would order another?"

Mario answered with a mischievous grin. "Your mind is written across your forehead in large type."

Octavio turned to his best friend and only conspirator. "Just one more try, Kikki, honest, one more try. If it works it works, if it doesn't it doesn't." He picked up his tequila, performed the ceremony of the sip, the lemon, and a lick of salt. "And nobody gets hurt, no pain, no hard feelings. Everything goes back the way it was."

"Only—"

"Only what?"

"Only I was hoping to watch you eat toad."

Octavio threw his free arm around his old friend and drew him in tight. "Kikki, you're the best!"

"Love can be so painful."

"If it doesn't hurt it isn't love."

Delia and Lorena had a valid and logical reason to meet for coffee at Lupita's tiny coffee and pastry shop tucked into a hidden crevice between two buildings on Calle Hidalgo. First, they didn't want to be seen together, second, they wanted to be sure they would be alone and in Tecate that's close to impossible. Lupita's little shop guaranteed both conditions. Lupita served a wide variety of beautifully decorated freshly baked pastries that everyone in Tecate made a special effort to avoid. From her coffee urn she poured a cup of evil liquid that, to anyone who'd lost their taste and olfactory senses, might pass for coffee. The little shop was cozy and richly scented with cinnamon and nutmeg. The two girls took a small table. Predictably, they were the only customers.

"Well, did Octavio make his move on you yet?"

"Oh yes!"

"Just as I thought."

"Every day! He confesses a love for me that he's carried secretly in a corner of his heart for years. He showers me with burning kisses and serenades me every night after I'm in bed!" Overcome with emotion, Lorena paused for breath. "When he sings *Júrame* I quiver all over!"

"He certainly wasted no time in pinning the horns on me."

"*Por teléfono.*"

"The immaculate deception."

Lorena thought she heard footsteps and lowered her voice. "Well, our clever scheme sounded good a few weeks ago, you would have Kikki and I would get Octavio. But it's not working out the way we planned. At this rate the only time you'll see Kikki is when he comes in for copies and Octavio will just be a disembodied voice on the phone."

"I'm disappointed too," admitted Delia. "I went out with Kikki and we didn't stir up any rumors. I felt sure the very next day Octavio would hear some gossip, he'd confront me and say '*aha!*' then dump me. You'd have Octavio and I'd have Kikki in my arms."

"Did he kiss you goodnight?"

"Didn't even shake hands. But deep inside I think he cares. Kikki is a man of honor."

"Should we try something else?"

"It takes time," Delia answered. "It can't be done overnight. Changing your entire personality is a long process. Try it sometime."

"I'm sorry, I guess I'm just being impatient."

"It's taken me several months to develop all those obnoxious mannerisms that make Octavio grind his teeth. I crack my knuckles constantly, I scratch my head at dinner, I bite my nails. Do you have any idea how long I've practiced laughing like a braying ass? It's not an easy thing to do." There was still no sign of Lupita but they could hear her in the kitchen doing something that required an electric mixer and the rattling of cake pans. "You can't imagine the hours I spend in front of the bathroom mirror practicing a repulsive contortion of my mouth until I've got it perfect." Delia demonstrated.

"*Ay!*" Lorena laughed, "You look just like a ferret! Wouldn't it be easier just to go to the *botanica* and get one of Doña Lala's boy repellents?"

"Oh, no! Those potions are non-selective. I'd lose Kikki and—"

"*Buenos dias, muchachas!*" the proprietress sang out as she came to their table. "*Café?*" She was a living replica of Mary See on a box of See's candies in her spotless full-length white apron, funny little hat, and granny glasses.

"Yes, Lupita," Delia answered. "Two coffees, *por favor.*"

"And some of your lovely little pastries," Lorena added with fraudulent sincerity only to encourage Delia to do the ferret face. She obliged.

Lupita brought them a cup of her infamous coffee and a plate of her lethal little pastries. "Just give me a call *muchachas* if you need anything. I have an oven full of little cakes in the back." And granny was gone.

"Why does she even bother to bake more? Nobody's going to buy what she already has."

"Sssh!"

The two girls looked at the plate of pastries in search of something that wouldn't require a stomach pump. It was hopeless. The marble cake appeared to have been made from genuine Carrara, the little yellow spongecakes looked like Brillo scouring pads. There were cookies artfully decorated and piped with swirls of Crest for Kids. The chocolate things were like something one would expect to find on the sidewalk.

"Back to the business at hand," Lorena began, "wouldn't it be simpler to just dump him?"

"*Como un saco de frijol?*"

"*Exacto.* Like a sack of beans."

"It wouldn't work. That's the problem with a small pueblo like Tecate—we're all family. His parents and my parents are friends from way back in their school days. Both sets of parents would be trying to get us back together again. They have their hearts set on our getting married. My mother is already taking me to look at wedding gowns! You can't imagine the pressure." Delia reached for a pastry and put it back. "No, breaking up has to be Octavio's idea if you and I are going to end up with the right man. Remember, Octavio is the only *novio* I ever had. It all started in high school."

"I well remember."

"My mother has a picture of the two of us naked in the bathtub."

"What!"

"Relax, we were four or five. I've heard marriage since I was fifteen. It was fun and exciting at first. But now it's getting scary." Delia was so wrapped up in her problem she took a sip of coffee. "Bleaagh! I'm having second thoughts. We change. We're not the same person at twenty-four that we were at sixteen. I've had the feeling for some time that Octavio and I are no longer twin souls."

Delia ran over to a mop bucket, emptied her cup and ran back. "This isn't high school, Lorena, this is real life. and I don't want to make a mistake. I don't want to end up like a lot of the women here in Tecate, keeping house, raising the kids, while my husband goes off to play. Octavio is sweet, he's nice. He'll make someone a wonderful husband but I realize now it would never work for me. I never had the chance to get to know other boys."

"Like Kikki."

"Thank God I realized that Kikki and I share the same heart before I could make a terrible mistake."

"How can you be so sure?"

"Because the mind can deceive us, the heart never lies. If my heart is telling me I'm in love with Kikki, then my heart must be right."

"And I've been in love with Octavio since kindergarten but you were always on his lap. I couldn't even get him to look at me. I date here and there or I'd never go out at all, but my heart and my body belong to Octavio."

Once again Delia summoned her courage, took a pastry, and inhaled the rich smell of cinnamon and vanilla. She couldn't resist nibbling a corner experimentally. Chocolate chips, toasted almonds with a sawdust filling. She wrapped it in a napkin. "But I have a whole new strategy, Plan A and Plan B."

"What's Plan A?"

"Plan A is nothing more than an innocent dinner."

"And Plan B?"

"Abduction!"

"What!"

"I just know Kikki is in love with me but he's too honorable to voice his feelings."

"Maybe he's afraid they're not returned. Boys are like that, you know."

"I know. Somehow I have to arrange a way to convey my feelings so he won't be afraid to express his. I must stir the embers I know are smoldering in his heart and release the words of love waiting to be spoken."

"Can you do it?"

"I can guarantee it. By this time next week you'll have Octavio in your arms and Kikki will be mine! Your only job is to be sure you answer your phone."

When Kikki walked into Copitec the following Wednesday he found the girl he feared to love loading paper into a printer. Delia reminded him of a French pastry. She was in a turquoise jersey and sequined stonewashed jeans. She wore a white belt and white boots.

"*Hola*, Kikki, *que onda?*"

I don't need copies I just came in here to eat you up! Kikki didn't actually say this but it was clear that's what he was thinking. "Could I have ten copies of each page in the folder?"

"Of course!"

Kikki handed her the folder with the ten documents that didn't need copying, but he figured a hundred copies would provide enough time to have a conversation. "That was a fun dinner last week. Let me know next time Octavio is too busy to take you out."

"That would be Friday. He says they're having some problems at the plant."

"That works for me. You choose the venue."

"Would you believe I've never been to Little Italy? Have you?"

"Lots of times. I know just the place. You'll love it."

"The only problem is we'll be getting a late start. I promised my mother I would do some things for her. I probably couldn't get away until almost nine or so."

"Oh, that's perfectly all right. Should I pick you up at home?"

"No! That is, we can save some time if you pick me up here."

"I'll see you here at nine, then." Kikki gathered up his useless copies, paid, returned to his office, and dropped them in the wastebasket. Champagne bubbles were bursting inside him.

The following Friday Kikki and Delia crossed the border a few minutes after nine. It was nearly ten when they arrived in San Diego. They parked the car and strolled down India Street side by side. Kikki admired her costume. She wore stretchy black pants and a black rayon blouse spattered with giant pompoms in shades of blue and plum and pink.

"This is positively magical!" Delia cried like a child when she caught a glimpse of the bay by night filled with boats at anchor. "What a beautiful sight! Just look at all the lights! I'm just sorry I've never been here before." She put her arm through his and snuggled close enough to press a few pompoms into his arm. "I'm glad I'm seeing it with you for the first time."

"Where would you like to have dinner?"

"You choose!"

"Your choice."

Lines formed at the door of all the restaurants. She chose the one with the longest line. "Oh, here, Kikki, can we eat here? It looks so charming."

"La Dolce Vita it is!" It grieved him to have to give up the soft pompoms pressing on his arm, but he led her in front of him and gave the hostess his name.

"Twenty minutes, *signor*."

Delia sneaked a peak at her watch. It was closer to forty minutes by the time the hostess called their name. *So far, so good.*

A young country girl in a red, white and green peasant costume showed them to an intimate table for two under a grape arbor. A candle glowed in a wine bottle, and from somewhere, the voice of Tito Schipa sang *Vieni Sul Mar.* They could have been in Tuscany.

"*Buona sera.*"

"*Buenas noches,*" they answered.

"*Parla italiano?*"

"*Ma non troppo,*" Delia answered. She knew it was wrong but she'd seen it written on her piano music and she was in a festive mood. Kikki just threw up his hands and grinned.

"*Me chiamo Bianca.*"

That, Kikki understood. "Kikki," he said, pointing at himself.

"Delia."

"*Un piacere,*" Bianca said with a smile. "*Vino?*"

Kikki could handle that one too. "Chianti."

They both ordered fetuccini a la primavera. The dinner conversation was gay and filled with laughter shared by a young man and a young woman standing perilously near the fathomless abyss of love from which there is no return. Kikki had to fight back an overwhelming urge to reach across the table, take Delia's hands into his own, and release the doves of love fluttering in his heart. I'm on assignment, he reminded himself, taking a breadstick. Wait! All Octavio wants is to unload Delia, he doesn't care to whom. Scrap the assignment! I'll confess my love this very night! No, better not. What if she doesn't feel the same way? What if she just sees this as a brother-sister relationship? I would just look sappy.

That inner voice came back to him. *What have you got to lose, your precious pride? Just do it!*

"I will, I will! Later."

"You will what?" his date inquired.

"Oh, er, uh — I will order another bottle of wine."

It was a leisurely dinner. Kikki ordered the second bottle of Chianti, then came lemon gelato and cappuccino.

"*Tutte bene?*" Bianca inquired.

"*Tutte bene,*" Kikki answered only to impress his date. He took the check.

"I hate to leave," Delia sighed.

"We can do it again."

"You mean it?"

"Promise."

Delia excused herself while Kikki took out his wallet and began sorting out pesos from dollars.

Out on the street again, they walked hand in hand toward where they'd left the car. Delia had checked her watch in the light of the ladies room. Eleven fifteen. "I'll never stop thanking you for such a lovely dinner and a great adventure," Delia gushed. She snuggled in a little closer. "I know it's late, but could we walk a couple of blocks? I've never seen anything quite so beautiful!"

The pompoms were back on his arm "Of course! We can do anything your heart desires." Kikki almost put a kiss on her face, lost his nerve again somewhere between intention and action, and Delia's damask cheek remained unkissed.

So much for Plan A, Delia thought. I don't think I've got him to the point where he wants to run away with me. Well, if I can't warm him up here, I'll go to Plan B.

They strolled and talked in sighs and whispers until Delia felt him suddenly stop dead. "What is it?"

"We'd better get moving. It's after eleven and the border closes at midnight."

"I feel like Cinderella."

"We'd better get in the pumpkin fast!"

Delia knew perfectly well they could never make it back before midnight so she wasn't at all surprised when Kikki screeched to a halt in front of the enormous iron gates that separate the land of the Golden Arches and Margarita-Land. "Damn! We're locked out!"

Okay, Delia decided, here goes Plan B. "Ooh! What do we do now?"

"There's nothing we can do. We're going to have to spend the night in the car."

"Oh, no!"

"Don't be frightened. I'll pull into the parking lot at the T.C. Worthy Market. We're perfectly safe there."

Kikki pulled in, turned off the engine, switched off the headlights. And there they sat. No one spoke. It was pitch dark. It was too quiet.

"I'm sorry, Delia."

"Oh please, don't say that. It was all my fault."

"No, no."

"Yes, I acted like a child. Oh, Kikki!"

"Sssh. Close your eyes and try to get some sleep."

They sat, each in their bucket seat, and closed their eyes. They listened to each other's breathing for half an hour. No one slept. Delia was restless. She couldn't get comfortable. She tried one position then another. Kikki did his best to stay in his place and tried not to get cozy. He pressed himself against his door, the armrest poking him painfully in the ribs, and pretended to sleep.

"Kikki?"

"What is it?"

"I'm cold."

Kikki put an arm around her to keep her warm. The console between them made it impossible to get any closer. "Better?"

"Mmm. Let's go to sleep."

They sat quietly, surrounded by silence and an immense darkness. They pretended to sleep for close to an hour.

"Kikki?"

"What is it?"

"It's too quiet. I hate to be a baby, but could you turn on the radio?"

"Of course." Kikki turned to a twenty-four-hour classical music station and again they tried to get comfortable. They dozed off with Debussy for what they felt was ten minutes but it was really closer to an hour.

"Kikki?"

"What is it?"

"Did I wake you?"

"No," he lied.

"My neck hurts and my right leg is asleep."

And my *nalgas* are numb, he thought, and I should have gone to the *signore* or the *signori*, I can never remember which, before we left the restaurant. He got out of the car.

"Where are you going?"

"I'm just going behind the building for a minute. Wait for me.'

Delia understood the nature of his mission. Quick as a flash she took her cell phone out of her purse. "*Bueno*, Mamá? Did I wake you?"

"That's all right, what is it?"

"We're locked out at the border."

"Oh, you poor thing! That happened to your father and me a couple of times. Your Nana gave him a scathing sermon when he brought me home. But I won't do that. I'll have a nice breakfast waiting for you and Octavio when you get in."

"I have a surprise for you, Mamá."

Kikki was back. Delia stashed the phone in her purse just as he opened the door. "I should have thought of this before. Come on." Kikki helped her out and they both got into the back seat. Kikki stretched out on his back and opened his arms. "Come."

Delia gently laid down on top of him on her back. "Am I too heavy?"

"Of course not." He folded his arms around her waist and held her close.

"Better?"

"Mmmmm."

Don't get carried away, Kikki had to remind himself again. This whole thing is a charade. Even if the stupid scheme is a success and Octavio and Delia do break up, that doesn't mean she has deep feelings for you. The dreamy adagio from Mozart's clarinet concerto K.622 lulled them to sleep. They slept soundly for nearly an hour before Kikki became aware of Delia's hair tickling his face.

"Delia?"

"Mmmmm?"

"Did I wake you?"

"No," she lied.

The inner voice was back. *This is your opportunity, cabrón, bury your silly pride. Take the leap!* All right, all right!

"Delia?"

"Mmmm?"

"Do you—do you love me?"

There was a painful silence in the dark car. Kikki's heart ceased its normal function of dilation and contraction. He whispered a final prayer to the Holy Virigin and prepared to expire during the 8.4 seconds it took Delia to compose her answer. "Kikki, I've loved you and you alone since eighth grade. I was just too dumb to know it."

"Enough to, to, to marry me?

"Yes!"

Beethoven's Pathetique sonata covered them like a blanket. And they both fell into an exhausted sleep.

The sound of cars and the growl of eighteen-wheelers lining up at the gate brought them both awake. The soft music was gone. It was light outside. The Americans were pushing open the iron gates. It was six o'clock in the morning.

They untangled themselves. Stiff and achy, they got into the front seat. Kikki turned the key.

Nothing.

He turned again. Still nothing. "The battery's dead."

"Oh Kikki!" Delia sounded like she was about to cry. "It's all my fault. I had to have the radio on." She covered her face in shame. "Oh, I'm so sorry!" But inside she was jubilant. Plan B was a winner!

"Sssh, no harm done, *mi amor.*" It was the first time the words *mi amor* formed on his lips. He liked the way it sounded. "We can walk three blocks to the plaza. We'll get a good breakfast and I'll get El Tigre to come get the car started."

Hopelessly rumpled, totally disheveled, and with unwashed sleepy faces, Delia and Kikki walked through the gate and back into Mexico. They inhaled the delicious aroma of fresh bread coming to them from the *panaderia*. They started across the plaza arm in arm, happy in love.

"*Buenos dias.*"

God, it was La Cucha!

"We'll make the early news on *Good Morning Tecate!*" Kikki gasped. "And I'll get the last *aha!*"

Delia had to restrain herself from leaping into the air for joy. Doña Fortuna is smiling on me today, she thought to herself, I couldn't have planned it any better even if I had paid the old hag!

Before the steam whistle at the brewery announced the noon hour with a deafening blast, the scandal had swept through Tecate like a SARS epidemic. The two conspirators in the convoluted plot now had to accept the harsh reality; sooner or later, or *a la larga*, if you prefer, the inevitable moment of truth would present itself and leave no option but to face both sets of parents and unravel the tangled web they weaved when first they practiced to deceive.

It cannot be denied that Delia and Octavio were people of resource, and by margarita time that same evening, the two couples got it all sorted out. The mothers could still buy a new dress, both sets of parents got to plan a wedding and throw a fiesta. The symposium ended with congratulatory *abrazos*, the girls got the right boy, the boys got the right girl.

Everyone in Tecate is still talking about the wedding, the first double wedding in the history of the Church of Our Lady de Guadalupe. Father Ruben officiated. The two couples, however, took separate honeymoons. Octavio and Lorena spent a week in Cancun, Delia and Kikki played on the pink beaches of Mazatlan and in their room at the Hotel De Cima.

Guadalajara Guadalajara
hueles a linda tierra mojada...

Mariachis played, the margaritas flowed. La Fonda was bursting with *alegría*. The four friends of a lifetime could hardly wait to get together as soon as they were back.

Beto arrived at their table. "Welcome back and *felicidades* to all of you!"

"*Gracias,*" the four answered in unison.

"I wondered how it would all end," Beto confessed.

"It ended well," Delia said.

"Another pitcher of margaritas, Beto, we're just getting started!" Octavio said.

"Oh, and bring us the appetizers," Kikki added.

"I don't think you spent your time on the beach." Octavio said to Delia. "You don't have much of a tan."

"First one to have a baby wins!" she answered.

Beto returned with the fresh pitcher of margaritas. "I'll be right back with your appetizers as soon as they come out of the kitchen."

"I think we made a boy," Lorena said.

"How can you tell?"

"It's already complaining!" Lorena laughed.

Octavio raised his glass. "And we want the two of you to be *compadres.*"

"Delia and I decided the same thing!" Kikki exclaimed. "We'll be double *compadres.*"

"Can we do that?"

"I'll check with Father Ruben."

"The appetizers are here!" Beto announced putting down a huge tray. "Let's see now, we have the guacamole dip, the salsa and chips, here's the chimichangas—and who gets the bean and toad burrito?"

*M*exican author Daniel Reveles invites us to join him for another helping of tales in *Guacamole Dip*. His previous books: *Tequila, Lemon, and Salt, Enchiladas, Rice, and Beans*, and *Salsa and Chips*, appear on required reading lists across the country. He enjoys a diversified audience of both non-Latino and Latino readers, probably because he takes the former to where they've never been, and the latter to where they *have* been.

PHOTO: JORGE MATEUS

Reveles began his career at Paramount Pictures in Hollywood as a "script girl," and remained in some aspect of the entertainment industry for many years, as a recording artist, songwriter, television producer, and disc jockey. He is credited with introducing the infectious Cuban rhythms of cha-cha-cha and merengue to the Los Angeles market, when no one else would, on his Spanish-language radio show "Fiesta Latina."

Nearly thirty years ago, Reveles got lost on his way to Ensenada, stumbled into Tecate, fell in love with the pueblo, and has remained ever since. He lives among jackrabbits and coyotes on a remote hacienda on the outskirts of town. When he isn't writing he plays chamber music, throws paint at a canvas, and can often be spotted roaming the town plaza for new material. He is presently in a stormy relationship with a computer, visit him on the web at: www.danielreveles.com

Selections from Sunbelt's Baja Bookshelf

Antigua California (University of New Mexico Press)   Crosby
The definitive history of the peninsula's mission and colonial frontier period.

Baja Legends: Historic Characters, Events, Locations Niemann
The author's extensive knowledge of Baja's colorful past and booming present.

Baja, Mexico: Through the Eyes of an Honest Lens   Healey
A photographic journey, featuring colorful places, people, and things.

Cave Paintings of Baja California, Rev. Ed.   Crosby
A full-color account of the author's exploration of world-class rock art sites.

Gateway to Alta California   Crosby
The groundbreaking trek through northern Baja California to San Diego in 1769. Color maps.

Guacamole Dip   Reveles
A collection of humorous and poignant stories, set in a Baja border town.

Houses of Los Cabos (Amaroma)   Aldrete
A stunning full-color pictorial highlighting architecture in and near the Cape.

Houses by the Sea (Amaroma)   Aldrete
The integrated architecture and natural beauty of Mexico's Pacific Coast.

In the Shadow of the Volcano   Humfreville
A couple and their young sons set up a camp in Bahia de los Angeles.

Journey with a Baja Burro   Mackintosh
Over 1,000 miles on foot, with his trusty companion, from Tecate to Loreto.

Mexican Slang plus Graffiti Jones-Reid
The hip talk and off-color eloquence of the Spanish commonly used in Mexico.

Mexicoland: Stories from Todos Santos
(Barking Dog Books) Mercer
These stories of Baja life range from satirical to dramatic.

Oasis of Stone: Visions of Baja Sur Berger
Essays on geology, flora, fauna; photography by Miguel Angel de la Cueva.

Ornamental Plants and Flowers of Tropical Mexico Trapp
How to select and grow just the right plants for this region.

Other Side: Journeys in Baja California Botello
Over twenty years of traveling—a love story, adventure, and inner journey.

Spanish Lingo for the Savvy Gringo Reid
The colloquial Spanish of Mexico, plus a guide to language and customs.

Tequila, Lemon, and Salt Reveles
The border town of Tecate comes to colorful life in this collection of stories.

The Baja California Travel Series (Dawson) Various authors
Select titles in this hard-to-find series of histories.

---

*We carry hundreds of books on
Baja California, Mexico, and the Southwest U.S.!*

www.sunbeltbooks.com
